Flying Fossils

Fossil Ridge Series

Book One

LYNNE GENTRY

TRAVEL LIGHT PRESS

FANTASY · DRAMA · ADVENTURE

Flying Fossil (Fossil Ridge Series, Book One)

Copyright © 2018 Lynne Gentry

All rights reserved.

Sign up for bonus information at: www.lynnegentry.com

This is a work of fiction. Names, characters, organizations, places, events incidents are products of the author's imagination.

Cover photo licensed by Shutterstock©2018

Edited by Gina Calvert

ISBN: 978-0-9986412-4-9

Dedication

For anyone caught between love and duty.

To the strong, beautiful older women who've loved me…

Women who fulfilled their purpose until the end.

Flying Fossils

Chapter 1

Sara: An Independent Mother

As usual, you're being overly dramatic, Charlotte Ann." I hug the phone receiver between my ear and shoulder, stretch the cord across the kitchen, then snag a butcher knife from the wooden block. "Putting a few dents in a lawnmower is hardly a reason for me to give up my ranch."

"Mother, you totaled a two-thousand-dollar *riding* mower!" My daughter's anger crackles on the line. "What if you'd been hurt?"

Contrary to Charlotte's insinuations, I'm not some fragile, rusty weathervane easily spun by the changing winds that sweep through these Texas Hill Country valleys. As per the invariant order of things, my feet have become deeply rooted in the rocky soil. I'm attached to this land tighter than the fossils that cling to the banks of the Frio River.

For forty-two years, I've been the mother. Charlotte the child. Simple laws govern our parent-child relationship. I'll admit, there are rules that allow for an orderly transition of power, if that sad time should ever come. But, I'll not be pushed into speeding things along simply because it suits Charlotte.

Trading roles with my daughter now would be like winter unexpectedly giving way to fall. Buds waiting to bloom would shrivel and die. There'd be no crops to harvest. Birds would never head north. Nothing would ever be right again. I know, because twenty-three years ago I was forced to go against the expected order of life. It was a tragedy that has ruined everything.

"Mother, did you hear me?" Somewhere in Charlotte's aggravation, I hear the little girl I used to know, the one who sat beside me on the piano bench...frustrated that she was having difficulty mastering Twinkle, Twinkle Little Star...worried that she never would.

I shift the receiver and whack a Bartlett pear into tiny pieces. "Don't worry, I'll pay you back."

"You know this is not about the money!" Charlotte barks.

"Then why did you bring it up?" I ignore my daughter's huge sigh and slide a piece of fruit through the bars of my ringneck parrot's cage. "Here you go, Polygon."

My bird waddles his perch shouting, "God save the Queen."

"Loyal and smart." I say as I wiggle the pear enticingly. "You need more roughage in your diet, my feathered friend. Can't have you getting backed up again."

"Mother, could you please stop talking to that blasted bird and finish our conversation?"

Polygon hops off his perch, wraps his claws around my arthritic knuckle, and begins to peck at the fruit. Touch is the sensation of touch I miss more than conversation. Which is strange, considering the complaints I lodged with Martin when I felt worn out by the constant pawing of third graders. Guess that goes to show how easy it is to take something for granted until it's gone.

I release the fruit and Polygon waddles toward his seed dish with a full mouth. "At least my bird listens."

Charlotte sighs. "I bought the riding mower to help you. The doctor said the strain of *pushing* a mower over that huge yard is putting your heart at risk." Her continued exasperation rattles me more than her exaggeration. "Obviously, power equipment isn't the answer."

"Anyone could've confused all those fancy pedals."

"You're seventy-two, Mother." She always manages to cite my age before overstepping the boundaries we've set in place. "There's no shame in admitting that you can no longer keep up with three hundred acres of rugged hill country."

I wipe the window with the sleeve of my robe and gaze at the pasture dotted with patches of this spring's fading bluebonnets. "No one was hurt."

"This time." The strain in her voice is as irritating as a mandatory fire drill.

"You want me to let the place grow up around my ears?"

"Of course not." She sighs to emphasize the stress I'm obviously adding to her very busy day. "But since you refuse to consider a move, I have to hire you some help."

I bite my tongue. Silence won't end this conversation with Charlotte, but it won't hurt her to believe it's the only defense I have left.

"I'm worried about you, Mother."

Charlotte's deep inhalation is my cue to take a seat because the recounting of my shortcomings that she feels honor bound to recite has grown into a rather long list. "In the last six months, you've flushed your dentures down the toilet."

"Just the lowers."

"You got lost on the way to town."

"Winnie found me and hauled me back home." I add, "Long before dark."

"I hate to think what would have happened if you hadn't run out of gas along her mail route."

Overstated dramatics always harden my resolve. Ask any child who was unlucky enough to have me as their teacher. "No law against trying a change of scenery."

"You don't like change, Mother," my daughter snips. "That's why we can't seem to have an honest and productive conversation about your future."

I sink into the chair and rest my elbow on the table. "Just because you think the old gray mare *ain't* what she used to be..." I cringe at that I've resorted to using slang. "...that doesn't mean I want to leave my home of forty-five years and move to Washington, D.C., Charlotte Ann."

Surely it wasn't that many years ago that Martin and I ignored a weathered *No Trespassing* sign, climbed an old, barbed-wire fence, shed our clothes, and jumped from a thirty-foot bluff with the abandon of two people with more nerve than sense. The moment our naked bodies slid into the crystal-clear water, we knew the Fossil Ridge Ranch was meant to be our little piece of heaven.

I've loved and lost on this land. I can't bear to leave any of it.

"I know this is hard," Charlotte whispers.

"How *could* you know? You only come home once a year."

"Mother, that's not true. I've flown to Texas four times since Thanksgiving. And if you don't start cooperating, I'm going to have to come home in April as well."

Without following the school calendar dates scramble in my head. "Four times?"

"Yes," she says. "I have a job, a teenager, and a marriage I'm trying to keep together. I can't keep dropping everything to..."

Her pause is my cue to say something that will soothe her conscience, to grant a pass that lets her off the hook. That's been our unspoken agreement for twenty-some years. I don't get a pass. She doesn't get a pass. That way neither one of us has to forgive the other. Slocums are like that. Charlotte may have taken on that fancy

McCandless surname when she married a good-for-nothing playboy, but roots deep as ours are tougher than weeds to yank out.

Charlotte's quiet. But I can hear her ripping the tiny gold treble clef back and forth on the thin silver chain around her neck. She's gearing up to issue my ultimatum. I suppose I should take some consolation in the fact that she still wears the little trinket I gave her years ago. Perhaps we're not completely lost to each other.

"If you want to stay on the Fossil Ridge, then you'll have to give this new guy a chance."

"He's already mowed over the bluebonnets in my front yard. They're beautiful this year, but he cut them down before they could seed. Next thing you know, he'll be toppin' my myrtles."

"I'll text him to be more careful. Please, for my peace of mind, can you just give this new guy a try?" Charlotte's breathing is becoming more rapid. Any minute she'll blow, unable to leave well enough alone. "That's all I ask."

"That's all?" Anger pumps through my veins and I spring from the chair, a taut rubber band aimed at the class bully. "If you call stripping my independence *guarding my heart*, Charlotte Ann, I'll take my chances with high cholesterol and a push mower."

I hang up the phone with a decisive slam and march to the counter. Sticky juice oozes from what remains of the mutilated mound of fruit.

Whatever happened to family taking care of family? My

neighbor LaVera's grown son takes care of her. Bo isn't pressuring his mother to leave her place, nor does he pawn off his responsibilities on hired help.

I swallow a bite of the vanilla-sweet flesh then poke a sliver through the bars of the birdcage. "Charlotte won't be satisfied until I sign over complete control of *my* life."

My bird abandons his preening and snatches his breakfast with his bright red beak.

"Sweet Moses," I snap. "Say something, Polygon!"

I know better than to encourage this feathered chatterbox to speak with his mouth full, but this traitorous deed by Charlotte has me in such a stew I'm willing to risk the undoing of my bird's etiquette training.

For once, Polygon behaves and remains silent. Although pleased the hours I've invested in my parrot's behavior has finally begun to pay off, I admit that at this very moment a word of encouragement, even a feathery nod would be a comfort. How many years has it been since I've had someone in my corner?

More than I care to count.

The screaming kettle gyrates above the gas flame. "We'll show Charlotte who can still take care of themselves, won't we, Polygon?"

I pour boiling water over a twice-used tea bag then wait for the water to brown. It's maddening that my life has come to recycling tea bags. Martin and I had planned to spend our golden years spoiling a passel of grandchildren. I shuffle to the fridge. My gnarled finger traces the photograph that curls beneath the World's Best Teacher magnet stuck to the door.

The little beauty sitting beside me and Charlotte is my only grandchild. Aria was eight when this photo was taken nearly five years ago. I haven't seen this little lioness in months. Busy teenager stuff, her mother claims. But I can't help but wonder if Ari has also outgrown her need for me. After all, she's probably taller than me by now, and well-past the age of appreciating anything I could teach her. And I'd planned to teach her so much. Her times tables. Piano scales. How to tell a barn swallow from a sparrow. The best way to free a fossil from the limestone that lines the river.

Some dreams are best forgotten.

I return to my tea, splurge and add a cube of sugar, then lift the rose-patterned porcelain cup to my lips.

My apple-green bird tilts his head, his beady eyes assessing my brewing storm. I blow steam in his direction. "You won't leave me, will you, Polygon?"

"C'mere." He waddles the length of his perch. "Pretty girl."

I rest the cup on a saucer and stick my finger through the wires and stroke the soft down above his beak. "If only family were as loyal."

I'd give anything to have my Martin pat my fanny as I wash up the supper dishes. Or have my ambitious Caroline hug my neck after I admire her work. Or have my sweet Charlotte crawl into my lap and beg for another song on the piano.

"Thank you for sticking it out, Polygon." Through tears, I look my bird in the eye. "Once I send Charlotte's new hire packing, we'll have our life back."

"Be nice." Polygon gives my finger a peck.

"Traitor." I recoil at his siding with Charlotte. "This has to be done, Polygon. And, no matter what anyone tries to tell me, I'm still the woman to do it."

Chapter 2

Charlotte: The Sandwiched Daughter

Frustration pounded Charlotte's temples. She stared at the blank screen of her cell phone. Her mother had hung up on her. Again. How could she help her mother if they couldn't finish a conversation?

Charlotte scrolled through her missed calls and pressed the number that had buzzed here three times in ten minutes. Drumming her fingers on desk, she waited for the call to connect.

"Mom, where have you been?"

"Sorry, sweetheart. I was on the phone with Nana."

"She okay?" Thirteen-year-olds shouldn't have so much worry in their voice.

"For now."

"You really should make her move here."

"I can't kidnap her. It's got to be her idea or she'll never be happy."

"Is she happy now?"

Mother will never be happy with me again.

Charlotte kept her thoughts to herself and shifted her guilt to the back burner. "Hard to tell."

"Maybe I should go with you next time."

Ari loved her Nana and enjoyed a special bond. Their connection to music and a love for the outdoors reminded Charlotte so much of the one she used to have with her mother. No matter how difficult Mother was becoming, keeping Ari away from Texas wasn't the answer. Sooner or later, Ari would have to be told about the river and none of them were ready for the unearthing of that secret.

"Mom, you still there?"

Ari's impatience jerked Charlotte free of the suffocating memory. "Tell me again what time I need to be at your recital?

"Same time as the last one."

"Look, I'm sorry for missing your Christmas show." Her excuses were beginning to sound thin so she didn't make one. It wasn't Ari's fault her grandmother backed the tractor through the side of the barn and got whacked on the head. And it wasn't Charlotte's fault she had to fly to Texas and make sure the concussion hadn't done any permanent damage. "I promise, I'll be there, Adds."

"Aria."

"Right, Aria." Charlotte scrambled to cross the growing divide between them. "Look, I'm planning to get off early, but just in case I get hung up, your dad has agreed to swing by on his way to the recital and pick you up." She left out the part about having to beg

James to come. "Want him to bring you a happy meal?"

"Mom, I'm not six and besides, I'm a vegetarian. Remember?"

"Sorry. I forgot." Charlotte slid her fingers up the sides of her nose and pinched the fact into the tiny space left between everything else she was juggling. "How about a salad from Wendy's?"

"Whatever."

"I had the black dress you wanted for tonight's performance shipped to the office. Loraine took it to the cleaners to be pressed. She'll pick it up then drop it by. You're going to look as beautiful as you play."

"What if it doesn't fit?"

"Aria, I'm doing the best I can, okay?"

"Caitlyn's had her dress for two weeks."

"Who?"

"Geez, Mom. My best friend, okay?"

"Oh, right."

"Caitlyn's mom had to hem her dress an inch. What if mine's too long?"

"There's scotch tape in the drawer next to the washing machine." Charlotte envisioned her mother of the year award swirling in the toilet. "Loraine will help you."

"Loraine is not my mother." Click.

I can't win.

Charlotte sent her phone spinning on the desk and lowered her head into her hands. A light rap at the door snapped her head up. "Loraine?"

"Expecting someone else?" Her paralegal, a clone of Annette Benning in a stylish pink suit and turquoise heels, stepped into the room toting a bulging brief case and a mug of something steamy. "Hope not, because it's time to go."

Charlotte glanced at her calendar, but she wasn't sure what day it was. "Where?"

Loraine's striking features scrunched into concern as she adjusted the leather strap digging into her shoulder. "You've got a meeting. On the Hill. In less than an hour."

"Right." Charlotte fumbled to regain control of her phone. "I know that."

She stared at the mound of files covering her desk, completely at a loss as to which white-collar cause she was expected to defend today. Mother's latest crisis and Ari's rightful need for attention had her so conflicted she couldn't defend herself right now much less make a decent argument on behalf of some giant corporation looking for a tax-sheltered loophole. Charlotte thumbed through manila folders all filled with the same thick, greedy, senseless weight.

Loraine held out the mug. "Coming?"

"That better be espresso, straight up."

"Always."

"Thanks." Charlotte took a distracted sip, while she flipped to the calendar on her phone in search of today's legal crisis. "When you drop off Ari's dress this afternoon, would you mind hanging around until she tries it on? She's worried it won't fit."

"I can staple. That's about it."

"You're a peach, Loriane. I don't know what I'd do without you."

"A peach? Is that a southern thing?"

"It means my head's in two places at once."

"Want to tell me what's really going on?" The same spot-on discernment that made Loraine invaluable during voir dire guaranteed this seasoned sleuth would nail anything less than a truthful answer.

Charlotte slumped in her leather chair. Endless and fruitless feuding with her mother, combined with her guilt for failing her own daughter, had worn her down. Her fingers went in search of the delicate silver chain that hung around her neck. She fished out the tiny gold treble clef and rubbed it as if by some magic the charm her mother had given her could make the weight on her shoulders disappear.

She'd spent years away from home, obtained an Ivy League law degree, and even married into money. None of it had changed her basic DNA. Her inherited chromosomes remained racked with guilt. At her core she was still a Slocum, and Slocums never aired their dirty laundry. Unlike her husband James, who relished tabloid coverage, she'd been raised to pretend problems didn't exist, while praying they'd go away.

Sliding the charm back and forth, Charlotte confessed, "Things are…tough right now."

"I guess that explains why you look like crap." Loraine navigated the tumbling stacks of files.

"Thanks for the encouragement." Charlotte dropped the music charm inside her blouse, the weight of her mother's token sat heavy on her chest.

In one swift movement, Loraine emptied a client interview chair, dropped the briefcase to the floor, and lowered her petite frame. She reached into her purse and pulled out a book. "I think you're finally ready for this."

"A book? I don't even have time to read emails."

Loraine thrust the book across the desk. "Make time."

The hardback was heavy as a brick. "How long have you been carrying this around?"

"Long enough that I'm seeing a chiropractor." Loraine shot a sly look over the top of her tortoise-shell glasses. "He's handsome, so it's a win-win for everyone."

Charlotte read the title out loud. "How to Survive Being the Ham of the Generation Sandwich." The cover picture of three happy females linking arms made survival seem possible. "Does it deal with how to handle a mother who crashed a brand-new riding mower into a tree?"

"Lord. Tree okay?"

"Loraine! Mother's seventy-two. She could have been badly injured."

An offended glare shot over Loraine's stylish rims. "Seventy-two is *not* that old, kiddo."

"You're a good thirty years from that."

"Seven."

"You're sixty-five?"

Loraine held a manicured nail to her lips. "Shhh...I'm not ready for the managing partners to put me out to pasture just yet."

"You look forty."

"A little work here and there is called job security." Loraine's laser stare cut through the smoke screen. "A person can putty and paste all they want, but one truth remains."

"What's that?"

"None of us are getting out of this world alive."

Each stunt her mother pulled made it feel like that day was barreling closer. "She could have been killed."

"But she's wasn't." Loraine's brow lifted without wrinkling her forehead. "Was she?"

"Loraine!"

"You need to fly out there?"

"Not unless she runs off my latest ranch-hand hire." Charlotte sighed. "What would you do, Loraine?"

Loraine's flawless poker-face revealed nothing of the self-sacrifices she'd made. "What does your local spy-friend say?"

Charlotte studied the woman she'd worked with for twelve years. Direct. Dependable. Sharp as they come. Taught her the ins and outs of DC. Covered for her inexperience on several occasions. Except for what happened at the office, she didn't really know anything about this woman. Not even her correct age. And yet, Loraine knew everything about her. She even knew about her old college roommate Winnie.

How could two lives intersect on a daily basis and one learn everything about the other while the other learned nothing? An awkward loneliness, the kind Charlotte experienced at her mother's silent dinner table, surged through her. She should pay better attention. Make a point to make friends and keep her family close. If she didn't, she'd end up like her mother—a half-crazed widow rattling around in a big house and forced to talk to birds.

Charlotte took a stab at rectifying her one-sided relationship with Loraine. "Mother's convinced Winnie's a communist. Any extra information I get from home is ascertained through covert operations and used with extreme caution." Encouraged by the smile her honesty had elicited from her paralegal, Charlotte ventured on. "You ever gone through anything like this?"

Loraine passed on the bait, skillfully returning the conversation to Charlotte's problem. "If this guy isn't to her liking, hire someone else."

"Who?" Charlotte pressed her fingers to the throb at her temples. "There isn't a soul left in Texas tough enough to work for Mother."

"Does she need help?"

Charlotte threw her hands in the air. "Remember when I had to fly home right before Christmas because she'd backed Daddy's old tractor through the side of the hay barn?"

Loraine shrugged. "Easy to mix up reverse and first."

"Last month, I had to go home because she shot at the neighbor's dog and smoked out half the county with a skillet of grease she left on the stove. She regularly flushes anything from her teeth to her heart medications. And she's been driving for three years without a license because she can't pass the eye test."

"Does she *want* help?"

"Loraine, what she wants doesn't matter. She needs—" Charlotte stopped. Loraine had done it again— cornered her using the same courtroom tactic she'd help Charlotte perfect—asking rhetorical questions until the witness tripped up, fessed up, or gave up. And Loraine had done it all without divulging a single clue about herself. "She needs what she'll never accept from me...help."

"How do you think your mother sees her situation?" The brilliant woman could have made a killing in civil litigation.

"She doesn't. She acts like she's twenty and going to live forever."

"And you? How do *you* see this working out?"

Charlotte parked her elbows on the edge of her desk in surrender. "Badly." She dropped her chin upon her folded hands. Truth be known, she'd spent better part of the past twenty-something years trying to rectify her mother's situation. "When Daddy died, Mother chose to stay, no, let me rephrase that. Mother *refused to leave* her precious river. Since then, she's flatly dismissed every option I've put before her. A room of her own in my home. A townhouse of her own close to her granddaughter. Even the final offer of moving her into Addisonville until she was ready to give up Texas. Nothing has budged her resolution to stay put." Charlotte let out a frustrated sigh. "I hate that river."

Loraine listened, her courtroom-face lacking condemnation and frustratingly impossible to read.

Charlotte continued on before Loraine asked questions, "Mother's nearest neighbor is half-blind and lives over a mile away. The closest medical facility, if Addisonville Memorial can be counted as a real hospital, takes a good thirty minutes to reach— assuming the Frio hasn't washed out the bridge on the twisty one-lane road. And, whether Mother likes it or not, I live four hours away by plane and rental car and I happen to have a life of my own."

"Sort of."

"I'm doing the best I can, Loraine."

"I didn't say you weren't. But if something happens, and you can't get to your mother in time, you couldn't forgive yourself, right?"

"I've got plenty I can't forgive. I don't need to toss in my mother to make my guilt complete."

A rap on the door frame drew their attention. Sid Waring, tall and distinguished in his tailored gray suit, did not look pleased. "Charlotte, did you forget the Senator and his subcommittee are waiting?"

"Coming, Mr. Waring." Charlotte jumped up. Coffee sloshed across her desk. "You won't be sorry you pulled me in on this."

Skepticism crossed his face as he watched her rescue files from the growing brown puddle. "The car's waiting. Bring your A-game."

Loraine tossed her a tissue, then held up the briefcase. "I've packed the files we need."

"I repeat, I don't know what I'd do without you, Loraine."

"Your head's in two places."

Charlotte grabbed her purse. "But if something doesn't give, it's going to be on the chopping block, right?"

Chapter 3

Sara vs. the Yard Man

Slipping out the back door, I'm careful not to let the screen slam behind me. The perfume of freshly mowed grass assaults my nostrils and raises my blood pressure several notches. A barn swallow swoops through the porch. Her piercing alarm shatters the country quiet I've come to love. I give the wild bird the space she needs to tend two chicks poking their beaks from the twiggy nest wedged between the porch roof and one of the eight porch pillars.

I navigate the stairs with the aid of the grab bar installed by the previous overzealous handyman Charlotte hired.

For the record, I only conceded to the addition of the stainless-steel handrail *after* Charlotte threatened to have one of those ugly ramps built. A person must pick the mountains they're willing to die on—wheelchair access is mine.

Fine line, I'll admit. But a necessary line nevertheless. And once lines are crossed, one must either concede or fight. And I never concede.

Which is the exact reason I'm sneaking down my back steps without so much as a stitch of makeup on this wrinkled face. One only has to be determined when heading toward a fight. Charlotte has crossed the threshold of my tolerance for the last time.

I peer around the corner of the clapboard farmhouse Martin and I restored forty-five years ago. Near my front door, the paunchy, overall-clad man who's just scalped my yard and obliterated my bluebonnets is whistling some tuneless ditty. He's toting a pair of hedge trimmers and mounting the stepladder beneath my prize crape myrtle.

From the pounding in my head, my blood pressure is hovering near the danger range.

I unspool the garden hose with the stealth of a goat-stealing coyote and hunker down behind the front porch foliage. I may forget to take my medicine or occasionally boil the kettle dry, but I still know enough to seize an opportunity when it knocks. My freedom is at stake.

I untangle my snagged housecoat from the shrubbery and shuffle out.

Charlotte's latest hire is balanced atop my rickety ladder. His rusty pruning shears are poised beneath a tender green branch.

I brace myself, aim the pistol nozzle at his chest, and clear my throat. "Step away from the crape myrtle, and no one will get hurt."

The surprised man stops mid-chop. "Morning, Miz Slocum." He positions the blades of that blasted hedge trimmer on either side of a drooping branch. "I'm used to ladders, Miz Slocum. But don't you go a frettin'. I'll tuck this here ladder away, put it back in the shed right where I got it. Soon as I finish doin' a little trimmin' on this here monstrosity." He flashes a buck-toothed grin that splits his ruddy face into two halves of an apple.

"Don't those buds mean a thing to you? It's too late in the season to top myrtles." Can't he tell that I mean business? I clutch the nozzle tighter, but I can see my seriousness is not registering. Where *does* Charlotte find these incompetent fools? Not a one of them knows which end of a hammer to hold. "You *are* finished, young man."

"No way am I'm lettin' a little old lady haul this heavy ladder back to the shed."

"Are you hard of hearing, or do you simply lack listening skills? I said, step away from my tree."

"Miz Slocum, Miz Charlotte paid me extra to cut back these branches. If'n I don't, you're gonna be a havin' all sorts of roof damage."

I tent one hand over my eyes, keeping a jumpy finger hooked around the nozzle's hair-trigger with the other. "Raymond Leck? Is that you?"

"Why, yes ma'am, it is." Relief releases his shoulders and he pulls the clippers free of the branch.

"The same impetuous, hard-headed rapscallion I had suspended from my third-grade class?"

He tucks the long handles under his arm. "Yes, ma'am," he says with a chuckle. "Thirty-five years ago." He draws a red bandana from his pocket.

"Then Raymond, do you have any doubts I'll do what I say?"

"No, ma'am." He mops his neck, red and leathery because of the hours he's spent in the sun. "You tol' me if I bit Corina Klump again, I'd be a spendin' a few days stacking wood scraps at my Pa's lumber yard."

"And did you?"

"Yes, ma'am." He stuffs the soiled bandana in his pocket, obviously unconcerned that a desperate woman has his forehead squarely in her sights. "Stacked lumber three whole days. But if I had it to do over again, I'd take another chunk out of that—"

"Watch your mouth, Raymond." I wave the nozzle at him. "You come down off my ladder, or I'll blow you into next week. And there isn't a school board in this whole county that can stop me."

"Miz Slocum, I—"

"You had your warning." I squeeze the trigger with the ease of someone half my age.

A blistering barrage of water surges from the barrel. The recoil sends me reeling. Any chance of remorse sails from my mind. I drop the writhing hose and lunge for the porch railing. I cling to the slippery wrought-iron as the hose whips around my feet like an angry chicken snake, periodically spewing watery venom at my face.

My feet flail the mulch-scented air, intersecting nothing solid. I open my eyes and discover I'm dangling above my flower bed. "Sweet Moses, don't let me crush the hyacinths."

Once Charlotte learns of this shenanigan, and that is the exact word she uses when my actions deviate from her orders, I will have no one but myself to blame as she pounds the last nail into my coffin.

Finding purchase, I right myself and plant my feet. Steadied against the porch, I survey the damage. The flower stems are neither bent nor broken. Spared the need to repair another mishap is a relief.

Now for a look at me. I slowly move one arm and then the other. So far, so good. Both legs are operational. My knees grind like corroded hinges, but at least they still work. Except for a bit of bruised pride, everything functions.

I'm relieved.

A broken bone would give Charlotte the excuse she needs to put me away. I shoot the Lord a quick prayer of thanks, then check for Raymond's whereabouts.

A long, low moan draws my attention to the lawn.

Charlotte's new yard man is flat on his back in the middle of a swath of freshly mowed St. Augustine. Soaking wet. Legs askew. His hat caught in the thorns of my prize-winning New Dawn roses, the yardstick against which all other climbers can be judged.

What if I've killed him? Panic addles my thoughts. I work to sort them into some kind of order. I hadn't meant to hurt him, only scare some common sense into that thick head of his.

"Raymond?"

He answers with another moan.

I'm relieved he's not dead. But I can't stop thinking about how close I came to once again being the heartbreaking headline in the *Addisonville Herald*.

Retired Educator Bushwhacks Former Student.

The newspaper's editor, Mitty Stringer the lug who barely passed third-grade English, hasn't had a story this good since...well, since the school board forced my early retirement.

Dragging the hose across my shorn lawn, I scan the distant gravel road and notice a tornado of dust headed this way.

Oh, dear. And me without so much as a swipe of rouge across my cheeks.

Who can it be? It's too early for the mail. It had better not be Sam Sparks. If that green-eyed land developer sets a foot on Fossil Ridge again, I'll teach him to dance the same buckshot two-step I taught the Wooten dog. No fake-tanned shyster is going to park me in some out-of-the-way nursing home to rust away like a forgotten plowshare. No, sir. If Sparky thinks I'll sit back and let him get his grimy mitts on my prime riverfront section of land, he sorely underestimates Sara Slocum.

Sparky's not the first slick operator to offer good money for my vista above the Frio. Though I no longer frolic in the crystal-clear waters that have carved a lazy S through my property, I will not relinquish the special place it once held in my heart. If Charlotte's inheritance is to be transformed into a swanky resort that siphons taxpayer dollars out of the pockets of the muckity-mucks from Austin, I'll push up my sleeves and do it myself.

I check my wrist to confirm the time. Leopard-looking spots mottle my paper-thin skin where my Timex should have been. I've misplaced my retirement gift...again. My best friend LaVera claims I ditch the imitation-gold timepiece on purpose. Maybe, subconsciously, I do. Some say that time flies as a person ages, but I find the days interminably long now that I'm... retired. Besides, watching that little second hand skirt those Roman numerals is like watching that ungrateful school board tick through their list of grievances at my dismissal proceedings. Stepping into that old mound of dog poo holds no attraction.

I inch closer to Raymond and nudge his still leg with the toe of the ballerina bedroom shoes Charlotte gave me for Christmas. "Crape murderer." Nothing. "Don't play possum with me, Raymond Leck." I prod him again.

His eyelids flutter open. "What the—?"

"Language." I hold up a palm in warning. "I hate that your disobedience left me no choice but to carry through with my threat,

Raymond." I plant my feet on either side of his twisted legs. Grass stains mar the tidy white bows of my non-skid slippers. With the nozzle barrel trained above Raymond's dazed eyes, I continue, "You know I only give one warning."

"Miz Slocum, I—"

"You agree to stay away from my crape myrtle, and I'll accept your apology. I'll even find you some honest work—some fencing maybe or barn painting—something to justify that ridiculous amount of money my daughter's paying you."

The ping of gravel draws my attention back to the road. I squint but cannot make out the vehicle escorting the plumy cloud my direction. It has to be the mail. LaVera Tucker lives over a half a mile away. My best friend's cataracts make it difficult for her to read a large print Reader's Digest without a magnifying glass let alone keep up with the goings on at my place or drive over here, even in an emergency.

But LaVera's deteriorating eyesight and arthritic joints don't seem to bother Bo Boy. LaVera's son has taken his widowed mother's aging in stride. Unlike Charlotte, Bo Tucker is not trying to put his sweet mama away. No, he is not. Bo Boy drives out from town every day and checks on LaVera, as a good son should. Maybe if I'd given my Martin a son, someone who actually wanted the ranch...Raymond's groans halt my mental tirade and spare my mind another useless trip into the past.

A bright purple Volkswagen beetle rounds the bend in my lane, dusting Raymond and me in a powdery, white caliche cloud.

"Sweet Moses, it's that Moretti woman." The last thing I need is Charlotte's paid snitch nosing around. I glance at the yard man. "You just lie still, Raymond. It would be un-American to let our disagreement slow up the U.S. Postal Service." I pinch my cheeks hoping to stir a respectable amount of color before Winifred reports back to Charlotte that I'm pale as death.

Winnie slams on the brakes. She sticks her head out the missing driver's side window. "Morning, Miss Sara." Her gaze lands square on me. As her eyes widen, I realize my position over Raymond may be interpreted as a tad compromising by someone not privy to the whole story. Too late to do anything about it now. I ready my answer for the question this is sure to raise. "Everything okay here, Miss Sara?"

Fully prepared, I tuck a strand of hair into my loosened bun. "Everything's peachy."

"Help," Raymond mumbles.

Winnie's bushy brows arch. "Oh, my." She exits the car she's hand-lettered in bright yellow: U.S. Postal Carrier.

I flash a glare at Raymond. "Now see the trouble you've caused." If my growl impresses upon this boy the need to obey the first time, we may have a future together.

He waves a limp hand. "Help."

So much for our future.

I glance across the yard. Judging by the speed of Winnie's gait, I have little chance of outrunning the Italian artist who moved to our little town and splashed color all over our respectably sedate community. I brace myself.

In short order, Winnie sidesteps Raymond's parked van, her tie-dyed skirt billowing in the breeze as she trots up the sidewalk bordered by faded jonquils. "Oh, my. I'll call an ambulance."

"I believe I would have called for assistance had there been a need, Winifred." I say rather tartly.

Winnie pauses for a moment, as if my sharp tone has sliced one of those abstract art canvases she hawks at her continual yard sale. She lets my rebuke slide as she finds that condescending smile she's used on me before. "Course you would have, Miss Sara. It's just that I promised Charlotte I'd watch out for you. Step in when she couldn't."

"Aren't you taking that sorority sister thing a bit far?"

"I owe Charlotte far more than the little I do for you." Winnie pats my shoulder.

The hair on the back of my neck bristles. I'm not one of her stray cats. But for once, I say nothing, leaving Winnie only two choices...put up or shut up.

"Why don't you let me have a look?" Winnie says, proving she rarely chooses to keep her thoughts to herself. "Patching the wounded was my specialty."

"Fossil Ridge is not the mission field, Winifred."

"Just let me check him, Miss Sara. Please, he looks injured."

I can see that my comment poked a hole in Winnie's perpetual desire to save something, but failed to deflate that eternal bubble of hope she floats around the county in. She won't rest until somebody repents. Better Raymond than me. I lift my foot. "Well, I suppose it wouldn't hurt to look him over." I keep a sure grip on the water hose. "You know not to move him, right?"

"Just gonna take a look." Winnie stuffs her skirt between her legs and squats beside the man whose bulging eyeballs still sport a dull glaze.

Sunlight catches random strands of silver streaking Winnie's coarse hair. Saving the world has taken a toll on this woman. I can think of no another explanation for her premature aging. She has no children and Lord knows how fast kids can put gray hairs on a mother's head. This girl is the exact same age as Charlotte, and my daughter doesn't have a wrinkle on her face or a hint of gray on her head. But then again, Charlotte doesn't have one hair out of place, and spends a small fortune maintaining her taut face and sassy bob.

Winnie's slender fingers gently brush away the grass clippings stuck to Raymond's forehead. Some folks consider me lacking in gentleness. This accusation bothers me. But just because I don't fawn over weakness, doesn't mean that I can't appreciate Winnie's ability to offer a tender touch. I want to be soft again. Really, I do. I miss…I don't let my mind recount all the things I miss. I know my prickliness doesn't help Charlotte and, for her sake, I've tried to smooth things over. But the softness within me turned to stone years ago. The weight sits in my chest and would take me straight to the bottom of the river. Staying afloat is the reason I never visit the water I once loved. Staying afloat.

"What's your name?" Winnie's question to Raymond jerks me back from the jagged ledge.

"Raymond," I interject.

"I know his name, Miss Sara. I'm checking to make sure he does." Winnie doesn't seem impressed by my lame attempt to spare this crape murderer any more senseless pain or suffering. "Anything hurt, Raymond?"

This question seems totally out of line and flies all over me. A true friend of the Slocum family would never side with an interloping sawbones. A Slocum prize crape myrtle was nearly destroyed. If Winnie cannot see that the real offended party in this instance is me, she needs glasses stronger than mine. I consider making this point just as Raymond pushes up onto his elbows.

His eyes cross. He frowns, as if he sees two of me, which I kind of hope he does. Maybe it will put the fear of God into him. I remain stoic to cement the possibility.

Raymond blinks and takes a labored breath. "Got the air knocked out of me is all."

I hide my pleasure and stash the tiny victory away for something new to ponder on those long nights that push back the dawn.

Winnie offers her hand and assists Raymond to an upright position. "What happened?" When he doesn't answer, she turns to me.

I shift the hose behind my back. "Mr. Leck...took a tumble off the ladder."

Raymond snaps up straight. "She can see that, Miz Slocum. What this lady's a wantin' to know is why a once respectable teacher is shootin' folks with a water hose?"

My anger gets the better of me. "Once respectable?"

Winnie's face screws into that pitiful-Miss-Slocum-look I can't stand. "Is that what happened, Miss Sara?"

"You telling Charlotte if it did?"

Chapter 4

Sara Loses to a Ladder

From the porch, I watch Raymond moan and groan. He's slumped against his van bumper, rubbing his temples as if the aspirin I gave him had not helped his headache. It's all I can do not to march over there and shake some sense into the boy. If his daddy hadn't succumbed to prostate cancer, God rest his soul, a simple note home would garner the apology I deserve from Raymond and all would be well.

Winnie tosses bundled mail from the Volkswagen's front seat to the back. The flying correspondence rouses the tattered-eared tabby curled upon a box stamped *Priority*. The cat stretches, leaps into the driver's seat, and plants its front paws on the steering wheel.

I would feel better about Winnie's insistence that Raymond receive medical attention if I could secure her firm commitment to silence. This unfortunate incident is not worth repeating, in my opinion.

But Winnie and Charlotte are wrapped tighter than kite string. And from the way Winnie hedged my inquiries, I'm certain Charlotte will know about my run-in with Raymond Leck long before the mid-day news airs. Even if Winnie swore on that dog-eared Bible she keeps handy, past experience makes me doubt her ability to keep her mouth shut about my business.

Winnie rounds the car and opens the driver's door. "You sure you weren't hurt, Miss Sara?"

"Don't you worry about me, Winifred." I keep a sharp eye on that arched-up alley cat, wishing Winnie had not stripped me of the water hose. If that scrappy feline bolted and took up country living, no bird would be safe. I realize Winnie is staring at me, obviously still unconvinced by my side of the story. I thrust my hands into my robe pockets and change the subject. "Let Dr. Ellis conduct a good look-see on Raymond." In an attempt at goodwill, I add brightly, "Have the bill sent to me."

Raymond fires an icy glare. "Who's gonna pay for my pain and sufferin'?"

So much for my goodwill.

"Making a mountain out of that little molehill on the back of your noggin has not improved your cognitive reasoning, Raymond. You did not complete the task you were assigned. You owe Charlotte a refund."

"I was blown off *her mother's* ladder…by *her mother*!"

"And did the dog eat your homework as well?"

Raymond's forehead wrinkles. "You ain't a makin' a lick o' sense, Miz Slocum."

"Me?" I cross my arms. "Apparently, you've never been on the receiving end of that mess you're making of the English language. Who was your teacher?"

"You."

Winnie covers her mouth, but not fast enough to dilute her snicker.

"I think you have me confused with that Crowder woman the board let go." I consider my response fairly civil considering I'm on the verge of ripping in to this hired tree-killer. No doubt he, too, will report to Charlotte. I look Raymond straight in the eye. "Your excuses are beginning to bore me, Raymond Leck."

He shakes a threatening fist. "You're gonna be hearin' from my lawyer."

I return the gesture. "If this hunk of junk you call a service vehicle sits on my property longer than twenty-four hours, you can count on hearing from my legal representative as well."

"Nobody's suing anybody." Winnie takes Raymond by the arm. "Let's get you to town, Mr. Leck." She stuffs Raymond's pudgy frame into her car.

Mumbling about my mental dexterity, Raymond tosses the cat into the back seat. I've always considered my hearing an asset, able to detect even the slightest of whispers amongst students. So, opting to let Raymond's crude remark slide speaks to my remarkable self-control. Hopefully my restraint will be mentioned in Winnie's report to Charlotte and add a point in my favor, but I doubt it.

Besides, Raymond has no idea how short-sighted those empty threats make him sound. But then again, the poor boy never was the sharpest crayon in the box. That he made it through school at all speaks to my extraordinary ability to guide even the slowest child through the great halls of learning.

I ease down the steps and shuffle to the end of the sidewalk. "Have a nice day." I flash my famous never-let-them-see-you-sweat smile and wave until the garish little car disappears around the bend.

Chalky dust settles upon my glasses. I pull them off my nose, drag the lens across the front of my robe, and set them back upon my least flattering feature. Martin liked my nose. Said the length of it made it easier for me to stick it where it didn't belong. He always claimed he admired any woman with that kind of gumption. If only my husband had managed to hang on to that wonderful sense of humor, I might not be running our ranch alone.

Taking stock in the acres of jungle surrounding my ever-shrinking yard, I wish Raymond had concentrated on brush-hogging the empty pasture instead of scalping my bluebonnets. Weeding flowerbeds and hand-pruning I can still handle, but operating the tractor wears me out more than I'll ever admit to Charlotte. The amount of work Raymond's departure has left would not have bothered me even a year ago. I can't tell if the bittersweet taste in my mouth is from my morning dose of iron or the bud of apprehension sprouting in my gut.

The hired man's termination will not please Charlotte. Adding Raymond's personal injury suit to the pile stacked against me might be the last straw. I would like to think my handling of this tree butcher will show Charlotte my deep reserves of mental and physical agility and ease that burr she's had under her saddle ever since her father died.

Charlotte thinks managing this place will do me in. Fresh air and hard work did not kill her father. Martin died of the same thing that's eating Charlotte. I'd hoped that in time, my girl would push through the darkness. I couldn't stand it if she let grief take her out as well.

I scoop up Raymond's forgotten tools. The next time Charlotte launches into one of her tirades on the dangers of old people living alone, I intend to raise Raymond Leck's rusty shears in triumph. But I can't stand the weight of the nasty things in my hands so I stomp to his van, open the door, and jam them beneath the seat. At least he'll have to spend a good deal of time looking for his shears before he can destroy someone else's nice trees.

I slam the door and decide to change into some work clothes, fire up my push mower, and finish the yardwork myself. But I need to hurry before the sun gets too high.

I head for the house.

The stepladder casts a shadow across the sidewalk. I pause and study the relic parked against the smooth bark of the crape myrtle. Why didn't I insist Raymond clean up his mess before he left? I pick my way through the small patch of hyacinths at the base of the crape myrtle.

The ladder towers over my head.

Don't do it.

"Polygon?" I eyeball the yard, worried I failed to latch the birdcage again. Bees dart in and out of the crape myrtles. I have the entire Fossil Ridge to myself. I tamp the sting of loneliness and remind myself that silence is golden. If my head hadn't been so full of noise that day, I might have heard...

Insides shaking, I dismiss the one memory I can't seem to forget and turn my attention back to the ladder. There's no reason I can't handle a ladder. I've done it a million times. I place a hand on each of the wooden legs.

Don't do it.

"Polygon, don't make me come up there." I shade my eyes and scan the trees.

Relieved when I see nothing, it crosses my mind that this urgent plea might be God trying to tell me something. But God has never spoken to me in words...through the sound of flowing water, yes. But never words.

Don't do it.

Maybe I should leave the ladder until LaVera's son takes his lunch break at the gas station and comes to check on her. I just hate to have to ask Bo Boy to stop by again so soon. Yesterday, I required his assistance to change the light bulb in the porch fixture. Seems any job demanding the slightest bit of muscle forces me to seek help. Which I'm more than capable of doing on my own. I'd ask for help more often if it wasn't so darn humiliating. Charlotte thinks I don't ask for help because I don't like people. Truth is, people don't like me…not anymore. Not that I blame them. I barely can stand the person I've become. Pieces of my mind are breaking off daily. It's become harder and harder to gather them up. The doctor assures me the descent will be slow and painless. But each morning is like starting the dying process all over.

Why couldn't I be one of the lucky ones? Die quickly. Like Mildred Culpepper. A heart attack took her out while squeezing tomatoes in the middle of the produce aisle. Except for dropping the tomato, the former home economics teacher died with her makeup on and her independence intact.

It's rather presumptuous to dictate one's own end to the Lord, but I'd much rather go out in a dramatic blaze of glory than sit around waiting on natural causes—or Charlotte— to steal my dignity one simple task at a time.

I know Bo Boy doesn't drop in to check on me because I offer him a little something for doing odd jobs. He always turns me down. Bo Boy comes by because each little visit gives him another opportunity to ask probing questions about Charlotte.

If Bo Boy thinks I've forgotten that sad look on his face when Charlotte showed him her law school acceptance letter, he's wrong. While I'll be the first to admit I wanted Charlotte to have the world, I didn't bargain on that sorry piece of swamp land she got when she married James McCandless. Would she have been happier married to a local and running a little two-pump gas operation on the corner of Main and Elm? I'll never know. A resigned sigh ruffles the tendril of snowy white hair that has once again escaped my normally tidy bun.

"Water under the bridge," I say, as if the ladder cares about my daughter's marital troubles. That I have taken to talking to inanimate objects concerns Charlotte more than my staying alone. But I don't see the harm. Unlike children, ladders don't talk back.

I tighten my grip on each of the ladder's wooden legs. No sense paying Bo Boy to do something I can handle myself. I try collapsing the ladder, but the paint-splattered braces are locked firmly into place. I flatten my palm and give the stubborn hinge on the right a swift hit. It pops loose. Pleased at my progress, I steady six feet of lopsided lumber with one hand while I reach around and whack the other brace.

Snap! The sudden smack of wood against wood catches my finger.

"Sweet Moses."

I jerk free and bring the swelling injury to my lips. Sucking my pinched skin, I watch the ladder dance left, then right. The folded contraption sways before me like the awkward hula girl Winifred hired for my surprise Hawaiian-themed seventieth birthday—a party no one attended, including Charlotte. Something came up at work, no doubt.

Without warning, the ladder stops spinning, a ballerina balanced on one toe.

Move!

The urgent command ringing in my head fails to uproot my feet. I'm rooted deep as the cypress trees shading the Frio.

Paint tray flapping, the ladder topples. In my direction.

Crack!

I go down hard. The back of my head smacks concrete.

Pop!

Pain rips through every inch of my body. Head pounding, I force my eyelids open. Blinking does not clear the stars swirling before my eyes. I try to raise my right hand to adjust my glasses beneath the wood flattening my face and pressing my elbow into my ribs.

How am I going to check out my situation if I can't even lift my head? Lacerating pain fillets the muscles from my frame. Bones are surely broken.

Oh, sweet Moses, not my back. Please not my back. What have I done?

My heart thumps against ribs that feel sharp as a pitchfork. Pulsing blood fills my ears and mutes the country melodies of insects and birds. If I don't get off this pavement, I'll fry like an egg. I struggle to move. My heroic efforts to wiggle even a big toe yield nothing.

Just to make sure I'm still alive, I whisper, "Get a hold of yourself." I labor to catch a breath, but the weight crushing my chest limits success.

First things first. Get this ladder off me, then call for help. Surely, I can rally some body part. I lick my crusty lips. No lipstick? Oh, how could I have entertained guests with no lipstick? I chide myself for letting my vanity get in the way. A second-rate yard man and an old-maid postal worker wouldn't know a good impression, had I made one.

I swallow back tears. I don't have time for useless waterworks or this inconvenience. The church's hospitality committee is expecting my hummingbird cake at their annual teacher appreciation banquet. Ironic I'm good enough to make cakes for teachers just not good enough to teach anymore.

That shindig is not until tomorrow, and Winnie has already brought today's mail. Not a single soul will miss me until Charlotte makes her Monday morning telephone call...and sadly, that's a whole week away.

The fingers on my left tingle. Hope jars the frozen cogs of my brain. Maybe I can slowly work my hand out from under my body. I force air into my compressed lungs. White hot pain sears my chest wall, but I manage to wrench my hand free.

Celebrating the victory, I open and close my fist. The burn of circulation returns. I grit my teeth and bring my freed hand toward the ladder pinning me to the ground.

Should I pull left or push right to remove it? I have to think this next move through carefully. Although I'd never admit this to Charlotte, I know my limitations. My strength will allow only one shot at freedom.

Running my fingers along the ladder's edge, I calculate the structure's location and determine that the majority of the weight is on my right. I opt to push.

Closing my eyes, I mentally count, "One. Two. Three."

I shove with all my might. Wood clatters upon the paved walk. Short, labored breaths instantly choke any exhilaration and rob me of any celebration. Excruciating spasms wrack my body. I cross my arms over my heaving chest but can't stop the scream shredding my insides. I hang on despite the shaking fit loosening my new dentures.

"Oh, sweet Moses. Sweet, sweet Moses."

Sunlight warms the cold sweat trickling down my face. Once the shaking subsides, I open my eyes. Through the shattered lens of my glasses, I can tell a blameless blue sky has replaced the earlier darkness I felt.

This is a comfort.

I don't care how bad Charlotte would think this situation, gazing into the beauty of the heavens is progress. Time spent lying upon the river's bluff, searching the sky, and listening to the water has been my salvation. A few hours flat on her back wouldn't hurt Charlotte.

"Focus on the good." I grab a breath. "Focus on the good." I snatch another short gasp of air. "Focus on the good."

Repeating my mother's mantra conjures visions of the tin lunch pail she placed into my quivering hands my first day of school. I was four years old and way too young for first grade. Momma had taken a job at the factory to help with the war effort while Daddy took a break from the bank to serve our country. And like so many children of the Great War, there was nowhere else for me to go.

The breeze carries the scent of Momma's lilac water. I let the smell fill my nose. No, that hint of sweetness is not Momma, but rather that of my own roses. I'm home. In the front yard Martin and I cleared ourselves. Calm settles over me. My racing heart slows to a limping thump. I breathe a bit easier despite the knife-like jab to my left lung.

There's nothing you and God can't do together, Sara Slocum, just as you have since Martin passed twenty-three years ago. Everything will be fine.

An overwhelming desire to sleep drags my eyelids shut. Various options spin like grating scribbles on a chalkboard. Each ugly picture creates another worry. I erase the images of walkers, wheelchairs, and nursing homes, leaving nothing but a blank slate. I try my best to relax. In a few moments, air seeps into my lungs and gently blows the cobwebs from my head.

I'll whittle this problem down, one step at a time, using the same patient method I taught my students as they learned long division. Show your work, and don't fret about what to do with that useless remainder.

Chapter 5

One Foot in the Grave

Why is my alarm beeping? I never sleep through the 5:00 a.m. Farm and Market Report.

I crack a crusty eyelid. The hazy-blue light of dawn chides my slothfulness. Getting rid of this muddy soup in my head will require two cups of tea before I fix Polygon's breakfast. I lie still, hoping a few more stationary moments will alleviate this headache without unnecessary medication. The constant beeping dashes any gains.

Must get moving if I am going to salvage the rest of the day.

I reach to throttle that blasted clock, but my hands and feet are tangled in the sheets. Working to free myself, I discover I'm bundled like a papoose and just as helpless. Pain needles my exhausted body and halts any plans of heading to the kitchen.

Why can't I get up?

Did I have a stroke?

Terror shoots through me. I take a daily baby aspirin. Without fail. Just as Dr. Ellis suggested. I couldn't have had a stroke.

Hyperventilating will not solve my problem, so I do my best to continue a shallow inhale and exhale. Struggling for breath, another thought, far worse than being made a drooling idiot by a stroke, seizes me.

Charlotte has buried me alive.

I don't know how she did it, but I've learned a good lawyer can get around the law. My hands continue to disregard my frantic commands to raise the roller shade between me and a clear understanding of my current situation. Ignoring the dull ache in my chest, I inhale slowly.

Fresh air.

I can't possibly be six feet under.

Embarrassment heats my cheeks. This has to be one of those crazy dreams, the same kind that tormented me for months after Martin died. I will my mind to step from the terrifying mist, but my body refuses to follow suit and my eyes refuse to focus.

In my blurred periphery, a form hovers. The gentle slope reminds me of my gabled roof. I must be home. My next breath comes a little easier. As long as I'm home, what does it matter if I have things a bit mixed up? I'm not counted tardy if I'm not up at the crack of dawn, and I don't receive a detention if I don't have all the answers.

"Mother?"

Why is my roof talking? I study the ridgeline, searching for the spinning weathervane. Those arrows have kept me straight for years and it seems I could benefit from being pointed in the right direction now. Inky clouds obscure the metal rooster. A summer thunderstorm has crept up over the craggy river bluffs. But the alcohol burn in my nostrils is not the sweet scent of rain. I'm confused, no doubt the result of that ladder lick I took between the eyes. What else would explain my headache and the reoccurring picture of Raymond standing over me saying, "Miz Slocum, you've gone and done it now."

Is that why I am spread-eagle on the front lawn with my robe tangled around my neck? Oh, dear. I should make myself presentable. No sense in showing my granny panties to God's entire creation. I struggle with my hands, but they do not lift, no matter how hard I try. I have no way to wrestle my clothes back into their proper position. Tears sting my eyes. Seems I went to bed robust and awoke eight hours later plum shiftless, one of those soap-opera-watching slackers Charlotte expected me to become after my retirement.

I shudder at the thought.

"Mother?"

Charlotte? The low and melodic voice reminds me of my youngest daughter. From her first utterances, long before Charlotte could walk, I thought her future was in front of a classroom, singing songs to children. That she ended up in law was her doing, not mine.

"Did you see that, Winnie? I think she's moving."

Another angled form joins the one hunched over me.

"Charlotte, I think that's just some of those reflex actions the doctor mentioned. Let me take you home."

Why is the mail lady on my front porch? Charlotte's the only one who ever sends me a package and that's only at Christmas. Then I remember Winnie and Raymond must have returned for his van. Good. The sooner that contraption is off my property, the better. That no-good tree scalper better not dilly dally if he knows what's good for him.

"What if she wakes up? What if she opens her eyes for just a split second and I'm not here?" Charlotte sounds ragged with worry.

"That ladder did a number on her head. I don't think she'll pry those swollen eyes open any time soon. Besides, you've been here for three days," Winnie says.

My head? I try to jump into the conversation, but my tongue is as dry as August pasture land and stuck to the roof of my mouth.

"At least come to my place," Winnie is saying. "Take a nap. Get a shower."

"Winnie, I can't. She looks so...helpless."

Helpless? I've never been helpless a day in my life, Charlotte Ann Slocum...McCandless. I tack on the McCandless purely out of respect for Charlotte and her dogged insistence that her husband's east coast name gives her credibility in certain circles.

"Miss Sara came through the surgery."

Surgery? What surgery? Winnie's overactive imagination is

trumped only by her overactive tongue. Would it kill her to keep her thoughts to herself just once? What can be gained by scaring Charlotte?

"Broken hip. Wrist. Ribs. Concussion." Charlotte shakes her head.

Broken? Hip? Wrist? Head? If Charlotte's saying I've suffered these injuries, no wonder every inch of me hurts. But how? Why?

"It's a lot. But your mother is tough as shoe leather."

"I know. She reminds me every chance she gets. But I can't ignore the facts, Winnie."

"What facts?"

"When people her age break a hip…they often die."

Die?

I try moving my hands, a foot, anything that will steer this ridiculous conversation in another direction. To my left, the sound of beeping intensifies and I make a mental note to get a new alarm clock.

Winnie clears her throat. "Some do."

"Ninety-something percent." Charlotte states the horrifying fact as if she's offering a summation before a hostile jury.

This is not comforting. I try fluttering my eyelids to get her attention.

"That means nearly ten percent don't," Winnie counters. "The doctor said that despite your mother's heart and her diabetes, she held up well through the surgery. You'll see, a little rehab and Miss Sara will be tending her birds and giving the next handyman what-for."

Charlotte snorts. "Can you imagine Mother in rehab? I can't even get her to leave the ranch long enough to fly up for one of Ari's recitals. How in God's name do you think I'll convince her to move to a rehab facility?"

Let me set the record straight. My daughter has never invited me to visit Washington. I wouldn't have missed a minute of Aria's life had they ever once included me. Receiving an occasional photo or a call on my birthday is hardly the relationship I envisioned having with my granddaughter.

I bite my tongue, as I have for years. Besides, now that I have one foot in the grave, there's no point in disagreeing. Charlotte thinks what she wants and once I'm gone, no telling what she'll tell Aria about me. I feel strength surge through me. If for no other reason than setting the record straight with my precious grandchild, I will live.

"I imagine your mother doing whatever it takes to get back on her feet."

"Winnie, what did I ever do to deserve a friend like you?"

"You know what you did for me. Watching out for your mother is the least I can do."

I'd gag if I could be certain my spittle wouldn't get hung up on this uncomfortable contraption lodged in my throat.

"Mother?" Charlotte's breath warms my ear. "Mother, I know you can hear me. Open your eyes, please."

I won't. I've never given credence to gloom and doom. And I won't do it now.

"Winnie, what if she's trapped in there? What if she can hear me, but I can't hear her?" Charlotte's lips brush my cheek.

I can't remember the last time my daughter kissed me. I must be dying. A swell of emotions long forgotten wash over me.

"All the tests ruled out brain damage," Winnie says. "I'm sure she's just worn out from the whole ordeal."

"I hate to think what would have happened if you hadn't taken that yard man back to the ranch." Charlotte pulls away and I wish I could grab her. "You can skip the details of Raymond's termination. He met me in the hospital lobby. Served me a piece of paper with a dollar amount penciled in beside every play-by-play grievance."

"Don't worry about Raymond. He'll settle down." Winnie's comment highlights her lack of experience with strong-willed children.

"Tell me what you think happened."

"Far as we could tell, your mother tried to put the ladder away and it got the better of her. How she managed to drag all those broken bones up the porch steps and half-way inside the front door is nothing short of a miracle."

That Winnie gives me no credit is no surprise. That she insists on underestimating Raymond is a serious mistake.

"Unless you walk on water," Charlotte says.

"Charlotte, I wish you could find some peace with your mother. Life is short."

My breath hitches in my chest. The river sucked the peace from our family so many years ago that I can scarcely recall the overrated feeling. I've tried. Late at night, alone in my bed, I've rummaged through the faded family snapshots stored in the crevices of my mind. Mealtimes, bedtimes, prayer times, holidays. But all I find is the sad picture of me eating alone in front of the TV. So how is it that a person can miss something they're not sure ever existed?

I force the air from my lungs in hopes of relieving the pressure. If someone asked

me to choose our family's most-likely-to-succeed-despite-the-devastation, I'd give Charlotte the place right behind me. I think she's done very well at finding some sort of footing and going on with her life. She got the education she wanted. Married the man she wanted. Had a child she mostly wants. Charlotte even follows my example and keeps herself busy.

I can't pinpoint the exact moment we decided staying busy was better than talking. Maybe it was after her sister's funeral. While I silently tackled the dishes in the sink, she'd silently tackled the clutter the crowd of sympathizers had left in the living room.

We didn't mean for the silence to go on, but neither of us knew what to say. At any rate, I think it's safe to assume we agree that the effort required to dismantle the wall between us would probably kill us.

But I can't help but wonder…does Charlotte miss me as much as I miss her? The question stirs something dormant, something reminiscent of hope. I listen for what Charlotte will say. I lie very still. Waiting. Afraid to water the brittle prospect with my tears. Afraid not to.

Charlotte clears her throat. "I don't know why she was trying to get to the phone. She hates talking to me."

Old fool. The empty lump in my throat will not be dislodged. I know better than to get my hopes up, but how much time does Charlotte think we have? This little accident has been a wake-up call for me. I'd be the last person to give Winnie credit for having an original idea, but she's right about how time flies. Yesterday, I was young and had forever before me. Today, I have death chiseling away at my bones. Tomorrow…my life will be over.

"You know you'd feel better if you could talk about it, Charlotte."

"Don't try to send me on one of your God-forgives-why-can't-you guilt trips."

"He does, you know…forgive," Winnie says.

"I envy people who believe strongly in religion. It gives them such a convenient place to dump their crap."

"God's big enough to take it."

"I'm not one of your Bible-study groupies, Winnie."

"You used to be."

"We were young. And stupid. And thought we could save the world. Well, let me tell you what twenty-plus years of a hard life will teach a person...," Charlotte pauses, and I wait, anxious to know exactly what she has learned.

"Stay out of the sun and wait two hours after eating before swim..." Winnie lets the word drop over a cliff. From the silence, I can tell Winnie's attempt at humor fell as flat as LaVera's angel food cakes.

"The world's not worth saving. In fact, very few things are." The bitter chill in Charlotte's retort jars me like a dissonant note.

What kind of mother sits back and allows circumstances to strip the lilt from a child capable of keeping the family in stitches? The same kind who thought she had all the time in the world. I try to shift out from under the crushing guilt, but I cannot move a muscle.

"Does your sky-is-falling attitude include your daughter?" Winnie asks.

"I don't need one of your sermons. I've heard them all before. Just give me the facts on Mother."

"Facts? You making a case against your mother?"

"Of course not."

"Really?"

Charlotte sighs. "Tell me how you found her, Winnie."

"If Raymond hadn't noticed her slipper on the sidewalk, I probably wouldn't have thought to go in to check on her."

"Don't beat yourself up. Believe me I know how difficult she can be. You got just a little taste of what I've been dealing with ever since Daddy..."

Here it comes, the truckload of guilt Charlotte loves to back up and dump on me. I brace myself. But she does not finish. The steady beeping of my alarm punctuates the silence.

"You're tired," Winnie says. I hear a chair slide across the floor. "Sit down, C."

"I can't sit and do nothing."

"Well, pacing isn't doing you a bit of good, and it's certainly not helping Miss Sara."

"Fine."

I can hear Charlotte plop onto the plastic seat, and not very lady-like I might add.

"That's better," Winnie says. "As I was saying, hopefully, I can talk Raymond out of suing. Except for a bit of bruised pride, he wasn't really hurt."

"How long before someone is? How long before my mother does something I can't fix?"

Winnie chuckles. "I don't fault Miss Sara for shooting the

Wooten dog. I might have done the same thing if that lop-eared mutt had chased my laying hens."

"Would you wave that same shotgun in the face of Sam Sparks?"

"If he was trying to push me off my land, maybe."

"What happened to 'Love thy neighbor?'" Charlotte's jab must have hit its mark because Winnie does not offer one of her snappy comebacks.

Come on, hippy girl. That I am rooting for Winnie sobers me. My head injury must be critical. Nevertheless, I cannot help praying this thorn in my flesh finds the words that will break through Charlotte's hard shell.

"Sparks Development is not bucking for any good neighbor awards and you know it, C."

Not the response I hoped for, but Winnie does bring up a good point.

"Do you really think me that shallow?"

"Not the Charlotte I knew."

"Things change." Charlotte's silence pricks my heart. "But you know that, Winnie. Whether or not Mother sells the ranch is the least of my worries. There's so much that can happen to her out there in the country. Rattlesnakes. Vagrants. What if she forgets to take her insulin or heart medication? What if she leaves the gas on and blows herself into eternity?"

I had no idea Charlotte considered me such a moron. Propane is far too expensive to fritter away. I understand budgets and the need to stick to them. For years, I stocked entire classrooms with glue, scissors, and anything extra using my own lunch money. I may not have my daughter's fancy Harvard degree, but no one's better than squeezing a dollar out of a dime. As for the serpents that slither onto my property, they've yet to land a good strike against me.

I should make myself get up and put an end to this nonsense. Send Winnie packing. Set Charlotte straight once and for all.

But I don't.

I just lie here, escaping into the coma I've been in for years.

Chapter 6

Charlotte's Home...I Must be Dead

The final bell rings.

Chairs scrape across the wooden floor as eighteen candy-cane-stuffed third graders push back from their desks and grab their coats. Laughing and shoving, the children duck under the sagging strands of popcorn and cranberries. When my classroom is finally empty, I sink into my chair. My head throbs as the sugar-high carries the noise of childish anticipations far from the building. My nerves could not have taken another minute of halls filled with holiday chatter of plans for family gatherings or visits from fake-bearded Santas. In the deserted quiet, I allow a sigh to escape my clenched jaws.

Christmas snuck up on me this year. That's what I get for hoping it wouldn't come, for wishing the blackened days of fall would tumble into winter and freeze solid before all the life ebbs from my veins. What a fool to think the world would skip Caroline's favorite day simply because she...I banish the raw thought to that dark crater in my heart. I'm swiping tears when my principal pokes her head inside the classroom.

"Sara, you still with us?"

Mrs. Rayburn means well. Even offered to hire an extended substitute so I could take a leave of absence. I didn't see how abandoning my students would make grief desert me. I don't trust my voice to convey the conviction of my answer, so I say nothing.

I glance around the classroom. Forgotten homework assignments and broken sugar cookies litter the floor as a cruel reminder that life is messy.

It's not right to bury the living with the dead. I know that as sure as I know Caroline would be terribly disappointed if I let her baby sister come home to a house without Christmas.

Charlotte, the polar opposite of Caroline, finishes her first college semester tomorrow. Pre-law. Such an unusual choice for a girl who's never had a logical thought in her life. I'm not sure Charlotte understands that she may have bitten off more than she can chew, but I've said as much as I dare on the subject.

Caroline, on the other hand, is lawyer material. My oldest loves a fight, always the last to back down. She's the one with her ducks in a row, making lists, checking them twice, crossing off accomplishments as she goes.

Was the one.

"Miss Sara?"

I attempt a nod, anything that will send the principal on her way and allow me a moment to get myself together. Charlotte is coming home. Caroline is not. Pretending otherwise will do Martin no good. That leaves me less than twenty-four hours to prepare Charlotte's favorite foods, sort the presents I'd stashed in the closet long before the funeral, and get my fruitcakes delivered to the nursing home.

The suggestion Martin made over our morning bowl of oatmeal rings in my ears. Cutting back on my baking for the shut-ins won't make things easier. Besides, how can I cut back without cutting someone out? Who can I ignore? Every one of those poor souls languishing in those drab, lonely rooms tug at my heart. No. Forgetting their hurts won't fix mine.

Take Cora Jenkins, for example. Every Christmas Eve, an aide helps that wisp of a woman clip gaudy snowflake earrings to her drooping earlobes and swipe rouge across her protruding cheekbones. Once Cora is all dolled up, she has the aide wheel her to the lobby. There she waits, patting the faded Christmas bow stuck to the crocheted afghan folded neatly in her lap. Not once, in five years, have I seen a single one of Cora's sorry offspring darken the nursing home with so much as a poinsettia. I know exactly how many years this optimistic mother has waited for her family to visit because I've counted the number of unclaimed throws stacked in the corner of Cora's dingy little room.

Thank God, that will never be me.

My girls will see to me...my girl. I cap the ever-present wellspring of tears, but the excess erupts over my rims. Charlotte loves me. In her own, distant way. Maybe we don't connect like we once did, but Charlotte would never stuff me in a cinder-block hole so small that if a mosquito bit me I would have no room to swell.

"Mother? I know you're in there. Please answer me."

Oh, dear, Charlotte's early. I'm not ready. The fruitcakes just went into the oven and I haven't crumbled the cornbread for the stuffing.

"Mother?"

The exhaustion in Charlotte's voice worries me. She's not been getting her rest. The doctor warned me about this, but I think he's just being overly cautious. Between dorm life and Charlotte's surprising determination to get into the best law school, this child seldom sleeps. But what good are dedicated efforts if she's too tired to enjoy life?

Martin claims the same could be said of me. He says Charlotte's overachieving tendency is my fault. I'm tempted to say there's no harm in wanting her to find something to make at least one of us happy, but I bite my tongue. I brush the cornbread from my hands. I used to think a few weeks of country air and good home cooking could put anyone right again, but now I'm not so sure.

"I'm coming, Charlotte." The words form in my head, but I'm unclear as to what has come out of my mouth.

"Mother!" Charlotte's glee is something I haven't heard since... "Oh, Winnie, look. She's moving her hands."

Someone squeezes my hand, pressing the tiny diamond Martin gave me into the knuckle of my pinky finger. I've known widows who removed their rings after a time, but mine will never leave its cherished place. Taking it off would mean forgetting that moonlight canoe ride down the Frio. Tragedy has taken many things from me. It will not confiscate that precious moment. Back before Martin decided the world no longer glimmered, he could be quite the romantic. I cling to that. When I can take his sulking no longer, that memory means more than any jewels money can buy.

"I think she's trying to open her eyes." The raspy voice close to my ear reminds me of the hippie who's been delivering my mail.

What on earth is going on?

"Do you think she knows it's me?" The heavy musk assaulting my drowsy senses awakens memories of Charlotte. Why would my own daughter ask such a silly question of me? Of course, I know it's her. Why is she home? Am I dead?

"Look at Miss Sara's wrinkled brow. She knows," Winnie says.

"Mother, don't try to talk. You've got a tube down your throat. Just blink if you can hear me."

What madness has possessed Charlotte? She no longer believes in games or frivolous recreation. I intend to get to the bottom of this nonsense. I blink. Twice, just to make sure she doesn't miss my intention. Relief eases the crease above Charlotte's perfect nose.

"Games?" The question sputters in my throat and dies before

making a clean exit. With this gravelly gullet, I sound like Ivan, the school's two-pack-a-day janitor. Ivan thinks his nasty habit is a secret, but there's too many ground butts behind the dumpster to blame them all on sixth graders. I attempt to clear my throat again. I can force nothing past the clog in my pipes. Mountain cedar always flares my allergies right when I have so much to do for the holidays.

"What is she insisting on saying, Winnie?" Charlotte's irritation isn't helping.

Winnie puts an ear to my lips, and I try again but achieve limited success. She straightens, and shrugs. "Sounds like gay."

"Lord, don't get her started on that subject." Charlotte's hand wraps around mine. "Mother, don't pull on your oxygen."

"Char—" I say.

"Don't try to talk, Mother." Charlotte tightens her grip and repeats, "Remember, you've got a tube down your throat."

Winnie places her hand on Charlotte's shoulder. "Maybe if you explain what happened? Tell Miss Sara where she is. Stuff like that. It'll calm her down."

Charlotte's doubtful gaze bounces from Winnie to me and back, sending a wave of panic rippling over me. I don't know what could have happened since the bell rang, but I can tell it's bad. My mind swims with the memory of Charlotte's pale face, streaked with mud and tears. Surely any news I must be told cannot be worse than what she finally managed to blurt out when she came back from the river dripping wet and...alone.

I wait, trying not to read more into her silence than my heart can take.

Finally, Charlotte draws a deep breath and lets the information pour forth. "Mother, you've had a little accident. Had to be brought to the hospital by ambulance. What in the world were you doing on a ladder?"

"Don't cross-examine her, Charlotte." Winnie's reprimand is soft, kind. "Just talk to her."

Charlotte releases my hand. "Talk to her? About what? You know I've never been able to talk to her."

Winnie sighs, then nudges Charlotte aside. She strokes my cheek like I'm a terrified two-year-old. "Miss Sara, you're in the hospital. Do you understand what I'm telling you?"

I give a slight nod, even though I'm furious Winnie is forcing her way into our lives. God forgive my little white lie to the girl, but I need some time to cool down, time to figure out what to say to Charlotte. How dare she bring her wacky roommate home without asking me? I do not like surprises. Charlotte knows I'm a planner, and yet she deliberately sprung this missionary girl on me.

Normally, I'd have so many holiday goodies stuffed in the freezer I could get by, but this year I'm not ready.

That's not true.

The freezer is chock full of all those funeral casseroles the ladies from the church brought in. I could feed Charlotte's entire sorority for a month.

Truth is I just don't feel up to company. God forgive me, but I'm not ready to pretend our broken family is whole so some California stranger with a cross-shaped tattoo and multiple ear-piercings can have a hill country Christmas.

I force my heavy lids wide as I can and glance around the room.

What has Charlotte done to my classroom? Nothing is where it should be. The desks are missing. The bulletin boards empty. Why did she mess with my seating chart and scribble names I don't know on the small dry-erase board under the clock? And what about this barrage of noisy machinery that have obscured the times tables?

Squiggly orange lines race across a dark TV screen. They beep to the rise and fall of my chest. I jerk, but can't turn my head enough to investigate this new-fangled set-up because my wrist is taped to the clear tubing running from a bag of fluid suspended above my head. I search the ceiling tiles. What happened to the red and green construction paper chain my students toiled over for three days? I close my eyes, hoping to rid the throb spreading to my temples. Did I have too much Christmas punch? Surely not. That would be so unlike me, but since the accident who can say what is or is not like me?

Charlotte waves from the foot of my bed and grinds out, "Ask her again, Winnie. I'm not sure she heard you."

Why does Charlotte keep insisting something is wrong with my hearing?

"You're in the hospital, Miss Sara." Winnie's mouth forms the words slowly, like she's chewing a wad of Christmas taffy. "Do...you...understand?"

I heard this Woodstock escapee the first time. I just don't believe her.

Hospital?

How on earth could I have ended up in the hospital? One moment I'm sweeping up popcorn, the next I'm laid out? This doesn't make sense. Did Winnie say morgue?

I stare at her, intent on burning a hole clear through that beaded headband pressing into her forehead.

"There you are." A smile softens Winnie's leathery face and lights up her powdery-blue eyes. "Raymond and I found you sprawled across the threshold of your front door."

"Mother, what were you thinking?"

Why is Charlotte shouting? My legs won't move, but there's nothing wrong with my hearing. And since when does she care what I'm thinking?

Winnie turns to Charlotte and puts a shushing finger to her lips. "What if we ask Miss Sara questions she can answer with a nod?"

"Right." Charlotte backs away, the flat of her raised hands pushing added distance between us. "You ask. Obviously, I'm no good at this."

"Your mother gave you a scare, C. But she's going to be okay." Winnie turns back to me. "Are you in pain, Miss Sara?"

I attempt to shake my head, but my neck seems locked in a vice. I move my eyes back and forth. Hopefully Winnie is smarter than I give her credit for and will recognize that I'm in a bit of a pickle here. I don't think it's asking too much to expect someone to do something about my inability to communicate freely.

"Your night nurse is named Kate." Winnie points to the name on the board. "Kate wrote her name right here. In case you forget."

"She can't talk, Winnie. How in God's name is she going to call for Kate?"

Winnie wheels toward Charlotte. "You want her to stay calm or not?"

One arm crossed over her chest, the other slinging the charm around her neck back and forth, Charlotte recedes into the shadow. I've seen this retreat before. This child of mine can grill someone on the witness stand until they melt into a puddle, but when it comes to dealing with life's sticky complications, her backbone has a permanent crook in it. How can one person be such a frustrating contradiction?

Winnie returns her attention to me and leans in close. She reeks of Dr. Sunshine's herbal tea and I think I'm going to be sick. "You've had major surgery, Miss Sara. Right now, they have you on some pretty stiff drugs."

Sweet Moses. Now I'm on dope. That explains my upset stomach. I knew no good would come from Charlotte's association with a child allowed to roam west coast beaches, or was it the bush country of Africa? I can't remember. Either way, Winnie's free-spirit ways tells me her parents did not understand the importance of structure during the formative years. Next thing I know, these two will hire a witch doctor. Well, I won't stand for it. I try to raise my head, my hand, a foot, anything, but not one single body part cooperates.

"If you continue to progress like you have the past few days, you'll be moved out of intensive care and into a regular room. Do you understand?" Winnie's smile expects a response.

I know the prospect of weeks without homework has pushed my students into overdrive, but how did a harmless little Christmas party get so out of hand? I manage a teeny nod, despite the intense pain flattening my head against the pillow. I've got to get back on my feet before Charlotte comes home for Christmas. I have to…for Caroline's sake.

Chapter 7

You're Gonna Do What, Charlotte Ann?

I don't have a timeline, James." Charlotte grinds her husband's name between clenched teeth. "The doctor didn't say how long...Look, it won't hurt you to act like a father for once."

That Charlotte would encourage a heated debate with her husband in my presence can only mean one of two things—either she's convinced I'm drugged beyond comprehension or she thinks I'm dead.

As my daughter paces the length of my hospital bed, I watch through the slits of my swollen eyes. Charlotte has that blasted cell phone sandwiched between her ear and shoulder. One day she'll wake up with her neck permanently welded into that awkward position. I've told her the same nearly as many times as I've told her to stop crossing her eyes before they freeze looking at her nose.

Slyly, I squint at Charlotte. I'm tempted to curse the ladder that ruined my glasses and, judging by everyone's refusal to bring me a mirror, my face. As expected, Charlotte's grimace matches the tenor of her conversation. If I were a betting woman, I'd wager fifty dollars she's on the verge of reaching through the airwaves and strangling her no-good husband. I've offered to do the deed myself. Many times. Why she swallows that man's impudence like a first grader at the mercy of a lunchroom bully is a mystery I may never solve.

Charlotte pivots at the head of my bed and storms toward the foot. With her stiffened back to me, I seize the opportunity to check for the smallest break in the dam of her emotions. Even without glasses, I recognize the huge chip sitting upon her shoulders—a foul mixture of unhappiness and an unwillingness to do a blasted thing about her strained marriage. A surge of fresh anger plumps my collapsed veins, but I say nothing. Avoiding another useless discussion doesn't mean I'm a coward. Martin would say it means I've finally learned putting my nose where it doesn't belong does more harm than good. And good is all I've ever wanted for Charlotte.

"No, James." Charlotte switches the phone to her other ear. "Ari can't drive herself to her private lessons...because she's only thirteen...Don't even think about letting her take the train...Are you kidding, a child alone in the city at night?...So how do you think I manage?...Figure it out...I've got to go." She snaps her engraved phone case shut then winds up like a pitcher ready to hurl the sleek silver contraption across the mound.

I can't believe my ears. A satisfied smile slides across my lips. I would have broken bones sooner had I thought forcing my daughter into an extended absence from Washington would aid her emotional development.

Suddenly, Charlotte wheels and catches me grinning. "How long have you been awake?" Scowling, she crams the phone into the pocket of her chic brown warm-up suit.

I'm far too busy wiping the Cheshire-cat smirk from my face to say a word, which is probably a good thing. After spending the past few days hacking through the thicket of pain-med confusion, I'm not certain I have the good sense to control my mouth. The only clear snapshot I have of this whole sordid ordeal captures Charlotte declaring my tongue a loose cannon.

Charlotte plants her hands onto her slender hips. "How long, Mother?"

I swallow, stalling for time, but her glare shrinks my smile like a cheap cotton sweater. "Long enough."

Charlotte bristles. She starts to say something, thinks better of it, then turns and opens the blinds. A flame-red sunset casts a glow over the tarred roof and gray air conditioning units comprising the view I'm sure will end up costing me a sizeable portion of my teacher retirement fund. Keeping her back to me, Charlotte breathes deeply, as if she can soak in the last bit of the sun's energy before the darkness descends upon us and leaves her to face me and another unpredictable night.

"Look, Mother, this isn't easy," she finally says.

My daughter has forgotten exactly who is confined to a hospital bed and who is not. The lapse does not set well with me. "For whom?"

Charlotte lowers her shoulders. She turns and I discover the sharpened edge of her anger has frayed a bit, revealing that familiar resigned worry at the center. My heart lurches. She leans against the marble window sill. A single green plant sent from LaVera's garden is the only proof I have that I used to be loved. Looking past me, Charlotte stares at the wall like a garage-sale shopper trying to make out one of Winnie's abstract pieces of art.

She lets out a slow sigh. "Everybody."

"James McCandless is a jerk. Always has been."

"Morphine is not your friend, Mother."

The way my assessment draws her fire means only one thing—I have hit the nail on the head. Her charming husband is not the charmer he claims to be. I know it. She knows it. And now she knows I know she knows it. A lesser person would use this crack to their advantage. Remind Charlotte she'd made her bed when she disregarded my advice almost fourteen years ago and married him. But when I look at her now, all I see is a reflection of my unhappiness. Any desire to gloat chokes my throat.

I change the subject. "Am I dying?"

Frustration obliterates the worry from my daughter's face faster than one of those deceitful carnival mirrors. "No." She steps forward. "Why do you ask that?"

"It's been almost a week, and you're still here."

Charlotte drops a stainless-steel lid over the cold mashed potatoes and untouched meatloaf on my bedside tray table. "Where else would I be?" In one fluid movement, she maneuvers the wheeled table away from the bed and toward the hall filled with the clatter of silverware and the squeak of rubber-soled shoes.

I don't answer right off. Instead, I watch Charlotte's stiffened back while the multitude of her past excuses flit through my brain.

Court. The office. Flying around the country. Entertaining clients. Redecorating a never-used summer house on the Cape. Possibly with Ari. Anywhere…but home.

I snuff the sorrow, knowing I'm partly responsible for this distance that defines Charlotte. That my mothering never measures up, no matter what I do. That I fail her every day in some big and unforgivable way simply because I expect her to survive.

I dig deep in search of some courage of my own. "If you've come to pull the plug, Charlotte…pull it and get on back to your life."

Charlotte abandons the meatloaf at the open door and returns to my bed. "And what? Miss all these wonderful meals and bedtime stories we love to share?" She lifts the pillow out from behind my head and punches at the indentation in the lumpy foam. "Medicare doesn't waste taxpayer dollars rehabilitating lost causes."

"So, I'm not dying?"

She flips the fluffed pillow, gently raises my head, and stuffs the cool side behind my flattened hair. "Have I not said that thirty times today, Mother?"

The tiny gold treble clef around her neck dangles in my face. She kept it. All these years. I start to reach for it, to ask her why?

But maybe I already have. So, I keep my hands to myself. "Have I asked thirty times today?"

Charlotte straightens and slips the charm inside her shirt, where I picture it resting on her heart. "At least."

Guilt pricks my conscience and hot tears escape. "I'm sorry. I don't mean to be such a bother."

For a brief instant, a little girl's love flashes in her eyes. "I know, Mother. You're sick." Charlotte snatches a tissue from the box on the shelf beside my bed and waves it in front of my face. "Crying can't be good for your nose."

"How bad *is* my face?"

Charlotte's eyes cut away. It's all the confirmation I need to know my old mug looks as bad as it feels. She lays a hand on top of mine and softens her features to deliver hard news. "Remember Rocky the Raccoon?"

"That abandoned little creature you girls found in the barn and begged your father to let you keep as a pet?"

She nods. "You're the purple and green version." Charlotte

squashed the beginnings of what could have been interpreted as a reassuring smile and immediately the summation seriousness returned. "But we're going to do whatever it takes to get you back on your feet, right?" She hurries on as if she has no stomach to argue should I be allowed to disagree. "The nurse said Dr. Ellis would come by sometime today. I guess the good doctor thinks we've got nothing better to do than sit around and wait." She hands me a tissue.

"I don't." I dab at my watery raccoon eyes, wincing at the bruising and trying hard not to touch my oversized nose.

"Well, some of us do, Mother."

"That's my point. Why are *you* still here?"

"Because *you've* had major surgery, been in the hospital for days, half out of your mind most of the time, and—" Charlotte adjusts the pillow behind my back. "—you're...my mother."

If *mother* could have been said with any less enthusiasm, I have enjoyed sitting through forty years of parent-teacher conferences. But that she'd said *my* mother surprises me almost as much as her attachment to the necklace I gave her after her first piano recital. Maybe I'm putting too much hope into both. But wearing a piece of jewelry is not the same as carrying someone in your heart. Calling me Mother is not the same as saying *my* mother.

I claw through the cobwebs in my head, trying to put my finger on the exact moment I went from being Momma to Mother, but the cold transition is lost among the keepsakes I seldom examine. What good would dredging that river of pain accomplish?

I did what I could.

Surely even God didn't expect me to do more. Besides, I can't go back and right the wrong, undo what was done, gather Charlotte into my arms in that funeral limo and assure her that what happened was not her fault. I didn't have the strength then. I don't have the courage now.

I search Charlotte's hardened features for signs of a thaw, but I find no evidence her proclamation will be followed by a warming trend. I wave the damp tissue in surrender. "The sooner I start this rehab business, the sooner I get home to Polygon."

Charlotte's face brightens. "Well, that's more like it."

"What do you mean?"

"Until now you've wanted nothing to do with trying to sit up, or trying to get out of bed, or any of it."

"That's because I've been busy getting ready for Christmas and the effort has worn me slap out."

"Christmas?" A puzzled look crosses Charlotte's face. "Mother, what on earth are you talking about?"

The fear darkening her eyes stops me cold. What did I say? My mind scrambles to sort out the tangled mess of current thoughts, past remembrances, and ideas that make absolutely no sense, even to me. In the end, my effort proves futile. I mumble, "Dreams, I guess."

More like dark, terrifying nightmares, but I leave out that unsettling tidbit.

Charlotte's expression softens. "That's the morphine, Mother." She gives my shoulder a placating pat. "Let's keep Christmas to ourselves, okay? I don't want Dr. Ellis thinking you have dementia."

"Why not? You do."

"I think once the pain meds are completely cut off, you'll return to your no-nonsense self."

"You're not worried I'll blow myself to smithereens?"

A sheepish-blush pinks Charlotte's cheeks when she realizes I've been listening in on all of her phone conversations. "Raymond Leck's not the only one who can play possum?"

"I was wondering when you'd get around to questioning the yard man."

A slight grin tugs at the corner of her mouth. "Professional habit."

"Ever think about getting my side of the story?"

"You haven't been able to tell me your name. How could you explain why you fired the help and hosed him off a ladder?"

"Don't get your back up, Charlotte Ann. In the future, you might remember that my memory may lapse, but my aim has never been a problem."

"So true." Charlotte's flinch tells me my reprimand hit the bull's eye. I feel a little guilty until she says, "Where is that doctor?"

"You need to slow down, because the stuffing just went into the oven and I've fruitcakes to make."

"Fruitcakes?" Exasperation furrows Charlotte's forehead. "Mother, what *are* you talking about? It's only April."

"April?" Panic pimples my flesh. What did I say? Did I bring up Christmas again? I struggle to regain control. "I know that. I'm just telling you how hard it is to keep things straight in this dark tunnel."

"That's why I'm here." She takes my hand. "I'm going to get you all lined out before I go back to Washington."

My mind snaps to attention, the point of Charlotte's extended visit suddenly painfully clear. "Lined out?"

"Get your rehab started here in the hospital. Arrange for an inpatient residential care facility. Decide—"

I rip my hand free of her grasp. "Wait one cotton-pickin' minute, little missy. Residential? What on earth is residential inpatient care?"

Charlotte tucks the blanket around my feet. "That's what I'm checking on. I have to find out what Medicare will pay for, if your extended care policy will make up the difference, if you can rehab here, or if you're going to have to go to Austin."

"Austin! I'm not going to Austin!" I throw off my covers. "Soon as my broken bones are mended, I'm going home."

"That's the thing. You can't stay in the hospital until you've healed." Charlotte flips the covers back over my lifeless legs.

"Medicare only allows so many hospital days, then its rehab until you're back on your feet and able to take care of yourself."

"Call Dr. Ellis and tell him to get his bony ass in here." My foul language echoes against the sterile hospital room walls the way our family's laughter used to bounce between the river bluffs during our annual Fourth of July canoe races.

A horrified look crosses Charlotte's face. "Mother, what on earth has happened to your mouth?"

I don't have an answer, at least not one she would understand. A healthy Sara, one who still had full charge of her independence, would feel remorse, struggle to regain her composure, apologize profusely, and never lapse again. No, I take that back. A healthy Sara would never stoop to using curse words to make a point.

I am no longer that Sara. Plain and simple. And I'm not sure how I feel about the change.

"My backside hasn't been bony since junior high." The booming voice hauls our attention toward the open door.

A hulking man in a white coat fills the metal frame. No telling how much of our conversation or my inexcusable language the doctor has heard. Embarrassed heat flushes both our cheeks.

My daughter is the first to recover from the surprise intrusion. She swoops her bangs behind her ear and takes a step forward. "You'll have to forgive my mother. She's not herself."

The doctor smiles and extends a professional hand. "Benjamin

Ellis."

Charlotte's eyes dart from the mammoth palm to the doctor's face and back as if she's connecting the dots on one of those worksheets I used to teach numerical sequencing. Once the picture is complete, recognition dawns.

"Itty Bitty?" Charlotte throws her arms around the doctor's thick neck, and then just as abruptly pulls away. Her rosy cheeks have flamed into fiery humiliation. She backpedals two steps, sucking the rare moment of reckless abandon inside herself the way a turtle retreats into its shell. "I haven't seen you since high school graduation. Who would have thought Itty Bitty would morph into...Big Ben." She gives that short-sheeted nervous giggle she's picked up on Capitol Hill.

"Charlotte Slocum?" Benjamin straightens his tie. "It never occurred to me that you would be here." The sudden darkening of Charlotte's face forces the doctor into an immediate backpedal of his own; not steps—because he appears to be leaning into her—but verbally this young man is definitely on the retreat. "But, of course you'd come home. Mrs. Slocum is your mother."

As much as Charlotte deserves the discomfort her old band friend's assessment of our relationship brings, I can't bear the cracks around her frozen smile. "Benjamin, I hate to interrupt this little class reunion, but I hope you've come to explain to my daughter why you're not busting me out of this hell hole and sending me home."

Benjamin's brows rise. "Hell hole?"

Charlotte steps between me and my doctor, her toned body shielding her shame. "Mother's had a bit too much morphine." The giggle again.

"You don't have to make excuses for me, Charlotte." I poke her rigid back with the TV remote control. "I don't make them for you."

"Mrs. Slocum?" Benjamin peeks around a board-stiff Charlotte for a better look at me. "Glad to see you so alert today."

Mentally applauding the doctor's willingness to disregard the hideous condition of my face and my unhinged tongue, I can only pray that he'll disregard Charlotte's interference and take the hint that I've not relinquished my health-care reins. Charlotte gives a resigned snort, steps aside, and retreats against the windowsill. Benjamin picks up the only chair in the room with one hand. He rotates it around, straddles the seat, and parks his elbows on the back.

We now see eye to eye, and I can't help but admire the direct approach I fostered in this fine young man. "Finally, someone who patch me up and get me out of here."

"You know I'm not a surgeon, Mrs. Slocum."

"You're my internist, Benjamin. I helped you prepare for the MCAT, remember?"

"I do." His smile is a winner. "My job is to get you off the meds and start some physical therapy now that we've got you a bit more…stable."

I cut a sideways glance in Charlotte's direction. "She seems to think my stability is still in question. Do you, Benjamin?"

The handsome doctor hesitates, shoots a help-me-out look at Charlotte. She shrugs as if to say he is on his own, so he continues, "I think you're still sharp as a Ginsu knife."

I pat his cheek. "You've always been one of my favorites, Benjamin."

He beams under the praise and I catch a glimpse of the freckle-faced boy who puffed up like a peacock when he finally mastered fractions. "Dr. Hunke thought that since you were a regular patient of mine, you might be willing to work with me, and between the two of us, we could make swifter progress."

"And who is Dr. Hunke?" I ask.

"He's your orthopedic surgeon." Benjamin's patient tone inspires me to ask for a little more clarification.

"And this Dr. Hunke operated on me?"

"Mother, we've gone over this a dozen times."

"I'm not speaking to you, Charlotte. I'm asking Benjamin." I smile at the young man beside my bed. "So, this doctor—what did you say his name was?"

Charlotte huffs. "Hunke, Mother. Hunke."

I hold up the flat of my hand silencing Charlotte without

breaking my gaze on Benjamin who's been watching our barbed exchange as if it was a tennis tournament. "So, this Dr. Hunke operated on me?"

The doctor sees his opening and joins the volley. "He did."

"Why did this Hunke fellow operate on me when I clearly would have chosen Dr. Stevens?"

Benjamin smiles at my clarity. "That's a fair question." He scans my chart. "Hunke was the doc on call when they brought you to Emergency. Stevens was trout fishing in New Mexico." The young doctor closes the chart. "I'm afraid your injuries wouldn't wait for Doc Stevens to catch his limit." He scoots the chair closer to my bed and strokes his mahogany beard. "Besides, have you seen Hunke? According to the nurses, his name suits him." That million-dollar smile is worth every dime Benjamin's parents spent on his braces.

"I've seen him. He doesn't hold a candle to my Martin," I say.

Charlotte throws her hands up in the air. "Mother, what do Daddy's looks have to do with anything? What I think Itty—excuse me, Ben—wants to know is why won't you cooperate with your surgeon?"

I let Charlotte's accusation go unchallenged. How can I explain that I feel as fragile and crumbly as one of LaVera's cheese straws? One false move and I'm certain to shatter. If that happens, even the best hot-shot Austin surgeon would be at a loss at how to put Humpty Dumpty back together again. What if Hunke is more handsome than he is medically capable of wiring my broken bones together? What if I never heal? What if I'm forced to go through life with yet another black-eyed misfortune for all to see and judge? I do my best to stiffen my shoulders and plaster a brave face on this mess, a mess that I can blame upon no one but myself.

"Exactly what are my injuries, young man? I don't want you to sugar-coat a thing, except maybe the part about my face."

"You sure, Mrs. Slocum?" Benjamin asks.

"To the last detail," I confirm.

"Very well." The doctor removes a marker from his jacket pocket. "You've got a couple of broken bones in your right wrist." He removes the marker's cap, then makes two quick strokes on the hard casing on my forearm. A black X appears on the bumpy surface. "Nice clean breaks. We don't anticipate any trouble with healing. Once we get you out of this contraption, you'll have to do some therapy to get your strength back, but nothing you can't handle." He offers that encouraging smile I so need to see.

"I'm left-handed." I point out. "I should be able to make do until I mend."

"That will get you through the next few days, but try to maintain natural hand activities, even simple ones like eating and brushing your teeth improve your mobility." He places his hand on my wrist, his span nearly covering the entire cast. "Some patients have a tendency to let their dominant side pick up the slack for an injured counterpart. You'll have to pay extra attention to that right side."

"I do not believe in slacking on any front, Benjamin."

His smile lights his green eyes. "Your lesson on the dangers of taking the easy road changed the course of my life, Mrs. Slocum."

Until this young man's praise, I'd had no feeling under this heavy cast. But now, a tingle of satisfaction zips from the tips of my fingers straight to my heart. So many years in the classroom. So many children. So many hours of grading papers. So many sleepless nights wondering if one over worked, under paid teacher could make a difference. To see the fruit of my labors—a fuzzy-peach of a man who is confident and fully capable of making his way in this world...well, it's nice to know my labors were not in vain. Benjamin's gratitude does more than ignite my senses, it ignites my courage.

"And my leg?" I asked, braced for the worst. "Why can't I move my leg?"

He ponders the best way to answer. "Well, now that's where the road gets rocky."

I clutch the edge of the stiff hospital sheet and gaze at Charlotte leaning against the windowsill. Lingering rays of sunlight catch the golden highlights she's added to her natural blonde. Even though worry has creased the corners of Charlotte's eyes, I marvel at the natural beauty she inherited from her father. She nibbles on her lower lip and picks at her expensive fake nails. So many things have robbed my child of innocence. That I share in the blame angers me.

Pulling the sheet to my chest, I summon my sparse reserves, praying I'm not too late to make it up to her. "Let's hear it then, Doctor. And do not spare the details."

Chapter 8

Ghosts and Fossils

Charlotte stomped the accelerator of her rental car and flew over the river bridge. She hated crossing the Frio, but there was no other way home.

Home.

Haunting memories chased the gravel spitting out from beneath her tires. She hadn't been back to the ranch in months and wouldn't have come then if Mother hadn't driven a tractor through the side of the barn and the contractor hadn't said the whole structure needed to come down. The visit had been a miserable failure she swore she'd never repeat.

As her car crested the hill, the headlights swept across a pair of flat metal cowboys that flanked the entrance to Fossil Ridge.

She'd never liked Mother's addition of the crossed-armed sentinels. Leaning casually against opposite hedge posts with their hats pulled down across their eyes and a boot jacked behind them, the cowboys looked bored or tired. Their unwillingness to lift their heads and really look at her whenever she did come around reminded her of Mother.

Charlotte braked to a stop outside the open gate. Her fingers drummed the wheel.

Coming home was a bad idea. She'd only agreed to Winnie's insistence that she spend the night at the ranch because she needed a break from the hospital. Major decisions should never be made when exhausted. She'd learned that the hard way. Twice.

She should have rented a motel room in town. It would have kept her closer to the hospital and spared her this added stress.

Charlotte lifted her glasses with thumb and index finger and pinched the mounting pressure. Anyone would be at the end of their rope after a week of listening to old Christmas stories that made no sense. Sorting through Mother's increasing disorientation was hard on a good day. They'd not had a good day since the difficult woman regained consciousness. No...there hadn't been a good day between them in twenty-four years. Her mother's current injuries had nothing to do with the real source of the pain and blame. That subject was so far off-limits, morphine couldn't even set it free.

Deep down Charlotte knew Winnie had been right to insist she take the night off. She was close to losing it. A moment of self-care was not selfish. It was necessary if she was going to maintain her sanity. And maintaining her sanity was the best thing she could do for her own daughter.

Charlotte's gaze locked on the silent cowboys. She gripped the wheel. "Move over boys, I'm coming in."

Her luxury sedan bounced across the cattle guard. Weeds high as the car's hood choked the wooden fence that lined both sides of the rutted drive. No point lamenting the disappearance of the immaculate fence rows or the appearance of the dangerous potholes. Everything had disintegrated since Daddy died, and she didn't need a stroll down memory lane to cement that fact. Her exasperating phone conversations with Mother kept the aching loss front and center every waking moment.

Rounding the bend in the long lane, the car's beams illuminated the front porch of the dark, three-story farmhouse. Modest. Sturdy. And, as far as she could tell in this light…remarkably unchanged.

Charlotte let the car coast to a stop. Tension had welded her hands to the wheel. Caliche dust sifted through the headlights' halogen glow and settled on the windshield. She killed the engine and sat in the cocoon of inky quiet.

Country tranquility stretched ten miles in every direction. The lack of civilization appealed to her mother, not her. She'd married to escape the loneliness. Mother, on the other hand, craved solitude and had married a soft-spoken country boy to get it.

The tap of the cooling engine lulled Charlotte into opening the door on a long, forgotten memory. She was seven and her sister Caroline was nine. It was nearly the end of May, and while the summer heat had already set in, it would be two more weeks before Charlotte and Caroline would be free to spend the long, hot days prowling the receding river in search of the perfect fossil, one that would make them rich. The smell of fresh peaches picked from the small orchard behind the house filled her nostrils.

"Quiet, girls. I need a minute to hear myself think." Mother lifted her flour-covered hands and shooed Charlotte and her sister toward their father.

Daddy, a wiry man, gifted with a sixth sense when it came to Mother, knew how the excitement of children anticipating the end of the school year took a toll upon his wife's noise limit. He kissed Mother's flushed cheeks, then turned to them. "Girls, I do believe it's warm enough for our first swim of the season. Last one to the river is a rotten egg."

Glad for any excuse to be with Daddy, they'd dropped their school bags and torn out after him. The screen door slammed behind them as they dashed to the Frio...three Musketeers in search of an adventure.

The clear, spring-fed river was a cold shock to the system, even on the hottest of summer days. Daddy believed true Texans never waded in slowly. That's why he'd climbed the giant live oak that loomed over the rocky outcropping, secured a heavy rope with thick knots, then threaded it through an old truck tire. The fight over who he launched first had been settled two years earlier when Caroline proved herself the stronger swimmer.

Daddy held the swing steady as Caroline took her seat. "Wait until you're clear of the sharp ledge before you let go," he reminded. "Then tread water until your sister has landed safely."

Caroline rolled her eyes at the reminder, then gave an obedient nod. With a mighty shove, Daddy sent her sailing over the water hole that remained deep even late in summer when the brutal Texas heat reduced the rest of the river to a mere trickle. "You're next, Beetle Bug."

He'd given her the name because of the way her body skated across the water's surface. Charlotte mounted the swing. At the height of the arc, she let go and plunged into the icy water. She and Caroline treaded water until their father landed with his cannonball right between them.

Their laughter echoed off the steep canyon walls as they kicked and frolicked. They dove after the little fish that darted about them. When they could no longer feel their fingers and toes, they pulled themselves onto the warm rocks.

Daddy slipped on his worn Red Wing work boots, leaving the ankle laces undone. They laughed about how his skinny white legs looked like they belonged on a chicken. He gave them a second to catch their breath. "Race you up the bluff," he shouted.

Dripping wet, they scrambled after him. They were nearly dry and starving by the time they climbed to the top and started racing across the pasture. But their father's wobbly cartwheels in his unlaced work boots and his white legs kept them laughing all the way back to the house. Even before they opened the kitchen door, the forgiving smell of cinnamon and sugared fruit greeted them.

Glorious peach pies cooled on the counter. Mother couldn't slice them fast enough. Charlotte and Caroline shared the three-legged stool. Mother and Daddy sat at the table. Together, they devoured delicious slabs of flaky crust dripping with peaches. And for that brief moment, everything was right with the world.

Shivering in the dark silence, Charlotte licked her damp lips. The salty taste jarred her back to the present.

What was she doing? She hadn't let herself remember swimming in the river or enjoying the spoils of Mother's baking frenzies for a long time.

Coming here was a bad idea.

Dredging up every happy memory she'd ever had here would never be enough to bury the sad ones.

She swiped her wet cheeks. She didn't want quiet. Quiet forced her to think, remember things that should be forgotten. Things like the keen of her father's unrelenting grief. The noise had been fingernails to a chalkboard for Mother. The disruption had forced the two remaining Slocum women to retreat inside themselves.

Those women had never been seen again.

Pressing her hand to her mouth, Charlotte smothered a repeat of the gut-wrenching scream that had shattered the Slocum family twenty-four years ago this month. She'd become adept at throttling the pain, but the effort was exhausting. Her primal cry for help had changed her mother. The ensuing silence had killed her father. The deadly combination had become a barbwire fence between her and her mother.

Charlotte snatched a tissue from her purse and mopped her eyes. She tossed the shredded tissue to the floor. She could no sooner forgive either parent than she could forgive herself. Never had she longed for the mind-numbing commotion of the city as much as she did at this very moment.

Desperate for fresh air and sound, Charlotte turned the key in the ignition and lowered the windows. The river's verdant fragrance, lush and teeming with the sounds of crickets and croaking frogs, assaulted her senses. Like a hungry child gorging on pie, she sucked it in.

She couldn't remember the last time she'd thought of pies or listened to chirpy wildlife serenades. Or even wanted to, for that matter.

Rare were the moments she and James had actually enjoyed the leafy backyard in their posh Virginian suburb. In fact, she could only recall the *one* time—the night Aria was conceived. James had never liked the historic brownstone she'd purchased when she first went to work on the Hill. In truth, he didn't like how her devotion to her job required her being close to the heartbeat of the Capitol. He'd kept on about his dislike of the cramped space until she finally gave in and agreed to a house far too big for just the two of them. The night they moved in, James coerced her from the mountain of boxes, grabbed a quilt, and led her out beneath the tree canopy. Side by side, they'd ignored the distant drone of traffic, and when they found each other, she'd allowed hope to bubble within her for the first time in years.

What a fool she'd been.

Tears flowed full force now.

She'd tried to forgive her husband. To put the hurt behind her. But someone had to be the adult—for Ari's sake—and it would never be James. Pinpointing the horrible instant her lot in life had become being the grown-up was easy.

It had happened long before James.

She didn't want to be the one who always had to pick up the pieces. And more importantly, why hadn't anyone noticed she sucked at cleaning up messes? Not one thing she'd ever tried to fix even remotely resembled the original when she finished.

Yet, here she was, patching and gluing her shattered mother as if she were one of those tiny broken barn swallow eggs Caroline insisted on trying to salvage every spring.

In an instant, the events of the past few days crowded out Charlotte's endless justifications and dumped a fresh load of guilt onto her already exhausted shoulders.

Accusation injected new life into old deliberations. Maybe if she'd lived next door? Checked on her mother daily? Helped with all the farm chores? Attentive daughters kept their mothers from breaking hips, didn't they?

"Stop it!" Charlotte pounded the wheel. "Sara Slocum doesn't need you, or anyone else for that matter." How many different ways did Mother have to say it before she got the message?

The surprise 70th birthday party she'd thrown for her mother had been a complete bust. Ari had wanted to give her grandmother a Hawaiian luau. She and Winnie had planned for weeks, even hired a girl from the high school drill team to do a hula dance. But Mother was so disappointed when none of her teacher friends came that the whole weekend went up in smoke. Ari was crushed. Mother had probably completely forgotten she'd even tried.

Texas wasn't big enough for the three of them. She'd do the honorable thing and let her mother have this place, even if it killed the old girl.

The insect symphony soured in Charlotte's ears. No matter how tempting, she couldn't leave her mother to her own devices. Mother's declining health had pushed their desire for mutual independence beyond their reach. There was no one else to fill in for Mother's increasing mental gaps. Coming home was no longer a choice, but a necessity that would kill them both.

Charlotte retrieved her purse and dug out her cell phone. She pressed a button and the screen glowed blue. Nine o'clock here, ten on the East coast. She punched her daughter's contact. Knowing James's lack of discipline, it was a pretty safe bet Ari's bedtime had been ignored.

"What do you want, Mom?"

Classical music played in the background. The girl had Juilliard on the brain and according to her piano teachers, more talent than Charlotte had ever had in her long, slender fingers.

"Good to hear your voice too, Ari."

"It's Aria."

"Right. Sorry." Given the lateness of the hour, she passed on addressing the razor-edged tone. Missing sleep never put Ari at her best. "Is your dad home?"

"I guess."

"What do you mean, you guess?"

"Haven't seen him since he paid for pizza. Want me to check his studio?"

"No!" Hurt, still white-hot fresh, straightened Charlotte's spine. She'd never set foot in that studio again, and once she finished mopping the courthouse floor with James, neither would their daughter. "I'll call him later. I want to catch up with you now."

"Whatever." Ari's tone was the audible sound of the door of communication slamming shut.

After what she'd been through with her own mother these past few years, Charlotte couldn't help but pound again. "How was your recital?"

"Same as the last one you missed."

The barb went straight through her aching heart. "You made it through Bach?"

"Beethoven."

"Right. Sorry."

Seconds ticked by as Charlotte groped for something else to say. How could she know so little about her own daughter? How could she be so much like her own mother? The realization nearly doubled her over. This couldn't be. She'd done everything she could to distance herself from anything that remotely resembled the matriarch of Fossil Ridge.

Yet, here she was some twenty-four years later, with more than miles between her and her own child. Something else to fix. Soon as she had things squared away here, she'd take the time to read the book Loraine gave her. See if the Ph.D. who'd lived this experience had any insights on what she could do to keep her from losing her daughter.

Aria broke the silence. "Nana gonna live?"

To suddenly realize that she'd been holding her breath and wondering the same thing hit Charlotte hard. "Of course." How much she should tell her child? She settled on a little as possible for now. "The doctors are saying she'll need rehab but she should walk again."

"She's a renaissance woman."

The unexpected insight caused Charlotte to chuckle. She'd underestimated her daughter and maybe that was the root of their problem. "Where'd you hear that?"

"I don't know. When are you coming home?"

Tough kid. Tougher question. Not so much the when of coming home as the where. Where was home? In the darkness she could make out the wrap-around porch of the house she'd spent eighteen years of her life...loving all of them until the last. Now it didn't feel any more like home than the various McCandless vacation properties scattered around the world.

Charlotte looked down. She didn't remember pulling out her necklace, but her fingers were rubbing the treble clef smooth. "I don't know, sweetie. Soon I hope."

"Whatever."

"You can stay with your father a little longer, can't you?" She hated making that concession, but until she had her mother situated, what choice did she have? She chafed at the injustice. Mother's latest shenanigan had effectively once again made her the smashed center of an Oreo cookie, sandwiched between obligations to parent and child. Balancing both. Failing badly.

"Caitlyn's sleepover is Friday night."

"Who's Caitlyn?"

"Geez, Mom."

"A little more information and a lot less attitude would go a long way in helping you win your case, young lady. Who's Caitlyn?"

"Am I on trial?"

"No, Caitlyn is."

Aria huffed, "My best friend, okay?"

"Since when?"

"Since third grade. Geez, you're cranky."

What kind of a mother forgets her daughter's best friend? Charlotte dropped the necklace and rubbed the regret throbbing between her eyes. "We'll see."

"I need to let her know."

"And I need a little more information." The conversation was veering off course, but Charlotte couldn't let it go. "Give me her mother's phone number."

"Geez, Mom. I'm not five. Don't call her."

"When you're a mother—"

"Why should I suffer because you won't let Dad live with us? It's not my fault."

Throttling the urge to blurt out where the blame belonged, Charlotte bit her tongue. Her daughter adored James McCandless the same way she'd adored Martin Slocum. Defending herself was as pointless as exposing him. Aria would no more believe her than she'd believed her own mother. "I'll call your father tomorrow and see what we can work out. All right, Ari—Aria?"

"Whatever."

Click.

Charlotte stared at the empty blue screen until it went black. The disconnect felt oddly familiar and painfully new. She hit the email icon and typed To Do in the subject line. *Take Ari to summer house on Cape. Search sky together. Find North Star.*

She re-read the message, added *Make Ari mine again*, then sent it to herself. She slid the phone into her pocket then dragged her laptop case across the seat.

"Might as well get this over with." She hauled herself out of the car and shut the door.

Except for the starry vastness, she stood in total darkness—the exact feeling she had every time she talked to Ari. She couldn't just brush aside her mothering failure. Fossil Ridge was proof that important relationships came with ticking clocks. As soon as she got back to DC, Ari would be her number one priority. Sid Waring owed her some time off. Charlotte popped the trunk and snagged her overnight bag. She took a cautious step toward her mother's house.

"Why didn't I ask LaVera to leave the porch light on after she fed Mother's bird this morning?" she muttered.

Computer bag slung over her shoulder and small duffle in hand, Charlotte trudged the dark walk. She stopped at the porch steps and let her fingers search behind the potted lantana. As expected, the key was hidden in the exact same place where it had been for the past forty years. Why did her mother even bother with locks? Everyone in the county knew the exact location of the Slocums' hidden key. Maybe this Christmas she'd forgo sending Mother slippers and have a sign made for her front door.

It's open. Wipe your feet before you rob me.

The key's jagged edge cut into Charlotte's clenched fist. She set her bags on the porch. After a few blind stabs at the lock, she pulled out her phone's flashlight and jammed the key into the slot. One hard twist to the right and the door creaked open.

Air stagnant with the smells of Mother's moth balls and the brandy-cask sweetness of Daddy's pipe tobacco wrapped around her like Caroline's hand-me-down coats. Charlotte wiped her feet on the mat then silently chided herself for sticking to the old habit. Mother wasn't here to monitor the tracking of her precious floors. Mother would probably never live in this house again.

Charlotte set her bags inside the door then groped the flocked wallpaper until her fingers found the entry light. A yellow bulb flickered to life. Every single piece of furniture, from the oak hall tree to the two wingbacks on either side of the fireplace, remained in the same spot Mother had placed them years ago. The predictability was strangely settling.

Charlotte went straight to the bay window in the living room. She reached around the piano where she'd spent so many hours dreaming of playing tunes kids would love and forced open each of the slender panes. By the time she finished, more sweat trickled down her back and her temper had risen. Her mother's refusal to have central heat and air installed made it blooming uncomfortable here, and for what reason?

"I'll pay for the upgrade, Mother," she'd offered during one of her Monday calls.

"Germs get trapped in a closed-up house," Mother had argued. "God invented open windows and summer breezes to blow away the cold and flu bugs of winter and who am I to question the wisdom of God?"

Who did Mother think she was fooling? Passing her shaky science off on God did not excuse her refusal to accept any tokens of love.

Charlotte tamped the resentment roiling inside her and opened the lid on the piano keys. She hit middle C. Out of tune. Of course. She'd told her mother a thousand times it wasn't good to have a piano by a window. But then, she'd told her mother many things that she'd refused to hear. Charlotte slid the lid over the yellowed keys.

She went through the quiet rooms undoing latches and banging on stubborn windows. A flip of a switch in the hall brought the attic fan rumbling to life. The draw of night air rearranged her hair and sucked the lacy doilies from the surface of every dusty antique.

Smoothing her bob proved to be a waste of time, but she'd rather tame flyaways than pull June bugs from her hair. Back before

Daddy installed the window screens, the attic fan brought in more winged creatures than it blew out. She'd spent many steamy summer evenings sprawled across crisp cotton sheets waging bug-crushing contests with Caroline.

Someone cackled behind her. Charlotte whirled, her feet slipping on the pine-planked floor. "Who's there?" She listened, breaths short and shallow, eyes darting. "Caroline?" The clatter of the fan's metal blades echoed in the empty house. "Just the fan." Charlotte took a couple of calming breaths. "No wonder Mother's losing it."

Grateful for the noise, Charlotte headed for the kitchen. She flipped on the kitchen light.

"Peek-a-boo."

Phone lifted like a weapon, her darting eyes sought the source. A large parrot fluttered in a cage tucked into the breakfast nook. "You really do talk." She set her phone on the counter with a relieved sigh and went to investigate the birthday present Aria had insisted they have shipped to her grandmother. "I guess I owe Mother an apology."

"Hello," the bird said.

She inched toward the cage. "You took ten years off my life." Charlotte squatted, bringing her face close enough to the wires to realize the newspaper lining needed to be changed before she returned to the hospital. She eased her index finger between the bars. "What's your name again, pretty fella?"

The bird's claws wrapped around her acrylic nail. "Peek-a-boo."

"Peek-a-boo?" Her laugh released a little of her pent up the tension. "That's not your name. I'm guessing it has something to do with the Pythagorean Theorem."

The bird cocked his head.

She drew her finger perch toward her, pulling the bird close to the bars and whispered, "You and I both know old math teachers never retire, they simply try to make all those stuffy formulas apply to real life. Tell me, my feathered friend, when was the last time you really had to know the hypotenuse of anything?" His beady eyes implied she might be the crazy one for carrying on like this, but she couldn't seem to help herself. "Let's see if I can't guess your name. Is it...Hexagon?"

Stony silence.

"Pentagon?"

Still nothing.

"Bird-be-gone."

Her new acquaintance abandoned her finger for the tiny swing with the bell.

"Can't take a joke?" Charlotte wiggled her finger, but she couldn't entice his return. "Hey, I didn't mean to cross some politically incorrect avian line."

Neck feathers puffed, the bird turned to the scratched mirror on the wall of his cage as if to say this conversation is over.

"Be that way." She stood. "But remember, I paid for you and I'll expect you to sing for your supper."

Charlotte reached for the mail on the gingham-cloth covered table. "Remind me to ask Winnie if she can deliver Mother's mail to the hospital so LaVera won't have to mess with it." She awaited his response like she expected a "yes ma'am." What was she thinking? In less than ten minutes after entering the front door, she was talking to birds...she'd become her mother.

The tiny bell above the bird's mirror tinkled.

"Okay, so you're not my secretary. I'll send myself an email." She tapped out a message then growled when it didn't send because of Mother refusing to get Wi-fi. She jammed the phone into her pocket. "I don't see that you're all that much company, bird."

"Don't bite."

"My bark's worse than my bite, so you can rest easy, pretty boy." Charlotte thumbed through the stack of Lillian Vernon catalogues and credit card applications. She cut a sideways glance at the parrot. "By the way, I know your name."

The admission she'd tossed his way seem to perk him up. "Get out."

She chuckled. "Don't worry, *Polygon*, I won't tell Mother that all her etiquette training has been a waste of good birdseed."

She opened the weekly grocery store flier and an envelope fell out.

"What's this?" She raised the thin missive toward the ceiling fixture, ignoring the pang of guilt her snooping aroused. "Sparks Development. The Ultimate in Country Living."

The bird sprung from his perch and clung to the bars. "Leave it."

"You know something I don't, Polygon?" She went to the sink and pulled the string dangling from a single bulb.

"Leave it."

"Get a grip, pretty boy." She raised the envelope again. "Someone has to look out for Mother's good." She tapped the envelope on the sink, adjusting the stationary inside. Lifting it again, she now had a clear view of the backlit words.

We regret that your delay has forced us to withdraw our offer.

"Over my dead body." Charlotte crammed the envelope into her pocket, grabbed her small suitcase from the hall, and stormed upstairs to her old room. Tomorrow, Mother would have some explaining to do. With any luck, some of it might actually make sense.

Chapter 9

I'm Not Going

LaVera, I am *not* exaggerating." I huddle close to the safety rail of my hospital bed, the phone receiver pressed to my mouth. "That beefy therapist is trying to kill me." I keep a sharp eye on the crack in the door.

"Simmer down, Sara. You've stoked yourself hotter than a two-dollar cookstove. That can't be good for your blood pressure."

I'm disappointed my lifelong friend and trusted cosmetics supplier has discounted the seriousness of my situation far more than she *ever* discounted my Avon orders. "Are you going to help me or not?"

Before LaVera can answer, the distant squeak of sneakers hoofing it down the waxed linoleum hallway incites a panic in me. I stuff the phone under the sheet, furious it hadn't even taken Charlotte two minutes to snag another diet Coke from the waiting room vending machine. If my child's not careful, consuming all that caffeine will lead to an addiction. Which is the exact reason I limit myself to one cup of weak tea in the morning.

My eyes are glued on the door while my ears remain

preoccupied with LaVera's garbled assessments and the squeak, squeak, squeak drawing near. I clamp a hand across the hidden receiver and prepare for the worst. All the reasons I could cite for calling LaVera go through my mind. None of them will satisfy Charlotte's suspicions.

Within the space of a few rapid heartbeats, the spine-jingling footsteps arrive outside my door. I listen with all my might, praying that by some miracle the rubber-soled shoes do not belong to Charlotte. I hold my breath. The squeaking slows, then stops. I feel myself turning blue, but I can't grab a breath to save my life. Seconds tick by as I wait for Charlotte to catch me red-handed plotting an escape. Then, without warning, the obnoxious squeak pivots and fades down the corridor. I expel such a huge sigh of relief it nearly blows me out of bed.

When did I become so afraid of my own daughter?

The ugly question collides with my recollection of the morning's events. Fire flashed in Charlotte's eyes the moment she walked in with my breakfast tray. In fact, smoke curled from her ears when I gave that little orderly a piece of my mind and sent him packing a moment ago. I don't know why Charlotte's wound tighter than normal today, but if it makes her happy to hunt the hospital's help down and apologize for my rude behavior, then more power to her. She's been apologizing for me for years, and I can't see that it's sweetened her sour disposition one iota. I fold any futile hopes that she'll spring me from this joint and stash them with the others better forgotten.

"Sara? You still there?"

LaVera's muffled shouts bring me back to the reason I called. Keeping check of the door, I wrestle the receiver out from under the bed sheets.

Just to be on the safe side, I whisper, "Please, LaVera. I want to go home."

"These exercises are for your own good."

I'm tired of everyone deciding my best interests. "Let's crank your arthritic leg ninety degrees off the floor, LaVera, and see how long you can maintain a Christian mindset."

"I'm just sayin' you're givin' up awful early in the game."

"Whose side are you on?"

"Yours." LaVera's dramatic pause irritates me. I'm not one of those small-minded heroines floundering around on the pages of her large-print Fran Lacy romance novels. "Remember when Gladys had her knee replaced?" she says.

I've always considered LaVera my best friend, but her audacity of referencing the neighbor I'd just as soon forget proves I am woefully mistaken. If she intends to smooth my ruffled feathers, the mention of Gladys Wooten is a poor course of action, and she knows it. "What does that woman's knee have to do with me?"

"Remember how Gladys carried on 'til Homer shut off her

automatic knee-bender?"

"Her husband never did have a lick of sense. And you know as well as I, that's a big part of the problem."

"And who does that remind you of?"

"LaVera, say what you mean. Don't beat around the bush with me."

"All right then. You sittin' down?"

"If I could sit and stand at will, LaVera, do you think that beefy therapist would lay another hand on me?"

"All right then. Here's the plain and simple truth of it. You refuse to rehabilitate and Dr. Hunke will have to loosen *your* frozen hip with that ball-peen hammer he took to Gladys' knee. Then you two know-it-alls can hobble around town arm-in-arm."

I'm in no mood for the mental picture of sharing so much as the fence row Homer Wooten and my Martin built together, let alone have my *real* friends thinking I'd associate with a backstabber like Gladys. "You are not my principal, LaVera."

"No. I'm your friend. And you ain't worked for Wilma Rayburn in seven years. But don't think for a minute I won't send you to her office for a good lickin'. Now quit that whinin' and start actin' like the Sara Slocum I know and love."

Truth, clear and irritating as a Baptist church bell, shames me. I'd miss LaVera terribly if something happened to her, so I understand her fear. But the Sara Slocum she knew, the one who pulled herself up by the bootstraps when she lost her daughter, and then again when she lost her husband, that Sara Slocum may as well be dead.

My bony fingers clutch the phone cord as if it's a lifeline LaVera can reel in. Blue veins ridge the once-smooth hands of the Sara I knew, but the stagnant tributaries carry none of the vim and vigor I vaguely remember. The person trapped in this frail body dreads her living daughter's return—a sure sign the old Sara Slocum passed from this life, leaving nothing but this pitiful stranger in the shell she abandoned.

"LaVera, if you are half the friend you claim, you'll get Bo Boy and bust me out of here."

I hang up the phone just as Charlotte breezes through the door.

She's fortified with caffeine, jumpy as a kidding goat, and juggling a near-empty soft drink bottle in one hand and a stack of papers in the other. "Mother, let's finish up your exercises, then take a look at this information I picked up at the nurse's station."

Charlotte's insistence I complete every painful exercise on my rehabilitation schedule does make me wonder if sitting in this freezing therapy room and watching me suffer gives her some perverse sense of pleasure. Why else would she stay in Addisonville longer than her usual twenty-four hours? I can't believe I'm wishing my daughter would go back to Washington.

"You ready to give those leg lifts another try?" Something about

Charlotte's sudden cheeriness doesn't feel right.

Since LaVera has obviously deserted me in my hour of need, I'm left with only two choices: face another round of grueling therapy torture or break myself out of here. Determined to save my strength so I can put up a decent fight, I grope for the bed rails on either side of me. "I don't feel up to any more of those ridiculous calisthenics today, Charlotte Ann."

Rare concession crosses my daughter's face. "Okay, let's take a break." She moves the phone and plops glossy brochures on my rolling chow table.

I feign indifference, but her overdone agreeability, coupled with a rare burst of chirpiness, gets the better of me. "What are these?"

Charlotte eagerly fans the stack so that I can get a good look at each pamphlet. Even without my glasses, I can make out the full-color pictures. Every page showcases either smiling old men tooling about in golf carts or flabby old women standing waist-high in blue pools and hoisting foam noodles over their swimming caps.

"Rehab-slash-assisted-living options." Charlotte's pacifying smile doesn't fool me for a second. I can spot a rat faster than a hungry alley cat.

I shove the table away. "I'm not interested."

"Well, maybe that's because you...aren't aware of all the wonderful...opportunities, Mother." She inches the table my direction.

"The only opportunity I'm interested in is the one that gets me home. Polygon is probably worried sick."

"LaVera's been taking great care of him during the day, and I checked him last night."

The idea of Polygon confined behind bars twenty-four-seven does not sit well with me now that I know exactly how it feels to be a prisoner of circumstances beyond one's control. "How was he?"

"Chatty...once we got to know each other."

"Did you give him his morning fruit? If he doesn't have his fiber he gets all backed up."

Charlotte nudges those fancy fliers toward me. "I found an apple and gave him several slices."

"Did you leave LaVera a note? I don't want him double-dosed with roughage. That can get a bit messy."

"I cleaned his cage and left a note."

Only somewhat satisfied, I slide the brochures back toward Charlotte. "Did you get my mail?"

Charlotte starts to say something, thinks better of it, then sighs. "It's in my purse." She paws through an alligator bag the size of a suitcase and sure to give her curvature of the spine before she's fifty. "Here you go." She tosses the bundle on my tray table. "I finished my chores, now can I go play, Mother?" Acidity has deflated her prior buoyancy.

I regret that once again I've said something that has shoved my daughter just beyond my reach. "What's got you more peevish than usual?"

"I'm not ten, Mother. I hold down a job. Try to keep up with your catastrophes. And I feed a cat and a child every day."

This unusual admittance behind the closed door of the life of Charlotte Ann Slocum McCandless surprises me. "You have a cat?"

Charlotte takes a step back as if she needs room to slam the hatch I've pushed open a crack too far. "It's Ari's cat. A Siamese." The hard line of her locked lips smacks of a reclaimed determination to limit our exchange.

"Cats are sneaky, you know," I say, just to egg her on.

"This one's a love," she growls through clenched teeth.

"They eat birds."

Charlotte crosses her arms. "We don't have a bird, Mother. You do."

"I know that." Still hungry for another insight, no matter how miniscule, I opt to change the subject. "You feed James, too?"

The question throws Charlotte off balance for a split second, but she recovers quickly and shrugs. "When he's home."

A mere tidbit into the state of her marriage, but enough to tide me over for now. "I appreciate you taking care of things, really I do."

Charlotte snatches her drink and finishes off the last slug as if she's obliged to wash down the compliment stuck in her craw. She swallows hard and then chucks the empty can in the trash. "Let's just say this place is getting to both of us."

"Let's." I shuffle the stack of mail. Nothing from Sam Sparks, and I am relieved. Maybe that used car salesman masquerading in a fancy business suit finally got the message. I'm not interested in his pesky offer, no matter how high he ups the ante. "This is mostly junk."

Charlotte plucks the pile from my hands. "Let me toss that for you, Mother."

She dumps the assortment in the trash container with a *thunk*, then spins to face me. I don't much care for the return of her forced smile.

"There, all gone." Charlotte brushes her hands, her gaze roaming the room—for exactly what, I'm not certain. "You need anything? Another pillow? A cold drink?" Her sunny attitude might fool a jury, but I'm her mother and this vacillating back and forth screams red-flag guilty.

"I'm fine."

"How about we watch a movie? They've got quite a selection of DVD's at the nurse's station."

"What's going on, Charlotte Ann?"

"Nothing. Is it bad that I want my mother to be comfortable?"

"Comfort is impossible in a hospital bed."

"And for good reason, too."

"Making a sick person miserable is not an acceptable reason."

"They don't want patients settling in and becoming unwilling to discuss the future." She pulls up a chair, continuing the conversation as if revealing my discomfort has granted her the go-ahead she's been fishing for all along. "Let's talk options."

The girl is slick and she is *not* going to let this assisted living thing go. "My options are simple, Charlotte Ann. Go home. Recuperate in my *own* bed. Live my life as I see fit."

"Your bed is upstairs."

"I'll sleep on the couch."

"Who's going to take care of you, Mother?"

"I'll take care of myself."

"How? You can't even get yourself to the toilet."

"LaVera was my right hand when you were born, and I imagine she'll be happy to step in again." I know I'm going out on a limb placing my dependency in the hands of the traitor who'd refused to bust me out of here, but I'll figure things out when I get back to the ranch—just like I always have.

"The blind leading the lame?"

"Unlike you, Charlotte, I have friends...plenty of them." Feeling a bit guilty about the exaggeration of my social circle, I let the void her life choices created sink in. She may have everything money can buy, but those empty eyes reveal what I've suspected all along. Charlotte has failed to cast a single crumb upon the waters. When she's old, what blessings will return to her? None. While I, on the other hand, may not have an abundance of friends anymore, I do have several favors primed to call in.

"Mother, you could have killed Raymond."

"I should have. Did you see what that butcher did to my yard?"

"This is the third lawn service you've fired in a month. I don't think we can convince anyone in town to take on you or your yard."

"I'll tend to things at Fossil Ridge the same way I have for these past twenty-some years…by myself."

"How?" Charlotte's chair screeches backwards as she leaps to my side. "You can't even get yourself out of bed."

"I will. You'll see."

"Mother, it's too much." Charlotte leans over the safety rail. "How will you keep up with the house? Drive? Start the mower?"

"I'll have Lester's Hardware bring over one of those clever electric mowers."

"And when you run over the cord?"

I scoot toward the opposite rail. "I'll buy a new one."

"Mother, if you would just read about all the wonderful offerings of assisted living." Charlotte snatches a brochure. She shoves the picture of a handsome gray-headed man standing at the foot of a winding staircase under my nose.

"Is it like the others?"

"Yes…and no."

"Which is it, Charlotte? Yes? Or no?"

"Yes."

I push the paper away. "I'm not leaving my home, Charlotte Ann."

"I'm not saying this is permanent. I'm only asking you to think about how we're going to get you well and back on your feet."

"No."

"Why do you always blow off everything I say?"

"Blow off?"

"Don't play dumb, Mother." Charlotte's voice rises. "Discount. Ignore. Treat as unimportant." Her hands wave like a baby barn swallow frantic to catch an updraft.

"I don't discount you."

"Yes, you do, Mother. I suggest something and you immediately turn up your nose." Charlotte paces the foot of my bed while tallying my offenses on her fingers. "Come to DC for Christmas, Mother. Can't. I don't have snow boots. Come in the spring to see the cherry blossoms, Mother. Can't. Who'll kid my goats? Come in the summer, Mother. Can't. Who'll tend my garden? Come live with me. Can't." She grabs a breath and shouts, "Do you see a pattern here?"

"I came to DC once."

"The day Ari was born. Mother, that was thirteen years ago."

"I don't think whether or not I visit the Capitol can be lumped into the same category as letting you put me away."

Charlotte stops her pacing, expended steam distorting her face like she's a summertime mirage. "Okay, Mother, I didn't want to say this, but this shenanigan you pulled with the ladder has left me no choice."

I told you that word would come up sooner or later. "A person always has a choice, Charlotte Ann."

Charlotte's glare burns a hole straight through me. "If we could get you settled into a senior living center now, while you're still able to make friends, think how nice that would be."

"Calling a compost heap for the aged a senior living center is an oxymoron."

I can't believe my very own child, with all her high-falutin' degrees, has fallen for the hooey in these slick brochures. I blame it on the dire decline of America's educational system. Young people just don't think for themselves as they used to. They believe whatever their computers or fancy phones tell them.

And I blame Martin. My dearly departed husband took the coward's way out when he bailed. Now I'm left to suffer the consequences alone. I bite my trembling lip.

"Mother, I can't stay here forever." Charlotte's tone has softened. "I have a family. I have a job. And both of them are half-way across the country."

"I have friends, and they're next door. And my friends won't let you stick me away and forget me like Cora Jenkins."

"Cora Jenkins? Mother, Cora died years ago."

"And she died alone." I cross my good arm over my broken one. "I will not."

"Your friends can't be around all the time. If they have any health left, they have their own lives." Charlotte puts her hand on mine. She means it to be comforting but her touch feels like a pillow over my face. "Think about how good it would be to have someone to talk to besides that contrary bird of yours." She offers a tiny smile.

I don't want to make life hard for Charlotte. She has a family of her own, such as they are, and they deserve her undivided attention. However, I have no intention of listening to groundless tirades touting the stimulating advantages of community living and round-the-clock Bingo tournaments. And I certainly will not sit still for any disparagement of Polygon.

"Take me home."

My daughter withdraws her hand and deposits determined resignation on her face. "I can't, Mother."

"Can't or won't, Charlotte Ann?"

"Both."

Chapter 10

Oh, Yes You Are, Mother!

Charlotte cranked the wheel of Raymond's old van, clipping the *Dead End* sign at the turn into Winnie's lane as she whizzed past. Negotiating with a small-time handyman nursing a big-time grudge had been her first mistake. Paying top dollar for this heap of his her second. Assuming brakes were included with this bucket of bolts would apparently be her last.

Frantic to gain some control, she pumped the squishy brake pedal. "Lord, I could use a little help here."

Her plea ricocheted off the metal walls of the cavernous hull, but it did nothing to slow the Dodge's charge toward the lemon-yellow cottage with grape-colored shutters. The times she'd let these exact words slip from her lips were too many to count. She knew better than to ask God for anything that required an immediate solution. As with everything else in her life, she'd have to handle this mess by herself.

Knuckles white and elbows locked, Charlotte jammed the brake against the plywood floorboard. The van's stubby nose reared and bucked against every ounce of her strength. And then, for no apparent reason, the van coughed, sputtered, and slowed. She reined the relic to a harrowing halt just shy of Winnie's front porch.

Dust swirled through the open windows and mingled with the interior stink of moldy grass clippings and old motor oil. Hands trembling, she laid on the horn, its rusty blast a startling jolt to her already hammering heart.

She blew out a relieved breath and congratulated herself that once again she'd managed. When would she learn that counting on God to resolve things was the same as expecting hell to freeze over? She hit the horn button again. She'd be the first to admit she deserved those eternal flames and the last to think she had any hope of escaping them.

Winnie appeared behind the chartreuse-trimmed screen door, a large cat in her arms. "This ain't the Dairy Queen drive-thru." A chameleon when it came to accents, Winnie sounded every bit hill-country born and bred. If Addisonville's resident hippie lost the Woodstock wardrobe in favor of Wranglers, tourists might mistake her for a native Texan.

"You coming or not?" Charlotte shouted through the missing passenger-side window.

Winnie surveyed their mode of transportation. "Necessity makes strange bedfellows."

Charlotte pointed at the faded purple VW parked under a copse of gnarled live oaks. "Is that why you're still hanging onto Little

Mulberry?"

Winnie placed her index finger on her lips. "Shhh. She prefers to be known as Bella."

"Since when?"

"Since she became a classic."

A smile curled Charlotte's lips. "You in or not?"

"Wouldn't miss it." Winnie kissed the cat, set him on the floor, and scooted out the door without even bothering to lock up. She floated down the steps, avoiding the odd assortment of sunning felines. She hiked her skirt and jogged to the van.

Charlotte stiffened at the sheer freedom in Winnie's gait, the lilt of someone without responsibilities. Winnie would beg to differ, but she couldn't really believe setting out a few cans of cat food or emptying a litter box every once-in-a-while was a real burden. A real job. Or a real stress. Overall, Winnie came and went like the same collegiate free-spirit Charlotte met their first day of law school.

Resentment tightened Charlotte's grip on the wheel. She'd been tied to something or someone for so long that even if she did cut bait and run she wouldn't know how to survive. She'd probably starve like a caged animal released into the wild.

Winnie heaved open the door, the hinges groaning in protest. She hopped up on the running board and hoisted herself into the front seat. "Told you Raymond would understand your predicament and lend you his van."

"If you count paying that bottom-feeder five thousand dollars as understanding, I'd have to call that old *friend* of yours downright philanthropic."

"I wouldn't call us friends." Winnie slammed the door. "For that price, I hope Raymond threw in his mower and weed-whacker." She swiveled in the passenger seat, scouted the empty space, and spun back around. "Just smells like it, huh?"

Charlotte jerked the gearshift into reverse. "Trust me, I got off cheap."

Comprehension darkened Winnie's eyes. "Five thousand to make a lawsuit go away is cheap by your standards, I'm sure."

"What else could I do?" Charlotte backed onto the quiet street. "Don't look so mortified, Winnie. Settlements happen all the time." She yanked the lever into drive and cautiously prodded the gas.

"Not in my world."

"No one lives in your perfect world, Winnie. They live in mine, and it's irreparably flawed. Nobody gets to have everything their way."

Charlotte regretted spewing bile all over the one person who didn't deserve another drop of the ugly stuff as long as she lived. Even worse, she hated how the strike activated Winnie's bristle-and-retreat syndrome, a malady she, too, suffered although she'd contracted the disease from a much more domesticated source.

Winnie's world had never perfect. In fact, most of her life had been hellish.

Charlotte sneaked a sideways peek at her passenger's clenched hands. Thick scars cross-hatching the leathery flesh had refused to fade with the passage of time. The sickening evidence turned Charlotte's stomach and condemned her all over again, her complicity in the horrendous ordeal undeniable. What kind of self-centered fool let her best friend rot in a refugee camp then begrudged her healing? Especially, when she herself hungered for the same peace that now sustained Winnie.

Charlotte shifted in her seat. She'd pay any amount of money to smooth out those ridges or push the memories of Rwanda and Winnie's emaciated body from her mind. But nothing worked, not even the excessive hours she continued to funnel toward noble deeds and humanitarian causes.

Regret flattened any hope of freedom. Charlotte fought back tears. Her own prolonged internment had nothing to do with foreign uprisings or unstable governments. The prison bars restraining her were fashioned from her overactive sense of honor and locked tight with her own guilt. Far more politically correct, but just as foul.

She tore her gaze from the jagged railroad tracks traversing Winnie's tanned hands and arms and focused on the massive live oaks, the sun-dappled road, and explaining why she'd chosen this route to solve her transportation problem. "This is an emergency,

Winnie. You can't rent a van in Addisonville, and I didn't have time to drive all the way to Austin or San Antonio to get one. You know how fast Mother can change her mind."

"You did what you had to do." All traces of Winnie's Texas twang had vanished. "Just like you did when you came for me."

"Don't give me medals I don't deserve." Charlotte swallowed the ache, choosing to avoid any eye contact in case today was the day Winnie retracted the forgiveness she could never accept. She quickly diverted the conversation from the past and back to their present mission. "I just didn't see how we could stuff Mother and all that medical equipment into the backseat of a Lexus."

"I guess that means you found a place that will take her." Winnie had taken the cue and once again let her off the hook she deserved.

"The Reserve."

"Sounds like a politically correct way of setting someone aside."

"I'm not setting Mother aside, I'm saving her."

"From what?"

"Herself."

"Hmmm."

The fast approaching stop sign robbed Charlotte of the opportunity to study Winnie's expression and sort out the level of her disapproval. "Hang on." Charlotte let off the gas and tapped the brakes, but once again the ancient fixtures gave her nothing. She plastered both feet against the biggest pedal and stiff-armed the wheel.

Winnie gasped. "Semi." She braced one hand against the console, the other against the door, and began praying out loud.

Catching a glimpse of danger barreling their way, Charlotte wrestled the van through the intersection and onto the shoulder. The eighteen-wheeler roared past, horn blaring. The van bounced over scrubby roadside weeds, decelerating to a crawl. Limbs shaking, Charlotte stared straight ahead, afraid to look at her friend.

"Miss Sara agreed to Austin?" Winnie's voice was shaky.

Charlotte got up the nerve to glance Winnie's direction. The color had not returned to her face, but the lack of judgment in her clear blue eyes said that this near-death experience would go unmentioned as well. Charlotte had never loved her friend more.

She blew out and stammered, "Not in so many words, but there again, I really didn't have much of a choice." She checked behind her. Coast clear, she eased the van back onto the pavement.

"Really?" Winnie cocked her head. "What about the Haven? It's local."

"That dump smells like Pine Sol, urine, and old men."

"How do you know? Did you go there and check it out?"

"Didn't have to. Every Christmas Mother made me and Caroline help deliver her blasted fruit cakes."

"That was thirty years ago."

"Winnie, urine is not a fine wine that gets better with age. Trust me, yellowed linoleum is a smell you never forget."

"I trust you, C. I always have."

Charlotte cringed at the assurance, the pledge of undying devotion in the return of her old friend's mossy drawl. If only she were worthy.

After a few moments of disconcerting silence, Winnie continued on, "How can your mother afford such swanky assisted living on a teacher's pension?" She did not wait for an answer, rapidly put two and two together on her own. "Oh, *she* isn't. *You* are. Right?"

"So, shoot me."

Winnie planted her flip-flop clad foot up on the mammoth shag-carpeted console. "Nope, I think I'll just tuck this piece of incriminating evidence away."

"Incriminating evidence?"

A well-pleased grin accentuated the simple beauty of her friend's face. "Proof beyond a shadow of a doubt that Charlotte McCandless has a heart."

Ah. So, what? She'd helped Winnie get settled in a new town and promised to keep her Harvard law degree a secret so she'd blend in with the locals. One look in the mirror was all the evidence Winnie should need to know that she'd managed just fine on her own. Even Mother did not suspect the brilliance tucked beneath the beaded headband bisecting her mail lady's forehead.

"Don't count on it." Charlotte stepped on the gas.

The van backfired and lurched, jolting them momentarily silent. Once they realized they had not been shot, or worse, stranded in the country, they looked at each other and laughed like two beach-bound college co-eds.

Winnie pointed at the speedometer. "Better drop below forty if you want us to keep our teeth."

Charlotte eased off the accelerator, the idea of taking her time far more appealing than the task before her. Their ride smoothed out, and they putted along in the comfortable silence of two old friends, wind tousling their hair. On either side of the road, craggy limestone bluffs towered overhead, casting ragged shadows on the winding two-lane highway. Charlotte tucked a silky strand behind her ear and inhaled the earthy combination of scrub cedar, Ashe juniper, and live oaks sporting the occasional ball of mistletoe.

Her father loved this rugged country. She scanned the rocky ridges, half expecting to see Martin Slocum, tall and strong, standing on one of the granite outcroppings jutting over the Frio and waving her home. Familiarity, the kind that anchors a person and gives them the courage to become all they can be, seized her. An intense longing swelled within her breasts, the pressure weakening the walls of her chest.

"You missed the turn." Winnie's shout over the roar of the van's engine snatched Charlotte back from the ledge and all the unanswered questions. "The hospital is the other way." She reached across and touched Charlotte's arm. "You okay, C?"

Charlotte swiped hot tears from her cheeks. "I'm going to get a few of Mother's things from the house. Try to make her feel more at home." Like she had a snowball's chance in August of that happening.

Winnie nodded at the explanation and probed no more. Charlotte scrambled to get her emotions in check. Now was not the time to fall apart. They were nearing the river bridge, and the crossing always demanded so much from her. Charlotte goosed the gas. The surge pinned Winnie against her seat.

"Where's the fire?" The roar of the engine gobbled Winnie's question, but that wouldn't keep her from expecting some sort of answer.

"I just want to get this done before Mother changes her mind." Charlotte pressed the pedal, and the van began to shake.

Crossing the cold, spring-fed waters at night, when darkness hid the scene of her crime, was one thing. Dallying on the trestle-span in broad daylight was quite another. She doubted she would ever acquire the stomach to look over those railings. They flew over the bridge, the railroad ties jarring every bone in her body. Charlotte kept her eyes forged on the gravel stretch of road on the other side. Once the van's back tires hit dirt, she released her breath.

They rounded the last curve before the Fossil Ridge. On the left, the neighbor's clean fencerows revealed a freshly-swathed meadow lined with grassy windrows drying in the morning sun and awaiting Homer's hay baler. A large wooden sign on the corner of the Wooten property caught Charlotte's attention. She slowed to read the hand-painted billboard.

For Sale by Owner.

"Gladys and Homer are selling?" Charlotte's foot searched for the brake.

"Already would have cashed their check if they'd had their druthers."

"Did I miss something?"

Winnie shrugged. "Rumor has it that Sam Sparks wants to build a resort on the Frio, put Addisonville on the map...or so *he* claims."

"Then why haven't the Wootens sold to him?" The inquiry had not sounded as nonchalant as she would have liked, but the idea of a mass buy-out had taken her completely off guard.

"River bluff property is worthless without river access."

"And Mother's the hold-up."

"No wonder Sid Waring pays you the big bucks, girl." Winnie smirked. "Now do you see why your sweet little momma took up arms and shot Homer's dog?"

"You're telling me Old Man Wooten's heeler was trying to herd Mother to a real estate closing?"

"Something like that."

"But the Wootens have been our friends for years. I can't believe they'd stoop to such underhanded tactics."

Winnie nodded. "Friends can become foes when there's gold in them thar' hills."

The idea of Mother fending off who-knows-what-kind-of coercion with nothing more than ninety-eight pounds of steely nerve and Daddy's old shotgun spotlighted a side of the curious woman she'd never considered, let alone knew existed. Maybe she'd underestimated her mother's ability to take care of herself. But then, her mother had always been a mystery and her biggest secret of all would probably never be answered to Charlotte's satisfaction. Sara Slocum would probably take the reason for her insistence to remain living in the very spot where so much had died to her grave.

Charlotte steered the van past the metal cowboys and over the iron-pole cattle guard. Skittish rabbits bounded back and forth, their fluffy tails vanishing in the waist-high weeds.

Cresting the last hill, the ranch house and scattered out-buildings came into view. Charlotte gasped. If she thought things were bad in the dark, daylight exposed the true state of the Slocum place, and it was ten times worse than she could have ever imagined.

Faded blue paint peeled from every board. A loosened shutter drooped across a dormer window making the sagging three-story structure look like a flirting geriatric.

Daddy would turn over in his grave. If she let Mother return to Fossil Ridge after rehab, the place would fall down around her ears.

Charlotte squinted. "Who's on the porch?"

Winnie leaned forward. "Who's the shirtless hunk pushing the mower?"

Charlotte raised her gaping lower jaw. "My old boyfriend."

Chapter 11

The Boy Next Door

Well, tie me up and tickle me pink. If it ain't our little Charlotte Ann." LaVera stood on Mother's front porch, her delighted face frozen on the dated-end of the cosmetic timeline. "Come up here and give this ol' girl a big ole hug." She opened her thick arms wide.

Charlotte obediently mounted the steps and was immediately swallowed in the neighbor's suffocating embrace. Honeysuckle talc wafted up from the sunken valley between LaVera's two mountainous bosoms. Visions of LaVera stomping up the porch steps, toting a gaudy, oversized-makeup bag swirled in Charlotte's air-deprived head. Once a month, for as far back as she could remember, she and Caroline dabbed on the potions in the Avon lady's sample canisters while Mother pored over the latest offerings in the new catalogue.

Charlotte melted into the fragrant memory. Mother had always said having LaVera for a neighbor was like living next door to heaven. At this very moment, swaddled in billowy clouds of perfumed flab, Charlotte couldn't agree more.

LaVera pulled back and clasped Charlotte by the shoulders. "Let me have a look at you." She pushed thick glasses tight against the bridge of her nose, lifted her jowly chin, then leaned in close. "You ain't changed a lick. Still pretty as a new penny." She dragged a hand across Charlotte's face. "And skin smooth as a baby's butt. Ain't that night cream a wonder?"

Fearful LaVera's Braille-type examination might uncover damage no amount of Botox could fix, Charlotte stepped back. She steadied herself against the rusty ironwork porch railing, stalling for a way to avoid confessing she'd given up Avon products when she gave up Addisonville. "You still peddling Avon door-to-door, Miss LaVera?"

"Oh, good heavens no, baby. Just a few phone orders from my regulars. Bo won't let me behind the wheel anymore with these." She thumped the wire frame of her coke-bottle glasses. "Cataracts, you know."

"There's a corrective surgery you can have."

"Sweetie, I know that." She leaned in closer still, her eyes blurry behind the dense lenses, her breath dank as an antique store. "I'd have to go clear to Austin to have it done, and who wants to navigate that traffic, 'lessin' they have to?" Immediately realizing her tactless *faux pas*, LaVera's over-blushed cheeks darkened. "Oh, 'ceptin' your sweet momma, of course. Don't you worry, Charlotte Ann, Sara will come around to the way things have to be." She rushed on, gushing frivolous dribble about how lucky she and Sara were to have such sweet children. She ended with, "Getting older has its advantages. If I could see real good, my Bo might not want to check on me like he does."

"That's not true, Momma, and you know it."

The baritone utterance came from behind her, its velvety smooth cadence striking an instant chord of recognition. Charlotte's heart stopped for a brief instant and then took off at a gallop. She silently chastised herself for failing to duck inside the house the moment the cessation of the mower had registered in her subconscious. Inattention to detail had cost her again. She'd recognized the dangers of facing the guy behind the mower long before she pulled into the yard, yet she neglected to prioritize devising a foolproof escape plan. Now here she stood, trapped between the porch railing and her ex-boyfriend's mother, with nowhere to run. She applied her best summation smile, the one she used to sway the favor of hostile juries and turned to face him as if there was no place on earth she'd rather be.

LaVera pushed Charlotte toward the edge of the porch. "Bo Boy, would you look who's here?"

Bo Tucker stood at the foot of the steps, his green eyes fixed directly on hers. Charlotte canned the urge to tidy her hair and check her lipstick, but the desire to knock twenty years off her life would not leave her heart.

He reached for the shirt draped over the newel post and began wiping the sweat from his muscular chest. "Good to see you, Beetle Bug."

Beetle Bug.

Daddy had coined the silly nickname the summer she learned to swim, and much to her chagrin, it stuck. Martin Slocum bragged to anyone who'd listen that his littlest girl swam like a beetle bug skating across the top of the water, refusing to put her face below the surface. She'd dropped the moniker, along with everything else that reminded her of the Frio, after her father died. Hearing it now, spoken with the same tinge of affection, roused a comatose inclination to dive into the water and disprove her father's boast.

Charlotte fought back the haunting image of an eighteen-year-old girl pounding against the current and Daddy screaming, "Dive, Beetle Bug. Deeper. She's drowning." She buried the horror Bo's use of the name had summoned as quickly as she could, throttling the burgeoning tears with the expert speed she'd lacked that summer day.

The concern creasing Bo's tanned face indicated he'd not missed her reaction. But he waited, saying nothing. Clearly, the next move had been volleyed into her court. Should she hug him? No, she was married. And he probably was too. She couldn't remember for sure. Well, a little side-hug couldn't hurt. After all, they'd practically grown up as brother and sister, except for that short-lived infatuation the summer before Caroline died.

Sweat trickled down Bo's neck and cut streaky paths through the dust and grass plastered to his chest. They weren't kids anymore, and that fact kept her rooted to the weathered porch decking, unable to do anything but mumble, "Good to see you too, Bo."

"Sorry, I'm such a mess." He lifted the faded orange University of Texas ball cap shading his face and raked his fingers through his wet, dark hair. "Not a very good impression after all these years, is it?"

Quite the opposite. Charlotte tamped the flood of emotions dredging up sketchy memories. What good could come from remembering the tingle of hot summer evenings and budding love? None. Her hopes of teaching music and settling down with the local football hero had drowned in the same greedy waters that claimed her sister. Cutting all ties to the past had never been meant to hurt him, although when she'd showed him her law school acceptance letter, she was certain she had. Leaving Addisonville had been a survival tactic. A way to keep her head above the whirlpool of people's whispered speculations and pity-filled stares. Nothing more.

Bo Tucker, with his broad shoulders and kind eyes, was a casualty of circumstances beyond anyone's control. Appealing the unfair verdict that ended their relationships would change nothing.

By the time she'd settled on a simple, casual handshake, Winnie had climbed out of the van and parked herself behind Bo, a dreamy stare glazing her eyes. The man, seemingly unaware of Winnie's bald-face scrutiny or Charlotte's resolved indecision, reset his cap and busied his strong, sure grip with the twisting of the chambray shirt into a tight rope.

Charlotte cleared her throat and opted for what should have been her first course of action. "Thanks for mowing, Bo." She pointed at the yard.

He gave a slight nod. "We were hoping you'd have Miss Sara with you—"

LaVera interrupted, finishing his sentences the way she used to. "And we know how she frets about the grass, so we thought it'd give her a bit of comfort to ride up and see things all shipshape."

"You've both been so good to Mother, but you don't have to do this. I can hire someone."

Bo glanced toward Raymond's van. "How's that working for you?"

A smile cracked the stiff façade of Charlotte's face. "Badly."

Unlike her relationship with James, admitting uncertainty or failure to Bo would not subject her to painful exploitation. Truth had always been the way between them and something about his impish grin told her nothing had changed. The ease at which she'd suddenly confessed her exasperation, and then laughed about it, stirred a disconcerting comfort she'd believed long-ago extinct.

LaVera took Charlotte's arm. "Then it's settled. We'll keep an eye on the place until Sara's able to come home." She dragged Charlotte toward the front door. "I remember how you loved my angel food cake, so I whipped one up. Why don't I cut us a little piece while you finish what I started on gettin' your momma's stuff together?"

Charlotte's stomach took a dive. How had she gotten herself into such a mess? She'd rather suffer indigestion from LaVera's rubbery cake than explain to the woman that her best friend would probably never live on the Fossil Ridge again. "Look, I don't want to impose on you two. Winnie and I...oh, Winnie, forgive me."

Charlotte freed herself from LaVera's hold and flew down the steps. She reached around Bo and dragged Winnie to the forefront. "This is my best friend, Winnie."

LaVera waved off the introduction. "Well, Charlotte Ann, this ain't the big city. We know our own mail carrier. I make Miss Moretti one of my angel food cakes every Christmas."

"That she does." Winnie's tight-lipped smile made it appear that she'd just choked down a bite. "I can see why Charlotte raves about them." She turned and offered Bo her hand. "Good to see you again, Beauregard."

"Winifred." He swiped his palm against his jeans, took her hand, and lightly kissed it. "Bella behavin' herself?"

"Whatever you did under her hood has her purring like a kitten." Winnie smiled and blushed, the spark that leapt between them unmistakable.

Charlotte observed the interchange, feeling like a third wheel and a real idiot for allowing her mind to tread over abandoned graves. "How do you two know each other?"

"I keep that temperamental classic of hers running." Bo shook out his shirt and shimmied into it. "And Winnie keeps me supplied in art."

"Beauregard is a first-rate mechanic." Winnie, mesmerized by his every movement, sounded every bit the love-sick school girl.

Bo laughed. "More like Addisonville's only mechanic."

"In that case, maybe we should have *Beauregard* check our brakes before we head back to town." Charlotte hated the edge in her voice.

Bo rubbed the stubble on his chin. "I've been trying to get Raymond to change out those brake cylinders for months. Last time he filled up, he just about took out one of my pumps. Don't know what I can do without my tools—"

"But he'd be happy to give it a good look-see while we finish up your packin', won't you Bo Boy?" LaVera turned and headed for the front door. "I'm slicin' cake and I ain't gonna be at it long. Charlotte Ann, you comin'?"

"Sure." Charlotte nudged Winnie. "Remember the reason we came?"

"You go ahead, C." Winnie's eyes went to Bo's. She was

practically glowing. "I think I'll give Beauregard a hand with those brakes."

"In that case, how about we scout about for tools?" Bo gestured grandly with a long, muscled arm and bowed toward the shed. "Ladies first."

Charlotte watched Winnie and Bo stroll toward the out buildings, laughing and chatting, tight as two old friends. She whirled and stormed the stairs, letting the screen door slam behind her. What was she thinking? She'd had her shot with Beauregard Tucker twenty-something years ago, and she hadn't taken it. She had no business wishing otherwise now. Not with James and their ruined marriage still unresolved. Not ever.

"I've laid out a few things on Sara's bed." LaVera shouted from the kitchen. "You head on up, pack anything I forgot. I'll be there to help you finish after I fix us a little snack."

Charlotte scraped her feet on the braided rug, shaking off the dust of what might have been, and traipsed across the entry. She grabbed hold of the walnut handrails and trudged toward the task she'd put off as long as she could. She'd give anything to pass this dreadful job off to Caroline. Never had she missed her older sister more than at this very minute. Her take-charge sibling would know what to do. Caroline would be the one searching the Internet for the best residential care. Caroline would be the one talking Mother down from the ceiling. Caroline would be the one deciding what

Mother would and would not need in her new digs. And Caroline would be the one hauling Mother's angry butt to Austin. Not her.

At the top of the stairs, Charlotte stood in the quiet hall. Dust particles swam in the light streaming in the far window. Photographs lined the walls. Ancient black and white ones, pictures of long-dead relatives she'd never kept straight. Maybe she should take a couple of the older looking ones, have Mother identify them, date them, give her some idea of who in the world they were. Once Mother was gone, there'd be no way to figure all that out. What was she thinking? Mother wasn't dying, at least not yet. They had time for all of this.

Time. The word was as deceptive as Winnie pretending she didn't know who was pushing that mower. One second you think you have forever. The next...it's over.

Feeling very alone, Charlotte turned the knob on her mother's bedroom door, a room she hadn't dared to open on her nighttime reprieve from the hospital.

The floral scent of jasmine with a hint of coriander, the unique blend of Mother's Bird of Paradise Avon favorite, lingered in the dark room. A nine-foot peak in the ceiling added to the empty, cavernous feel. Light streaming in from the hall showcased an unusual bedroom fireplace squeezed between two dormer windows. Charlotte went straight to the mantel. She dragged her finger along the underneath side of the polished oak. The cup hooks where she and Caroline hung their Christmas stockings were still there.

Still there.

Her eyes drifted to the picture of her and Caroline, probably taken when they were about six and eight. Charlotte ran her finger over the dusty glass, letting her mind carry her back to that day when she and her sister were laughing and clinging to the rope of a tire swing as it soared over the sparkling Frio.

Take the photo or leave it? She dropped her hand and decided she'd think about what to do while she finished packing.

The closet door stood slightly ajar. Charlotte crossed the room and pushed it open. She pulled the string and dull light shone from the lone bulb. Daddy's things were gone. In their place, Mother had spread her dresses on the rod, each hung in color-coordinated order. Her shoes were neatly paired together on a wire rack on the floor. Charlotte shoved the clothes aside, half-hoping to find keepsakes of her childhood hidden behind Mother's sensible wardrobe.

Varying sizes of shipping boxes were stacked floor to ceiling in largest to smallest order. Boxes she instantly recognized.

"What the...?" Charlotte ripped down the first box and a card fell out. "Merry Christmas, Mother. Love Charlotte, James, and Ari." She yanked the lid off and tore through tissue paper that appeared to have never been touched. "The robe I sent her. Two years ago. I can't believe this." She threw the box on the floor and grabbed another one, recognizing the writing on the card. "Merry

Christmas, Mother. Love, Charlotte." The perfume and bath salts she'd sent from France. She let the box drop at her feet and opened the next one. Diamond earrings. A pair of sandals. And the next. Expensive stationery. And the next. Sandals. Same thing. Nothing touched.

She twisted the soft leather sandal she'd special ordered from a cobbler in Spain. "She hasn't used a single thing I sent."

"Cake's ready," LaVera called from the doorway.

Charlotte wheeled. "What is all of this?" She waved the sandal over the looted pile.

The tubby woman took in the mess and sighed. "Guess they're things Sara was saving, baby."

"For what, LaVera?" Charlotte threw the shoe across the room. It bounced off the mantle and hit the floor. "To be buried in?"

"For you."

"Me? I don't know what you're talking about, LaVera. Why would I want this stuff? I gave these things to her. I sent gifts I thought she could use. I wanted her to have something special."

"She has somethin' special. She always has."

"And what is that?"

"You." LaVera paused as if the weight of the burden she'd helped Mother carry needed a moment to shift to its rightful owner. "She just wanted you."

A wave of guilt washed over Charlotte, its force flattening her like a tsunami. Charlotte put a trembling hand over her mouth, yet she could not keep her tumbling emotions in check. The tick of Mother's wind-up clock sounded in Charlotte's aching head. Tears streamed down her cheeks.

"LaVera, I know you think I'm being selfish by not bringing Mother back to her home and caring for her myself, but what am I supposed to do? I have a family, a job, a life. I can't help it that I live far away."

"Beetle Bug, the weight you tote around on those pretty little shoulders is of your own gathering. Not mine, or your momma's." LaVera took her hand. "Let me show you something." She waddled over to the bed, dragging Charlotte along. The suitcase lay open, everything packed in neat little rows. She dropped Charlotte's hand and lifted the corner of the robe on the top layer. "Here you go. I found these on the front porch." She pulled out a pair of grass-stained Dearfoam slippers. "I'm sure she had 'em on when she fell. Your momma wore these every chance she got, and I think she'd take up walkin' a lot sooner if she had 'em on her feet again."

"I can't believe she still has these." Charlotte stepped forward and took the slippers. "They're twenty-five years old." She turned them over and examined the threadbare soles. "I gave them to her the Christmas before...Caroline died. Saved every dime I made babysitting the Smith twins." Fresh tears stung her eyes.

"Meant the world to her. She bragged about it for weeks."

LaVera gave Charlotte's shoulders a squeeze. "One more thing I think she'd want." She went to the nightstand beside Mother's bed and opened the drawer. Stooping, she crammed her arm in as far as it would go and felt around. "Yep. Here it is." With a big grin, she retrieved Daddy's pipe and handed it to Charlotte. "Sara would never admit it, but I think she lights this up and takes a puff every now and again just so the place will smell like Martin."

Charlotte blinked back tears.

"She tries to act tough. But losing your sister and daddy has been harder on your momma than you'll ever know, baby."

Charlotte lifted the robe and returned the slippers to their place in the suitcase. She opened her hand to the pipe. LaVera deposited it gently into her palm. Charlotte caressed the curve of the ebony stem. The lip of the mouthpiece exhibited the gnawed evidence of Daddy talking with the pipe clenched between his teeth. She drew the burled bowl to her nose and closed her eyes. She inhaled the ghostly aroma of the man she'd adored.

LaVera's sniffles jogged Charlotte from the past. She willed herself to open her eyes and face her mother's best friend. Tears had leaked out from under the old woman's rims.

"Thank you, LaVera," Charlotte managed around the lump in her throat.

LaVera nodded and swiped her damp cheeks. "Let's get some cake into you so you'll have the strength to wrestle your momma into that van." She patted Charlotte's shoulder.

"I'll be right there. Let me try to clean up the mess I made."

An understanding smile crossed LaVera's face. "It's all any of us can do." She wiped a tear from Charlotte's cheek. "But once my angel food dries out it's hard as concrete. I'll be in the kitchen. Polygon's got dibs on the crumbs."

Digesting the bewildering possibility that her mother still thought her special, Charlotte slipped the pipe into her pocket. She picked up the sandals, sandwiched them inside the shoebox, and stacked it neatly in the closet. She returned all of the forgotten Christmas gifts to their place in the stack, the sting of their rejection no longer so strong. She went to the mantle and took down the picture of two inseparable sisters sailing over the Frio.

Her heart clutched at the sight of that blasted swing. If only she'd gone first that day.

Using the corner of her shirt, she dusted the glass. Caroline, with her thick ebony hair and eyes dark and mysterious as the river after a rain, was a stunning child. As a young woman, no man could walk past Caroline without taking a long look. And whenever her older sister caught men gawking, she'd raise her chin and square her shoulders in a way that demanded their respect. She would have been a force to be reckoned with on the Hill.

Charlotte kissed her sister's photo. "I miss you, Line." She tucked the frame between the slippers and Mother's flowered robe.

"I miss all of us."

The sum total of a life...folded and stashed inside one tiny carry-on bag. When her day came to be *dealt with*, what would her daughter pack for her? Would Ari even come after all the times she'd failed to show up for her? Charlotte brushed the terrifying guilt aside and scanned the room.

Nothing of value struck her. Once she knew the exact set-up of Mother's new living quarters, she'd fly back and change out the apartment's standard furnishings with pieces from home. For now, this one suitcase would have to do. She zipped the bag.

Laughter drifted up the stairs. She carried the bag down, set it in the entry hall, then followed the sound to the kitchen. At the bay window that overlooked the Frio, everyone had gathered around Polygon's cage. Winnie cooed at the bird sitting upon her finger stuck through the wire bars.

Charlotte cleared her throat. "I hope you're not feeding him cake. Mother would have a cow if he gets plugged up."

Winnie glanced at Charlotte, her face flush with excitement. "Did you know this creature talks, C?"

"Peek-a-boo is all I could get him to say."

"Really? That's odd, because he's shared his life story for me."

"Winnie, Polygon doesn't have a life story. He's a bird."

"A very sensitive one, in case you haven't noticed, and basically what it's come down to is this—he claims that wherever Miss Sara goes, he goes."

All eyes were riveted on her. Winnie's blue ones. Miss LaVera's hazy ones. Bo's kelly- green ones. And Polygon's beady ones.

"Don't be ridiculous, Winnie. We can't take a bird to The Rreserve."

LaVera handed Charlotte a plate of cake. "Well, Sara was afraid you'd say that, Charlotte Ann, so she phoned this morning and told me to ask Bo to get on that computer of his and doodle this Reserve."

"It's Google, Momma." Bo's kind correction was guilty stake to Charlotte's heart.

"That's what I said." LaVera poked a piece of cake through the bars of Polygon's cage. "Anyway, right there on Bo Boy's fancy screen it said that pets are welcome."

"In fact, they encourage—" Bo began.

"Their lonelier residents to get one." LaVera finished for him. She wrapped a chunky hand around the birdcage handle. "Polygon's a sittin' on fresh papers. I've got a stack of the *Addisonville Herald* piled by the front door. That's about all that bi-monthly rag's good for anyway. And I've packed his birdseed and a few pears 'til you get a chance to settle him proper."

"Here, Momma, let me get that." Bo set his cake plate on the table and took the cage.

"Mother doesn't need a—"

"Just tote him right on out to the van, Bo Boy, and slide him in the back." LaVera waved him out of the kitchen.

"I'll get the door." Winnie rushed after him.

"Ain't they a pair?" LaVera flashed a pleased smile. "I didn't think there'd ever be anyone as good as you, but shame on me for limiting God."

They were a pair all right, a pair of *ex*-friends in her book. "LaVera, Mother can't even take care of herself, how in the world is she going to take care of a bird?"

She patted Charlotte's cheek. "I know this ain't easy for any of us, but especially not for your momma. The only thing that'll make her happier than havin' you along to fight with is having that blasted parrot you gave her to talk to."

Charlotte slammed her plate on the table. "But I'm not along. Why is that so hard for everyone to understand? I'm dropping Mother off and flying back to DC. Today. I've been away from my life for nearly three weeks. I have a job I'm on the verge of losing, a teenager who needs her mother, and a husband who...who knows what James is doing."

LaVera let Charlotte's steam hit her full force without so much as an eyebrow raise in judgment. "It's never easy doin' the hard things." She clasped Charlotte's arm. "And no one's had to do more hard things than you, Charlotte Ann...unless it's your mother." She led her away from the empty birdcage stand. "One more thing before I forget." They stopped in the entryway and LaVera lifted a worn book from the seat of the hall tree. "Long as Sara has her Bible and her bird, ain't nothing she cain't do. Slip this in her suitcase for me, will you?"

Charlotte eyed the cracked cover with contempt. LaVera dropped the Bible into her hands, the weight as condemning as the thought of leaving Mother with no one but a bird to fend for her.

Chapter 12

Show Time

A sudden bolt of lightning split the sky and sent Charlotte and Winnie diving into the van.

Breathless and flushed, Winnie shimmied into the front seat. "Beauregard Tucker is top-of-the line. Good as they come. And without a doubt, the most handsome man I've ever laid eyes on." Cooing like the homing pigeons Mother had once tried her hand at raising, Winnie plastered her face against the window.

Charlotte ground her disgust between locked jaws and jerked the shifter into gear. "A regular Mr. Bojangles."

Another shard of lightning ripped the roiling clouds apart with an anger that mirrored her current frame of mind. LaVera's assault with worn slippers, old pipes, and a Bible hadn't knocked her off track or caused her to waiver. Winnie's ridiculous crush wouldn't stop her either. She knew what she had to do and was determined to do it.

But instead of getting the heck out of Dodge, she sat with both hands glued to the wheel. Her gaze teamed up with Winnie's in a google-eyed observance of the unique mother-son pair huddled together in the middle of the yard, right there in plain view, as if they conspired to deliver one last parting shot.

Another boom of thunder sounded. Bo wrapped his arm around LaVera and hurriedly shepherded her back to the safety of the porch. The caring look that passed between parent and child had been brief, but effective.

Charlotte gave herself a mental kick for allowing this exchange of undying trust and unconditional love to get to her, to make her question The Reserve plan all over again. If she'd done what she should've done and kept her eyes on the road, she'd have missed the whole thing. But she hadn't. And now it was too late.

Once again, she'd seen something she'd never forget.

It wasn't the terrifying sight of watching her sister sink or the nauseating guilt of finding her father lifeless body face down in the water. The horror came in knowing this kind of love would always be beyond her reach. Jealousy irritated every raw nerve in her body. She punched the accelerator and spun out of the circle drive.

Texas-sized raindrops pelted the van's windshield and breached the crack in the driver's side window as the van flew down the lane. Charlotte cranked the window lever, but the glass refused to meet the seal. Assisted living was the absolute best option for Mother. The neighbors, and *Winifred*, would just have to deal with defeat.

Feeling every-bit the selfish, ungrateful daughter, Charlotte twisted the wiper knob. Frayed rubber and warped metal smeared the glass. Bo made giving up dreams look easy. The irony slung back and forth like muddy rainwater.

She'd gone in search of life and found death. The demise of everything she valued had come to pass, just as Winnie predicted. Faith. Marriage. Friendships. Her relationship with her daughter. And, despite what she told herself, even the once-strong connection she'd once had with Mother.

The losses, each one greater than any human being should have to bear, had sucked away her very essence, the core of who she was and had hoped to be. Not swiftly like the currents of the Frio's floodwaters, but slowly day after day, the deadly force eroded the banks of her being. Before she realized the extent of the damage, any remnants of hope had been carved away, leaving her as scarred and pitted as the Texas limestone, her emotions fossilized.

Bo Tucker, on the other hand, willingly agreed to what she had flat-out told him was a death sentence. During Bo's junior year of college, his father died of an unexpected heart attack. Bo left the University of Texas and a shot at the Heisman to take over Leon's gas station. In doing so, this gifted athlete exchanged a bronze trophy for what turned out to be a golden life of happiness.

Injustice boiled within her and tightened her grip on the wheel. Knuckles white, Charlotte forced her blurry focus on the slick road ahead.

Mother claimed God had a unique sense of humor. Without

question, the current dismal state of her life gave the cock-eyed theory some weight. But why she'd been singled-out to bear the brunt of God's distasteful jokes had always frustrated her and would probably never be answered to her satisfaction. This latest round of second-guessing herself was not the least bit funny.

The van bounced through water-filled potholes impossible to detect, jarring Winnie's lips from their locked position. She cleared her throat and took another stab at conversation. "Are you not speaking to me because we have a bird in the backseat?" Winnie poked at Charlotte's ribs. "C'mon, C, lighten up. It would be asking a lot of LaVera to have to check on Polygon twice a day."

Charlotte refused the weak attempt to sweeten her sour mood. Being one-upped by a pickled Avon lady was bad enough, but that her supposed friend aided and abetted the crime hacked her even more.

"I took you along for moral support, so I'd have someone on my side. But no, you were too busy drooling over Bo Tucker to keep your focus where it should have been. What were you thinking?" She stomped the gas and the van fishtailed around another waterlogged corner.

Winnie clawed the dash. "What was *I* thinking?" She righted herself. "A better question would be, what are *you* thinking? What's it gonna hurt if your mother has a bird? Can't you give the old girl something, Charlotte?"

"Don't think because you moved to Addisonville and weaseled your way in tight with the locals that you have any idea of what I have or have not given to my family over the years."

Winnie sat back in her seat, arms crossed over her chest. "This is about your old boyfriend, isn't it?"

"For Pete's sake, Winnie. Have Bo Tucker."

Sheets of water pummeled the van's roof, intensifying the empty tin-can feeling churning inside Charlotte's belly. At the blue hospital sign, she slowed and whipped the van under the covered entrance, stopping on a dime. Whatever magic Bo had performed on the brakes had done the trick. So why was she still seething?

Winnie looked at Charlotte. "This bitterness is going to kill you, you know."

"The sooner the better."

Winnie shook her head and reached for the door handle. "It's your show. It always has been." She got out of the van and slammed the door. "I'm going home."

Charlotte jumped out. "Go ahead. Leave me to deal with this alone." Wind drove rain under the overhang, soaking any dry clothing the window leak had missed. "See if I care."

"You've forgotten how to care." With a cutting wave, Winnie strode toward the street, not even taking the time to look back. Rain straightened her wiry curls, her flip-flops smacking a hasty retreat through the puddles on the pavement.

"Yeah?" Charlotte shouted. "Well, then how come that's all I've been doing for the past twenty-five years?"

Winnie ignored her tantrum and kept walking.

Charlotte kicked the tire. She left the van unlocked and the keys in the ignition. With any luck someone might steal the heap and pawn that stupid bird. Then she'd ship Mother to Austin in an ambulance and spare herself the torture of being trapped in a vehicle for hours with another person who hated her guts.

She marched through the automatic hospital doors and made a beeline to the open elevator. She punched the two, and the doors on the ancient contraption groaned shut. Water dripped around her feet. As the elevator lumbered up, she blew hot air across her wet lips. Why did giving an inch, even on such a minor point as taking a bird to a nursing home, seem like such a major deal?

With a ding, the doors creaked opened, and she got off on Mother's floor. She ducked into the nearest restroom. One glance in the mirror confirmed the mess the rain, the leaky van, and the Tuckers had made of her. She wiped streaked mascara from her face and wrung excess water from her shirt. Once she'd put herself back together, she headed for the nurses' station.

"Hey, Molly." Charlotte pulled her vocal pitch out of the anxious range. "Sara Slocum ready to go?"

"She's packed. But I'll let you decide if she's ready." The spunky little redhead snapped her fingers at the two burly techs leaning against the wall. "Come on, boys. It's going to take all of us to manage this show."

Show? LaVera and Winnie had used the same word. That's the thing she hated about small towns and the very reason she had to get out of here as soon as possible. Everyone knew everything about your business.

Charlotte joined the techs treading on the heels of Molly's squeaky shoes, the dread in her stomach rumbling to the clipped rhythm their small army made in the empty hall.

Molly paused at the door. "Want me to go first?"

"I wouldn't do that to my worst enemy." Charlotte eased past the relieved woman.

Molly and the techs waited for a second, then flanked her.

Mother sat in a wheelchair. Her bad leg stuck straight out like a drawn sword. The bouquet of Get Well balloons Ari had ordered and had delivered all by herself fluttered above Mother's flattened bed-head hair.

"Ready to go, Mother?"

"You're soaked to the bone, Charlotte Ann."

"It's pouring out there, but don't worry, I'm parked under the portico."

"Then how did you get so wet?"

"Long story."

Mother studied her as if debating whether or not she wanted

details. "You have my bird?"

Charlotte caught Molly's see-what-I-mean look. Mother was not going to make this easy. "He's whistling Dixie in the back of the van."

"Van?"

Letting the question slide, Charlotte hoped she would not have to explain how she came into the possession of Raymond's vehicle. "Your chariot, Mother...and it awaits." She busied herself with the lonely plant on the windowsill.

"Where did you get a van?"

"Raymond."

"Sweet Moses."

Molly slipped behind the wheelchair and unlocked the brakes. "You ready to roll, Mrs. Slocum?"

"Do I have a choice?"

Charlotte stashed the dying plant with the leftover hospital paraphernalia on the rolling cart and changed the subject. "LaVera sends her love, Mother."

"Love, schmove. If LaVera loved me, she would have had Bo Boy bust me out of here." Mother adjusted the pillow under her arm cast. "Molly, feel free to give my bed to someone else. I won't be back."

Molly grinned. "We're gonna miss your spunk, Mrs. Slocum."

"Not as badly as I will, child." Jaw set, Mother waved toward the door.

The nurse and two techs trundled her out of the room and off to the elevator.

Charlotte glanced at the rumpled bed. How had their lives become such a tangled mess? She sighed and pushed the loaded cart into the hall. She trailed the entourage at a safe distance, dragging herself along. At the elevator, Molly held the door open. The medical personnel and Mother's wheelchair had taken up most of the four-by-four space.

"You coming or not, Charlotte Ann?" Mother's bad leg was aimed at Charlotte like an accusatory finger. "I seem to recall that this whole rehab ordeal was your idea."

"Why don't you go ahead, Mother. It's a bit crowded for me. I'll wait for the next one."

Molly mouthed the word *chicken* and let the door close.

By the time Charlotte reached the portico, the techs had Mother's wheelchair backed against the running boards under the van's open side door. The gaping dark hole, plus the panic glazing Mother's face, reminded Charlotte of how Jonah must have looked as the whale swallowed him whole.

She left the cart and hurried over to Molly. "How're you going to get her into that middle seat? I thought the running boards would help, but there's no way she can manage the height."

"We'll have to lift her."

"We?" Charlotte's voice squeaked.

"Best if you learn so you can manage her unloading." Molly explained. "Jerry will climb in the van, hook his arms under hers and hoist her up while Ben and I steady her leg." Molly turned to Charlotte. "When we get your mother clear of the wheelchair, you maneuver that chair out of the way. Think you can do that?"

Charlotte nodded, her eyes transfixed on the bone-chilling fear stirring the liquid pools forming in her mother's eyes. This was going to hurt, and it was all her fault.

Chapter 13

Prison Bus

Let's keep this right leg supported as we ease Mrs. Slocum onto the backseat, Jerry," Nurse Molly places one hand under my knee and the other under my injured hip. "One. Two. Lift."

She holds my shaky appendage steady as the strapping young man I taught in third grade backpedals carefully into the van, hefts me over the running board, and slides my backside snug against the armrest.

Pain jolts my entire body and spurs another round of shameful howling. "Sweeeet Moses!"

Molly's face contorts into an ugly grimace that no doubt mirrors mine. "You're doin' great, Mrs. Slocum. Hang on 'til we get some pillows stuffed around you."

I suck air through my clenched teeth while squeezing the phooey out of Jerry's arm, but I cannot get a grip on myself. I entered the hospital limber as a well-chewed piece of gum and exited a petrified pretzel stick. A kindergartner could snap me in half.

"I'll get them." Charlotte, pale as that awful summer day, runs to the cart and snatches bedding from the cart's bottom shelf. "These work?"

"Perfect." Molly tosses a pillow to Jerry, and he tucks it behind my back. "That better, Mrs. Slocum?" Molly and Jerry cast doubtful looks at each other while they wait on me to catch my breath.

This uncontrollable gasping and blubbering has made me appear a fool in front of my former students. I take a very uncharacteristic course of action and lie. "Yes, thank you."

Molly offers a commiserating smile and steps up into the van. She lifts my good leg and places it gently next to the bad one. "Try to keep 'em parallel. I think it will make your ride to rehab a bit more comfortable." Molly uses all the pillows, cramming them into every available nook and cranny that has formed between my rigid body and the lumpy seat. Satisfied I'm not going anywhere, she asks, "How about another pain pill before you head out?"

Tempting as her offer sounds I can't have these young minds polluted with the notion that suffering is an acceptable reason to resort to drugs, so I lie again. "I'm good, thank you, dear."

Molly pats my arm, letting my untruths go unchallenged. "We'll miss you, Mrs. Slocum."

She and Jerry back out of the van and close the sliding door with a resounding clang. My fate is sealed, and every far-fetched scenario that included Charlotte changing her mind is dashed.

Propped and stuffed tight as a bell pepper, I finally catch a deep, cleansing breath. I inhale and exhale slowly, twiddling my thumbs to the ragged rhythm ricocheting off the tinny walls of the van. I am still alive, despite feeling very much the opposite. The insides of my nostrils burn with the oily reek of yard equipment. Why Charlotte thought forcing me to ride in Raymond's vehicle would bring me comfort, I don't know.

I glance at the driver's seat and wonder how the world would look from Raymond's perspective because it's not looking too good from mine. I spot the rusty blades of his evil hedge trimmers sticking out from under his seat. This whole mess is Raymond's fault. If only he'd left my myrtles alone, none of this would have happened.

A great homesickness t-bones me. I cave in the middle, my heart a sinking bowling ball that rolls the alleys of my useless legs and strikes my toes.

"Peek-a-boo."

I perk up quickly, blood rushing to my craning head at a dizzying speed. "Polygon?" My eyes search the cavern-like space behind me.

Polygon's cage is wedged between my rented wheelchair and the back of my seat. The angle affords me a bird's-eye view of my parrot sitting on his swing, his steady black eyes gazing into mine.

"It's good to see you, friend." I reach as far as my hip allows and stick my finger through the bars. Immediately he pecks a welcome on my nail. "You up for this, boy?"

Polygon rips off a shrill wolf whistle. At least he's on board for come-what-may, which is more than I can say for me at the moment.

Wiggling my finger in appreciation of his loyalty, I watch Charlotte and Molly through the window. The nurse is giving my daughter last-minute instructions on how to care for me. Everything about this picture goes against the invariant order of things. Charging a child with parental custody is life turned upside down.

I remember leaving this very hospital with Charlotte forty-two years ago. I had a toddler at home, a colicky infant in my lap, and a bad case of second thoughts. The nurse wheeled me out to the car without a single word of advice on how to raise more than one child, or how to love the second when you loved the first more than your own life. She offered nothing on how to cope with the demands of two children only two years apart. Stiff-lipped, she stuffed me next to Martin and handed me the tiny pink bundle without so much as a wish for luck. I wasn't home five minutes when I learned what mothers have known throughout the ages…the sacrifices made to accommodate the second one wouldn't matter because the love comes easy.

Brow furrowed, Charlotte signs the stack of papers on Molly's clipboard and then jumps into the driver's seat. She swivels around. "How you doing back there, Mother?"

I choke back the urge to scream *if you loved me, missing a few weeks of work wouldn't matter.* "A road trip is probably the last thing I need right now, but I'm obviously no longer behind the wheel of my own life, am I?"

Chapter 14

There is No Such Thing as Forgiveness

The rain stopped at the edge of town, much to Charlotte's relief. At least she wouldn't have to battle the forces of nature and Mother at the same time.

She flew down the highway, one hand on the wheel the other adjusting the rearview mirror. She'd never aspired to be one of those neurotic mothers with eyes in the back of her head, but an extra pair of eyes would come in handy about now. Grasping for some sort of handle on Mother's current state of mind, Charlotte's attention darted between drying blacktop and the speechless women sitting directly behind her. She fiddled with the mirror, framing her passenger squarely in her sights.

Acting like she was a bound-and-gagged hostage, Mother stared out the window as if the hills had disappeared into the hazy blue mist hanging over the valley. With each mile, the clouds dissipated and her mother's mood darkened.

Certain the ceasefire was only temporary, Charlotte took advantage of the peace and concentrated on the future, the benefits this new arrangement offered the entire family. Mother would be safe. Not having to worry about her burning the house down around herself might even be a bigger plus than the promise of excellent care and opportunities for social interaction. Although, she had to admit, alleviating Mother's loneliness would certainly take the pressure off of her. Maybe even give her a chance to build a relationship with Ari. Nothing but good all the way around.

Charlotte ventured another quick glance into the mirror. "Have I told you about The Reserve's forty-seat, in-house, movie theater? Great digital set-up. The movie room even has a popcorn machine." No interest registered on Mother's grim face. "And surround sound."

A swift mental kick poked a hole in Charlotte's overblown thoughts. Could she have said anything more idiotic? The last movie Mother saw in a theater was probably one of the Disney movies she and Caroline had begged to see.

Charlotte's mind scrambled through the oppressive tension in search of The Reserve's list of amenities. Arts and craft studio, exercise room, beauty salon and spa, billiards parlor, cigar lounge, game room, and something poolside called a Safari Hut. All designed to give seniors another shot at community life. None of these selling-point extras would engage Mother. Then she remembered the gardens.

"Oh, did I mention the beautiful landscaping? You'll even have your own terrace. We can stop and pick up a few potted plants, if you'd like."

Surely the offer of a place to stroll among beautiful flowers or grow a few in some pots would penetrate Mother's hard shell. She waited, hoping she'd stumbled upon the spark that could rekindle the fire she suddenly missed. Cutting her eyes back and forth between the road and the sour reflection in the mirror effectively closed the book on that addlebrained idea and sent her careening down a different path.

"I have lovely flowerbeds...at home."

"We've talked about this, Mother. You can't go home...your bedroom is upstairs, the only bathroom is not wheelchair accessible, and you couldn't drive to town for your daily therapy sessions."

"My couch is comfortable."

Unwilling to ride the hamster wheel of this argument again, Charlotte changed the subject. "You know, I should be able to come see you much more often." She checked the mirror. Despite the skepticism of Mother's raised brows, she felt encouraged and compelled to charge ahead. "Flying in and out of Austin will be much more convenient. I won't have to rent a car or make the two-hour drive to Addisonville. Just hop a plane in DC, land at Bergstrom International, and catch a cab to The Reserve. I should be able to do that at least...once a month."

"Will you bring Aria?"

"Sure. When I can. She's pretty busy. School and teenage stuff, you know."

Mother's brows slowly deflated, but she said nothing. Worn rubber meeting the road and Polygon fluttering about in his cage joined her flat-line response.

Salty tears trickled down Charlotte's face and wet her lips. She hurriedly retracted her moistened gaze from the mirror and aimed her blurred focus on the long stretch of road ahead. How could this be the same mother who'd read to her every night before bed, taught her to roll a pie crust, and smothered her with kisses. Were those true memories or wishful imaginings? The silent woman staring a hole through the back of Charlotte's head was nobody's mother.

Charlotte's hand searched the door pocket for a tissue. She would not allow Mother the pleasure of knowing that years of her cold-shoulder treatment was getting to her.

Why did she try? What did it matter? Nothing she did ever pleased this impossible woman. Charlotte fingers located an old Dairy Queen napkin in the console. Willing herself not to think about how long it had been there, she swiped under her nose, recounting with each pass the twenty-five years of wasted efforts. Giving up Bo Tucker. Going to law school in Caroline's place. Securing the job Caroline would have gotten at one of the nation's top law firms. Marrying and having Caroline's family. Yet none of her personal sacrifices were enough to blot the blame. Mother kept a detailed ledger and managed to smear her shortcomings into every conversation they'd ever tried to have.

The wheels pounded the pavement with the *thu-thunk* finality of the judge's gavel. In some respects, having her guilt officially declared and the sentence delivered would be far better than this perpetual pussy-footing around the facts she and Mother both knew to be true. She'd let her sister die and grief had sent her father to the river that day he fell in. Offenses so great, she deserved Mother's inability to forgive her.

Tears under control, Charlotte sneaked another peek into the mirror. Mother, stone-cold silent, had resumed her vigilant inspection of the countryside.

Like a serial murderer returning to the scene of her horrendous crime, Charlotte cleared her throat and tried again. "Don't you think Polygon looks good?"

"He still has feathers."

Charlotte laughed out loud, surprised by the splinter of an olive-branch Mother had begrudgingly offered. "I'm sure he'll have the ladies fawning all over him."

A pleased smile crept to the corners of Mother's lips. "He *is* a bit of a Casanova, isn't he?"

"You've done a great job teaching him."

A sly smile softened her mother's features. "He's been one of my flightier students, but a quick study."

Charlotte's cell rang and the warm moment instantly cooled. She grabbed the phone off the console, mentally cursing the intrusion that had immediately swept any trace of progress from her mother's face. The number on the caller ID belonged to James.

"I better take this, Mother. Could be Ari." She punched the button. "Ari?"

"Char? Where have you been?"

"James, this better be an emergency." She knew the tone of her voice would spur Mother's questions, but she'd have to worry about that later. Her husband had ruined more than an opportunity to build bridges, and she didn't care who knew. In fact, telling Mother the truth about their separation might actually be a relief.

"You need to come home immediately."

"I'm coming tonight. But later. After I get Mother settled. I emailed you my flight times."

"Ari needs you now."

"It won't kill her to wait a few more hours."

"It might." The brevity of his tone quickened Charlotte's pulse.

"What's happened? Tell me she's all right?"

"Charlotte Ann?" Mother's white head appeared in the mirror. "What's wrong?"

"Not now, Mother," she snapped.

"Are you in the car with Sara?" James didn't wait for her answer. "Good. I'm glad someone's with you."

His uncharacteristic appreciation of her mother alerted all

Charlotte's senses. "Quit stalling. Tell me."

"Pull over, Char."

Like Pavlov's trained dog, she obeyed his calm directive and jerked the wheel. "Tell me Ari's all right." The van bounced off onto the shoulder.

Mother held on to her seat, her white head gyrating up and down. "Charlotte Ann, what on earth is going on?"

"Hush, Mother." Charlotte slammed on the brakes and threw the shifter into park. "Now, James. I want the truth now!" She clutched the wheel.

"Aria got into a little bit of trouble last night."

Charlotte felt her grip slip. "What kind of trouble?"

"She and three friends were...arrested."

"What? How did you let that happen? When did she get picked up? Where. Is. She?"

"Whoa. Slow down. Which question do you want me to answer?"

"Pick one, James. It doesn't matter. You're going to answer every single thing I ask and for once, you're going to tell me the truth. Start with where they're holding her?"

"Juvenile detention. Somewhere close to the Hill."

A semi whizzed by, rocking the van and Charlotte to the core. She couldn't even conjure the picture of her child locked up, scared and alone, and trapped with the thugs of the inner city. The startling realization hit her hard. Somewhere along the line, Aria had become more than the fulfillment of Caroline's dream. Aria was her child, her baby, and she'd rip steel bars out with her bare hands to get to her if she had to.

Charlotte cleared the rage building in her throat, determined to get to the bottom of this. "Since when?"

"About two o'clock this morning."

"What was she doing out at two in the morning?"

"I don't know. She spent the night with that girl."

"What girl?"

"The one who had a birthday."

"But Caitlyn's party is Friday."

"Char, it's Saturday."

"That can't be right."

"Check your precious calendar. You know, the one you live by."

Endless hours sitting in a hospital had blurred one day into the other. She wouldn't know today's date if she hadn't just written it fifteen times on all those forms Molly made her sign. But knowing today was the middle of June didn't help her name the actual day of the week. She pulled up the date. Saturday.

"Okay, so I lost track. I've been busy. That doesn't explain how you let our daughter end up in juvie?"

"I didn't."

"What do you mean, you didn't? The only time I've ever asked you for help, and you can't even watch her for a few days."

"Maybe if she had a mother—"

"Don't even go there, James. You're her father. Where were you?"

"Do you want to hear this? Maybe possibly come up with a way to help our kid? Or would you rather spend the conversation slapping tar and feathers all over me?"

Charlotte cringed at his logic and the cunning way he shirked any responsibility and passed the buck to her. "What happened?"

"They waited until the girl's parents were asleep. Climbed out a window. Took several cans of spray paint, took the train downtown, then tagged the walls of a Metro rail station. A security guard saw them. Called the police. They hauled them in. Ari called me."

That last piece of the puzzle he forced into place, with expert precision, stung badly. "Why didn't she call me?"

"Well, I don't know, Char. Maybe she thought her mother was too busy."

Charlotte ignored his jab, her lawyer instincts kicking in and taking over where her marriage and parenting skills had obviously failed. "You haven't gone down there, have you?"

"Contrary to what you think, I'm not stupid. I've been trying to get a hold of you. See what we should do."

"I don't have good reception in these hills."

"Makes it easier to block everything out, doesn't it?" He paused as if her guilt needed a moment to multiply itself. "You want me to call Saul?"

Charlotte clenched the phone. If she could throw it at him, she would. "Are you kidding? Send *your* attorney to the courthouse? Ari's picture would be on the cover of every tabloid before the evening commute. I won't do that to her."

"You're saying you want me to let Ari sit in juvie until you get your mother tucked in for the night?"

"I want you to crawl back under the rock you slithered out from under and do what you do best—let me handle this. I'll call Loraine. I'm sure Sid Waring can pull some strings. Once this mess is cleaned up, hopefully Loraine can slip Ari out a back door before your paparazzi Nazis get a whiff."

James sighed. "You want Loraine to bring her here?"

"No. I want my daughter home. Safe and sound. And as far away from you as possible."

"Before you get all self-righteous, Char, maybe you should stop to think about where she got the paint."

His accusation and her realization collided with a nauseating efficiency. "From your studio?"

"Cleaned out my entire cabinet."

Charlotte couldn't breathe. "Are you saying Aria planned this?"

"Looks that way."

"You don't know that."

"I know most people don't pack spray paint for a sleepover unless they want to get high or paint something, Char."

"Why would she do such a stupid, stupid thing?"

"Ever occur to you that maybe she was trying to get your attention, so that maybe, just maybe, you'd come home? Hell, I've tried it myself."

"Don't lay your shenanigans at my feet, James. Painting a wall doesn't come anywhere close to what you've done. And, for the record, my being gone has nothing to do with the string of bimbos that file in and out of your studio."

She had him, and his silence confirmed he knew it, but she was shaking so violently she could scarcely enjoy the victory. "Stay away from that courthouse, and stay away from me and my daughter, James McCandless." She snapped the phone shut. Immediately her mother's concerned face filled the rearview mirror.

"Don't say a word, Mother. Not one word."

Chapter 15

Hide and Watch

Loraine, I'll have to call you back." Charlotte tosses her phone onto the empty passenger seat and brings the van to a screeching halt beside the uniformed gate attendant. She cranks the window down. "Slocum. Sara Slocum."

The guard's eyes are concealed by the shiny bill of his khaki-green uniform cap, but I suspect the young fellow's hesitation to open the gate stems from the once-over our transportation deserves. "I'll need some ID, miss."

"Can't you just check the list?" Charlotte's first words since James called her about Aria are taut with nerves.

"ID, please."

Charlotte digs through that piece of luggage she calls a purse. After a few seconds, she retrieves a wallet, yanks out her driver's license, and shoves it into his gloved hand. "I'm sure she's on your list."

He takes the laminated card. After a quick glance, his head ping-pongs between the license and Charlotte as if she's a potential car bomber. I can hardly fault the young man's caution. Paint peeling, hubcaps missing, and overloaded to the point of blowing all four bald tires, I'm sure we look like escapees from *The Grapes of Wrath.*

"I'll have to call for back up." He stuffs the license in his pocket. "This says McCandless."

Charlotte stiffens. "Not for long."

His hand goes to the gun in his holster. "Excuse me."

"Easy boy." Charlotte raises both hands, palms out. "Sara Slocum is my mother, and she's roasting in the back."

A muscle twitches along his clenched jaw, but he leaves the weapon strapped in its place. He steps forward and warily peeks inside Charlotte's lowered window. I squint, determined to make out the name on his badge.

Kevin.

Or is it *Keith*?

Without my glasses, I cannot be completely certain, but decide to go with Kevin.

Kevin conducts a visual inspection of the van's interior and then of me.

He takes in everything about me…from my disarrayed hair to the tip of my useless toes. A small shake of his head, and I get the distinct feeling Kevin's a bit disappointed I'm not a terrorist.

I nod and smile. "I'm scheduled for move-in today, *Kevin*. I'm a bit road weary. So, either pick up the pace, or risk the embarrassment of explaining to an Austin news team how The Reserve's newest tenant succumbed to heatstroke at the gate designed to keep her safe."

Charlotte whips around. I love the mouth-gaping shock on her face. It's all the evidence I need that she has been waylaid by the depths of my reserves. Pleasure courses through my veins for the first time in days. I'm tempted to believe this enlightening moment will inspire Charlotte to turn around and head for home, but I know better. This is a puny victory at best. Changing my daughter's mind is like pouring concrete: either you get things smoothed out before it sets up, or you're stuck with a lumpy mess.

We have a lumpy mess. I was as anxious to be rid of her as she was to be rid of me.

Until the last fifty miles.

This rare peek into her life has given me a new understanding...pricked compassion I thought long-since dead.

Hide and watch, as my mother used to say, has its advantages. Had I not eavesdropped on my daughter's conversations with Sid and Loraine, I would have no inkling of the impressive skills she possesses. Charlotte leapt through hoops of legal red tape like an expert high hurdler. She cajoled her boss to call in favors on one line while instructing Loraine to make a beeline to the courthouse on the other. I'm more confident than ever she'll survive this latest upset, with or without me. Hard as it is to fathom that I did something right, I believe Charlotte's decisive actions prove that despite my mistakes, I have raised quite a girl. Quite a girl, indeed.

But whether or not my precious granddaughter will fare as well still concerns me. Charlotte's work keeps her away from home every day and most nights. And from what little I gathered from the shouting match she had with James, while the cat's away that dirty rat plays and plays.

I agonize over Aria's future in the same way I pray for Charlotte's. The faster I can get on my feet and go home the sooner Charlotte can scratch my name off her list of worries and focus on her daughter. Much as I hate to admit it, I'm going to have to cooperate. For now.

"Wait here." Kevin executes a pivot turn and steps inside his little glass house. He retrieves a clipboard and scans the list. Confirmed error blushes his baby-smooth cheeks. Kevin returns the license with prompt precision and without apology. "These days, we can't be too careful. Welcome to The Reserve, Mrs. Slocum." He jams the clipboard under one arm and dismisses us with a snappy salute.

Charlotte's smile does little to warm the cold dread I feel creeping toward my puffed-up bravado. "Mother, you can ride shotgun on my defense team any time."

I muster an appreciative nod, but inside I'm frantically tamping a host of fears, dying here, alone and forgotten, being foremost among them.

Heavy wrought-iron gates high as a maximum-security prison fence swing open. Charlotte spins around and puts the van into gear. "Now this is service."

She prompts the gas and we lurch into a different world, one that's foreign and more unsettling than the year Wilma Rayburn reassigned me from third grade to middle school math.

Lushly-landscaped cobblestone streets wind through the well-manicured property. Park benches and cast-iron street lamps every twenty or thirty feet lend to the feel of a city unto itself. At every cross-hatched intersection, yellow warning signs sport pictures of golf carts. I'm reminded of the deer crossing signs posted along the hill country roads. Is it as difficult to get golfers to cross at a designated spot as it is a deer? Any self-respecting deer would feel slighted by all this safety hoopla devoted to darting old geezers. I blink away the tears. Any self-respecting deer would rather run broadside into a speeding car than be caught dead here.

Charlotte slows to the requisite five miles per hour and follows the black arrows pointing the way to the main building. After a couple of wrong turns and what seems like several minutes of being lost in a live oak forest, I volunteer to toss breadcrumbs so that we can find our way out. Charlotte and I share a much-needed laugh. And then we crest the bluff.

There it is...The Reserve. The sight of the massive, four-story structure decked top to bottom in hill country sandstone knocks the humor right out of me. Hand-hewn rocks, rich in varied buff-colored tones, bring to mind the distant villas of Tuscany. Not that I've ever been to one, but I've seen them featured in the travel magazines Martin and I used to drool over. I half expect to hear Italian music— the kind Vinny plays over the Pizza Hut loud speakers. Deaf and mute to Charlotte's pointing out of this and that, I take in the grandeur of my surroundings, feeling every bit the plain and simple country bumpkin that I am.

In the middle of the circular drive a shimmering, quartz dolphin spews water fifteen feet into the sticky air. We follow the signs marked *Main Entrance* and head toward the expansive porte-cochere shading two beveled-glass doors. Beams the size of tree trunks are supported by four stone pillars. Ceramic pots, bigger than the galvanized stock tank I use to water goats, flank each dry-stacked column. Exotic flowers crown the planters with generous bouquets of cardinal reds and hyacinth blues nearly as breathtaking as my New Dawn roses at their peak. I make a mental note to call LaVera. If I don't remind her to keep the soaker hose going on my flower beds, I won't have a plant left when I can get home.

A black limo idles under the fancy carport. Several people dressed in very classy funeral garb mill around the open U-Haul trailer hitched to a long black car. Charlotte pulls in and parks our van right alongside two women. One blonde. One brunette. Each with a firm grip on the opposite posts of a vintage headboard.

Our muffler backfires, and the two snooty broads stop their tug-of-war long enough to turn up their noses and drag the mahogany piece closer to the trailer. Their urgency to clear a space for us is probably based on the same observation that made Kevin think twice.

If I've ever craved my lipstick, it is now. I run my tongue over my dry lips. "Can I afford this, Charlotte Ann?"

"No." Our eyes meet in the rearview mirror. "But James McCandless can." Once I catch her meaning, she fires off a quick wink, and then she's out the door. Before she goes, she leans inside the open window. "Stay put until I find someone to help us unload."

I point at my legs. "Just where do you think I could go on these toothpicks?"

"Mother, can you at least give this place a chance?"

I shrug.

"I'll leave the windows down so you can get some air." Charlotte's eyes slide toward the unhappy neighbors. "I'll hurry."

In a flash, she skedaddles around the U-Haul crowd and disappears behind those two enormous doors. The lobby doors are as tall as my hay barn. I feel even smaller. I close my eyes and blow out my breath like a deflating balloon. A sudden crash startles me and I become aware of the shouting right outside my window.

"You got Mimi's jewelry. I get the Florida timeshare and *all* of her furniture." The frosted-blonde with the short skirt is staring at the fallen headboard. "What's left of it, anyway." She waves a piece of broken bedpost in the face of the heavy-set brunette. "Look what you did to my inheritance."

"I don't know why you want this old stuff. You don't even like antiques."

The blonde stomps across the headboard, her stilettos making mincemeat out of the splintered wood. "*You* didn't even like Mimi."

The brunette's nostrils flare. "That's not true."

"Mimi always liked me better, and you hated us both for it."

"I can't believe you." The brunette rips off her jacket, her thick arms revealing remarkable muscle definition. I've seen enough playground fights to know that blonde better back off, but she stands there like my completely clueless neighbor Gloria Wooten. "Were you here every holiday and birthday? No. I was." The brunette throws her jacket on the pavers and thrusts her face at the blonde. "Did you take the old woman to Luby's every Saturday for the vegetable platter? No. I did." The brunette jabs chubby hands upon rounded hips and squares herself up. The crowd backs up, giving the raving lunatic ample room. "You haven't seen Grandmother in ten years. Dumped every bit of her care on me. Now you show up at the funeral with your hand out. Well, I'm gonna give you exactly what you deserve."

Before the blonde can get a word in edgewise, the brunette flies at her and takes her down like a football tackling dummy. A flurry of hair, hose, and heels rolls onto the grassy knoll. Three security guards burst through the lobby doors, and within seconds they wrestle the snarling women apart. After much shouting and cussing, the officers manage to stuff the bloody blonde into the limo's front seat and manhandle the smirking brunette into the back. While two guards keep the women in the car, another guard supervises the remaining family members as they quickly throw pieces of the headboard into the U-Haul and dive into the departing limo.

I sit in the silence, stunned by what I've just witnessed. Does life always end in a cat fight?

I remember when Papa died. I'd already made my peace with the fact that Burl Addison didn't care for Martin. True to his word, Papa disowned me when I married the starry-eyed country boy. Despite the hurt of being ostracized, I wanted a memento. A tiny piece of my father. Something that connected me to him. Something that said I had been the little girl he showed around his bank that smelled of paper money. My brother wouldn't hear of it. Burl Junior said I'd made my bed and now I had to lie in it, even if it meant I wasn't welcome at the funeral.

I shouldn't have been surprised when Burl Junior showed up at my ranch a few days later, but I was. Junior was mad as a stirred-up school board. He accused me of taking Daddy's brass nameplate from the bank. Why did something so small matter to Junior? He'd gotten everything else. The house, the bank presidency, the investment portfolio, our father's blessing...everything. All I wanted was my daddy's name: Burl C. Addison, President. I know for a fact Burl Junior would have torn me and my house apart looking for that placard if Martin hadn't been twice his size.

I poke my finger in Polygon's cage and smile. Burl Junior never was the sharpest crayon in the box.

"Mother, these nice men are going to help you." Charlotte's appearance at the window startles me back to the present. "I'll get your suitcase."

The side door slides open and two brawny techs in spotless white coats wait for me to give them the go ahead. The back doors open and another tech removes my wheelchair. I take a fortifying breath and allow them to gather my useless limbs and deposit me into the empty chair. One tech adjusts my leg support. One gets behind me and unlocks my brakes. One runs ahead and stations himself by those massive lobby doors.

"My bird," I say.

"Let's get you settled first, Mother."

"It's too hot to leave him in the van."

Charlotte sighs. "All right." She passes my suitcase off to the spare tech and returns for Polygon.

"Get her out of this heat." The door tech says to the young man pushing me.

I hold up my hand. "If you don't mind, young man, I'll wait on my companion."

He shrugs. "Anything you say, Mrs. Slocum."

His hint of sarcasm rubs me wrong. No one listens to what I say anymore. But what can I do? I can't stomp off. So, I wait, all clench-lipped and pea-green envious that these young men are years away from the embarrassment of foggy memories and brittle bones.

The slicing whir of a distant weed whacker reminds me of my run-in with Raymond. No doubt about it, my yardman has his faults...not putting tools back where he got them for example. I knew he was on the lazy end of the success spectrum the moment he ambled into my third-grade classroom. Yet, I think no less of him. He has done his best with what God gave him. I'm grateful Raymond tries to make a living and more than a tad regretful my short temper added to his difficulties.

Suddenly I miss the company of people I know, even the dumb and prickly ones. They are the folks I have history with. I'm too tired to start relationships from scratch. For the first time in my life, I feel old. Stiff and stodgy, and set in ways that do not want to change.

Charlotte returns, birdcage in tow. "Happy now?"

Even though I'm not, I nod. The tech opens the ornate doors. A blast of air-conditioned cold, tinged with the floral-masked smell of death hits me. I shudder.

"You catchin' a chill, Mrs. Slocum?" My chair chauffer asks.

I can't seem to stop my teeth from chattering. "It's must be cold enough in there to hang meat."

"You'll get used to it."

The tech wheels me inside, Charlotte trailing behind. He parks me under a glittering chandelier. Unlike the lobby of Addisonville's nursing home, this light and airy room is not populated with wheelchairs draped in rotting corpses. Instead, fully-dressed and vibrantly alert patrons sit in plush, overstuffed chairs and sip goblets of sparkling water. They toast each other across the polished side tables. At the base of the *Gone-With-the-Wind* staircase, several couples glide over pristine marble floors, waltzing to soft, classical music playing in the background.

The tech pats my shoulder lightly. "I'll tell the boss lady you're here."

Before I can agree or disagree, my wheelchair driver has disappeared down the long hall to my left, and just as quickly the other two techs vanish down the hall to my right.

All conversations, dancing, and the clink of glasses cease. The strains of Beethoven are the only sound. Residents look my way, whether it is with pity or understanding, I'm not sure. Polygon flutters to his perch, and I know curiosity cannot be ruled out.

"Want to look around, Mother?"

"I've already seen plenty."

"Mrs. Slocum?" An attractive redhead, dressed in a navy-blue suit, unreasonably high heels, and a cloud of perfume extends a jeweled hand. "I'm Paula Jennings. Welcome to The Reserve." She turns and greets my daughter. "You must be Charlotte. I believe we've spoken on the phone." They shake hands as if solidifying some secret deal.

I decide then and there that I don't care for this young, slender Paula Jennings.

"If you'll come with me, we'll knock this little orientation out of the way as quickly as possible. We don't want Mrs. Slocum to miss her first official dinner hour." Paula takes the handles of my chair, and we fly down the hall, her heels clicking out a taxing pace. "You have a good trip, Mrs. Slocum?"

"Considering that I've been spirited away from my home, learned that my granddaughter's been arrested, and confirmed what I've known all along—that my son-in-law is the south end of a north-bound donkey, I'd have to rate the trip as right up there with a yearly mammogram."

Charlotte nearly drops the birdcage. "Mother!"

Paula stops my chair, comes around, and squats so that she and I are eye-to-eye. "I think we have just what you need, Mrs. Slocum."

I don't appreciate the coy twinkle in her olive orbs, but I play along. "Three hundred acres of wide open spaces and a killer view of the river?"

Charlotte sits Polygon's cage down hard. "Mother."

Paula waves off Charlotte's reprimand and whispers to her, "Let me handle this." She smiles at me as if my hearing's gone bad, then brushes a hair from my face. "Something even better."

Every atrophied muscle in my body twists tighter than a new guitar string. "What could possibly be better?"

"Spa days."

Chapter 16

Lipstick on a Pig

You sit right here, Mrs. Slocum, while I check the spa's availability." Paula parks my wheelchair in front of her glass-top desk. "Your daughter did all the pre-admission paperwork so we'll skip right to the fun part." She motions for Charlotte to take the seat beside me. "Our hot rock massage is our best seller. Unfortunately, they're usually booked weeks in advance."

She settles into a plush desk chair, adds a rhinestone-studded pair of readers to her perfect nose, and bangs out something on one of those fancy computer keyboards. "I'll see if I can't get you the *New Tenant Special*, it's almost as good. I know people in the spa, and I'm sure I can pull a few strings and have you worked in right away." She smiles sweetly. "Steam some of that nasty tension right out of you."

I return the smile, secure in the knowledge that Miss Jennings has no idea that boiling me like a lobster will only harden my shell. Keeping one eye trained on The Reserve's pretty warden, I realign both my resolve and my slipping knee pillow.

"Here we go. There's a tiny slot between rehab and free time."

Paula pushes a button on the computer and a slip of paper spits out of the machine on the credenza behind her desk. "Keep up with this. Your first treatment is complimentary."

Charlotte takes the paper. "Sounds fun to be pampered a bit, doesn't it Mother?"

"Lipstick on a pig." I say, keeping a laser bead on Miss Jennings.

Paula catches my disapproving drift but continues on. Admirable trait, I must concede. "Let's get started on this paper work, shall we?" She opens a file, fans a stack of brochures, and deals them across the desk like the three of us are about to play gin rummy. "Let me start by saying that The Reserve is green."

Exactly the way my stomach feels at this very moment. "Really? It appeared a bit more buff-colored to me."

"Oh, Mrs. Slocum, aren't you a card? I can see you're going to keep us all pleasantly entertained." She points to a glossy brochure decorated with a simple maple leaf logo. "Green means that we've designed our facility to benefit our seniors while saving the planet."

I raise a brow, waiting on her to explain how excessive tree-trunk-sized rafters and carpets thick as sheep's wool could possibly benefit me or the world.

"For example, our buildings are designed to let in as much natural light as possible. Studies show that exposure to light can drastically reduce depression in the elderly while improving both their physical and mental health." She flips to the back page of the green brochure, while my mind stays put, hung up on being lumped into a category I've avoided my entire life.

I mull the term *elderly*. When had I joined the ranks of the blue-hairs?

Paula races ahead. "You'll find that your private residence has several windows, natural-fiber floor coverings, and environmentally-friendly, low-fume paint on every wall."

"Green is good, Mother."

"If we're talking grass, Charlotte Ann." I keep my eyes on Paula. One look at my daughter, and I'm liable to turn into a sobbing, begging, pleading mess, and I won't do that to my granddaughter. She needs her mother.

"Maybe we should move on. Perhaps go over the daily schedules." Paula sorts through the brochures in her hand and plays her trump card. An elegant table setting is featured on the full-color front cover. "At The Reserve, we believe dining should be an experience. For the early riser, we have the Nook. It's a manned continental station of pastries, cereals, and fruit. Our full-course breakfast is served from seven to nine in the main dining room. Lunch starts at eleven thirty and is served until one. Light snacks are available all day in the Safari Hut. Dinner begins promptly at four, with service until six." She cocks her head, appearing every bit the wary cardinal. "Do you think you'll be joining us in the dining room for most meals or do you prefer to cook?"

"Mother's an excellent cook. Pies are her specialty." Charlotte scoots forward in her seat. "But I think it reasonable to assume Mother will be using the meal plan until she achieves a little more mobility. Don't you, Mother?"

That Charlotte has asked my opinion is not nearly as astounding as her mention of the pies. She remembers the pies. I'm floored. Inside, I smile. Outside, I remain poker-faced since it is the only way I will win the cruel hand I've been dealt. "A person would be hard pressed to go hungry here."

Paula's red lips form a courtesy smile. "In that case, I'll go ahead and make your table and seating assignment." She turns to her computer and her lacquered nails fly across the keys.

I can't believe she thinks I'm going to sit here and let her push me around like a second grader. "I'll have an assigned seat?"

Paula nods, her nails tapping out a Morse code of who-knows-what. "We rotate everyone once a month."

"If I promise to be good, can I sit wherever I please?" I make sure she cannot overlook the sarcastic edge in my voice.

She pauses and sums me up over the rim of her glasses. "Oh, Mrs. Slocum, you are a cutie. But, no." She whirls back to the computer and the clacking begins again. "Studies show that eating with others and forming relationships improves digestion and increases longevity. And, Mrs. Slocum, we are all about longevity here." She pecks the button again and the printer shoots out another slip. "Here we go." The paper is ripped from the printer tray and placed before me. "Your tablemates are true treasures. There's Lauralee Macy, distant cousin of the department store Macys..." She lowers her voice. "...with an unfortunate Sears connection somewhere in her lineage." Shaking her head, she returns to the list. "Then we have Ira Conner, independent oil man. And finally, Teeny McElroy of the sausage and kielbasa McElroy's."

I'm flabbergasted. Miss Jennings has pared the sum of these people's lives into pithy titles. I wonder what she'll tell my tablemates about me. Meet Sara Slocum of the dilapidated Fossil Ridge Ranch, no connection to the Rockefellers, and only slightly off her rocker.

Charlotte gathers up the slip and adds it to the growing pile. "What about her rehab schedule?"

"Let's see." Paula rifles through the file. "I see that we're a little behind the curve on our rehab."

We? I'm the only one in this room who's been subjected to rehab torture.

"Mother had a bad reaction to pain meds."

"That's a shame." Paula's comment reminded me of all the parent-teacher conferences I conducted. "Opioids aren't for everyone."

Sitting behind my desk and having to deliver sad news to parents that their child was performing below average, I found the best method was to just spit it out, tell it like it was. But now that I'm on the receiving end of disapproval, I question every word I ever said. I venture a quick glance at Charlotte and see on her face the same look I saw on the face of poor Mrs. Leck when I told her Raymond was so far behind it would take a miracle for him to catch up.

"Mrs. Slocum's primary care physician is in Addisonville," Paula says. "I think it best we have her re-examined by our staff doctor." She looks at the file again. "He'll set up her rehab appointments and see that she's assigned to a physical therapist. The therapist will devise a plan and oversee her progress and report back to our doctor."

All her bases covered, Paula closes the file on my physical health. In my opinion, her priority should be whether or not I can live here and maintain my mental health. Of course, no one asked me.

"Great." Charlotte says. "Mother's anxious to get back on her feet. Aren't you, Mother?"

I nod, although I'm already expecting the worst.

"Now, as for her current mode of transportation..." Paula looks down her nose at my wheelchair.

"It's a rental," Charlotte explains. "It's the only one the Addisonville drug store had in stock."

"Well," Paula says with a placating smile that sands my stiffened spine. "Why don't you allow me to secure something a little easier for her to use...especially with that broken arm."

"Like what?" Charlotte asks.

"We have a custom-designed line of sleek, motorized scooters. Our less-mobile residents are welcome to zip around on them...for a small fee."

"I thought the goal was to get Mother on her feet?" Charlotte's razor-sharp tone tells me that she's not appreciating Paula's tone any more than I. Normally, I'd be grateful we've finally found something upon which we agree. But I'm too angry and hurt at the moment to claim any comfort.

"It will be several weeks before she's fully mobile. In the meantime, we like our residents to have full and meaningful days. It'll be much easier for Mrs. Slocum to keep up if she has a power scooter." Before Charlotte can argue, Paula pulls out another brochure and slides it our direction. "Now that we have that settled, let's talk schedule. After breakfast, she'll be taken to the rehab gymnasium to exercise with her personal trainer. She'll have time for a quick shower, then a light lunch. After a short nap, she'll go to our indoor pool for water aerobics or perhaps some swimming—"

"I don't swim."

Paula's brows arch. "You don't know how, Mrs. Slocum? Or you don't enjoy it anymore?"

Charlotte and I exchange heated glances. Charlotte's index

finger warns me to let her handle this. "We'd both prefer other activities."

Paula rests both elbows on her desk. She steeples her fingers and smiles just like she's a school principal ready to let loose on a disobedient child sent to her office. "Mrs. Slocum, here at The Reserve, we believe that old dogs can learn new tricks, so to speak." Her gaze leaps those fancy readers and drills right into me. "There are very few skills, swimming included, that people cannot master. Why, I can't begin to tell you the number of residents we have who've started a second career in their sixties, and even a third in their eighties."

"No water rehab." Charlotte's firm tone is an electric charge in the tense air.

Paula's attention has definitely been captured, but from the way her back arches up, I'm not in the clear yet. "Very well." She turns to her keyboard and taps out a sentence. "So noted."

"A few more points for your records, Miss Jennings." Charlotte rises from her chair, her posture board-straight perfect, her jaw set. "First of all, we pay you to see to *Mother's* every whim. Not the other way around. Am I clear?"

Paula maintains her level eye contact. "Very."

"Secondly, *Mother* is never to be referred to as an old dog." Charlotte hitches her purse strap over her shoulder. "And, in closing, when it comes to new tricks, this woman could teach you more in an hour than you've obviously learned in a lifetime." Charlotte puts both hands on my wheelchair handles. "We're ready to be shown to her apartment."

Paula stands. I would too, if I could. Charlotte's tremendous cross deserves an ovation. I'm encouraged that this display of fortitude means she will take hold of that sorry husband of hers in a similar manner.

"Very well." Miss Jennings tugs on the bottom edge of her jacket and snaps it back into place. "Mrs. Slocum, you're required to complete these forms in the privacy of your new home and return them to me first thing in the morning." She hands me a folder marked *Directives*. "Also, you'll need to wheel over to this line for your ID photo and fingerprints."

"Fingerprints?" Charlotte voice has risen several notches.

"In the unfortunate event Mrs. Slocum might not be able to speak for herself, emergency personnel would have easy access to a secure website using a fingerprint scan. Your mother's medical history could be pulled up within seconds. It's the latest in residential care technology." Paula removes an ink pad from the drawer.

"LaVera wears a medical bracelet on her wrist." I'm hanging on to the wheelchair armrests with all my might. "Can't I just have one that says I'm a diabetic with an unpredictable heart?"

"Our finger-print system frees our residents from lugging extra objects around."

Charlotte frowns and thinks a minute before she grants the go-ahead. I'm left with no choice but to hold out my hand. Paula rolls the pads of my fingers across the ink and stamps the tiny squares on her form with the squiggly ridges that are uniquely mine. Charlotte puts the stack of forms in my lap then pushes me over to the blue-tape line on the carpet. Paula steps behind the camera tripod. I refuse to say cheese, but she snaps my photo anyway. I'm sure I've had better photos taken by those traveling school photographers.

In less than two minutes, a laminated card shoots out of the printer. Paula punches a hole next to my mug shot and threads a shoestring through the opening. She drops the tag around my neck and I am officially incarcerated.

Chapter 17

Throw Away the Key

The door clicks shut. The jangle of Paula's keys disappears down the third-floor stairwell. So that's how she maintains an hour-glass figure. I make a mental note that as soon as I ditch this wheelchair or Paula's power scooter, I intend to do the same. Get my legs back, not my figure. Rigorously hiking those stairs will surely put some muscle on these spindly fence posts and help me walk out of this place and all the way home if no one will come for me.

"Mother, where do you want me to put Polygon?"

Charlotte's question gets hung up in the fog of my very bad dream. Jagged metal cuts into my palm. I open my tightly clasped hand and study the key Miss Jennings left for me at the end of our five-minute tour of the entire apartment.

One small living room, tastefully furnished with pull-out couch for the occasional, pre-approved, overnight visitor. One wheelchair-accessible bathroom, complete with roll-in shower and handy seating bench. One small bedroom, a queen-sized bed flanked by nightstands and lamps for reading after lights out. One efficiency kitchen, the miniature fridge stocked with sparkling water and prune juice.

"Don't get too comfortable here, Mrs. Slocum," Miss Jennings had said. "As your care needs decrease, so does your floor level. You're on three now. Work hard and you'll move to two...as soon as a room is available."

I knew full-well her implication...I'd get a new room if someone else who'd worked hard died. "I can't imagine how exciting it must be to live on the first floor."

"Absolutely."

Unable to leave well-enough alone, I had to ask the question I now regret. "Who lives on the fourth floor?"

She'd hesitated for a moment. "Four is reserved for our critical care patients." With that Paula dropped the key into my hands, wished me luck, and left me and Charlotte to sort out the rest.

I squeeze the key until I can stand the pain no longer. I am mistaken. This is no dream. It is a nightmare.

Charlotte's hand touches my shoulder and I'm prodded back into the very gloomy present. "What if we put Polygon by this nice big plate-glass window?"

How long has Charlotte been standing there holding that huge cage? "If you're sure there's no draft. He enjoys a view."

She clears the lamp and knickknacks from an end table and pushes it in front of the window. "This do?"

"I suppose."

Charlotte places the cage carefully on the table and Polygon flutters to his perch. "While we wait for them to bring up the rest of your stuff from the van, why don't we see if we can finish this paperwork?"

"I don't have my glasses."

"Shoot. I meant to say something to Miss Jennings about your glasses. Hang on. Let me see if we have any information in our file." She picks up the folder my warden left on a dinette table so small it could have been built for the Seven Dwarfs. "Okay, here we go. They have an on-site optometrist. His office hours are on Wednesday mornings from nine to eleven. Think you can get your appointment scheduled this week or do you want me to do it from DC?"

"I've done my own appointments for years. I'm sure I can manage this one as well. Where will I get my glasses?"

Charlotte flips the brochure over. "They have their own optical shop."

"You think that's where Paula gets her readers?"

A true belly laugh, not that short-sheeted nervous giggle I can't stand, escapes Charlotte's pursed lips. "They were hideous, weren't they?"

"LaVera wouldn't even wear them."

We laugh until tears fill our eyes. I've never enjoyed my daughter so much as I do right this moment. How good it is to hear the laughter I remember, hearty and rich with the sound of joy that comes so easily before tragedy. Martin and I had always marveled at this child's sense of humor and quick wit, the way she could brighten the whole mood of the family with one little snicker. The familiar melody stirs the embers of my soul, but I don't have a stick of emotional kindling left to catch fire. Only tear-sodden dread. Dread of the silent, dark hole her departures always leave.

Charlotte wipes her eyes, and I can see she's not looking forward to what we both know will not be a pleasant job. "I'll read this stuff and show you where to sign." She opens the *Directives* file. "Looks pretty standard. A Power of Attorney. A Living Will. And a DNR."

"A DNR?"

Chewing the corner of her lip, I know Charlotte's stalling, seeking a palatable answer where none will be found. "Do Not Resuscitate."

So, I am dying. I've known for some time that my heart was not good, but to hear language that decides the rate of my fate…I admit that's more than a bit disconcerting. "I don't want to talk about this now."

"No one ever does. But we have to. They need to know what you want." She pauses. "I need to know."

I'm shocked. I just assumed she'd know to bury me on that little plot of land near the bluff in the high pasture. Right next to her sister and father. There's fear in her eyes, but I don't know what I can say to make it go away. "You know what I want."

"I have no idea, Mother. We've never talked about any of this before, not even when Daddy..." Charlotte's face goes slack. She lets the unfinished sentence hang in the air, stiff as a piece of sun-dried laundry.

What does she want from me? If I give into her grief pangs, my own dam will break. "You'll figure it out. I did."

"No life support?"

"Whatever happened to letting nature take its course?"

"No feeding tube?"

"No."

"Antibiotics?"

"I want treatment stopped sooner rather than later, Charlotte Ann."

"So, you do have an opinion."

I raise my chin and look her square in the eyes. "Maybe you should have checked me into the fourth floor."

Horrified astonishment creases Charlotte's face. "No."

"Am I dying?"

"Not right this minute."

"But I will. There, I said it. Isn't that what you've been waiting to hear? I won't live forever. You'll be rid of me and free to go on with your life."

Charlotte allows the blunt reality to paralyze her, as if I'd hit her smack between the eyes with novel, yet terrifying information. I don't know why I do this, speak without a thimbleful of consideration to what she must be feeling, but I seem to do it more and more frequently.

Suddenly Charlotte thumbs through the papers as if her wits have returned and she's determined to find some clause that spares me the inevitable. I'm afraid she will be disappointed yet again. I wait. Eventually she closes the folder. Just as I predicted, she has come up empty-handed. But that doesn't stop her from trying another tactic.

Slow and steady she removes a page. "In the meantime, what if you lapse into a coma and word leaks out that the Slocum family lawyer did not have her own mother's affairs in order? Do you really want your last act on this earth to embarrass me?"

I snatch the blasted form from her and scribble her name in as my decision-maker. "You have the power. Make the most of it." I hand her the paper. Our talk is over, the warm, fuzzy feeling we shared moments before cooled.

"Mother, I don't want this..." She swallows, turns from me, and then tucks my signed forms into the file.

"Then who, Charlotte Ann?"

I know this isn't fair. I don't want her carrying the entire burden of my future on her shoulders. This weight should be borne by families. By siblings of like mind and thought. Sisters and brothers who can step in when the others are at the end of their rope. But for some reason, I can no more control my tongue than I can resurrect Caroline from the dead. And I won't pretend that I can. My filter has been shut off, and I have no clue how to turn it on again. I press my lips tightly.

"I'll drop these by Paula's office on my way down to see what's taking them so long with your things." Charlotte starts for the door.

"Tell Paula I prefer to dine in tonight."

She stops. "Are you sure you don't want me to meet your tablemates?"

"I would hate for my last act before you leave me here to embarrass you in any way."

With a firm bang of the door, my only daughter leaves me alone to stew in the juice of my reality. Sometime between yesterday and today, I've aged and I can't do a blasted thing about it. I breathe in and out trying to remind myself of why I can't give up. Not just yet. I have a granddaughter who needs a mother totally unencumbered by my care. I have to cut Charlotte loose.

Wheeling myself over to Polygon's cage, I pray the urge to call off my plan will subside. "We'll figure out a way to cope, won't we friend?"

"Taking care of business." My parrot chirps, then begins to preen like he's expecting company.

I'd love to tell him he's wasting his time. From the visual inspection the uppity city-people in the lobby cast our way, we don't have a snowball's chance of undoing the damage caused by our first impression.

I open the door to his cage and stick my arm in until my shoulder presses against the wire. Using my finger, I lift all the newspaper layers lining the bottom of his cage. I grab hold of something brass and heavy. After a few tries and some wrestling around, I free the tarnished nameplate. For the last few years, this bird has guarded my inheritance.

I shake excess birdseed onto the soiled papers. "The day Burl Junior dies is the day this can proudly be displayed once again."

Polygon tilts his head.

I brush away the last remnants of downy feathers and study the bold, sturdy letters. *Burl Addison.* My whole growing-up life, I took pride in the name that carried clout in Addisonville. When Papa said the railroad would have to find another route, that's what the Union Pacific did. When Papa said an interstate would wreck my wholesome small town, the highway commissioner snaked his four-lane miles away from Addisonville. When Papa said, don't come home if you marry that Slocum boy, I didn't. But I know Papa loved me, cross as he was. I know he did. I pray Charlotte knows the same.

Tracing the letters of my father's name, I feel his presence.

Large and imposing. Only this time he's smiling, and I know he'd say he was sorry if he could. Polygon hops over to his mirror and pecks at his reflection.

"All of us need a reason to live, Polygon. Until the day we die, all of us need a reason to keep going."

Chapter 18

This Is How It Is

Put my mother's suitcase on the bed." Charlotte directs the uniformed fellow pushing my belongings on a rolling cart. "I'll make room for her medical supplies in the bathroom." She flits around the apartment rearranging this and that, obviously in a hurry to dump me and flee.

I've always thought that children were only as good as their raising. The theory is one I've stood by, especially when board members brought parental complaints to my attention. It's rare when children surpass the unfortunate influences in their home. What is also equally as rare is for a child to fail in spite of having everything.

I watch Charlotte. Her face is tense. Her mind is miles away. She's failing at everything. Taking care of me. Motherhood. Being happy.

So much for my apple-doesn't-fall-far-from-the-tree theory.

A change creeps over me the way the smell of rain awakens hope after a long, dry spell. It is not a hammer to my hard shell, but more of a realization. I want Charlotte to excel as a mother. I want her to be happy. I want my daughter to be better than her raising.

"Careful with that suitcase," Charlotte snaps at the bag boy. "I don't want her walls banged up. Mother can you scoot your chair out of the way so he can get in the bedroom?" She's bossing the poor moving man and me with the skill of a first-grade teacher, reminding me again at how far she strayed from her calling. "Mother, how about you come to the bedroom?"

"Make up your mind, Charlotte Ann. Do you want me to scoot or to come?"

"Come," she hollers from the bedroom. "I need to know where you want your things."

I don't want my belongings placed here. I want them returned to my house and put in the same drawers and closets they've been in for forty-some years. But Charlotte needs to get back to Aria, so drop the name plate in my lap, wait until the moving man is clear of the extra-wide door, then wheel myself into the bedroom. "Just keep them handy."

Charlotte surveys the empty closet with it's low-hung shelves and waist-high clothing bar. "That should be easy enough." As she flings the suitcase upon the bed she notices the name plate. "What's this?"

I hold out Papa's name plate. "A little something I've been saving for Aria."

Charlotte runs her finger over her grandfather's name. "Caroline and I used to peek in the bank window and watch him behind his desk."

I take the placard out of her hands. "I'm sorry Burl Addison never had much to do with you girls. That was my fault. Not yours."

She starts to say something, but then turns and quietly unzips the suitcase. The hurt look I catch in her eye unsettles me.

Charlotte paws through my bag and produces my flowered robe. "LaVera picked your sleepwear." Any hurt she'd been on the verge of expressing has been banished and the equilibrium restored to the distance we've nurtured for so long.

She shakes out the wrinkles. Bird of Paradise wafts in the breeze. The faint fragrance fills me with such a powerful homesickness I'm afraid I'll pass out.

Busy spreading the robe across the pristine white bedding, Charlotte misses my episode of nostalgia. "Soon as we get things squared away," she says, "I'll help you sponge off. Then we'll dress you in something more comfortable." She rummages through a pile of sensible undies and produces a pair of grass-stained slippers. "Look what LaVera found."

"My Dearfoams." My enthusiasm generates a pleased expression on Charlotte's face and eases the gulch-sized creases she's had in her forehead since James called. "Those bootie-things they had on my feet in the hospital made the floor slicker than snot." Curious as to what other treasures my daughter and best friend believed I couldn't live without, I lean forward. "What else do you have in there?"

"Something...I hope it's all right..." Charlotte hesitates. "I wanted you to have this."

I gasp.

Of all things. It's the picture I can't bear to touch. The lights suddenly go out.

"Mother?"

When I come to my senses, Charlotte is squatted in front of me and mopping my face with a cool cloth. "I can take the picture with me if it's going to upset you."

"No." My voice sounds as shaky as my insides feel. "Leave it."

The doorbell rings and both of us jump.

Charlotte checks her watch. "That's probably your dinner."

"At four o'clock?"

"Paula says they like to give residents a chance to digest before bed." She sets the picture on the nightstand. "After we get something in your stomach, we'll take some meds and put you to bed. Can you keep this cloth on your forehead?"

I take over my resuscitation while she goes to answer the door. Taking my eyes off the children in the picture is impossible. Where have they gone? An ache, fresh as the day everything happened, knots my insides. Fault and blame, the very architects I cursed all these years, had carved the exact same divide I had accused Papa of digging between us. I overhear Charlotte explaining to the jailor delivering my rations that she is *not* Mrs. Slocum. I want to shout out that she is my daughter and that I love her. But the words are buried too deep and I cannot find them.

"Mother, I've got your food set up in the kitchen. Can you wheel in here or do I need to help you?"

When I don't answer, she hollers again. I don't know why she's taken up this unladylike shouting. I have a broken hip, not eardrums. Along with the fact that she keeps testing my ability to care for myself. She doesn't think me well enough to live in my own house, yet she wants me self-sufficient enough so that she can leave me here without feeling guilty. I refuse to answer. Head pounding, I drop the damp cloth in my lap, release the wheelchair brakes and snap free of the hold of the past. I wheel myself to the table.

"Good for you, Mother." Charlotte claps like I just won the three-legged race and then lifts a silver-domed lid from the tray. "Ta da." Grilled salmon and sautéed vegetables are arranged in a beautiful presentation on a gold-rimmed china plate. "Doesn't this look fabulous?"

I would never have guessed a little piece of fish and some undercooked vegetables could make someone so happy. "Where's yours?"

"I'll grab something at the airport."

"You want me to eat alone?"

My question leaves her speechless. She scrambles for an answer.

"No. Of course not." She opens the little fridge and removes a bottle of water. "I'll sit and visit while you eat."

"I don't need a lunchroom monitor." I take one bite. It looks better than it tastes. Pushing the rest around on my plate, the tines of my fork scrape the china. "I'm not very hungry."

"The trip was harder than we thought. Sorry about that."

"What will you do with Raymond's van?"

"Leave it at the airport. Pray someone steals it."

I smile, an idea suddenly coming to me. "Bo and LaVera would be happy to come get it. Maybe they could sell it for scrap metal and get some of your money back."

"Good thinking. I'll call them on my way to the airport. You want them to stop by here and check on you?"

She bit. "Well, I hadn't thought of that, but I guess it wouldn't hurt for LaVera to see how I've come up in the world. Maybe Bo will dump her here when he's tired of her." I hadn't meant that quite as caustic as it sounded.

Charlotte let the comment go, quickly concealing any wound my jab had made with a thin-lipped smile. "I'll help you get into bed. When I'm not here, an aid will assist you."

"I don't need someone tucking me in."

"Well, their job is to make sure you've had your meds and—"

"Spy on me."

"Help you."

The key is still in my left hand. "How will they get in?"

"They have a master key."

"Without my permission people can traipse in and out of my house all night long and there isn't a thing I can do about it?"

"Mother, you never lock your doors."

"At home."

"I know this is all really new and different. Please, just give it a chance. Can't you do that?" Her face was that of the little girl in the picture. Not happy and care free, but one of hopeful naiveté. "For me?" She has me over a barrel and she knows it.

I shove another bite of salmon into my mouth and nod.

But whether or not I'm giving any of this a chance remains to be seen.

Chapter 19

Don't Look Back

Charlotte hurried through the twisted corridors of The Reserve. Tears hounded her quickened steps. Leaving her mother with people far better equipped to withstand the stony face of abandonment should be a relief. But it wasn't.

She'd been reading her mother's expressions her whole life. But something unfamiliar had entered her mother's eyes right before she left. Fear. She'd expected devastation, anger, and defiance. But she'd never seen her mother afraid. Mother was putting on a brave face, but underneath that impudent determination, she was terrified.

Charlotte burst through the heavy beveled doors and dashed to the van. She climbed in and wilted. Oddly, the repressive heat of the oil-tinged darkness freed her tears. The emotional toll of this whole ordeal had been far greater than she bargained for. She rested her head against the steering wheel. This was the best place for Mother. She was safe and would be well-cared for. Then why was she feeling so much dread about returning to her own life?

Aria!

The thought rocketed Charlotte bolt-straight. She'd not talked to

Loraine since Sid Waring managed to secure Aria's release. Last she knew, Loraine was on her way to the holding center. Mother had kept her so busy these past few hours she hadn't even thought to check to make sure someone had saved her daughter.

What if Ari was still sitting in jail?

Now, who was the bad mother? Shaking, Charlotte pawed through her purse for her cell phone.

Her assistant answered on the first ring. "She's sulking in her room. Only moderately repentant I'd say. And if she says *whatever* one more time, I won't be held responsible if someone locks her door and throws away the key."

"I owe you, Loraine."

"No, you owe this child. Despite her limited vocabulary, I suspect she's quite a girl."

"Throw in a southern drawl and you'd sound just like Winnie."

"The more I learn about your tree-hugging friend, the more I think I like her. Tell Winnie that for me, will you?"

"She's not speaking to me right now."

"Who is?"

Loraine was right. Charlotte's on-the-outs list was getting longer and longer. Winnie. Mother. James. Aria. Probably her boss. And if she didn't handle this thing with Ari right, Loraine would add herself at the very top.

She had to get home. Sort this mess out. "Settling Mother took longer than I expected." It felt like a way of telling the truth without admitting how awful it was being needed in two places at once. "I think I can still make that late flight. It'll be close." Charlotte checked her watch. "I hate to ask, but can you—"

"Already put my stuff in your guest room. I'll get Ari fed and tucked in. You make sure you're here to wake her up."

"Loraine…were you able to keep this under the radar?"

"Mission accomplished. Now you accomplish yours."

Charlotte hung up the phone and reached for the key. Something in her pants' pocket jabbed her leg. She reached inside and withdrew her father's pipe. Holding the bowl to her nose, she breathed in the faint trace of tobacco. This last remaining trace of Martin Slocum really belonged to Mother. Guilt skittered down her spine. A good daughter would run it up to the third floor as proof that she wasn't totally heartless.

But everyone knew that wasn't the case.

Charlotte placed the pipe on the console and cranked the key. The van started on the first try. Finally, something worked like it should. Keeping her eyes on the winding road, she left The Reserve. If she dared look back, she'd be lost.

Chapter 20

Alone in a Foreign Land

Flat on my back, I lie sandwiched between crispy sheets. They smell of industrial soap and cellophane packaging. Except for my jagged breaths, my new bedroom is draped in the suffocating quiet that comes after a child leaves. I crave the sounds of the country, the hoot of an owl or the whistle of the wind skirting the bluffs. I listen for the occasional tinkle of Polygon's bell, glad for his company and the noisy distraction from the pain in my chest, but he's settled for the night.

Through the thin walls I hear a bang and then the sound of a woman calling out. At first, it's a low moan. Like the howl of an animal in pain. Within seconds the plea escalates to a high-pitched scream begging someone to come. Where is that automatic call button Charlotte tethered to my nightstand?

I push myself up, find the button, and punch the lighted nurse's hat icon. A distant voice asks the problem. "Someone's hurting. In the room next to mine. I'm not sure of the number."

"That's Mrs. Scott."

"I don't care what her name is. Send someone. Quickly. She

needs help."

"She'll sleep as soon as her meds kick in, Mrs. Slocum. Try turning up the volume on your TV if the noise is bothering you." Before I can say I don't watch much TV, the person on the other end of the line clicks off.

I sink back onto my pillow. Lonelier than ever. Lacing my fingers through the waffle-weave of my blanket, I lay rigid, trying to remember what my life was like before Caroline died and the bottom dropped out of my world, but I can't. I pull the blanket up around my ears but it doesn't block out Mrs. Scott's exhausted sobbing.

Charlotte left the light on in the bathroom. The yellow glow slashes a line in the darkness, but it does nothing to illuminate the black well all of this has dug in my soul.

I sit up and reach for the drawer in my nightstand. That I'm expecting to find Martin's pipe speaks volumes about the depth of my despair. I close the empty drawer, the shameful slam upsetting the framed photo. Like a fish out of water, I flop back onto the bed. Why did Charlotte insist on leaving that particular memento? Stretching as far as I can without toppling out of the bed, I snag the corner of the frame I haven't touched for years. The dust disappears under the cuff of my gown sleeve.

Hands shaky, I hold the black and white picture in the sliver of golden light and study the glee-lit faces of two little girls I once knew better than I knew myself. This summer day from long ago dances in my memories so often it feels like it happened yesterday. For a moment, I allow myself the rare exception to dwell on its perfection.

Caroline's eight. Charlotte six. They've spent the afternoon swimming in the Frio with their father. He's an artist with a camera and he couldn't wait to develop the roll he used up on our girls. After their swim, they burst into my kitchen, dripping wet and ravenous. I snatch two towels and wrap them tight, confident their bundled bodies are safe from the dangers of growing up.

The air conditioner clicks on smoothly and jars me back to the fading photo. What happened to my babies? Longing to touch those perfect faces, I clasp the frame to my chest. "God, forgive my failure."

Sorrow plunges me into a familiar darkness, an abyss of overwhelming loss. My first journey to this horrifying place was nearly twenty-five years ago. I remember stumbling over the loose rocks of the high pasture as I sprinted ahead of Charlotte. I skidded to a stop at the jagged edge and frantically scanned the deep hole thirty feet below. On the far side of the river, Martin was tugging frantically at the rope tangled around Caroline's feet. I dove into the icy water and swam with everything that was in me. But I was too late.

One year later, Martin did not come in for lunch. I knew where he'd gone. The same place he'd gone every day since Caroline died. I scrambled through the thorns and briars of the pasture. When I arrived at the bluff, I found his shoes on the ledge. His shoes. Why did he take off his shoes? I scanned the pool below and saw him floating face down, the current carrying him toward the bridge. I dove and swam to him, but he was gone. It took everything that was in me to drag him to shore. Once again, I was too late.

Eyes squeezed tight, I clutch at my heart and wait for the ache to subside. I search the back of my clenched lids, but Martin and Caroline have disappeared below the dark surface of the water and I can no longer see them.

"I'm coming!" I can still hear the terror in my voice. Feel the water pressing against my chest. Back and forth I go. Wrestling to free each one. Failing at both.

Several pummeling beats thud against my chest, and then slowly the pain eases. I open my eyes, frightened by the strange surroundings, the smell of new carpet and fresh paint. Exhausted, I'm tempted to give in to sleep. A flush of warmth forces my eyes to remain open. I half expect God, or at the very least one of his angels. Light seeps around the edges of the window blinds. Nowhere near the blinding beam the Apostle Paul experienced on that fateful road, but enough to remind me that God is here.

Caroline is gone. Martin is gone. Charlotte is gone. But God is here.

I will not cry again.

Chapter 21

Uprights. Walkers. Creepers. Leapers.

Señora Chokum, rise and chine." My nurse opens the blinds and sunlight streams in.

I cover my eyes. "No thank you, Esmerelda."

"Today we're going to take a chower." The little Cuban aid Paula assigned to my cell block marches to my bed and lowers the rail. She leans over me and I catch a whiff of fresh air and sunshine. "The boss lady she say, 'We no let our new resident waste anudder day.'"

"I don't want a shower." I pull the bedding above my nose.

"You chink."

"What?"

She waves her hand past her perfect nose, takes ahold of my blankets, and throws them off me. "Whew! While you chower, I change des cheets."

I lie here shivering, nightgown up around my throat and my useless lower extremities fully exposed to a person I met less than thirty-six hours ago. Esmerelda's creamy, caramel-colored skin makes it impossible to guess her age. Her confidence is the kind people acquire after weathering difficult circumstances. The determination in her eyes reminds me of Charlotte, strong on the outside, broken on inside. I liked Esmerelda the moment she smiled at me with those straight, white teeth, but I have no desire to cooperate with her.

"We sit you up, no?" She slides one hand behind my shoulders and takes a hold of my hand with the other. "Uno. Dos. Tres."

In a flash, she has me upright. I wait for the dizziness and nausea to pass. "What time is it?"

"Time to make hay."

I can't help but laugh. "I haven't heard that expression in years. Do they say that in Cuba?"

"No. Mister Ira, down the hall, he teached me. You like to make hay, no?"

"I like to get things done." I wonder if this Ira fellow is the same independent-oil-man tablemate I have yet to meet, but I don't ask. Having to eat my breakfast in the dining room will answer my questions soon enough. "Time to make hay. Explore my new world."

"Good." She smiles, her dark eyebrows disappearing under a skirt of board-straight bangs. "I start de chower, no?"

Ever the teacher, I correct her English. "Yes." I cringe as she slides a plastic sock thing over my arm cast. She helps me stand. I've been off my legs so long they feel like two wet noodles. The room is whizzing around me.

"You ride the power chair, no?"

I knew the moment Paula drove that small tractor into my room that I had no business touching anything that even remotely resembled the riding mower I'd crashed into a tree. That's how this whole mess started. I lower myself into my rented wheels. "Nothing wrong with the transportation I brought."

She lightly taps my plastic sleeve. "You can do the new chair yourself."

"No."

She sighs and wheels me into the bathroom, lowers the hinged seat, and cranks on the water. "I help you in, no?"

"I can do it."

"Cho me."

While the steam builds, she eases my gown over my head. Naked as the day I came into this world, I cross my arms over my sagging body and wait until she has everything in place. I've no choice but to disregard the brush of her arm against my bare breast as she lifts me from the chair and slides me onto the wet seat.

"I help you champoo, no?"

"No. I can do it."

She smiles and shoves the bottle my direction. "Cho me."

The plastic sleeve is a mitten over my swollen fingers. I fumble with the flip cap until I eventually manage to squeeze enough shampoo into my palm to work up a decent lather. Once my scalp is scrubbed, I stick my head under the stream of water and rinse. Pleased at my progress, I take the washcloth and shower gel Esmerelda passes around the curtain and tackle the stench my spit baths had missed.

"Señora Chokum, you finished, no?"

"Yes."

Esmerelda reaches in and shuts off the water. She pushes back the curtain and then wraps a plush towel around my head and another around my body. Before I can change my mind, Esmerelda has me dried off, powdered, and dressed for my first foray into the dining room.

"You ready to make friends, no?"

I'm my own good company. I don't whine or complain, and I get along with myself real well. "No."

"We go anyway." Esmerelda wheels me past the dresser mirror and I catch a glimpse of my reflection.

My hair has dried in the shape of a wild sage bush and my face is the color of dried craft paste. Usually when I look in the mirror, I see the woman I used to be. Young, happy, and wrinkle-free. But today I see a sour, old woman. The truth is seldom pretty.

"Stop, Esmerelda." I open the top drawer and find my lipstick. A few quick strokes and a respectable amount of color is added to my pursed lips. I cap the tube. "That'll have to do."

The clock chimes seven.

"You have de key, Señora?"

"No." She hands me an orange elastic-coiled bracelet attached to the key Paula left me. "I'm not used to having to lock my door."

"Better safe than sorry."

"No one is ever really safe." I slip the bracelet onto my wrist and away we go with Esmerelda humming something in Spanish and me fretting silently in English.

I've refused to eat since Charlotte brought me here. I'm starving, but as a matter of principle I'm not going to choke down a single bite.

To get a handle on my nerves, I strike up a conversation with my chipper chauffer. "Have you worked here long, Esmerelda?"

"Two years."

"Have family close?"

"*Si!* My brother, Carlos. He serves the eggs." We're flying down the hall. "You have family, no?"

"No." I'd rather have nerves than discuss Charlotte. "Not close anyway."

At the elevator, Esmerelda pushes the buttons. We exit on the first floor. The sterile opulence of the lobby reminds me that I have no business here. We round the corner and two white-coated attendants open the dining room doors. I'm greeted by the smell of coffee and the clank of silver on china. A few graying heads briefly turn my way, but most have not allowed my arrival to interfere with their breakfast.

"We find your table, no?"

"I guess."

"Good." Esmerelda wheels me through the maze of walkers, wheelchairs, and canes, greeting each equipment owner as though they were her long-lost friends. When we arrive at a corner table overlooking an expansive view of the golf course, she stops. "Good morning, Señora Lauralee. Señora Tee-nee."

Lauralee, a shriveled snippet of a woman whose chin barely clears the table line, is nibbling on a prune skewered on her fork. Teeny, a woman with linebacker shoulders, hands the size of dinner plates, and a huge red bow sitting on top of her curly white perm like Mickey Mouse ears, struggles to get a spoonful of Cream of Wheat to her mouth.

Esmerelda removes one of the two empty chairs and scoots my wheelchair under the pristine table linen. "Ladies, this is Señora Chokum."

"Slocum," I correct, soberly.

Esmerelda's brow furrows in confusion. "What I say, no?"

It'll take much longer than I'm going to give this place to refine Esmerelda's grasp of the nuances of the English language so I sigh and nod.

Esmerelda unfurls the silverware bundle and places more

utensils than I use to set my entire Thanksgiving t
of my bone china. "You ladies make her welcom
the napkin in my lap.

I turn to thank Esmerelda, but she's already beelined it to the buffet where she's smiling at the handsome young chef erasing yesterday's menu from a blackboard. The chalky dust filling the air reminds me of my fondness for the classroom and how far removed I am from those days. The chef must be Esmerelda's brother Carlos. The family resemblance is closer than mine and Caroline's.

Pangs of longing rip through me. Longings to gather my own eggs. Fix my own tea. And to have my family around me.

"You're the newbie in 302, aren't you?" Lauralee's voice is gravely as a two-pack-a-day smoker. The bony arch of her spine reminds me of Martin's fishing pole when he hooks a big one. "I'm Lauralee Macy." She cocks her head slightly to her right. "This is Teeny McElroy. She's one of them damn Yankees. She doesn't talk much, but when she does, she'll swear she's never been north of the Mason-Dixon Line. She can't remember from one minute to the next, let alone seventy years ago. We don't remind her."

Teeny doesn't even look up from her bowl of hot cereal.

"Nice to meet you both." I flip my coffee cup over and motion for Carlos. He slips out from behind the buffet and heads my way. "Young man, is there any way I could have hot tea?"

"No *problema*." Carlos leaves me with nothing to do but return curious stares of my tablemates.

Lauralee stabs another prune. "That wheelchair permanent or temporary?"

"Temporary." I have no intention of going into my plans to heal as quickly as possible and walk out of her on my own two feet.

"Broken hip?"

"If you must know, yes."

"Broke mine a few years back." She waves her fork at her walker. "Never did get my legs back." Her eyes twinkle at my horror. "Here's your tea."

Carlos places before me a miniature silver pot of hot water and a tea bag on a little silver tray and a plate heaped with sausage, eggs, and a beautiful apricot pastry. The delicious smell is making it harder to stick to my plan to starve myself to death.

According to the unopened tea bag's fancy label, the tea is some sort of exotic fruit blend. I prefer a plain black tea, but the idea of using a brand-new tea bag has an appeal I can't resist. I rip into the packaging and drop the plump bag into the hot water. Jiggling the string up and down like I'm fishing for bream, I let my eyes drift to the empty chair at our table.

Lauralee notices my curiosity and says, "Ira sits there. When he's not messing with those silly birds."

"I have a bird," I say with pride.

She considers my statement, as Carlos approaches our table with a coffee carafe. "I'm a cat person myself. But you and Ira should hit it off nicely." She puts a thin hand over her full cup and Carlos moves on. She lifts the cup. Coffee sloshes over the sides all the way to her lips. "I'll be happy to show you around."

I agree to Lauralee's proposal for two reasons. One, horrifying as I find her straightforwardness, it's also surprisingly refreshing. And two, I doubt that this bent little candy cane will have the stamina to tie me up for long. No sense putting off until tomorrow what needs to be accomplished today. And today, I must make progress toward figuring out how to break myself out of here and get back to my own kitchen. I need a lay of the land, so to speak.

Teeny, head down and determined to get that last raisin on her spoon, says nothing. Lauralee chats non-stop while I break my hunger strike and down the apricot pastry that tastes every bit as good as it looks. Carlos removes our dishes. I don't have a clue what I should do next. If I was in my own home, I'd feed Polygon. I glance around for Esmerelda to ask her to help me back to my room.

"You have thirty minutes between breakfast and rehab." Lauralee pushes back from the table. "Digestion can't be hurried at our age, but trying to tell young people anything these days is like spittin' in the wind." She grabs hold of her walker and pulls herself from her seat. "Ready?"

Eye-to-eye with a woman who resembles an upside-down letter L, I ask, "For what?"

"Your five-cent tour." She follows my gaze toward Esmerelda. "Don't worry, I'll have you back in plenty of time for your workout. Believe me, after that sadistic therapist finishes with you, you'll be thanking me that you were late."

"I need to feed my bird. Maybe tomorrow?"

"Tomorrow's a luxury none of us can afford." Lauralee apparently doesn't take no for an answer. "We can swing past your place."

I unlock my brakes. "Nice meeting you, Teeny." She says nothing as I back out and strain with my good arm to wheel myself after Lauralee.

"A good shot of WD-40, and that chair would be a lot easier on you." Lauralee pushes the elevator button. "We'll see if we can find Ira. He's real handy at fixin' things." Before I can agree or disagree, she continues. "We're on the first floor. Dining room, gym, and swimming pool are on this level." She waves her hand as if she's painting a picture for me, but thankfully she doesn't make me wheel to those locations. "I call the first floor Geezer's Glen. This is where the Uprights live."

"Uprights?"

"Those who can still get where they're going on their own two feet. Uprights party in Geezer's Glen until six or seven every night. The rest of us poor schmucks call it quits after slurping up our 4:00 dinner." Lauralee laughs at her own joke. "Teeny can't remember her name most days, but she can still cut a right smart rug. Ira takes her for a spin around the dance floor every Friday night. But he keeps it short. The eight-second rule, you know."

I shake my head. "Eight seconds?"

"It only takes a man eight seconds around here to decide he's in love," Lauralee explains. "Best way to avoid another trip to the altar is just not to make eye contact. Unless you're looking to marry again. Are you, Sara?"

"Absolutely not. Martin was the love of my life," I say. "Are Ira and Teeny in love?"

"I can't remember." Lauralee howls at how easily I fell for her story. "You're going to be a fun one, Sara Slocum."

"You always this happy?"

"Just as easy to be happy as not. The choice belongs to each of us." The elevator door opens and she shuffles in. "Coming?"

I wheel after this eighty-pound sage like a stray dog hungry for a home. "Where to now?"

"My floor. Vertigo Village. Home of the Walkers." The door closes and she punches the number 2 with the bulging knuckle of her crooked index finger. "Walkers need a little mechanical help to get around. Canes, crutches, or walkers. Third floor, where you live, is called Bedpan Alley. It's for the Creepers." She looks at my wheelchair. "No shame in it. Just how life goes sometimes, honey."

"And the fourth floor?" I ask.

Lauralee's shoulders stoop a bit more. "The fourth floor is for the Leapers."

"Leapers?"

The humor slides from her face. "It's the place where all of us fossils eventually take a flying leap toward heaven." Lauralee runs her eyes over me as if she's assessing my floor assignment. "Flying Fossil. It's what we call it when someone passes to the other side."

I can't help but think about the name of my ranch. Martin and I had named it The Fossil Ridge because of all the tiny fossils sprinkled on the ridge along the river. But now that I think about it, so much hurt had sunk to the bottom of that river, grown hard and crusty like a fossil. How would it feel if that hurt took wing and flew away? Would the relief finally set me free?

The elevator dings and we get off on Lauralee's floor. "Come meet some of my neighbors, then I'll show you the arts and crafts room."

I follow her down a carpeted hall, contemplating how close my new living quarters are to my final reward. We wheel around the corner and stop at a little alcove where four women are seated at a game table and arguing over a deck of cards.

"Girls, this is Sara Slocum. In case you're worried you've met her and have just forgotten her name, she's new." Lauralee introduces all the women at table, but my mind has skittered away, combing my memories of the fossils on The Fossil Ridge.

I'm suddenly back on the bluff that overlooks my river. The water level has begun to recede under the sun's glare. I navigate the path down to the riverbed and gaze upwards. Entombed in the craggy limestone are scores of fossils. Tiny white creatures that have been held prisoner for centuries. I run my finger across their rigid shells, pick at them until my nail breaks, but I cannot set them free. The sudden roar of water turns my head upstream. I've heard this sound before. Every spring, when the rains turn the river into a raging torrent. The riverbed is no longer safe. But my feet refuse to move.

"Run, Mother!"

"Charlotte?" I scramble up the path and throw myself onto the jagged ledge and fling my legs to safety as a wave of water gushes past. The flood is over as quickly as it came. Still flat on my belly, I peer over the edge. The fossils are gone. Washed away. Free at last. The layer of stone that bound them has been sanded smooth.

I turn with a smile, but Charlotte is crying. Inconsolably. Is this how it will be when my release comes? When I leap? A mixture of happiness and sorrow for my daughter? No, having Charlotte within reach is a dream. When my time for leaping comes, I will be alone.

"You play cards, Sara?" Lauralee's tug on my sleeve pulls me back to the second floor. These Walkers are either oblivious or in denial to the ticking clock within each of us. They're only two floors away from leaping into eternity and they want to know if I play cards.

I nod.

"Schedule her in, Ivy," Lauralee says.

Ivy clicks a pen. "Is that Sara with or without an H?"

"Without," I say. "Always without."

Ivy jots down the correct spelling of my name then coughs into a hanky.

"Are you coming down with something, Ivy?" Lauralee asks.

"It's only allergies." Ivy dabs her mouth.

"Hmmm." Lauralee is not convinced. "At your age, you need to tell someone. Don't mess around with it."

"Age!" Ivy sniffs. "Why is everything about our age here?"

The comment launches the foursome back into their argument. From what I can make out, they're arguing over whether Ivy, who's eighty, should leave Ira alone. Lauralee motions me on, but I'm glued to the conversation.

"Eight-second rule," Bea shouts.

"You're just jealous, Bea Comstock," Ivy says.

Bea smacks a card on the table. "Maybe I should try using more of that blue shampoo and going around with my robe unbuttoned to my naval the way *some* women do." Bea's goading tone and accusing gaze slide toward Ivy.

"My heart will give out long before Alzheimer's gets Ira." Ivy adjusts the bed swirl on the back of her blue-tinged hair. "Odds are, he won't even remember loving me, so I don't see the harm."

"You never dreamed you'd live to be this old so you spent up your money, didn't you, Ivy?" Bea slaps another card on the table. "Ira's got a pile of it."

Ivy pounds the table with her fist. "Bea Comstock, you take that back."

Bea calmly draws another card. "Once a gold-digger, always a gold-digger."

Ivy throws her cards on the table. "If you don't shut up, I'm going to reach across this table and snatch that ratty rug right off your bald head."

"Come on, Sara." Lauralee gives my wheelchair a push. "This won't be pretty." Once out of earshot, Lauralee whispers, "Don't ever bet against Ivy. After she got divorced, she didn't even leave her ex-husband enough money to get a haircut."

We travel the hall at a snail's pace. Lauralee sets her walker as far out in front of her as her arms will reach and then shuffles to catch up. Me? I wish my arms would fall off so I'd have a good excuse to go no farther. I've seen enough of what my future holds if I stay in this place, but Lauralee is determined I get my nickel's worth.

"This is the arts and crafts room. Ira hides out in here." She lowers her voice. "Can't say as I blame him. Everyone calls Ira an independent oil man, but he's really an old goat farmer from

Hillsboro. Didn't have a dime to his name until Mobil Oil discovered natural gas on his dusty little acreage." She opens the door and we make our way inside the brightly lit space. "He may not be able to see what he's eating for lunch, but he can still fix anything with a little baling wire or twine."

Across the room, a bald man sits at a table troweling a lumpy, brown mixture onto a dried corncob. Curled in his lap are two teacup-sized poodles. One black. One white.

"Ira," Lauralee shouts, "This is Sara. She's our new tablemate. Her chair needs a squirt of WD-40." If Ira heard her, he doesn't act like it. Lauralee whispers, "His wife Oleta became a Flying Fossil last Christmas. He's been *creative* ever since."

I nod, remembering how I took up birds after losing Caroline and Martin. I start to back out.

Lauralee shakes her head. "Go ahead and talk to him." She turns for the door.

"Where are you going?"

"My morning constitutional. Those prunes keep me regular as clockwork." She whips her walker around. "We'll do your floor tomorrow."

"Wait," I say. "I thought you said tomorrow was a luxury we couldn't afford."

"Procrastinating when nature calls an 87-year-old woman is more foolish than putting off until tomorrow what should be done today."

"Before you go, can I ask you something?"

"Make it quick. I forgot to put on my Depends."

"Do you know Mrs. Scott? She's in the room next to mine. Three hundred something."

The smile slid from Lauralee's lips. "Don't see much of her anymore."

"Last night, I heard her calling for help, but no one seemed concerned."

"Not much to be done. She's a sundowner, honey."

"Sundowner?"

"It's what the nurses call someone whose dementia gets worse at dark. They leave a light on for you, but when it doesn't seem to help anymore, men with white coats move you up to the Leapers. It's only a matter of time before they take her to the fourth floor." With a sad shake of her head, Lauralee heads for the nearest bathroom.

Charlotte's accusations pound my thick skull. You forgot to turn the kettle off again, Mother. Stop mixing your medications, Mother. You got lost between the house and the barn, how can I trust you with car keys? I haven't dared tell her that the nights are the worst. Memories of Caroline and Martin are jumbled in with actual events of the day. Sorting them is difficult. How long before men in white coats carry me upstairs?

"You just going to sit there or can you give me a hand?" Ira's cloudy, brown eyes stare a hole straight through me.

Feeling the need to connect with someone real, to ground myself in the present, I wheel over to the table. "May I ask what you're making?"

"Bird bait."

"You're trying to catch a bird?"

"Nah. Just hopin' to lure that pesky woodpecker away from the tree outside my window and get him to take up residence on this side of the building." Ira doesn't seem demented to me. Maybe he's just been acting looney to keep the gold diggers at bay.

"What's in it?" I ask, testing his memory skills.

"Peanut butter, lard, and cornmeal."

"Hope your woodpecker is not a finicky eater."

A low chuckle rumbles out of Ira. "The way he's goin' after that live oak bark, I doubt it."

I notice a nectar feeder sitting on the table. The plexi-glass cylinder is filled with bright-red liquid. "And that?"

"Sugar water for the black-chins."

"They have hummingbirds here?"

"That we do. I'll hang this feeder on that hook right outside on that veranda and you'll witness some of the fanciest flyin' you ever did see."

"Those little devils will divebomb that sugar water before you can say soup's on."

A smile lights Ira's face. "You sure know birds."

I puff up a little. "I have one."

"You don't say."

"A ringneck parrot. Apple green. He'd still swear like a sailor if I hadn't introduced him to the Lord." I know I should feel ashamed for the pride in my voice, but my display of mental agility coupled with the genuine interest on Ira's face makes it so I don't. "His name is Polygon."

"Interesting name for what sounds like an interesting fellow. I'd love to meet your feathered friend."

I smile and point at the sleeping dogs. "Your pets?"

He waves a half-finished cob over their curly coats. "Goodness and Mercy."

"Which one's which?"

"Does it really matter? Long as they follow me all the days of my life, I'm set." He grins like he's got more wit than Johnny Carson. Amazing how everyone in this place fancies themselves a comedian.

Ira scoops up Goodness and Mercy and sets them on the floor. "Wait here, girls." He takes the handle of the hummingbird feeder and indicates I should follow. "This spring we had a family of turkey vultures nesting just the other side of that small creek."

I crank the wheels on my chair. "Where?"

Ira removes the binoculars hanging around his neck. "See that small ledge in the cliff face?"

Our fingers brush as I take them from him and it's like a spark of electricity arcs between us. "Turkey vultures would rather steal a nest than build their own."

"Had a brother-in-law like that." He pointed at the bluff across the creek. "Look for a little heap of leaves and scraps of vegetation."

I adjust the focus. "I see it."

"Once those vulture chicks fledged, it was somethin' watching those parents trying to keep 'em all fed. Reminded me of me and Oleta a-scratchin' out a living for our six."

I hand him the binoculars. "So many children."

He returns the glasses to his neck. "Oleta always claimed kids were cheaper by the dozen, but thank the Lord, He stopped us before we had a chance to find out." Another chuckle shakes Ira's belly.

I remember my classroom days. Children everywhere. The smell of leftover lunches and playground sweat so strong sometimes I could barely breathe. While I'd loved every minute of teaching other people's children, wrapping my arms around my own at the end of the day was what I lived for. How could someone be so lucky to have six of their own to love? When you're only blessed with two, it's a terrible blow to lose one. I lower my eyes to conceal my envy.

"If I grease your wheels, would you give me a hand with this feeder, Sara?"

Something about the way he says my name...not Mrs.

Slocum...not Miss Sara...but *Sara*, jerks my head up. No one has called me just plain *Sara* in years. I've been seen as someone's wife, mother, or teacher for so long it feels strange to have someone see just me.

Then I remember the Lauralee's eight-second rule and pull my sweater closed. "Thank you, Ira, but no. I'm late for therapy."

Chapter 22

Playing Catch Up

Charlotte stared at her haggard reflection in the dark kitchen window, absently pouring herself another cup of coffee. Trying to be in two places at once had taken quite a toll. How had her life come to this? Sandwiched between her mother and her daughter. Failing both of them.

"You're up early." Looking remarkably put-together in her matching robe, gown, and slippers, Loraine padded around the island and helped herself to the last of the coffee.

"Never went to bed. Kept wanting to go into Ari's room and make sure she was safe."

"Why didn't you?" She took a sip, turned up her nose, and poured the dregs down the drain.

"Didn't want to wake her."

"That's not it."

"I'm sure Ari was tired when you brought her home."

"She's a kid. They bounce back real fast." Loraine rinsed the pot and began making fresh coffee. "You didn't wake her up because you don't know what to say."

"I know what to say."

"What? That's she's grounded for the rest of her life?"

"Is that what my daughter told you I would say?"

Loraine made a zipping motion across her lips. "Attorney-client privilege."

"This isn't easy."

"No, but the kid deserves a fair hearing. I told her I'd speak to you on her behalf...pro bono." Loraine flipped the switch on the coffeemaker.

"I'd love to hash this out, but I've got to get to the office."

"No need to rush. I saved your daughter and then I saved your job."

"For now. You can't cover for me forever."

"And you can't keep telling yourself Aria's going to be fine." Loraine filled her cup. "Go wake your daughter. Let me handle Sid." She started for the door. "And lay off the caffeine. You look like crap."

Brewing coffee gurgled into the glass pot like the plethora of confused thoughts percolating in Charlotte's head. She hadn't even had time to think about her job these past couple of weeks. No telling how many deadlines she'd missed. Thank God for Loraine.

Now if only Loraine could step in and tell her what to do about Ari. If she did nothing about this ever-growing crack in their relationship, the risk was great that she and Ari would end up like her and Mother—distant and glad of it. If she did try to work things out and screwed it up, she could make things worse. How could she ensure a winning chance for their relationship?

Charlotte turned back to the window, searching the predawn darkness. Winnie's accusations, vivid and sharp, came back to her. She hadn't forgotten how to care. After Caroline's accident, it just seemed a far less painful way to live. Charlotte rubbed her throbbing temples. One thing she knew for certain, she cared too much about Ari to make things worse.

Charlotte reached into the pocket of her sweatpants where she'd stuffed two other important matters. The letter from Sam Sparks would have to wait. She pulled out her father's pipe. Cupping the bowl in the palm of her hand, she closed her fist. Would her father have continued going to the river if he'd believed that Caroline was not the only one who needed him? Past due tears stung her eyes. She didn't have time for grief, for useless second-guessing. Charlotte swiped the hot trickle that had squeezed through the crack in the dam, snatched her phone, and punched the first number on her Contacts list.

"James, we need to talk."

"Ari okay?" Her husband's sleepy voice had that husky edge she used to love waking up to.

She started to say *no thanks to you* but biting his head off wouldn't achieve the results she was after. "She's still in bed."

"When did you get home?"

"Late." Charlotte rushed on before wisdom took hold and she talked herself out of saying what had been pounding in her head since she'd left her mother in that awful place. "James, Aria needs boundaries."

"Here it comes."

Charlotte felt her jaw tighten. Where did he get off thinking the worst of her? He was the one who...she stopped her descent into the dark hole his infidelities had gouged in their marriage. "I'm not pointing fingers."

"That's a first."

She pictured him sitting up in bed and raking his hands through his lush head of hair. "We need to come to some sort of agreement."

The click of his cigarette lighter was followed by a prolonged inhale and exhale. "I told you I wouldn't fight you on custody."

"Aria obviously needs extra supervision. More than I can give her right now."

"It's not my fault your mom's a nutcase. I've got a shoot in New York."

"Ari needs *both* parents. Fathers matter. I'm willing to put our issues on hold until we've gotten her through this...whatever *this* is."

"What does that mean?"

"I think you need to move home...for a little while."

"That house is a lot of things, but it's never been a home, Char."

The truth was an arrow through her heart. She'd hated this house and resented him for making her sell the little brownstone she'd loved so he'd have more room for his lavish parties. "For Ari's sake, I think it's time we made it a home."

Another long exhale on his end. "So, you want us to play nice until our kid's back on the straight and narrow?"

"I want us to present a united front."

"Let me think about it."

"What's there to think about? Either you believe our daughter is worth some grown-up effort on our part, or you don't."

"I didn't say I wouldn't come, but…"

Charlotte waited, hoping he'd spare her all the reasons he wouldn't change his schedule. She wasn't the only one who had trouble prioritizing her life list. For once she wished James would move her and Aria to the top of *his* list.

The last of the coffee bubbled into the pot, the quiet on the other end of the line as empty as the coffee maker's water reservoir. "Do what you want, James. You always have."

"Our kid got into a little trouble. They all do. Don't make a federal case out of it, Char."

"It's a cry for help, and I'm not going to pretend that I don't hear her anymore."

"You're making a big deal out of nothing."

"Don't ever call my daughter *nothing* again." Charlotte jabbed the red disconnect button.

Hands trembling, she stuffed her father's pipe back into her pocket. She climbed the stairs and knocked on the guest room door.

"Loraine?"

The door opened and Loraine appeared, fully dressed, briefcase and bag in hand. "Well?"

"Tell Sid I'll be a little late."

Loraine's raised a questioning brow. "And when he asks why?"

"Tell him...I have pressing family business."

"Good girl." She kissed Charlotte's cheek. "This is a decision you will never regret." Loraine brushed past Charlotte and started down the stairs.

"Loraine? I have to know. Do you have a family?"

She stopped, turned, and answered with a watery-eyed shake of her head.

"What happened?"

"I chose to believe I could have it all...the law...the career... the demanding hours." She swallowed hard. "It was a lie that cost me my son."

"You have a son?"

"Had." She adjusted the bag strap cutting into her shoulder. "Brian was killed in a car wreck his freshman year in college. I didn't even know his major until I emptied his dorm room." She descended the stairs, stopping to throw over her shoulder. "By the way, just between us, I *am* a lawyer."

Stunned at how blinded she'd been by her self-centered focus, Charlotte asked, "Why are you not practicing?"

"Life's too short to let work define you." Loraine flashed a wave over her shoulder, her heels clicking on the stair rungs.

Charlotte spun and headed for Ari's room. What else had she missed?

She quietly opened the door. The crown of her daughter's blonde head peeked out from under the covers. Charlotte crossed the fluffy rug and sat on the edge of the bed, her breath catching in her chest.

"Aria." She stroked the long, slender hand resting on the pillow. "Ari, wake up."

Her daughter stirred, rolled over, and opened her eyes. When her vision cleared, shame snapped her eyes shut. "I'm sorry, Mom." She flipped herself face down and pulled the cover over her head.

"Ari, stand up."

"What?" was the muffled reply.

"You heard me." Charlotte tugged at the blanket, but Ari held it tightly in place. "Stand up."

"Why?"

"I want to hug you."

Aria rolled over and flung the blanket away from her face. "Hug me?"

Her question didn't surprise Charlotte. As Aria had grown older, they'd touched less and less. But the doubt in Aria's eyes stung. She missed kissing the sweet spot behind her baby's earlobe. She missed her baby. "Yes, hug you."

"Don't you mean kill me?"

"Maybe later." Charlotte tugged the blanket away from her daughter's long, slender frame. "First a hug. Then, some breakfast."

"Won't you be late to work?"

"I'm not going to work."

Ari's brow furrowed in wary doubt. "I'll be late for school."

"You're not going to school today?"

She pushed herself up in bed. "What?"

"You have some serious explaining to do, my love." She brushed a curly strand away from her daughter's face. "And your mother promises to do some serious listening."

Chapter 23

Friends in Low Places

Stand up straight and hang on tight to the back of that chair, Sara."
Lauralee leans on her walker, reading from an exercise printout
she'd saved from her own hip stint in physical therapy. "Now, slide
your bad leg out to the side. Keep your toes pointed forward." Her
orders bounce off the walls of my small apartment living room.
"You can do it."

I take a deep breath in anticipation of the pain. "How many
more?" These private, after-dinner sessions with my tablemates are
about to kill me. Everything strong and good—my faith, my
determination, my hope—was shattered in the fall.

"As many as it takes to get you transferred from Creeper to
Walker." Ira seems to think our mutual interest in birds gives him
the right to start a war within my soul. "Toes forward." Ira shifts
Goodness and Mercy in his arms. "And hold."

Teeny is standing between Ira and Lauralee, an amused twinkle
in her eye as she quietly watches my efforts to regain mobility. Ice
cream drips from the paper cup and wooden spoon I used to bribe
her continued silence. Teeny's real name is Ethel Marie. According

to Lauralee, Teeny started drifting in and out of dementia after her husband died and has refused to answer to anything other than his pet name for her. Lauralee claims Teeny has not said more than a few words since her family left her here. Nearly a decade ago. But I can't take the chance that Teeny might suddenly find her voice and rat me out and my plans to leave here. Thus, the ice cream.

Teeny's huge red, white, and blue bow has slipped to the side of her head. Lauralee says Teeny chose this Fourth of July hair ornament in support of my commitment to gain my freedom from this blasted scooter. Teeny has been institutionalized so long she wouldn't know freedom if it bit her in the backside. But it's not Teeny's fault that her soul has deserted her body. Life steals from us, bit by bit. Knowing the final assault has yet to come, but not knowing when to expect the blow, is one of the hardest parts of getting older.

A sharp pain warns that I've stretched too far. I pull my leg in, pondering my dilemma. It's nice to have human companionship again. I've even started to think of Ira, Teeny and Lauralee as friends. Leaving them behind pains me almost as badly as these exercises hurt my legs. But I can't bear to think of how it will end for me if I stay here. Either some horrible disease will wipe my mind, or someone I don't even know will be wiping my butt. If my plan works, the third option, the one no one wants to talk about but everyone is wishing they had the guts to do, will be swift and painless.

Teeny lifts her soggy cone in a salute of solidarity.

I smile at her and slowly slide my legs together. Pain radiates from my hip and shoots down my leg and up my back.

Lauralee withdraws the tissue tucked inside the cuff of her sleeve and dabs Teeny's mouth. "That's better, dear." She wads the tissue. "Keep this up, Sara, and you might be moving into the empty apartment next to mine. Ivy will be pea green with envy because we'll be two single gals havin' all kinds of fun."

I slide my leg out and in. "You said this would be fun."

Lauralee shakes her therapy notes at me. "At our age, we don't have time for slothful moods. Now snap out if it." She pushes the tissue under the hem of her cuff. "Thanks to our coaching, you've come a long way in three weeks. Keep it up and you'll be a gold medalist at the Geriatric Games."

Medals are for winners. The jury's still out for me.

I shake my head at the bossy little candy cane who's become my shadow. "How do you do it, Lauralee?"

"Do what?"

"Keep going."

"The alternative doesn't appeal to me." Lauralee wheels her walker around and lowers the little seat. She lifts the cane dangling off the side and comes around and sits with a relieved sigh. "I'm planning to live to be at least a hundred."

"Why on earth would you want to live that long?" I slide my straightened leg out again.

"People who reach one hundred receive one of those congratulatory centurion letters from the President. I want one...unless there's a democrat in office. Then I'll settle for a cake with enough candles to set this place on fire."

I drag my bad leg back into a parallel position with my good one. "Why didn't I listen to that voice telling me not to move the ladder?"

Ira places his dogs on the little couch in my tiny living room. "Had you taken care of yard equipment before?"

"Handling equipment is a must on a ranch."

Lauralee rubs her knees. "And you thought, I can still do it, right?"

"Yes." My extended leg quivers against the pull of gravity. "How did you know?"

"I haven't always been one to sit around and cheer on friends." Lauralee smiles at me and warmth ripples over my cold insides. "I raised a family. Traveled. Had dinner parties. And even worked at Papa's department store in Austin. Whenever I look in the mirror, I still see a twenty-year-old." Resting the can between her legs, she rubs her hands together. "But that's not how my son sees me. He said it was time I started acting my age. I see no good reason for that. So, I refused to use the handrails he had installed by my sunken tub. Nearly drowned before I was able to drag my broken body out and call 911." Lauralee shifted in the seat. "You ready to talk about who put you here?"

"My ungrateful daughter." I hobble out from behind the chair and lower myself to the seat. "She believes I'm no longer capable of doing what I used to."

"And what was that?" Ira joins his dogs on the couch.

"Besides raising a family and running a ranch, I taught third grade for forty years," I add.

"Once a teacher. Always a teacher," Lauralee says.

I pick at the lint on my pants. "Not according to the Addisonville School Board."

Lauralee taps her cane on the tile floor. "You know the one thing this classy joint is lacking?"

"An open bar?" Ira says.

Lauralee frowns. "Mental stimulation, Ira." She directs her attention back to me. "Sara, what if you offered to teach a class?"

The idea's preposterous, but before I can poo-poo the suggestion, hope snags the loss deep within me and drags it into the realm of possibility. "On what?"

My bird, as if he can sense this change in me—this nugget of excitement to reclaim some purpose—begins flapping and squawking and carrying on.

I limp over to his cage. "Hush, Polygon." Math? Geography?

Science? Ideas are pinging between my ears as I slide a slice of apple through the wire.

"Tank you," Polygon chirps then snatches his snack and hops up to his perch.

"Good boy, Polygon," I say.

"Birds!" Lauralee's face glows like she's had a heavenly vision. "You can teach on birds."

"What could I teach anyone about birds?"

"Everything," Lauralee grins. "I don't know a thing about taming a wild creature. It would be far more fascinating than the dietician's lectures on collard greens and the importance of having plenty of fiber in our diets."

My eyes dart from Lauralee to Ira to Teeny. All of them are smiling and nodding. Their encouragement is something I haven't felt in…well, I can't remember the last time I felt encouraged. "I suppose I could teach a few things on training a bird how to talk, but I'll only do it if Ira teaches with me." I wipe the apple juice from my hand. "What do you say, Ira? Think you could give a lesson or two on attracting birds?"

Ira sits up a little taller. "I could demonstrate the best way to make a corncob feeder."

"Perfect!" Lauralee is beside herself. "You two are a match made in heaven. Ivy won't like it one little bit, but then I don't like Ivy. Do you, Teeny?"

Teeny shakes her head and her bow slips to the other side.

Lauralee is a downhill train once she gets rolling, and from the tap, tap, tap of her cane, she's rolling. "Teeny and I will get started on the announcement posters. Now, who wants to speak to Miss Jennings about reserving the activities room?" Lauralee lays a bead on me.

The less I have to do with that uppity director, the better. "All the staff here is so young. Why would Miss Jennings allow an old woman to teach a class?"

A sly smile crosses Lauralee's lined lips. "The key to a long life is to stop acting your age and live until you die."

Chapter 24

Let's Make a Deal

Charlotte tapped the unopened envelope on her desk. Mother would never forgive her for meddling in her affairs. But then, what was one more unforgivable offense on her mother's growing list?

Legal wheels spinning, Charlotte concluded she could argue, that in light of her mother's current pain-med regimen, she was not of sound mind. Therefore, any legal or financial decisions Sara Slocum made could be easily overturned. As her mother's closest next of kin and her legal Power of Attorney, it was Charlotte's duty to step in. Protect her mother from making a catastrophic mistake.

After all, the exorbitant costs of maintaining her mother's long-term care must be taken into consideration. Especially, if James decided to follow through with his threat to divorce her. She'd fight for child support and equal division of anything they'd acquired jointly, but her carte blanche access to the McCandless family money would end the minute he filed.

And while she made a decent living, her salary was not enough to raise her daughter and support her mother. The Reserve cost nearly five thousand dollars a month. Of course, Mother would argue that she didn't want to live in one of Austin's premiere assisted living facilities. She could have done her rehab in the comfort of her own home or spent a few nights in the local nursing home. But the Addisonville Nursing Home hadn't made a single improvement since Charlotte used to go with her mother to deliver her Christmas fruitcakes. The place reeked of elder neglect. She couldn't live with herself if anything happened because lack of funds had forced her mother into second-tier care.

Selling Fossil Ridge Ranch made the most sense.

Mother would no longer be saddled with the burden of maintaining a large property and the sizeable selling price Charlotte intended to procure would assure her mother's comfort at The Reserve for the rest of her life.

Charlotte slit the envelope's seal. She pulled out the single sheet of paper and punched in the contact phone number listed on the letterhead. "Sam Sparks, please." She gave her maiden name in hopes that the deal with the real estate developer wasn't as dead as his last chance notice had implied.

"Miss Slocum? Sam Sparks here." The real estate developer sounded surprised, pleased, eager, and a little winded when he came on the line. Funny how the smell of money sent scavengers scurrying toward a prospective carcass. "How can I help you?"

"It's Mrs. McCandless, and a further explanation as to why you're interested in the Fossil Ridge Ranch is why I'm calling, Mr.

Sparks."

"I'm sure you're charming, Mrs. McCandless, but I can only discuss this matter with Mrs. Slocum or a close relative."

"I'm her daughter, Mr. Sparks."

"Oh." The uptick in his lilt indicated she'd snagged his attention. "Sam, please."

"According to the notice you sent my mother, the option period for your proposed purchase of the Fossil Ridge Ranch expired while my mother was recuperating from a serious...accident."

"I was saddened to learn that our sweet Sara suffered quite a fall."

"Let's not play games, Mr. Sparks." Charlotte tapped the point of her paper opener on her desk. "If you're still interested in building a resort along the Frio, I'd appreciate the opportunity to review your proposal on behalf of my mother."

"Mrs. Slocum is the sole deed holder, according to our records. And she's made it very clear she isn't interested in selling." He didn't mention he'd filed a complaint when she sprayed the tailgate of his fancy pickup with buckshot. But he didn't have to. They both knew Charlotte had hired Winnie to smooth that one over with the county sheriff.

"Things can change, Mr. Sparks."

"By what authority are you acting on Mrs. Slocum's behalf?"

"I'm not only her daughter, but her legal adviser." Perhaps she'd stretched her reach a hair, but he didn't have to know that just yet. "If you could fax me the details, I could possibly present your terms in a more...*advantageous* light for all of us."

"Well, you may be too late. I have managed to generate considerable interest downstream." He was slippery as a Capitol congressman, but an amateur compared to the people she dealt with on a daily basis.

"And when the river dries up in summer, then what will you do?"

"I can see you know the Frio, Mrs. McCandless." He took a deep breath. "For the sake of transparency, it's only right that I let you know that your mother's neighbors have countered."

"We both know the Wooten property does not have river access." Charlotte let him squirm a minute, then said, "A hill country river resort without a river is...well, less than premium, wouldn't you say?"

"How soon can you deliver Fossil Ridge?"

"You send me a deal Mother can't refuse, and I'll fly to Texas to work out the details and acquire her signature in the next two weeks."

"I've heard your mother has relocated to Austin. I could drive over and—"

"Stay away from my mother and her land, Mr. Sparks." Her tone left no room for negotiation. "I'll call you when we have a decent offer to discuss."

Chapter 25

Can't Beat 'Em—Might as Well Join 'Em

Señora Chokum, where jou want me to set dis bird?" Esmerelda's been more help than any aide I've ever had in my classroom.

"Right here will give me easy access to his cage." I pat the corner of the table in the activities room that I've claimed as my desk. "Let's leave him covered a few more minutes." I can hear Polygon fluttering about. "Hopefully, he'll calm down. I'll lose all credibility if he starts swearing."

Esmerelda's brows shoot up. "Already he say—"

I hold up my palm. "Ringnecks can have foul mouths when they're forced to change."

"Surprised you've managed to hold *your* tongue, Sara." Lauralee places a pile of freshly sharpened pencils on my desk. "If I hadn't pushed you to try your hand at teaching adults, you'd still be moping around like a useless old woman." She points to my cane. "Look at you. Haven't used your scooter since you agreed to this little educational adventure."

These past two days have taught me it's useless to argue with Lauralee. She'd insisted on adding glitter to the feathers of the birds

Teeny drew on the advertising posters. The two of them plastered the sparkly announcements of my bird workshop all over the first three floors. I have to admit, Teeny has quite a talent when it comes to art and Lauralee has a way with words. It never would have occurred to me to entitle our little workshop session: *Finding the Frontiers of our Feathered Friends.* According to Lauralee, the alliteration would be as alluring as my lesson on exploring the finer points of becoming a bird enthusiast.

Personally, I think if we're going to draw a crowd it will be because Lauralee also sent out fifty invitations which included: *FREE birdseed cookies and hummingbird punch* beneath the meeting time and location. Adding a few frosted sugar cookies sprinkled with poppy seeds had been my idea. Sweets, plus the fact that a person can only take so much Bingo, will surely prod people from their complacency.

Some teachers pray for empty seats, but I've always loved a full classroom. The more eyes I can make light up with a new fact or a newly mastered skill the better. Truth be known, I'm more than a little scared my skills have rusted over, but I'm excited to prove this part of me still exists.

"Carlos." I wave to the handsome little chef carrying two big trays of cookies. "We'll set up the refreshments on the back table. It's been my experience that too much sugar during class makes it difficult for students to concentrate."

He nods and delivers the trays to Teeny who's agreed to man the refreshment table. Satisfied Teeny and Carlos have things well in hand, I turn my attention to Ira. He and Esmerelda are carefully arranging corncobs, small dishes of peanut butter, and baggies filled with birdseed on the activities table while Ira's dogs, Goodness and Mercy, sit on a nearby chair with their faces turned adoringly toward their master.

Ira reaches over and pats the heads of his dogs with a shaky hand. From the flush of his cheeks, I can tell the thought of speaking in public is scaring him to death.

"Your display looks real nice, Ira," I say in hopes of calming his stage fright.

"I'm not much of a public speaker." He drags his hand over his face. "What if I can't remember what comes first...the peanut butter or the birdseed?"

I steady his hand. "Follow my lead and stick to the script." I point to the lesson plan Lauralee typed up for us. "You'll do fine. Nobody knows more about attracting birds than you."

Lauralee wheels her walker up to me and Ira. "Almost time."

I glance at the clock at the back of the room. "Open the door, Esmerelda."

"*Si, Señora.*" She props the door open. "I go get your neighbor, no?"

Lauralee and I had debated on whether or not to include my

howling neighbor, but in the end, I said I'd dealt with children with all sorts of peculiarities. Speaking out of turn would be nothing. Besides, it was only four o'clock in the afternoon and I never heard a peep out of her as long as the sun was up.

"Yes, please, Esmerelda. Thank you." I hurry to Polygon's cage and slowly lift the towel and gently tap one of the wire bars. "Today's important. I'm expecting you to behave yourself, young man."

He dances around squawking, "Lighten up!"

Ira chuckles as I hurry back behind the desk, smooth my skirt, and seat myself. Hands clasped, I peer at the door where Lauralee waits with the stack of handouts Miss Jennings had reluctantly made on the office copier. Nothing fancy. Just a few facts about Ringneck parrots and tips on how to train one.

Anticipation, great as any I've ever experienced on the first day of school, thrums through my veins. I feel more like myself than I've felt in years. In fact, I'm almost giddy. So much so, I haven't dared to answer any of Charlotte calls. Her keen ears would quickly pick up any excitement that might have seeped into my tone. I'm not ready to concede to her *I told you so*.

Sooner or later, I'll have to answer her calls and when I do, I'll confess. She was right. I *am* enjoying human interaction. But I don't have to confess just yet. It won't hurt her to stew a bit more…even though her messages have increased in desperation. Something about unfinished business.

I can't imagine what *business* we have left to discuss. LaVera and Bo are keeping an eye on things at the ranch. Charlotte's back to her life in Washington. And I'm conveniently tucked away and officially out of her hair. It seems to me our *business* is concluded.

Determined to let nothing ruin this day, I push away the last message Charlotte left on my recorder and breathe in through my nose and blow slowly through my mouth. Just like I used to do before a new batch of third graders hit my door, I mentally recite my teaching mantra: never smile before Christmas.

"Someone's coming," Lauralee shouts and gives me a thumbs-up.

Miss Jennings bustles to the door. Buttoned-up tight in her periwinkle suit, she waves off Lauralee's offer of the handout. Lauralee will not be ignored. She slaps her cane across the entryway and thrusts a copy at the director. "Everyone who attends today's workshop will need a class syllabus."

"A syllabus?" Miss Jennings glances at the stapled packet. "This isn't a lecture series."

"It will be if we publish."

"Publish?"

"Sara and Ira have lots and lots of thoughts on birds," Lauralee says. "Absolutely fascinating stuff."

"Allowing residents to present one little talk is hardly a lecture series." Miss Jennings puffs up like rooster. "Whether or not we add Mrs. Slocum's class to our events calendar will depend upon interest and..." she scans the empty room. "So far there doesn't seem to be any—"

"Excuse me, Miss Jennings." Lauralee lowers her cane. "You're blocking the door."

Miss Jennings glances over her shoulder, sees the line forming behind her, and whips her head back toward me. I fight the chuckle rumbling up my throat. I'd go to all this effort again just to incite the shocked look on her face. Mouth agape, Miss Jennings steps aside.

The shy woman I met in the spa's beauty shop shuffles in. She wiggles her fingers at me in an excited hello and I nod, gratefully. Before she is even seated, one of Ira's poker partners strides through the door and marches straight up to Ira's table and offers his hand in a show of interested support. I suppose if one is still lucky enough to be such an agile Upright one should flaunt it. As Ira and his friend are discussing the merits of smooth peanut butter over crunchy, two of Teeny's female dance partners waltz through the door. They giggle at something Lauralee says, then stop by the refreshment table to hug Teeny before taking chairs on the front row.

For the next ten minutes, residents from the first three floors amble in or wheel themselves in. Ira and his buddy rearrange a few chairs to make room at the tables for walkers and scooters. Esmerelda arrives with my neighbor, Mrs. Scott. This is my first glimpse of the frail little woman. She's nothing but a bag of bones, but her eyes are bright and completely absent of any sign of the madness I hear coming from her apartment every night. Apparently, sundowners are normal during sunlight hours. Who knew?

I marvel at how, just like the children I taught, these elderly students are already teaching me something.

Nearly every seat is taken when Ivy and Bea appear to the door. Bea greets Lauralee warmly, but Ivy's scowl matches the chip on her shoulder. Lauralee shouldn't have teased her about dying her hair a deeper shade of blue in hopes of Ira mistaking her for a blue jay. "The man can't see past the end of his nose." Lauralee had told her. "Besides, anyone who knows anything about birds knows it's the male birds who have the beautiful plumage."

Ivy snatches the handout and joins Bea who's been forced to take a seat directly in front of my makeshift desk.

I remind myself that there's never been a student I couldn't win over with patience, kindness, and a little encouragement.

The room reeks of liniment, sour socks, and apathy, but I'm filled with hope.

"Good afternoon." I ease around my desk. I feel more vulnerable without my cane, but I've never been one to let anything come between me and my students. "I'm Sara Slocum." My arm extends toward Ira who's hiding behind Polygon's cage. "My co-teacher and fellow avian lover is Mr. Ira Conner."

Ivy's lip raises in a smile that looks more like a terrified snarl.

"The beautiful bird I'm going to tell you about is my Polygon." I tap the top of his cage lightly, Polygon's signal to waddle the length of his perch. "Not only do ringnecks make excellent pets, they are wonderful companions." I stick my finger through the wire and my bird steps on. "Say hello, Polygon."

His green head cocks toward me. "Hello."

Everyone claps. My startled bird flutters from my finger and lights on his perch. He immediately begins a nervous pacing that concerns me just a little. Most parrot owners have had their bird's wings clipped, but I couldn't bring myself to do such a cruel thing to a creature meant to fly. Perhaps I should have reconsidered that position…put his comfort ahead of my notions of what a bird would or would not want.

"Ringnecks are very smart, very wary, and sometimes as moody as a hormonal woman." I pick up a piece of sliced apple. "But like most ladies, they can be won over by something sweet." My attempt to bring humor falls flat. The faces staring back at me are blank. The classroom is no place for a deflated ego. I'm going to have to do something quick if I'm going to maintain interest.

I decide information is the key to sparking their interest. So, I begin to tackle some of the myths about parrots. Males can talk as much as females. Parrots are very social. And contrary to what you may have been told, birds do make good, devoted pets. "I don't know what I would have done without Polygon's company."

"Where'd he get such a strange name?" Ivy blurts her question without bothering to raise here hand.

Instead of reminding her of proper class protocol, I say, "I'm a retired teacher. Mathematics was my specialty. His personality has many sides. Thus, the name Polygon."

"What can he say?" Ira's friend shouts from his seat.

Unwilling to let the class get away from me, I jump in with an answer. "He's not a Macaw." High expectations curbed, I go on to explain. "Those birds can learn more than a hundred words. For a ringneck, Polygon has a fairly large vocabulary."

"Then let's hear him talk." Bea's insinuation that I'm lying flies all over me.

I'm quickly losing control, but since I can't keep them in for recess or even threaten to make them clean the boards, showing Polygon's range seems the best course of action.

"Very well." I turn to my bird, who currently has his back to me…a sign that it will take every ounce of my skill and effort to coerce him into a cooperative mood. "Polygon, are you tired?"

"Nite. Nite," he says and buries his beak in his chest feathers.

Laughter ripples through the room. Until I've earned the respect of my students, I'll settle for being entertaining.

"It's time to wake up, Polygon."

He lifts his beak and says, "Be nice." Then he drops his beak amongst his ruffled feathers and plays possum again.

A quick scan of the smiles in the room tells me that I'm back in business. Capitalizing on their current interest, I say, "Oh, Polygon. Don't pout. It's time to wake up."

"Witch," he squawks.

Everyone bursts out laughing. They're leaning over and asking each other what he said like first graders who have no concept of asking permission to speak. Before I can take steps to regain control, someone shouts the B-version of the word.

I gasp, mortified that for those hard of hearing Polygon had been misunderstood...or worse...that I'd misunderstood and that my bird *had* actually cursed. And done it despite my stern warnings.

Ira taps my shoulder. "You told me to let you know when your time was up." He points at his watch, but his eyes are filled with kindness.

I still have three minutes, but I know a lifeline when it's tossed my way. Only a first-year rookie would insist on trying to salvage this mess.

Diversion was my only hope. "Thank you, Ira."

Knees shaky, I hobble back to my seat behind the desk. My gaze slides to Ivy. The little gold digger is primping her blue hair with the flat of her hand. It's easy to see that Ivy has every intention of becoming teacher's pet—Ira's pet.

Trying to pass myself off as something I once was—a capable, engaging teacher—isn't the worst of it. I can't stand that my inability to teach one small feathered creature to control his tongue has made me the laughingstock of The Reserve. Every humiliation I'd ever suffered at the hands of the Addisonville school board comes flooding back.

Before I can crawl into my hidey hole, Ira is proudly showing a peanut-butter-smeared corncob and asking me to help him assist those interested in making a feeder.

Swallowing the last of my pride, I grab my cane and make my way to the craft table to congratulate him. To my surprise, the residents crowd around me. They're remarkably kind about my presentation, but what excites me most are the questions I've stimulated. I'm doing my best to answer each one when suddenly, there's a scream on the other side of the room.

Goodness and Mercy start barking and leap from the chair.

As I turn to see what's causing the commotion, apple green wings swoop over my head. "Polygon!" I drop my cane and reach up with both hands, but he's flying too far above me. "Don't open the door!" I push through the crowd, scramble to his cage, and grab an apple slice. "Polygon!" Yelling only sends him zooming back and forth, dipping lower with each pass until he's grazing the tops of the sea of white heads.

"Catch that monster!" Ivy screams, then throws her arms over her head to shield her new hairdo.

I wheel on her. "Did you let him out?"

Ivy straightens from her crouch. "I just opened his door a crack and he shot past. Nearly knocked my glasses off."

While Ivy and I exchanged daggered glares, canes and thin arms swat at my poor, disoriented bird. Putting Ivy in her place is a battle that will have to wait. I yank my attention back to Polygon.

"Please, everyone," I plead. "Sit down and be very quiet." I shout a command at Ira. "Get your dogs."

"I'm trying," he says as he dashes after them with a treat. "Goodness and Mercy, heel."

Miss Jennings punches numbers on her phone. "Security. We have a code...we have a loose bird. Bring a net."

"Please, don't let them open the door," I beg. "Everyone, just get real still and he'll settle."

Polygon makes several swooping passes. He ignores the apple I'm holding above my head. So, I drop it by his cage and try extending my finger. He zips past, beak in the air, treating me as a traitor, like I was the one who wanted him to forget he was meant to fly. His wings are weak from lack of use. He tires quickly and, to my relief, he lights on a curtain rod. His head whips side to side, his eyes wild. I know that look. He's searching for an escape route...an open window or door.

Quiet blankets the activities room. Goodness and Mercy are quivering in Ira's arms, but at least they're no longer barking. My heart is thundering in my ears. My feet are frozen to the spot. Ideas of what to do next are mired in terror.

Miss Jennings heels click on the tile as she strides toward him with a rolled-up syllabus. Before I can stop her, she eases under his perch. Face raised, she lifts her paper, "Here, birdie, birdie, birdie."

Polygon turns his beak to the wall and wiggles his tail feathers.

I shout, "Run! Miss Jennings!" But I'm too late.

Poop rains down on Paula's forehead and drips onto her pristine suit.

"Ahhh," the director simultaneously screams, swipes at the mess, and swats the rolled-up paper just inches from my smug Polygon. "Get that blasted bird!"

Polygon launches himself into the air. He darts back and forth across the room. Goodness and Mercy leap free of Ira's grasp and weave in and out through the walkers and wheelchairs in an effort to keep up with Polygon's flight.

"Polygon, no!" I can see he's becoming more and more frantic but I don't know what to do. I find my teacher's voice and shout, "Everyone, sit down!"

People drop into chairs or sink upon their walker seats.

"Hungry, Polygon?" At the sound of Ira's easy, mossy drawl, Goodness and Mercy stop dead in their tracks and look to see what Ira's up to.

I look over and see my fellow bird lover slowly lifting a

corncob.

Polygon lands on a curtain rod opposite of Miss Jennings. I can tell from the quirk of Polygon's head, he's debating between Ira's offering and this rare chance to make a run for it. Goodness and Mercy, believing Ira's offering them another treat, yelp in glee and dash toward their master. They hit Ira's arm with a force that sends the corncob flying.

Before I can think of a way to make up the loss to Polygon, my bird leaps from the rod. Wings spread wide, he soars around the room faster and faster. He dives toward the corncob Goodness and Mercy are tussling over, pulls up at the last second as if he's suddenly realized he'd never win over to snarling canines, then sails toward the bank of windows.

"Polygon, stop!" I shout.

He slams headfirst into the glass.

The sickening crack is one I recognize from the many times barn swallows have crashed into the clean windows of my house. It's the sound of a bird's neck breaking.

As my beloved Polygon falls to the floor in a green-feathered heap, there's another sound...it's the deafening crack of my heart breaking.

"Sweet Moses." I hurry to him as fast as I can. "Polygon," I whisper as I snag him with my cane.

But it's too late.

Polygon has become a flying fossil.

Chapter 26

I'm Not Dead Yet

Here you are, Mrs. Slocum." Paula Jennings has caught me with my nose pressed against the glass of the lobby door. "I've been looking all over for you.

I pivot slightly, careful to keep my cane steady, and try to act like it's perfectly normal for a Creeper to have made herself at home in Upright territory. "I'm still here, Miss Jennings."

From the corner of my eye, I catch a brief glimpse of the director's dismay at my refusal to call her Paula. The pinched smile is her admission that she's glad we'll never be friends. Not after Polygon. Not after her ruined periwinkle suit.

She tugs the hem of her new, mustard-colored jacket. "You've made tremendous progress in the four weeks that you've been under our care." She points to my cane. "But until your therapist releases you, we'd prefer you explore The Reserve with either your scooter or the aid of your walker."

"I'm not exploring," I say, keeping my gaze on the circle drive. "I'm waiting on friends."

"That explains the message I just received from the gate guard."

Miss Jennings steps up and places her phone under my nose. "There's a Mrs. LaVera Tucker demanding to see you. Do you know her?"

LaVera's eyes are huge in the picture on the screen, but I'd know my friend anywhere.

"Tell Kevin or Keith or whatever that poor gatekeeper's name is to let Mrs. Tucker in." I crane my neck. The curve in the front drive blocks my view of the huge gates that are supposed to keep the riff-raff out, but everyone knows the gates are there to keep the residents in.

"She's not on your approved visitor list."

"Add her." The solution seems simple enough. "LaVera is spelled with a capital V on Vera."

"Adding a new name is not that simple."

"I can see you've never met LaVera, Miss Jennings." I point to her phone. "Old Avon ladies never take no for an answer."

"We'll need to phone your daughter—"

I bristle. "Charlotte Ann has no say over who I entertain. LaVera and Bo Boy are *my* friends." I hadn't planned on standing for so long. This wait forces me to shift my weight off of my bad leg. "They've driven all the way from Addisonville. Surely, you can't object to offering them a cup of tea and one of those birdseed cookies left from my workshop."

"They're several days old."

I push my new glasses snug against my nose. "LaVera's a terrible cook. She won't know the difference." Trashing friends is unlike me and totally uncalled for, but like Polygon, this place has made my tongue go mad.

"I'm afraid if we bend the rules for you, then we'll have—"

"A riot on your hands?" I don't hide my intent to win this argument. "On second thought, let's do call my daughter, Miss Jennings. She's an attorney. On Capitol Hill. I'm sure she'd be only too happy to encourage the Texas governor to launch an investigation into The Reserve's treatment of the elderly."

Paula glares for a second, decides not to call my bluff, then types a message into her phone. Two minutes later, I hear the annoying buzz of a...Volkswagen bug.

I plaster my nose to the glass as the mail lady's car putts to a stop under the porte-cochere. "What on earth is *she* doing here?"

I rub the window with my sleeve. There's no doubt about it, Winifred Moretti is at the wheel. Stranger still, Bo Boy is riding shot gun. LaVera's big frame is squished into the back seat like she's a reused wine cork. I don't know what surprises me more: That LaVera would bring Charlotte's friend to spy on me or that Bo is hopping out and running around to open Winnie's door *before* he helps his own mother. Maybe it will take the two of them to uncork LaVera. Then I see the way Bo is smiling at Winnie as they come around the hood of the VW with their arms linked and my heart sinks.

Winnie likes Bo.

And Bo likes Winnie.

Call me naïve, but I've secretly held out hope that somehow, someway Bo and Charlotte would find each other again. Bo's attachment to this free-range chickadee is an unexpected blow.

LaVera crooks an arm out the VW's open door. From her frantic waving, she needs air and she needs it fast. From the irregular beating of my heart, I need Bo and Winnie to keep their display of affection to themselves.

I yank open the heavy door and step out into the heat.

"Miss Sara!" Winnie releases Bo and runs to me. "It's so good to see you on your feet again." Before I can tell Winnie to keep her distance, she wraps me in a hug that smells of that nasty incense stuff she burns in her paint studio.

By the time she's done smothering me, Bo has pried his mother free.

The top of LaVera's helmet hair has been bent to the shape of the car's curved roof. Sweat drips from her upper lip. Little rivers of bright red lipstick snake her chin. I've never seen my Avon lady in such disarray, but that's not what worries me. Anger shoots from her filmy eyes and hits me square in the face. Not bad aim for a woman who claims to be blind. LaVera sees what she wants to see. That's how her husband was able to carry on with one of Daddy's peppy little bank tellers for so many years. I, on the other hand, can spot trouble a mile away. And this is no neighborly visit.

My cane can barely hold me up under the weight of possibilities. "What's happened?' I can barely spit out my next question. "Is it Charlotte?"

LaVera hefts her huge handbag over her shoulder. "I told Bo Boy, my friend Sara Slocum would never throw in with the Wootens. But that was before I saw this." She waves her hand at the massive glass doors of The Reserve. "Obviously, money talks."

"LaVera, I think you're overheated." All hopes of receiving the comfort I need after the loss of my precious Polygon goes out the window. I take a shaky step toward her. "You're not making sense."

"Tell her, Bo Boy." LaVera won't even look at me.

Bo steps forward, obviously pained to say what he's been instructed to say. "Miss Sara, why did you sell Fossil Ridge to Sam Sparks?"

"What?" The driveway seems to shift. "I've done no such thing."

LaVera whips a Polaroid picture out of her bag. "Then why is there a *Future Home of Sparks Resorts and Spa* billboard beside your entrance gate?"

"Since when?" I snatch the picture from her hand. It's true. The fancy sign covers all but the jacked boot of one of my metal cowboys. Suddenly, the trees and the VW bug are swirling around me, making it impossible to sort through this misunderstanding.

"Since this morning." LaVera sees my shock and her fire dies down a little. "You didn't know, did you?"

All I can do is clutch my cane with both hands and shake my head.

"Let's get her inside." Winnie takes my arm, but thanks to Lauralee's workouts my feet are firmly planted.

"Charlotte's done this." The betrayal is a gut punch similar to...no, she can't have done this to me.

"Now, Miss Sara, we don't know that." Winnie's placating tone stiffens my spine.

"We don't, but *you* probably do," I accuse. "You're Charlotte's best friend. Did she send you here to make sure I stay out of her way?"

"Charlotte and I are not speaking."

"Since when?"

"Since the day I told her she shouldn't bring you here."

Conflict of interest splits me in two. Winnie has never been a favorite of mine. Discovering that she stood up for me is sobering. Charlotte hasn't had many friends other than Caroline. They were inseparable. That Charlotte would risk losing the only friend she's made after she lost her sister is...confusing. Why would she do that?

"This is what I know," I say. "Charlotte made sure the hospital kept me dead to the world until she could stick me in this mausoleum, have my will probated, and sell off *my* property!" I hold out my palm. "I need your phone, Winnie."

Winnie's in the middle of some cockamamie explanation as to why Charlotte would most likely ignore her call when Paula pops outside.

"Everything okay here, Mrs. Slocum?" The Reserve's director sounds like she's concerned about me, but from the lusty, eight-second look she's giving Bo Boy, my well-being is not her mission. "I'm sure your friends would like to get out of this heat. Have you told them it's tea time?"

"Tea time?" LaVera's nose is so out of joint she can't see that I'm mad as a barn swallow who's just discovered a snake in her nest.

I'm also mortified.

Charlotte has put me in a horrible position. My friends believe I've sold them out. If they are still my friends. Right now, I'm not sure, and I can't say as I blame them.

"Have a cookie, LaVera," I say. "That'll give you something to chew on besides me while I get to a phone and figure this out."

Paula hooks Bo Boy's arm. "Let me show you and your lovely mother around."

"This place is too rich for our blood." LaVera's breezy clip past me sends a chill that rattles my bones.

I hobble after her and head straight for the lobby phone.

Winnie trails after me, but her head is swiveled in Bo's direction. "Do you need Charlotte's number, Miss Sara?"

I wave her off. If Charlotte can't have Bo Boy, there's no way I'm letting him fall into Paula's hands. "Numbers stick with me…even when friends and family don't."

Chapter 27

Truth is Stranger than Fiction

I'm worn to tatters. I don't know which was worse. Fighting with Charlotte or trying to convince LaVera that I will not sell her down the river. I don't know which stings worse. Charlotte's betrayal or LaVera's belief that I would ever do anything to hurt our friendship.

The need for some commiseration drives me away from my empty birdcage out to the handrail in the Walker's hall.

Lauralee, Ira, and Teeny were disappointed when I denied their request to meet LaVera and her son. I hate that Ira believes his dogs caused Polygon's death and that I'm holding some sort of grudge. That wasn't why I wanted to visit with LaVera alone. Old friends have a lot of history. I didn't feel like being sandwiched in the middle of old and new while feeling like I had to be the one to bring everyone up to speed.

But now that I've lost the confidence of my old friends, I see the error of trying to keep my relationships in nice, neat, separate boxes. I hope it's not too late to apologize to my new friends. They're all I've got...now that Polygon is gone. After spending a few weeks actually being around humans on a regular basis, I've come to realize how perilous it is to rely on the counsel of a flighty bird.

If I'm to have any hope of fixing this mess, I can't afford foolish mistakes. I must remain sharp. No more mixing up my meds or confusing the days of the week. No more boiling the kettle dry, or saying what I think, or refusing the help of a yard man...that last one will take some work.

The door to Lauralee's apartment is open a crack.

Clack. Clack. Clack. Ding.

I knock, but do not receive a response.

Clack. Clack. Ding.

Cigarette smoke curls around the door. The Reserve is a smoke-free environment, according to Paula and all the posted signs. Either Lauralee has company or Lauralee's apartment is on fire.

"Lauralee?" I push the door and it swings open.

"Can't stop." Lauralee mumbles around the cigarette hanging from the corner of her mouth. "I'm on a roll." She hunches closer to the massive desk taking up the center of the room and pounds away on a manual typewriter. "The hero is about to sweep the heroine off her feet." She waves me in. "Clear off one of those chairs and keep quiet."

Stepping into Lauralee's small living room is like stepping into a smoky library. Floor to ceiling oak bookcases line every wall. Stacks of books fill both side chairs and half of the small loveseat. I hobble to the nearest set of shelves for a closer look.

Rows and rows and rows of paperbacks. Some yellowed. Others a little newer. Some books are very recent, judging from their sharp colors and pristine pages.

All of the spines bear the same name: Fran Lacy.

LaVera would think she'd died and gone to heaven if she saw this collection of her favorite author's books. Too bad for her she got so ugly. "You must really love the work of Lacy," I say, already forgetting my rule to quit saying whatever pops into my head.

Lauralee glances at me without removing her hands from the keyboard. "I *am* Lacy." Her fingers march across the keys and words splatter the paper.

"Really?" I drag my finger along the spines. "You wrote all of these?"

She rips the page from her typewriter and whirls in her chair. "Everyone goes on and on about Cartland, but I can write her under the table. Have for years."

I've made judgments about this woman without knowing all the facts and it shames me. "You write romance?"

"*Steamy* romance." Lauralee drops her finished page on a stack beside her typewriter, removes her cigarette with v'd fingers.

"I thought you worked for your father."

Lauralee blows a smoky cloud my direction. "I totaled Papa's accounting sheets during the day and did what I loved at night…wrote."

How wonderful to have something age could not steal. "There must be a thousand books here."

"Nearly two thousand." She stubs her cigarette amongst the mound of butts in a cut-glass ashtray. "Smoking is something I still have to keep a secret. My pen name, not so much anymore…now that Papa's dead. I couldn't even kiss my husband in front of Papa without sending a blush to the old man's cheeks. Oh, how I miss kissing. Don't you?"

"Kissing is not what I miss about my Martin."

She notices the curt clip in my voice and motions for me to sit in the only available spot. "Visit with your friend not go well?"

"LaVera didn't come all this way to check on my emotional wellbeing."

Lauralee pulls a new cigarette from a shiny case. "Is she shopping for a retirement center?"

"No." I sigh and release the ugly truth. "My oldest and dearest friend came to accuse me of selling out. I've never sold out in my life. Not even when the school board offered to renew my contract in return for the name of the person pilfering canned goods from the school cafeteria."

Lauralee taps the cigarette on a pile of paper. "I could tell right off you were a person of principle."

"Exposing that desperate woman would have been tragic. Her family was poor. The children were thin as reeds." I drop onto the loveseat. "They don't pay lunchroom ladies enough to even buy themselves a reduced-priced lunch let alone feed their families."

Lauralee lights the cigarette, takes a deep drag, then releases a perfect ring of smoke that quickly encircles me. "Something tells me there's more behind the ever-present frown on your face than social injustice."

The truth is so ugly I can barely stand to let it roll off my tongue, but Lauralee's face is so lacking in judgment, I spill everything. "My daughter is trying to sell my ranch right out from under me."

"Have you talked to her?"

"I tried."

"What did she say?"

"Mother, are you still alive?"

Lauralee's not buying my version of this story. "Sarcasm rarely resolves anything."

Revisiting the argument is a pain I'd rather avoid, but I'm in too deep to back out now. "Charlotte said,"—I can barely spit out the hurtful words—"I'm only thinking ahead, making plans with your best interest in mind. What if this kind of offer never comes around again?'"

"And you said?"

"I'm not dead yet, Charlotte Ann. And until I am, Fossil Ridge remains my home."

Lauralee lets me stew for a few minutes, when she finally speaks

I know I'm in for a story. "My son and I have similar discussions. He says, Mother, when are you going to give up writing and start acting your age?"

"What do you tell him?"

She takes time to blow another smoke ring. "Stewart, I know you mean well, but I'm not going to sit around and wait for my joints to calcify and my arteries to clog. I see no good reason to act old. As long as I can string two words together, I'm going to keep writing.'" She pats the stack of paper. "I've never missed a deadline. I'm going to write until they pry this typewriter from my cold, dead hands." She leans forward. Eyes trained on me, she points a half-smoked ciggy in my direction. "You understand, Sara?"

I did. All of it. If I wanted to be in charge of my life I had to do more than whine about it. I had to do something. "I've got to get home."

"What will that accomplish?"

"Once I pin back the ears of that sleazy land developer, word will get around that Sara Slocum is still the sole owner and boss of Fossil Ridge Ranch. Charlotte can have the ranch when she pries it from my cold, dead hands."

Lauralee studies me through the thick lens of her glasses. "Life is a novel filled with today's short stories." She rests her smoldering cigarette on the ashtray. "Whether or not our stories end well…that, my friend, is up to us."

This woman has done more with her life than fill a room with books, she's filled her life with purpose. I'm hungry to do the same. "I've got so many things to set right and I feel like time is running out."

"We've all got scars." She slowly unbuttons her shirt and points to a fleshy pink scar where her breast used to be. "All we can do is unzip our hearts."

"Will you help me escape, Lauralee?"

She picks up her burning cigarette and takes a long, contemplative drag on the glowing stub between her fingers. "You'll need a plan."

"And a car."

"Ira's got the car."

"Really? I thought his kids had taken away his keys."

"His keys. Not his car." She taps ash atop the butts. "He keeps it under a tarp in the parking garage."

"What good is a car without the keys?"

"Ira, may be going blind, but he's not as demented as Ivy would have us believe. He's got a spare key taped under his medicine cabinet."

"Think he'd loan it to me?"

"Ira didn't need eight seconds to decide he'd do anything for you, Sara." She took a short drag. "Any man who'll smear peanut butter on a corncob for you will certainly loan you his car."

"You've been writing fiction far too long, Lauralee."

"Truth is always stranger than fiction."

"His children are good to him. I don't want him to know about my ungrateful daughter."

She blew a perfect smoke ring. "Leave Ira to me."

Chapter 28

Prison Break

I wait until Esmerelda has completed her last bed check. The moment the door clicks shut, I roll out of bed, fully dressed. From under my pillow, I retrieve an envelope addressed to Miss Jennings and set it on my bedside table. There's no way I want sweet Esmerelda blamed for my escape.

I mount my power scooter, yank the charger cord from the wall socket, and back my motorized vehicle as close as possible to Polygon's cage.

Ira helped me bury Polygon in the garden beneath a hydrangea bush, but I could no more leave his cage behind than I could leave the small plot of land where I buried my Caroline and Martin.

Considerable effort is needed to maintain my balance while wrestling a large birdcage, but I'm determined. After a few tries, my robe ties are threaded through the wires and Polygon's cage is secured to the back of the scooter seat. From behind the dresses in the closet, I retrieve a small bag packed with the things that matter...my Bible, Dearfoams, meds, and the photo of my girls on that awful tire swing. I drape the bag's strap over the scooter's handle bars and mount the seat.

Next door, Mrs. Scott is in full sundowner mode. Her howls rattle the art on the walls. I glance at the clock. Freedom from dining schedules, hallway designations, and demented neighbors is only moments away. The clock strikes ten. I unlock my door and peer into the dimly lit hall.

All clear.

An overanxious press to the throttle shoots the scooter from my apartment. I zip to the elevator and jab the down button. Looking over my shoulder, I half expect to encounter Esmerelda. That sweet girl would be heartbroken by this shenanigan. Fortunately, the elevator arrives and I'm safely tucked inside without having to come up with an explanation.

I hold my breath as the elevator plummets to the garage level. The door dings and I exit into the dim coolness of the underground.

"Sara," Ira whisper-shouts. "Over here."

As my eyes adjust, I spot Ira. He's holding Goodness and Mercy in his arms and standing with Lauralee, and Teeny beside a tarped object.

I press the throttle and shoot toward them. "What are y'all doing here, Lauralee?"

She points to the typewriter in the basket of her walker. "Teeny and I are going with you."

Teeny holds up a plastic bag stuffed with bows. "Go."

All of us are done in by the sound of Teeny's rusty voice, but I'm more undone about the thought of taking them with me. I can barely take care of myself, how could I take care of this decrepit crew?

"I'm not running to the store," I say. "I'm going home. My ranch is ten miles from the nearest milk and bread. Eleven miles from marginal medical help."

"I'm tired of just writing about adventures," Lauralee says. "I want to take...I want to take...one...just..." Lauralee seems so excited she's having trouble finishing the sentence.

"One more—?" I ask.

Lauralee nods, but her eyes seem a bit frantic.

Ira raises his dogs so I can see a bag dangling from his arm. "Me, too."

"Sweet Moses." I swing my legs off the scooter.

"Let's loooad uuuuh."

"Lauralee?" Ira says.

His concern whips me around.

Lauralee's expression is one I can't decipher. Her eyes are suddenly very wide. Her lips droop on one side. Drool trickles from the lower corner. But the words she is trying to say are stuck in her throat.

"Lauralee!" I lunge. Lauralee's slumped body is a dead weight takes both of us to the garage floor.

"Sara!" Ira rushes to us, but his arms are too full to lift either of us. "What should I do?"

"Get help, Ira. Now!"

Chapter 29

Freedom Foiled

What were you thinking, Señora?" Esmerelda tugs a clean gown over my head. "You could have re-broken your hip."

"The ER doctor said I'm fine." From the corner of my eye, I spot the envelope addressed to Miss Jennings. I wait until Esmerelda turns to untie Polygon's cage then snatch the letter and stuff under my pillow. "Why didn't they take Mrs. Macy to the hospital?"

"She has the orders."

"What orders?"

Esmerelda returns Polygon's cage to the table. "The ones that say do not make me live when I cannot live on my own."

The forms Charlotte wanted me to sign. The ones with all the ugly questions I've never wanted to answer for myself. Not after the way Martin took things into his own hands. Torn between not wanting to look back and not wanting to face the future as an old woman, I've pretended I have plenty of time. Well, I don't. No one does. Sooner or later, death comes for us all. I just hope it comes for me before I lose myself in the fog.

I have to work hard to get my lips around the question I must ask. "Where did they take her?"

"The fourth floor."

"Which room?"

Esmerelda's eyes dart toward the door, as if she's expecting someone to bust in and snatch her away if she tells me too much. "Room 412."

"I need to see her." I grab Esmerelda's hand. "Please, before it's too late."

She shakes her head. "Miss Jennings say to put you to bed. Let you get a good night's rest."

Miss Jennings had also said that come morning she would summon me and Ira to her office to discuss why we were in the garage past curfew. What the angry director didn't say was how in the world she expected any of us to rest tonight when it was obvious Lauralee had suffered a stroke. Lauralee Macy is a national treasure. A gifted writer. My friend.

"Please, Esmerelda. I need to tell her...I need to tell her thank you."

"You want I lose my job, Señora?"

"Of course not. I'm sorry. I wasn't thinking." Tail between my legs, I crawl into bed and let Esmerelda tuck me in.

The moment the door clicks shut I pick up the phone and dial Ira's room. "Get Teeny. Come to my apartment as fast as you can. We're going to find Lauralee. Before it's too late." I start to hang up. "And Ira, best to leave Goodness and Mercy in your apartment. I'm sorry, but we can't risk them giving us away."

Ten minutes later, Ira and Teeny are at my door.

"You sure this is a good idea?" Ira asks.

"Never been more sure of anything in my life." I'm worried the ding of the elevator will give us away, so I leave the scooter attached to the charger in my apartment and pray I can make it up one flight of stairs with just a cane.

Unlike the first floor where the Uprights gather for decaf coffee or flutes of champagne, or on the Walkers' floor where Ivy and Bea play cards and argue with their partners, the lobby of the Leaper floor is totally empty. Quiet. Deathly quiet.

"Which way?" Ira's whisper warms my neck.

I lean away from his trust and check the numbers on the wall placard. "This way."

At the nurses' station, a stocky woman in need of a root touch-up sits with her back to us. Her fingers tap the keys of a computer.

"I should have brought Lauralee's typewriter. She would want her typewriter." I whisper to Ira.

"We can bring it tomorrow." Ira nods toward the nurse. "How are we going to get past that old battle axe?"

"Follow me." Gripping the handle of my cane, I shuffle toward the nurses' station, mentally rehearsing explanations for our presence on the fourth floor. On the outside, I appear calm and confident. On the inside, I praying for the Lord's help.

Without the wailing sundowners or blaring TVs, every click of the respirators and beep of the heart monitors echoes in the hallway. Unsettling as those sounds are, it's the smell of decay I can hardly stomach.

To my right, a door has been left open to a dimly lit resident's room 408. Call it morbid curiosity or call it fear, but I can't stop my gaze from slipping inside. A skeleton-thin woman is curled into a ball. Her hand is a bird claw clutching the rail. Like Polygon, she's hanging on to life by a thread, but her wide eyes are searching for an open window.

Bile rises in my throat. I yank my focus back to the task at hand. But at the next open door, Room 410, I'm peeking in again—a rubbernecker who can't get enough of tragic scenes. A slumped shell of a man is strapped into a wheelchair. His chin rests on his chest, making it impossible for me to make out his face. With that full-head of silver hair I surmise he might have been quite the lady's man, but what does it matter now? Like the woman in the room we've just passed, he too is alone.

The nurse swivels in her chair and the three of us freeze. I hold my breath and pray she won't look up. We don't really have a plausible explanation for being on the Leaper floor at this late hour. Then, as if the Lord is finally listening to me, a high-pitched alarm goes off and the yellow line zig-zagging across the nurse's computer screen goes flat.

My heart stops. Lord, don't let it be Lauralee?

The nurse calmly turns back to the screen, then her chin lifts toward the clock. She sighs, pushes up from her chair without noticing us, then ambles past 412 and makes her way to a room at the end of the hall. She doesn't call a Code Blue or summon help. For the poor soul she's attending, it is already too late.

"Come on," I wave Ira and Teeny on and we duck into the room marked 412.

Lauralee lies in the middle of a hospital bed. She's frail as a barn swallow chick. Her glazed eyes are fixed on the ceiling and her drooping mouth hangs like a cupboard door with a broken hinge.

Feeling like a trespasser in another's death scene, I reach over the bedrail and touch the paper-thin skin of her hand. "Lauralee?"

Her countenance remains vacant. Sorrow wells up within me.

"She won't get her letter from the President." Teeny's matter-of-fact voice jerks my head up.

I don't care about letters from the President, but that Lauralee won't get hers makes me mad. This is not the ending a steamy romance writer would have written for her life. "We can't leave her here." I say.

"Where would we take her?" Ira hands clutch the rail on the opposite side of Lauralee's bed. "She's outlived her husband and her child."

"Her son's not dead," I snap. "His name's Stewart and they argue."

"That was ten years ago." Ira's sad headshake awakens me to the ugly truth.

"Lauralee's all alone?"

Ira nods. "She came here to die. Just like the rest of us."

"That's not true," I argue. "Lauralee has purpose. She has books to write. Friends who need her."

"Sooner or later,"—Ira's voice is calm, as if he's given this situation considerable thought. —"we're all leapin' from the fourth floor, Sara. Until then, all we can do is try to make it to the table every night."

"There's no *we* on this floor, Ira." My raising volume is sure to get us kicked out, but I'm determined to be heard. "No one should have to die alone."

"Or live like this." Ira's eyes are watery with the same fear I'm feeling.

It takes bravery to walk into a classroom of rowdy third graders. It takes bravery to stand at the grave of your child. It takes bravery to bury a husband who's basically deserted you. But I'm not brave enough to become a Flying Fossil on my own.

I shake my head like I'm priming some sort of rusty courage pump. "I've been dying every day for the past twenty-some years." Right then a new plan coalesces. "Thanks to Lauralee, I've finally started living." I weave my fingers through Lauralee's frail ones. "You're the best teacher I ever had. Thank you, my friend. I'll never forget what you've done for me." Holding on tight, I lean over and kiss her forehead. When I pull back, I see one of my tears slid into the hollow of Lauralee's cheek.

"Sad as it makes me to desert you Lauralee, I know you'd kick my tail if I hung around to watch you die. So, I'm leaving. Like we planned." I swipe my eyes and turn to Ira and Teeny. The look I give them is an invitation to freedom. Freedom from the boredom. Freedom from dying alone on the fourth floor. Freedom to live until I'm not. "It's what she'd want. And she'd want y'all to come with me."

"Goodness and Mercy, too?" Ira asks.

"Long as they follow us all the days of our lives," I smile through my tears.

Chapter 30

Prison Break 2

The fire alarm blares outside my apartment door. Having Ira set it off at midnight was my idea, but still, the blast was startling.

I open the door and peer out. The chaos I hoped would ensue is in full swing. Two attendants are punching numbers on the code box outside my neighbor's locked door.

The burly one spots me. "Probably just a drill, Mrs. Slocum," he says. "Stay put. We'll be back for you after we carry Mrs. Scott out."

I ease back into my apartment and close the door. Soon frantic footsteps no longer pound the hall and Mrs. Scott's wailing and screaming can no longer be heard.

I peer into the hall again. All clear. I drop a towel over Polygon's empty cage. Mount my scooter. Squeeze the throttle and shoot forward.

Ira said I would have about five minutes before the automatic shut-down of the elevators. A jab to the down button opens the doors immediately. Luckily, the elevator is empty. The ride to the garage level is fast. I wheel into the adequately lit space. The distant wail of approaching fire trucks speeds me along.

I park my scooter alongside Ira's covered car. "Ready?"

Ira smiles, both dogs snuggled into the crook of his arm. "Your chariot awaits." He yanks the tarp.

The canvas slides off a beautiful 1955, two-door Cadillac coupe. Azure blue. White-wall tires. Shiny, inverted gull-wing chrome bumpers.

"Oh, Ira," I gasp. "She's a beauty."

"Beauty's more than skin deep on this old girl." He rubs his hand gently over the hood. "Under her shiny shell, Trixie's spry as a teenager in love."

"Trixie?"

"Oleta named her." With a lilt in his step, Ira sets his dogs on the front seat. Then he unloads my bag and Teeny's sack of bows and puts them in the trunk along with a small bag he's hastily repacked. "Allow me, Teeny." He flips a latch on the front passenger seat and slides half of the split-bench forward.

Teeny folds herself like a hibiscus and wiggles into the expansive backseat. Once she settles her body blooms and her smile grows bigger than the hair bow that brushes the car's ceiling.

Ira nods toward Polygon's cage. "This coming with us?"

"If you don't mind."

"Mind? It's my fault this cage is empty."

I swallow the lump in my throat. "Don't ever say that again, Ira.

It was Polygon's time and he went out flying like a bird should."

"Thank you, Sara." Ira carries Polygon's cage around to the other side and settles it beside Teeny. "Keep an eye on this, Teeny. I don't want Sara to lose a single feather before she's ready." Ira comes back around and hands me the keys. "You better drive."

It seems a bit late to bring up the fact that I haven't had a driver's license in several years. "But it's your car."

He shakes his head. "My kids are right. I'm blind as a bat."

I thrust the keys back at him. "Don't know if I can drive a standard."

"Trixie's fully automatic. Even has power steering." He smiles and pushes the keys toward me. He's not letting me off the hook. "She'll be easy on your legs."

If I'm going to have to do this, perhaps it's best not to mention that the last time I backed my little 1999 Ford Escort from the shed I scraped the mirror off the driver's side. "All right then."

After I'm settled behind the wheel, Ira's dogs squeeze between us as he gives me a quick rundown on the switches, including the lights. "Let's leave the high beams off 'til we're clear of the property. There's a service entrance at the back of the grounds that is never locked."

The starter turns over on the first crank and Trixie roars to life. Fortunately, the firetruck sirens are so near, I don't think anyone would have heard the car start up.

"You'll have to guide me out of here," I try to sound upbeat and confident but inside I'm a bowl of Jell-O.

"Just take her real slow to start."

I nod and slip the column shifter into reverse. I can't tell you how relieved I am when I back free of the parking space without putting a single dent or scratch on Ira's beautiful car.

We creep past the other parked cars and finally make it to the garage exit. I brake for a passing firetruck with its lights flashing and siren screaming. My heart's racing. To my left, firemen are jumping out of trucks and swarming the lobby.

"It's now or never," I tell Ira.

"Go easy on the gas pedal," he warns. "Trixie's got a V-8 that can do zero to seventy in eighteen seconds. She'll get out from under you if you're not careful. Turn right."

The steering wheel is larger than the one on the tractor I use to brush hog the pastures. I've driven school buses that weren't this long. When we arrive at the closed gate, Ira gets out. As he fiddles with the latch, I check the rearview. No one is following us, and Teeny is still smiling. Wishing Lauralee was with us is a waste of valuable time and clarity I'm going to need.

Ira waves me through, shuts the gate like a good goat farmer would, then gets back in. "I got us out of here. It's up to you to get us to your place, Sara. Think you can do that?"

"A person never forgets the way home." I mentally cross my

fingers and turn onto the street.

Ira reaches across the expansive seat and flips on the headlights. "Feels good to be back on the road. Going on your own schedule. Making your own choices." He scoops up his dogs. "Hang on, girls."

His joy over reclaiming his freedom washes over me. Freedom I haven't felt in years. For this, I have Lauralee to thank. I refuse to beat myself up for leaving her to die alone, because to stay there and watch her die would have been to deny the greatest lesson that spunky little candy cane taught me. Living until we're not is the only way to live. For her sake, I'm going to live and love for as long as I can.

Glare from all the street lights and headlights makes the street signs hard to read. "We need to head west. Toward..." I can't remember the name of the town. "Toward...it's a town... with lots of little shops." The jumble in my head sends panic racing through my body. What if Charlotte is right? That I do forget things like how to get home? Suddenly, a number pops from the fog. "Highway 290." Numbers have yet to fail me.

Ira taps the frame of his glasses. "The signs are blurs through these Coke bottles."

"Don't worry. I've got this," my voice is as shaky as my confidence. "You just watch for a gas station. I don't know what kind of mileage Trixie gets, but according to the needle we've got less than a half a tank."

Ira leans over and checks the gauge. "My kids didn't want me and Trixie to get far, did they?"

"How did they know you still had a key?"

"They've all got a fair share of their momma in them." He chuckled. "Never could pull a thing over on that woman."

The number on the exit sign is 290. I check it twice. "Here's our turn." Hands gripping the wheel, I eased into the flow of traffic. "Should be in…" I can't remember the name of the town, so I cover with, "Should be at our turn in an hour."

"Mind if I lower the window?" Ira asks. "I love the hum of white walls on pavement and the girls love to sniff the breeze."

"I think we could all stand a bit of fresh air." I press the gas and we sail down the highway. Goodness and Mercy perch on Ira's lap and stick their heads out the open window.

Every so often, I glance in the rearview. Teeny's head is resting against Polygon's cage. Her eyes are closed, but a grin still lifts her lips. From the corner of my eye, Ira is gently caressing the car's interior as if he's touching some treasured memory. In the glow of the dashboard lights, I see a tear trickle down his cheek. I'm not the only one who misses what life has taken from them.

It feels good to give again. Even if it's just a few moments of freedom in a borrowed car. I haven't felt this useful in a long time. Now I know how Lauralee managed to keep a smile on her face and hope in her heart. She gave. She gave her wit, a listening ear, her wisdom, and her friendship.

But giving two friends a road trip is one thing. Taking on the well-being of two dogs and a couple of people with one foot in the grave and the other on a banana peel...well, that's crazy. What am I going to do with these two when I get them home? The house is big enough for all of us, but Charlotte's right. The bedrooms are upstairs. The only bathroom will have to be completely remodeled to accommodate a wheelchair, should any of us need one. And the odds are great that sooner or later, one of us will need one.

I push the fear from my mind and decide to worry about the details later. Right now, I'm excited to be going home and beyond excited to have someone to share that home with again.

The only problem I really need to deal with is how to formulate a plan to deal with Charlotte. She will not be happy when Miss Jennings reports my escape.

My eyes jump to the flashing sign on the side of the highway.

SILVER ALERT.

Flashes in big orange letters even Ira would have no trouble seeing.

SILVER ALERT. BLUE '55CADILLAC.

TX LIC #NVR DUN

I push Ira's arm. "Wake up!"

He shakes himself alert. "Find a gas station?"

I point to the flashing sign. "What is Trixie's license plate number?"

"Never Done. Why?"

"Why would you buy a plate that says that?"

"Wife bought it for me." He rubs his hand over his bald head. "According to her, it seemed like I'd never be done sinkin' money into this car."

I glance in the mirror, half expecting to see flashing lights. "We've got to get off the main highway. This car is too easy to spot."

"Why?"

"Because according to that flashing sign, we're fugitives." I ease over to the right lane, praying the driver behind me is too busy talking on the phone or something to notice our vanity plate. "Trixie sticks out like a pretty girl at an all-boys school." My eyes scan the road for an exit sign. "We've got to take back roads."

Two miles later, we luck out. I zoom for the exit and peel right so fast the front tires snag a little pea gravel from the shoulder. Goodness and Mercy fly out of Ira's lap and land on the floorboard. Polygon's cage crashes into the back of my seat. Teeny lunges with both hands and pulls it upright again. The car swerves and bucks along the service road until I finally wrestle the wheel and my racing heart into submission. I screech to a stop at the first intersection. There's not another car in sight. I'm clear to go, but I can't lift my foot from the brake. Air doesn't seem to be getting to my lungs.

My thinking is muddy. Confused. Afraid.

Goodness and Mercy scramble back to the safety of Ira's lap. Ira touches my arm lightly. "You okay, Sara?"

I manage a shaky nod. "Just trying to get my bearings."

I've had foggy spells on and off for the last five years. Brief moments when I go into a room and can't remember why I went there. Retracing my steps and giving myself time to think has always cleared the fog. But tonight, I don't have that option. Retracing our route would mean facing Miss Jenkins and confessing to Charlotte that I had gotten lost. Frightening as that sounds, I'm more terrified by the honest truth. Retracing our route is impossible because I'm so turned around, I couldn't find my way back to The Reserve if I wanted to.

In an effort to be helpful, Ira points across the intersection. "Is that green thing up ahead a sign?"

I stick my chin over the wheel and squint. "It is."

Dallas 96 miles.

All of the solutions whirring around in my head come to a dead stop. I pull back against the seat. "Oh, no."

Ira shifts. "What's the matter?"

"The good news is we're still in Texas."

"And the bad news?" Ira asks.

"We're headed north."

"I thought you said Addisonville is west," Ira's attempt at being helpful is not helping.

I shove aside mental cobwebs and conjure a blurry version of the Texas map that hung in my classroom. "I've been going the wrong direction."

From the draw of Ira's brows, my explanation has not inspired his confidence. "For how long?"

"Since we left," I admit.

Teeny leans forward. "Turn that way." She points left then settles into her seat and rests her head against Polygon's cage.

"Well, at least it's a night for a drive," Ira says.

I appreciate how Ira is trying to remain calm and not push me over the ledge, but my knuckles are white against the brown leather of the wheel. "I wish I'd agreed to carrying one of those mobile phones my daughter is always yammering about."

Ira's face brightens. "We have a mobile phone."

"Oh, Ira." Chastising him is the pot calling the kettle black, but hopefully he can forgive the pressure getting to me once he sees the sunrise over the Frio. "Why didn't you say so sooner?"

"You didn't ask." Ira leans over the dogs and opens the glovebox. A heavy black receiver sitting on a base like the phone I have on my bedside table at home slides out.

"We can't call Miss Jennings. She'll sic the Highway Patrol on us." I gnaw my lip. "Charlotte's just going to yell. And LaVera isn't speaking to me. Who do you think we should call?"

Ira shakes his head. "Doesn't matter what I think."

"It does, Ira," I argue. "Call the wrong person and we'll be playing Bingo at The Reserve for the rest of our lives."

He lifts the receiver. "This blasted thing never has worked like they do on the TV shows." He pops the button on the base like he's trying to rouse a dial tone. "I thought about yanking it during the restoration but decided I couldn't do that to Oleta. She loved pretending to chat with Bogart as we drove down the road." He hangs up the receiver. "Funny, the things we'll do for those we love."

The click of the glovebox is a needle prick that lets the air out of my shoulders.

Other than keeping the piano, how long has it been since I've done something so outrageously selfless that Charlotte would know how much I love her? The least I can do is trust that she has my best interest at heart.

I look at Ira. "Fifty-fifty chance Teeny's right."

He nods. "You're bound to see something you recognize."

"And if I don't?"

"No shame in turning around, trying a different direction."

"Right." I lower the blinker lever. Sucking in a deep breath, I lift my foot from the brake and make the turn. Trixie's headlight beams sweep across a fence row as saggy as my confidence. The car bounces onto an empty two-lane highway.

Nothing looks familiar.

Desperation bursting through, I've no choice but to confess, "Ira, I'm lost and I don't have a driver's license."

He rubs his dogs' ears. "I don't have collision insurance on this car anymore or a gas card."

"Well, aren't we a pair?"

"Two halves of a rotten apple." Ira pats my arm with a chuckle.

I grip the wheel and drive into the unknown.

Chapter 31

Which is Worse?

Charlotte laid aside the real estate papers Sam Sparks wanted executed. She hadn't talked to her mother since the heated conversation that followed LaVera's drive to Austin to spill the beans. Sparks Development did not have the right to plant a sign on Slocum land before the deal was signed. But she might have mitigated the damage if she'd done the courageous thing and flown to Austin and reasoned with her mother. In person.

After all, Fossil Ridge legally belonged to Mother. The ranch was her home. Mother's mental capacities may be failing, but she deserved the courtesy of being able to dictate the terms of how and when she would say goodbye to the home she loved.

Charlotte picked up her phone and scrolled to her mother's new number. Hopefully, the woman had calmed down enough to accept an apology. If not an apology, then perhaps Mother had at least become more rational now that her meds were regulated. Maybe she was even beginning to remember how much she used to enjoy social interaction. Maybe she was starting to settle into her new surroundings.

And maybe, just maybe, snowballs stood a chance of surviving a Texas summer.

As Charlotte's finger hovered over the call button, Loraine burst into her office waving a newspaper. "Have you seen this?" She slapped the tabloid down on Charlotte's desk.

NY Jets Cheerleader Accuses Celebrity Photographer of Sexual Misconduct

The ugly caption was splashed over a photo of James smiling at the curvy brunette on his arm.

"So that's what he was doing in New York." Phone in hand, Charlotte opened her desk drawer and grabbed her purse. "I've got to get to Ari."

"Too late." Loraine scooped up the paper and tossed it in the trash. "She's already seen this garbage."

"How do you know?"

"School just called." Loraine's sober face caused Charlotte's heart to skip a beat.

"And?"

"Aria's in the principal's office."

"Why?"

"For smashing mirrors in the bathroom."

"Call the school." Charlotte hoisted her purse strap over her shoulder. "Tell them I'm on my way." She charged around the desk.

"Already had your car brought up from the garage." Loraine

stopped Charlotte. "Go easy on her."

The principal was a short, stocky woman with a thin reputation for being fair. "Restitution must be made. A three-day suspension is mandatory. And I expect Aria to return from her time of reflection with a ten-page report stressing the value of respecting public property."

"Send me a bill." Charlotte nodded to Aria. "Get your backpack. Let's go."

They rode in silence all the way to the house. Neither mentioned the tabloid or the reason for Aria's unusual behavior. The moment they pulled into the drive, Aria hopped out, slammed the door, and stomped into the house.

Charlotte started to go after her, but she didn't know what to say. That she was sorry? That she wanted to break a chair over James's head? That some choices haunt you for a lifetime?

She climbed the steps to their front door, threw her keys into the crystal bowl on the entry table, and caught her reflection in the mirror. Dark circles under her eyes. Anger clenching her jaw. Worry wrinkles slashing her brow. When had she become a worn-out, middle-aged woman?

No wonder James…no! She refused to let him off the hook. This time he'd gone too far. He hadn't just humiliated her, he'd hurt their daughter.

Charlotte picked up the bowl and threw it at the pitiful excuse of a mother staring back at her. Shattered glass showered the marble tiles.

"Mom!" Aria stood at the top of the stairs, her face a combination of horror and understanding. "You okay?"

Charlotte shook her head. "Am now."

A tiny ripple of solidarity lifted the frown from Aria's lips.

A buzzing cell phone drew Charlotte's attention to her purse, but she didn't have the strength to fish it out.

"Aren't you going to get that?" Aria asked.

"No."

"What if it's Dad?"

Yeah, what if it was? She had plenty to say to him. None of it good.

Charlotte ripped the phone from the side pocket of her bag. "James, you're going to regret—"

"Mrs. McCandless?" The interrupting voice sent a cold chill racing down Charlotte's spine. "This is Paula Jennings. The Reserve's—"

"What's happened?"

"I...we...had a fire drill last night," she hesitated. "Your mother and two other residents managed to steal a car and...escape."

"What?"

"Mrs. Slocum, Ira Conner, and Teeny...uh...Ethel Marie McIlroy are currently...at large."

"At large?"

"Missing."

"When did this happen?"

"The fire drill took place around midnight. We didn't have a full accounting of all the residents for approximately another two hours. When these three residents could not be located, we immediately notified our security and conducted a thorough search of our grounds, which as you know, are quite extensive." Paula hurried on. "That's when we discovered the tarp."

"Tarp?"

"The one that usually covers Mr. Conner's antique Cadillac. It was lying on the floor of our private parking garage. The car was gone."

"Were they abducted?"

"We believe their exit was...planned."

"Are you blaming my mother for this?"

"Mrs. Slocum left a note."

"What did it say?"

"Well, I wouldn't put a lot of stock in everything she said...especially since your mother's been slightly...agitated."

"But the last time we spoke, you assured me Mother was making good progress with her rehab and in making friends."

"She was. But, I believe, the unfortunate death of her parrot was more than she could bear."

"Her bird died?"

"Yes, in a rather bizarre accident."

"Your entire story is rather bizarre, Miss Jennings."

"There was another strange event earlier in the evening."

"Another event?"

"Your mother and her three tablemates were in the parking garage when one of the women in their party had a stroke. Surprisingly, your mother had the wherewithal to summon help...sadly, Mrs. Macy has since passed away." Paula cleared her throat. "They offered no explanation as to why the four of them had gathered in the garage...I assumed it was to admire Mr. Conner's automobile. He frequently loves to show it off to the ladies. Usually, I'd get to the bottom of something like this immediately. But they were all so exhausted by the trauma of witnessing a medical emergency that I decided it best to let them rest. I planned to deal with them this morning. Give them a stern lecture on the dangers of prowling around the grounds after curfew. Obviously, that lecture will now include leaving the grounds without permission."

"When you realized the car was missing, and possibly my mother along with it, why in the world didn't you notify me?" This was a lawsuit waiting to happen and Charlotte fully intended her tone to imply that Miss Jennings should feel the same fear that was racing through her veins. "She's a diabetic with a heart condition. If she doesn't take her meds regularly, no telling what might happen."

"Once we found your mother's note, we followed protocol. Notified the proper authorities and provided them with ID photos and fingerprints, as well as the medical documentation of Mr. Conner and Mrs. McIlroy's diminished capacities as well as your mother's medical history. They immediately initiated a Silver Alert. Texas has a high rate of successfully locating missing seniors. However—"

"However, *my* mother had been missing several hours by the time the alert was officially launched, right?"

"Technically...yes."

"And don't the statistics support the fact that if missing seniors are not located within twenty-four hours the odds of serious injury or death greatly increase?"

"The tendency to wander is one of the most challenging behaviors to manage for those with dementia and..."

"Yes or no, Miss Jennings, does time play a factor in finding them alive?"

"Yes, but Mr. Conner's children don't allow him to keep much gas in the car. Only enough to start it up every once in a while."

"But enough to drive off the property?"

"Yes."

"No telling how far they've gotten."

"It would help if you could give us an idea of where your mother might be headed."

"I know exactly where she's headed. The problem is this, Miss Jennings: my mother won't have a clue!" Scenarios of Mother lying in a ditch flashed through her mind. "I'm getting on the next plane to Austin. By the time I get there, you better have my mother in your possession."

Chapter 32

Bisected by Duty and Love

Winnie, it's Charlotte." From the corner of her eye, Charlotte watched her daughter as their Uber driver wove in and out of traffic trying to get them to the airport on time. Aria's stony silence and icy glare had made it abundantly clear that she wasn't happy about being forced to fly to Texas. That made two of them. "Please don't hang up, Win."

"I was wondering when you'd call."

Hope pounded in Charlotte's ears. "Have you heard something? Do you know where she is?"

"Who?"

"Mother!" Charlotte's exasperated tone drew an over-the-shoulder glance from the college-age driver who was successfully darting around traffic snarls while texting and eavesdropping. He made multi-tasking look disgustingly easy.

"Not my job to keep up with her anymore, remember?"

"I deserve everything you want to throw at me, Win, but can you please just tell me if you've seen her?"

"Last I saw Miss Sara, she was spitting nails at everyone in that fancy nursing home where you'd abandoned her."

Bisected by duty and love was not a defense. Charlotte opted to stick to the facts. "She's stolen a car and escaped from The Reserve."

"Good for her!"

"Winnie, they can't find her." Charlotte didn't try to hide her desperation. "She's lost somewhere between Austin and who-knows-where. She could be in Oklahoma or driving straight into the Gulf for all I know. If they don't find her, I'll never forgive myself."

"Okay, calm down, C." The vinegar was gone from Winnie's voice and Charlotte knew she'd been forgiven. "Start at the beginning."

Charlotte let out a relieved sigh and relayed the brief conversation with Miss Jennings as well as the useless information she'd managed to extract from the Texas Highway Patrol. One blue antique Cadillac, three addled seniors, and one empty birdcage had completely disappeared. "I don't have Bo's cell number and LaVera's not answering. Could you possibly drive out and ask LaVera if she's heard from Mother?"

"I don't know that your mother would call LaVera. They did not part on good terms."

"My ability to sabotage relationships must be hereditary."

"Then there must be some strength in your DNA too," Winnie said.

"I don't know about that, Win."

"The day I found your mother stranded on my mail route, she was hot, tired, and a little bit confused, but she was not resigned. Purse slung over her arm, she was walking away from her stalled Ford. When I mentioned she was going the wrong direction, she said, 'I'm not going to sit here and mold.'" Winnie's tone softened. "C, since your sister died you've put one foot in front of the other. You may go the wrong direction every now and then, but you keep moving forward. What better legacy could you give your daughter?"

The shot of truth was as uncomfortable as an oversized vitamin lodged in her throat, but Charlotte did her best to choke it down. "I'll check in with you as soon as Ari and I land in Austin. If by some small chance Mother has managed to make it home, I'll save my wrath for The Reserve's director and drive straight to the ranch."

"Bo and I picked up Raymond's van from the airport garage," Winnie said. "You'll have to rent a car."

"None of this would have happened if I'd listened to Mother and not hired Raymond in the first place."

"Hindsight is an exhausting master." Winnie quickly followed up her truthful assessment with offered assurances, along with promises to gather a search party and ask everyone in Addisonville to pray. Always with the prayers.

Winnie's undying faith was an irritant Charlotte preferred to avoid, but tonight, she'd had more than one reason for calling her old friend. Her mother was a car thief. Her daughter seemed intent on acquiring a criminal record. And if mother hadn't been located by the time she landed in Austin, she'd be guilty of murdering one inept assisted living director.

Yes, if ever Divine help was needed, it was now.

Charlotte clicked off her phone and turned her focus on the quiet child plastered against the opposite side of the car. Aria had been somber and despondent since she'd been told she was coming along. Charlotte could almost feel her daughter secretly plotting to break free. The wiry little blonde was so much more like her grandmother than her. Headstrong. Brilliant. Extremely independent. And sometimes a royal pain in the backside. Curse DNA.

Teen rebellion was a normal part of life. Every family expected it. Hundreds of books had been written to prepare parents on the subject.

Elderly parent rebellion, on the other hand, was a completely different animal. Reversing roles meant she had to managed Mother's safety issues, direct her healthcare, see to her proper nutrition, and eventually take over her finances. How did anyone assume control of their parent's life without dishonoring or devaluing them? Every time she turned around, she was telling her mother no. She felt like she was constantly disciplining a petulant two-year-old and she didn't like it. She didn't have enough grown-up experience or the guts to parent her parent.

In truth, she had little experience to fall back on when it came to rebellion.

She'd always followed the rules. Caroline was the wild one.

Her older sister and Mother were always at odds, disagreeing on everything from hairstyles to boys to colleges. When Caroline died, Mother lost her sparring partner. Charlotte had no idea how to fill that role. So, she'd done the only thing she knew to do: never ripple the waters. But that tactic failed as well. The more perfect she tried to be, the more distant Mother became.

It wasn't until Charlotte decided to go against the grain...to pick up her sister's dropped reins...to irritate her mother so badly she wouldn't miss Caroline...that she felt she'd sparked the anger her mother needed to live.

Charlotte raised her hand to sweep a stray curl from Aria's face. Her daughter flashed a quick glare and low snarl. Charlotte pulled back a nub...not a bitten hand...but a broken heart.

She'd expected she and Aria would have the typical teen fights about inappropriate clothes and curfews. They'd always been two different people with two different views. She loved Aria's fearless nature. Wished she had more of it herself.

But the intentional defacing of public property was so unlike the little girl she'd once known. Admittedly, Aria was no longer a little girl. Sometime during Charlotte's numerous court cases and extended jaunts to deal with her mother, her own daughter had grown up. The growing distance between them was killing her.

It was easy to see that Aria's actions were more than tantrums, they were cries for help. They were a child's inability to process what was happening to her parents. And frankly, Charlotte wasn't sure she understood it herself.

She should have cleaned her husband's clock twelve years ago. Aria wasn't even a year old the first time she walked into her husband's studio and caught him kissing one of his models. In the end, she'd told herself fighting with Mother was all the conflict she could stand.

Sticking her head in the sand had created far more trouble. She should've known better than to try to hide her hurt. Daddy and Mother had tried to hide theirs. Her father was a guilt-racked, grieving man and her mother was a vindictive perfectionist who couldn't forgive. Both thought they were keeping their cold war secret, but she'd seen it all. Every blaming look. Every flinch whenever her father reached for her mother. Everything...but her father's desperation to make the hurt go away.

"Why do I have to go to Texas?" Aria's question snapped Charlotte from the sins of the past.

"Because she's your grandmother."

"I haven't seen her in months."

"Well, all of that's going to change."

Aria cast her a suspicious glare. "Why?"

"I promised her."

"Then she better not count on it." Ouch! Hurt bubbled in Aria's accusation.

"Sometimes things happen, Ari. Things you can't control."

"Like Dad?" She shook her head at Charlotte's surprise then rolled her eyes. "Geez, Mom. I can read. Dad's all over the Internet. Everybody at school was talking about...what he did."

The humiliation in her daughter's voice was a gut-punch worse than anything the tabloids had printed. "Is that why you broke the mirrors?" Her daughter's heavy shrug was almost more than Charlotte could handle. "It's all right, you can tell me."

"Caitlyn said he was going to jail..." Aria's voice cracked.

"Your *friend* said that?"

"She's a tool."

"A tool?"

"She was using me."

"For what?"

"She knows how hard it is to book a shoot with Dad."

"So, she thought you could get her scheduled on his calendar?"

Aria nodded. "She wants headshots so she can run away from home, lie about her age, and audition for Broadway." Aria was losing her war with the tears and Charlotte was on the verge of losing her lunch.

She'd been so distracted she'd lost touch with her daughter and her friends. "Was the spray paint her idea?"

Aria's head bobbed slightly. "She said if I didn't do it, she'd tell everyone what an awful person my dad is and that I wouldn't have any friends when she finished."

"I'm so sorry, Ari." Desperate to stand between her daughter and the pain, Charlotte reached for Aria, but her daughter pulled away. Her offer of protection was too late. The damage had been done. While she was taking care of her mother, her daughter had been hurt. If she'd been in DC, where she belonged, she could have spotted this little tool and...and what...put her daughter in a glass cage?

Charlotte released the breath she realized she'd been holding for decades. "I don't know what will happen with your dad, okay?" The admission was glass in her mouth. "The woman wasn't a minor. So, it's not a given that he'll go to jail. We'll talk about what your father...did...later...when..."

Aria crossed her arms and stiffened. "I'm older?"

Charlotte inclined her head toward their driver. "When we have a minute and some privacy."

"I'm thirteen. I know what sexual misconduct means." Aria pointed at the driver making no attempt to hide his interest in their conversation. "Everyone knows."

"Then you know why you're stuck with me."

"I also know that you hate it more than I do."

"That's not true, Ari."

Aria whipped her head toward the window. "Dad needs a lawyer."

"Your Grandmother McCandless has hired him one of the best."

"You?"

"No."

She spun in her seatbelt, her eyes blazing. "But, you're a lawyer."

"I can't represent your father."

"Why not?"

"For one, I don't practice that type of law."

"You got me out of juvi."

"Which, by the way, cost a lot of money and you're going to pay me back."

Her scowl turned hateful. "No wonder Nana ran away." She spun back to the window and growled, "You're awful."

"So everybody says."

****

Other than telling the flight attendant that she'd like a Coke, Aria didn't say another word for the entire flight.

In the silence, memories of her own peer exile erupted from the depths with such force Charlotte reached for a barf bag. She held on tight as her mind dragged her back to the summer after Caroline's death, the summer when none of her friends knew what to say. So, they didn't talk to her at all. But sound carries on the river. She'd lay in her bed with the windows open and listen to their parties upstream.

Bo Tucker was the only one who hadn't treated her like the lonely monster she'd become. She knew what it was to be pushed to the outside and she hated that she'd failed to protect her daughter from that feeling.

"Watch the bags while I get the keys to the rental car." Once Charlotte had their luggage stowed in the trunk and her silent daughter belted in the passenger seat, she called Winnie. "Is she at the ranch?"

"Afraid not." Winnie went on. "But LaVera's flipped on every light at Fossil Ridge and put on the coffee. She said making Sara feel welcome in her own home was the least she could do after I explained to her that she'd falsely accused her dearest friend of selling out."

"Thanks, Winnie."

"Real friends do what they've got to do...I learned that from you, C."

Winnie went on to say that she and Bo had sent searchers in several directions while they personally planned to scout the backroads to Fredericksburg. If they didn't find Sara there, they planned to take Highway 290 East toward Austin in hopes that Mother had somehow remembered the proper highway number.

According to Ira's oldest daughter, whom Winnie had thought to contact on her own, the car didn't have much gas. So, unless they had an active credit card (which none of them did) or cash (which Ira might have had because of his tendency to stash things—like a spare car key all of them knew he had but never thought he'd use) they could all hope that the fugitives hadn't gotten far.

"We'll find her, C," Winnie said. "Try not to worry."

"Too late for that." Charlotte turned into The Reserve's drive and stopped at the gate house. "I'll see if she left any clues in her apartment, then call you when I'm heading your way." She held her license out to the guard who'd detained her the last time. "And Win...thanks. I owe you."

"Never as much as I owe you, friend."

"Mrs. McCandless?" The guard handed her license back. "Miss Jennings is waiting for you in her office."

"Is this a prison?" Aria's assessment brought the guardhouse, wrought-iron fencing, and speed bumps into proper perspective.

"Depends on how you look at it."

"It looks like a prison."

"You're right." Charlotte parked under the covered entrance. "Come on. Let's get your Nana's stuff. She's not coming back here."

Chapter 33

Rest Stop

My heart has finally regained a steadier rhythm, but Ira and Teeny have been so quiet for the last twenty-five miles I'm not sure their hearts are still beating. I wish they'd say something. Blame me for getting them into this mess. Blame is something I understand. Know how to dish it out as well as steel myself against it. Acceptance and blind trust make me as nervous as a gas gauge needle plummeting toward empty. Which is exactly where Trixie's gauge has been steadily heading. With each passing mile, the arrow falls closer and closer to that dreadful E.

I may not remember how to get home, but I know traveling with the windows down and Ira's upgraded air conditioner turned off will only take us so far. We can't even make it back to The Reserve without fuel, even if I remembered how to get back there.

Hot air whistles in my ears. The sound summons memories I no longer have the mental or physical strength to fight off…memories of the night Charlotte was born.

Darkness had done little to lower the heat of that long ago Indian summer. I'd felt the twinges of labor most of the day. Determined to finish my lesson plans in case I couldn't make it to class the next day, I'd waited until the last minute to tell Martin it was time to go to the hospital. I cradled our sleeping Caroline as Martin's old pickup bounced across the cattleguard. The urge to push struck so forcefully I knew we'd never make it to Addisonville. I asked Martin to lower his window so I could breathe. But the night air was hot and sticky and of no use when it came to blowing away the pain.

I don't remember climbing the steps of LaVera's porch or following our neighbor to her bedroom. Despite the whistling wind, I can still hear her cheering me on as I labored to bring Charlotte into the world.

Had I known this pain ripping me and my daughter apart was the beginning of being forever connected—would I have done anything differently?

I listen intently to the whistle of the wind. But the answer is as lost to me as the way home.

Maybe Charlotte's right. Maybe I'm no longer fit to run my life. Maybe it's time for this old fossil to follow Polygon's lead and fly.

I search the reach of the headlight beams for a sign, a landmark, a familiar building. Anything that will jar my memory and direct me to the road that will lead us to some help.

Spirits faltering, I remember the day Caroline decided to run away. By the time Caroline had reached the age of six, it was becoming increasingly evident that her quick temper had to be nipped in the bud, especially her torments of Charlotte. My stern reprimand called for her to be kinder to her little sister. Instead of acquiescing, Caroline promptly announced that she was running away. I wasn't too worried. In fact, I gave her a pillowcase and told her to pack. Brash and bossy as Caroline could be, she hated being alone. She wouldn't go far and she wouldn't be gone long.

I failed on two accounts that day.

Not only did I miscalculate Caroline's powers of persuasion, I completely underestimated Charlotte's undying loyalty. Charlotte was the one who'd been mistreated, and yet, without the slightest hesitation, she heeded her sister's bidding and loaded her bicycle with a pillowcase she'd stuffed with a doll, her piano book, and a peanut butter sandwich she intended to split with Caroline...because Caroline never thought ahead, she'd explained when I asked why she was rummaging around in the pantry.

As they pedaled away from the house, I thought it sweet that Charlotte would follow her older sister off a cliff if Caroline asked.

Had I only known how devastatingly true that would be.

"Sara?" Ira tugs on my arm. "Me and the dogs are going to need to find a gas station and a tree."

"Oh," heat flushes my cheeks. "We'll keep our eyes peeled."

Teeny leans forward. "Rest stop." She pointed to a distant sign. "Two miles."

"Thank you, Jesus," I whisper.

Within minutes, we're pulling into a well-lit, deserted roadside park. The facility is fairly new, or at least that's what I tell myself since I have no recollection of having been here before.

I wheel Trixie into one of the empty spaces in front of a Hill Country stone structure reminiscent of the German-styled buildings in Fredericksburg.

"Fredericksburg!" I shout, elated that something has finally jogged my memory. "That's the name of the town I couldn't remember." I ease the gearshift into park. "We need to head toward Fredericksburg. From there, we can take the back roads south."

"Can we just sit here a minute and look at each other?" Ira acts relieved we've made it this far without a scratch or dent.

"I thought you needed a restroom."

"Oh, yeah." Ira taps a finger to his forehead. "This old brain can't always keep up with my bladder."

Unsure what to do with this information, I look over my shoulder. "Teeny, you need a break?"

Her bow bobs with the nod of her head and she clambers out after Ira and the dogs.

My hip could use a little loosening up so I pull the keys and ease myself out into the predawn quiet that blankets a small playground and a couple of picnic tables. A stainless-steel drinking fountain glimmers under one of the pole lights. All the wind and worrying has left me so parched, I'm willing to break a teacher's number one rule: never drink from the communal fountain.

I take a moment to peek under the towel covering Polygon's cage. The emptiness hurts. I drop the towel and head toward the fountain. A large, plexiglass case captures my attention. A map. A big, red star marks our current location. Doing my best to let my eyes adjust to the bright lighting, I drag my finger along the highway lines in search of Addisonville. "I found it." I say out loud. "We're only seventy-five miles from home."

Pangs of longing shoot through me. I know in that moment I won't ever go back to The Reserve. No matter how this night ends.

I want to get up with the sun. Sweet as Esmerelda is, I hate how she bursts into my room uninvited and throws open the curtains. Much as I've enjoyed Carlos's cuisine, I want to feed my chickens, gather my own eggs, and scramble them with bits of ham. I want to reuse my tea bags until the water no longer turns brown. I want to mow my own grass and smell the clippings and I want...

"Sara?" Ira is standing beside me staring at the map. Goodness and Mercy are sniffing the ground around my feet.

"I found Addisonville." I thump the glass. "Right here. See?"

He inches closer, until his nose is nearly pressed against the map. "Reckon we should write these road numbers down?"

I start to tell him I never forget a number, but after my performance tonight, I know that's no longer true. "Excellent idea, Ira."

"Be right back." He rushes to the car and returns with a notepad. "Can you call them out to me? The print's way too small."

"We should be home by the time the sun comes up." I squint and begin to list the highway numbers, taking extra care to keep them in descending order and making a point to ask Ira to make the additional note of whether we turn right or left.

I call out the last number. "Let's go."

Ira deposits the pad in his shirt pocket. "Better wait on Teeny." He nods toward the restroom. "I think she's still on the can."

About that time Teeny exits the restroom, drying her hands on her skirt.

"Let's get a move on," I say again.

"Don't you need to go?" Ira asks.

"I've got a bladder of steel." Which is only true because I haven't had a drop to drink in hours. For now, my sugar levels seem good enough. They could get a little shaky if I don't get some fluids in me, but if I start drinking, we will have to stop more and if we have to stop more, we have a higher risk of being spotted.

"How's the gas holding up?" Ira asks.

"We're only a few miles from Stonewall."

"Hopefully no one will rat us out if they spot us when we stop."

I shake my head. "Folks who work in those all-night places are too busy watching for riff-raff."

"Hope you're right, because I don't think I could push Trixie more than a couple yards downhill."

"You folks lost?" The strange voice that snuck up behind us makes me jump.

Goodness and Mercy growl and tug at their leash.

I turn to see a middle-aged man with a scruffy beard and tight tee-shirt blocking our exit.

Wishing I had the shotgun I used on the Wooten's dog, I loop my arm through Ira's. "Just taking a break."

"That Caddy yours?"

I squeeze the keys inside my fist. "It is."

"Couldn't help but overhear your concern about gas."

"We hope to fill up in Stonewall." My clipped tone is intended to clear him from our path, but it doesn't work.

He's eyeing us carefully, like maybe he's seen the flashing sign about some missing senior citizens. "Bet she's a gas guzzler."

"We'll be fine." I take hold of Teeny's sleeve with my free arm, but she's rooted to the spot. "Teeny, let's go." Teeny's bow slides with the side to side tilt of her head, but her feet don't move. "Teeny!"

The man eases toward my human chain. "I've got a gas can with a couple of gallons," he points toward a semi idling across the parking lot. "It's not much, but it'll get you to Stonewall."

How had I missed the approach of an eighteen-wheeler? I stop tugging on Teeny's arm. "We don't have cash?" It's a lie. Charlotte had given me a twenty for incidentals. I'd remembered to stick it in my bra, in case of an emergency.

He holds up empty palms. "Free of charge."

"Nothing's ever free." I suddenly realize from whom Caroline had inherited her short fuse and it shames me.

"Lady," the trucker lowers his hands. "I don't know why three seniors are traveling the highways at this time of night, but if you were my relatives, I'd want someone to help you."

While Ira watches the trucker empty his gas can into Trixie's tank, Teeny and I sit in the car listening to Ira jaw on about how hard it is to find a good mechanic these days. Goodness and Mercy are curled up beside me. I'm tapping the wheel and giving Ira the stink-eye, but he can't seem to let the trucker go. I keep checking the rearview for flashing blue lights. I'm about to blow a gasket worrying about the possibility of a highway trooper spotting this shiny blue Caddy sitting under a yard light when I feel a hand on my shoulder.

"I'd sure feel better if you'd follow me to Stonewall, ma'am." The trucker's trusting smile knocks my blood pressure down a notch. "There's a station just off the highway, but it's easy to miss."

I crank the engine. "So many things in life are, young man."

Chapter 34

Life Lessons

Despite our premiere security force, The Reserve is not a prison."
With a wave of her hand, Miss Jennings invited Charlotte and Aria
to take the plush seats in front of her desk. "We lose people all the
time. That's just to be expected."

Charlotte's grip on Aria's shoulders tightened but they both
remained standing. "For five thousand dollars a month, losing my
mother is not what *I* expected." The lawsuit was forming in her
mind. "Not only have you lost my mother, you failed to alert me
when you sent her to the emergency room for a possible hip fracture
or when she suffered the tragic loss of her bird."

Miss Jennings stiffened. "The class was Mrs. Slocum's idea."

"Class?"

"She was teaching a workshop on training birds to talk when her
parrot made his unfortunate escape."

"My mother asked to teach?"

"Yes, and she's really quite good." Miss Jennings offered one of
the stapled packets on the corner of her desk. "She had a syllabus for
everyone, plus a well-planned, age-appropriate, hands-on activity."

Flipping through the lesson plan was like flipping through vivid recollections of rainy weekends curled beside Mother as she read Little House on the Prairie. Never was Mother's affection simply a way to while away the hours. She always had a point and some sort of interactive way to cement the point. Once, after they'd finished their reading, they'd spent the afternoon making bread. Another time they'd churned cream into butter. The day Mother had tried to teach them to quilt, Charlotte stuck her finger with a needle and cried. Mother had been frustrated, but her eyes were never brighter than when she was teaching. To anyone who'd listen...but especially her girls.

Were these past few years of conflict really Mother's way of trying to teach her? To give her hands-on insight into the difficult and degrading aging process? To show her that giving up yard work was more than giving up her independence. It was giving up her dignity. Was Mother's intent to leave her with the most valuable lesson of all: that life is really all we know. It's why we struggle to hang on to it. Good or bad.

Her refusal to learn these lessons well was a guilty knot in Charlotte's stomach. She'd been so stuck on the story—the tragic tale of loss—that she'd missed the application. If something didn't change in her approach to life, one day she too, might find herself totally alone.

Miss Jennings pushed back from her desk. "The hardest part is waiting."

"No, Miss Jennings." Charlotte squeezed her daughter a little closer. "The hardest part is knowing I never should have brought my mother here."

Chapter 35

Road Block

I follow the kind trucker's taillights to Stonewall. He insists on paying to fill Trixie's tank and leads us all the way to Fredericksburg. Ira disagrees with me when I send the trucker on his way, but I don't need help to get to Addisonville. I may not remember to turn off the fire below the kettle, but I can still follow directions. The highway numbers the trucker rattled off match those Ira and I had already copied down.

For better or worse, we're on our own.

If it weren't for Teeny's snoring and the hum of the tires, I could hear my excitement beating like a butterfly trapped in a jar.

It's still too dark to make out landmarks, but the gentle increase of the highway's incline builds my confidence with each passing mile. I loosen my death grip on the wheel and smile.

"We should be home by sunrise."

"Good." If Ira doesn't believe me, he's keeping his doubt to himself.

There won't be a stitch of food fit to eat in my refrigerator. But thanks to the trucker's generosity, I still have the folded twenty in my bra. He wouldn't even allow me to take his name and address so that I could reimburse him once I have access to my checkbook again. His chivalry gives me hope for the next generation.

"We'll stop at the Get-in-Go in Camp Wood and pick up a few things for breakfast," I whisper.

"I could eat a cow...hoof and tail." Ira sounds upbeat, but he's rolling the directions between his palms and squinting at the highway. "Road's kind of lonely without that young trucker."

Admitting that I miss having an eighteen-wheeler go before us like the pillar of fire that led Moses through the wilderness will only worry Ira more.

I scour my brain for a distracting change of subject. "Lauralee told me you have a ranch in Hillsboro. Are your children running it for you?"

"Nah." Ira turns his face toward the window. His shoulders seem to slump a little. "After Oleta passed, they pressured me to move to town. My oldest son gave running the place a try, but when he turned sixty, he and his wife retired and bought an RV. After they hit the road, it was too hard on the others to keep up with the goats and their jobs and families." He rubs his knees. "I sold everything but the mineral rights and divided my estate. When the kids aren't too busy spending their inheritance, they drop in to check on me."

Charlotte has her reasons for sending me off. But getting her hands on more money isn't one of them. Thanks to a good job and that no-good husband of hers, she's flush with more than she can spend. Her hurry to sell the ranch has everything to do with her desire to be rid of the past.

"You miss your ranch?" I ask Ira.

"Me and the girls are looking forward to the smell of country air again." Ira turns to me, his face wet in the light of the dashboard. He strokes his dogs. "Tell me about your Fossil Ridge, Sara."

Next to talking numbers and birds, there's nothing I enjoy more. Besides, what good will it do for Ira and me to hash over how little we see our children and how much that hurts?

I tell him about how Martin and I didn't have a pot to pee in after we married, but we had plenty of muscle and energy. "A friend told us a small ranch was for sale several miles outside of town. We borrowed a car and drove out to see it. The property was overgrown and the abandoned house needed much more than a coat of paint. But we loved the bluff-side view of the river the moment we laid eyes on it. Martin had to drive clear to Leakey to find a banker who'd give us a loan." I leave out the part about my father refusing to help us in any way. "Forty-five years ago, three thousand dollars sounded like a million."

Ira chuckled. "We bought our place for two thousand. I didn't think Oleta and I would live to see it paid off." He bends an ear my way and his genuine interest unleashes a flood dammed up inside me.

I tell Ira about all the years spent patching and repairing everything from shingles to fence posts. I yammer on about how I took a job teaching school to help make ends meet and how, in the process, discovered what God had meant for me to do with my life.

"Lesson plans and tardy slips?" Ira teases.

"That, and seeing young eyes light up as the world opens up."

"You're good at it. It's been a long time since I've seen that moldy group at The Reserve stay awake through an entire presentation."

We laugh, but when our eyes meet, we both grow sober.

"I'm sorry we couldn't bring Polygon with us, Sara."

I shake off tears. "He's flying high." I reach across the seat and take Ira's hand. "He's free."

To keep from crying, I give Ira's hand a quick squeeze, let him go, and tell my new friend more about life on Fossil Ridge. But I don't tell him about the nights Martin and I took a blanket to the river's edge, listened to the water, counted the stars, and made love. I can't forgive Martin for the way he left me, but the way he loved me while he lived is a treasure I'll never share with anyone.

"Sounds like you polished a piece of hill country rock into a jewel." Ira's comment carries me back to the early days of living on the ranch.

"Sweat equity, Martin called it. The majority of the land sits up on a bluff overlooking the Frio. In the summer, when the heat sucks the river down to an ankle-deep trickle, I take our girls to the rocky bed to search for fossils. The bluff sparkles with more stony oysters and sea urchins than the beaches of Yucatan."

"Your girls still at home?"

I jerk my eyes off the road and look at him like he must be joking. "Do I look thirty?"

"You said you *take* your girls to the river."

"Took." One little slip of semantics and I'm suddenly drowning in the memories. "Took my girls." My voice is shaky and I can tell Ira knows there's more to this story. "My oldest has been dead nearly twenty-five years."

He shakes his head sadly. "No parent should ever have to bury a child."

His pity angers me. I don't want his pity. I want an ally. "My youngest lives in Washington. She was my passive child. Rarely expressed herself. A lot like her daddy, holding everything inside. But, unlike him, Charlotte came out of her grief fighting. She rose up with anger and put holes in the walls, went to law school, and now she kicks politicians around just for fun." I can tell by the smile on Ira's face, he thinks I'm kidding. "She plans to sell the ranch and lock me up at The Reserve. She'd deny this ungrateful little scheme if I asked her point blank, but a spade is a spade." I swerve to miss a dead skunk in the road. "At least your kids come to visit once in a while."

"My kids know who they're dealing with. Don't always like stopping their lives to check on me, but they know their momma would be sorely disappointed if they didn't do their duty. I give Oleta all the credit for their attentiveness." He unrolls the paper with our directions. "Are those flashing lights up ahead?"

I yank my gaze back to the road. Two patrol cars straddle the highway about a half mile in the distance. "Road block. Hang on." A hard jerk on the wheel sends us careening onto an unpaved, one-lane back road.

Goodness and Mercy slam into Ira.

Teeny's body slides across the seat and her head hits the glass. "Where are we?" She's rubbing the knot forming on her forehead.

"Taking the scenic route," I chirp. "Faster this way." The Lord is going to strike me dead for all these lies.

Chapter 36

Is it My Fault?

Did you know one in nine people over the age of 65 get dementia?" Aria scrolled through her phone. "Six out of ten of those will wander away from their caregivers." She looked up from the screen. "Approximately 125,000 seniors disappear every year." She slaps the phone face-down in her lap. "Geez, Mom. Why didn't you tell me Nana was sick?"

Charlotte pressed the accelerator on the rental car. "Googling missing seniors is not helping." She pointed to the ditches along the highway. "You're supposed to be looking for a big blue car...an old one."

"I know what I'm looking for."

"How would you know what a '55 Cadillac looks like?"

"Googled it." Aria picked up her phone again. "Just because I can multi-task, doesn't mean you have to bite my head off."

"Sorry." How could she explain that nobody can do two things at once forever and do them both justice? "I'm worried."

"You should be." Aria returned to the article and started to read out loud. "If a senior is not found within twenty-four hours..." she paused, her face white in the dash lights. "They may never be found."

"I know, Ari."

Never to be found was not an option. Here she was, in the middle of the night, driving through the Texas Hill Country like a crazy woman trying to fix her mother's messes when all she wanted was for someone to fix the messes in her life...letting her sister die, her failing marriage, her daughter's rejection. She needed her mother. She'd laugh at the irony if she wasn't so mad at the woman right now she could cry. "If you're going to keep digging up facts, try to find something that might actually be helpful in locating your grandmother?"

"Like what?"

"Like any patterns to their behavior. Where do they tend to go? How far do they usually travel? Anything."

Aria bent over her phone again, her hair a curtain between them. "It says Alzheimer patients don't wander without an actual cause. They're typically going somewhere, looking for something, and don't actually consider themselves lost."

"I know she wanted to go home."

"Then why didn't you take her?"

"Because..." Charlotte stopped the rant dying to roll off her tongue. Aria was just a child. And children didn't deserve to carry adult guilt.

"Because of me, right?"

Charlotte shook her head. "It's complicated, okay?"

"Nana's lost because of me, isn't she?"

"No." Charlotte pounded the wheel. "Nana's lost because she's a stubborn woman who has always refused to accept my help."

"Adults *are* complicated." Aria went back to scrolling through her phone. "Oh no." She held her phone screen toward Charlotte, her eyes huge. "This shrink says that lost seniors don't usually reach out for help. They can't remember how."

Charlotte inhaled and exhaled slowly, mentally examining this pivotal piece of information…a fact she'd failed to acknowledge, let alone assimilate into her dealings with her mother. She'd lost major court cases by overlooking smaller pieces of evidence. She knew better than to assume anything. Why hadn't she done her homework? Taken steps to understand her mother. To protect her from herself. Tattoo her name and contact info on her arm or something. Help her remember the good and be grateful for the possibility that she could forget the bad.

"Mom?" Creeping panic squeezed Aria's tone. "You okay?"

Charlotte nodded. "Mr. Conner's children didn't allow him to keep much gas in the car. I'm hoping they ran out of gas before they got too far."

"What if they didn't?"

"I'm doing the best I can, Ari."

"You don't have to do it all alone, you know? I can help."

Charlotte tore her eyes from the road and let her gratitude land on her daughter. "When did you grow up?"

"While you were either working feverishly or saving Nana from herself in Texas."

"Sorry I missed it. All of it."

"Mom, kids are like seeds. They sprout while no one is looking."

"Oh. My. Goodness. Now I really feel old." She reached for the treble clef hanging around her neck, wishing it could fix her relationship with her daughter as easily as it had helped her with stage fright. "Give me your best ideas, Einstein."

A tug of a smile lifted the corner of Aria's lips. "We need to create a website, get on the local news, make posters...does Nana have any tattoos?"

Charlotte laughed out loud at Ari's uncanny ability to read her mind. "Not that I know of. Why?"

"Without any specific identifying marks, she's just an ordinary, white-haired senior."

Rubbing the treble clef hanging around her neck, Charlotte conjured images of her mother at the piano. Her mother chasing a fox from the henhouse. Her mother putting one foot in front of the other when so many other women would have curled up and died. "There's nothing ordinary about your grandmother."

"I can only go by what I remember."

"We're going to change that." Charlotte reached for her daughter's hand. "I promise."

Aria let her hold on for a brief instant then slowly pulled back. It wasn't complete forgiveness, but it was a start, one that Charlotte would take and strive to initiate with her own mother. She turned her eyes back to the road and Aria buried her nose in her phone.

"It says they'll go until they get stuck...they're especially attracted to water."

Charlotte's breath whooshed from her lungs. She dropped the treble clef. "The river." She pressed the accelerator to the floor and zipped around the car poking along in front of her.

"Whoa, Mom." Aria grabbed the dash. "I know I may not have room to talk about breaking the law, but I think the speed limit's only 55 through here."

"She's headed for the river."

"Where Caroline and Granddaddy died?"

"Yes." Charlotte pressed the accelerator to the floor. "Call Nana's house. Tell LaVera we'll be there in two hours."

Chapter 37

Home at Last

I've quit fighting the panic and have chosen to rely on my mental muscle memory. It's a simple theory. One I employed in my classroom when a child had difficulty recalling math facts for the quiz. My theory relied on the possibility that simply repeating a fact was not enough to forever engrain the fact in the child's head. I tapped into their visual learning with flash cards. Their tactile learning was tackled with hands-on illustrations with actual objects and hours and hours of problems worked at the board and on paper.

Each exercise was designed to dig a trench through my students' young minds. Once the pathway was established, all I had to do was come along and sprinkle in the facts. Little seeds of knowledge.

"Two times two is four," I would say until the answer took root and a permanent connection was made to the fact. Two times two equals four.

Always.

I've pinned my hopes on the possibility that driving the back roads, paths I've taken again and again over the years, works the same way. That somewhere deep inside this fog, my heart knows the way home.

My eyes are growing heavy and I'm plum tuckered out. To Ira's credit, he's fought off his own weariness to keep me awake.

"Looks like the sky is beginning to lighten." He points to the iron trestle of a bridge not ten car lengths ahead. "Recognize anything?"

I blink twice. "That's my river." When we pull into my drive, it'll be hard not to jump out and kiss the ground. "I'm home."

"I knew you could do it, Sara." Ira reaches behind the seat and tenderly nudges Teeny awake. "We're here, Teeny."

The gentle giant rustles in the seat and leans forward. Her bow has slipped to the side and her face has three red indentations from leaning against Polygon's cage. "Not much to look at."

"Wait until you see the sun come up over the Frio." My excitement will not be dampened, not even by the sound of Trixie rattling across the rusty, pony-truss bridge.

Our headlight beams sweep across the metal cowboys who've greeted me for years. Right next to one of my boys is that ugly Future Home of Sparks Resorts sign LaVera had her panties in a wad over.

"I guess you were right about your daughter sellin', Sara," Ira says.

"I am *not* selling." We bounce over the cattle guard. As we round the curve in the lane, I see that light shines from every window in the house.

Home. I'm finally home.

"Someone's expecting you," Ira says.

My heart sinks. Surely Charlotte couldn't have beat me home. But who else would it be? I'm sure Miss Jennings was as duty-bound to call my next of kin as she was to report us to the Texas Highway Patrol.

"Let me do the talking." I grip the wheel as Trixie rumbles to a stop near the sidewalk that leads to my front door.

Before Ira or I can maneuver our stiff limbs from the car, LaVera flies out the front door. "Sara!" She thunders down the steps and pokes her head in Ira's window. "Sara, are you all right?"

"I'm good, LaVera," I say. "No, better than I've been in quite some time."

"Sara, I'm so sorry." LaVera doesn't need long explanations. "Forgive me?"

"Always." And like that, LaVera and I are good. "Charlotte here?"

"On her way." LaVera sticks her head inside the car window. "Who do we have here?"

"New friends," I say.

"Well, your old friend hopes your new friends are hungry." She opens Ira's door. Goodness and Mercy leap from the car. LaVera chuckles. "Your chickens have been off a bit since you've been gone, but I managed to gather enough eggs to make a good-sized scramble."

"Sounds good. I'm starving." Ira clambers out, stretches then extends his hand toward LaVera. "Ira Conner."

LaVera gives his hand a firm shake. "LaVera Tucker." She nods toward Teeny. "And she is?"

"Teeny McIlroy." Ira slides his seat forward and offers his hand to Teeny. He hauls her out of the back seat. "She's a woman of few words."

"Good thing," LaVera says. "I can talk enough for the both of us."

Everyone has a much-needed laugh and I'm reminded again about the things a person never misses until they're gone.

I fish my cane from the seat and hobble around the hood. LaVera meets me halfway and wraps me in a big hug. "Charlotte wanted me to call the minute you showed up, but I can find a few things to do in the kitchen if you need a moment."

"She comin' to take me back to Austin?"

"She's traveled all night because she's scared half out of her mind."

"That I'll do something crazy?"

"I think you've proved that's possible." LaVera reached up and smoothed my wind-blown hair. "Girl, you're a hot mess." She takes my hand. "Let's get you freshened up, spritz you with some of that perfume you love, and get your new friends settled in, okay?"

"Thank you, LaVera."

"Thanks for finding your way home."

"I'm not going back to Austin, LaVera."

"How about we get a cup of tea and a biscuit in you before you make any rash decisions."

Hand in hand, LaVera and I lead Ira and Teeny into my house. The faint scent of Martin's pipe tobacco envelops me the second I walk through the door.

"Restroom is down the hall on your left," LaVera tells Ira and Teeny. "Bedrooms are upstairs. Leave your bags here and I'll help you tote them up after breakfast." LaVera heads toward the kitchen. "I know y'all must be plumb tuckered out."

I should feel tired, but I don't. In fact, I feel stronger than I've felt in years. "I promised Ira and Teeny they could see the sun come up over the river." I lead them to the back porch.

The pinking sky frames the rugged countryside in a rosy glow. "The river is that way. Hear it?"

Teeny nods enthusiastically.

Ira smiles. "Can smell the water from here."

"The sun will come up over that ridge. When it hits the water, it's like the fossils come to life."

My rooster crows and a ray of golden light breaks through a bank of gray clouds. The windmill blades creak with the rising of a slight breeze.

"Any second the birds will come to life." As if the feathered creatures heard my cue, their morning chatter floats from the gnarled branches of the live oaks in my yard.

Ira inhales a long, satisfied breath. "Glorious."

"Breakfast," LaVera calls from behind the screen door. "Let these biscuits get cold and you'll be able to use them as hockey pucks."

We shuffle back inside and sit at the table snuggled into my bay window. LaVera has outdone herself. She's rummaged around and found my best china. It's the dainty floral set I got a piece at a time with every fill-up at her son's gas station, but still my best. Steam rises from mound of bacon and a pile of scrambled eggs. Hard, brown biscuits are artfully arranged into a stack on a platter.

Friends fill my table. It's been a long time since it's been anyone but me at this table.

Too long.

LaVera keeps the coffee and tea coming. Nothing like fresh eggs and they melt in my mouth. Ira, Teeny, and the dogs are also eating like they haven't eaten in weeks. But it's more than a physical hunger we're satisfying. It's a deep emptiness that each of us has had and we're sucking in the country air and camaraderie like escapees from a prisoner of war camp.

Ira is the first to wipe his chin and push back from the table.

"LaVera," Ira pats his belly. "Mr. Tucker is a mighty lucky man."

"He was," LaVera says. "He just didn't know it."

Realizing he's just stepped into something, but not sure what, Ira switches direction. "I'm needing a bit of shut-eye."

Chewing a big bite of biscuit, Teeny nods agreement.

"Would you mind showing them to the spare rooms, LaVera? I don't think I'm quite ready to tackle the stairs."

"Happy to." LaVera sets the coffee pot on the stove. "I brought some of my special soaps and lotions. Y'all just help yourself."

"Come on, girls." Ira's call sends Goodness and Mercy lumbering after him.

Stairs and knees creak as the three of them trudge to the girls' old rooms. I'm left to soak in the solitude of my kitchen and the view of my river. Sunlight dances on the fossils that the lower water level has exposed along the bluff. I sip my tea and let the peace of this moment wash over me.

My gaze wanders to the giant live oak and the small family cemetery it guards. Swallowing a lump, I yank my attention back inside and let myself finally look at the empty stand where Polygon's cage used to hang. I asked Ira to leave it on the porch, saying I'd like to clean it good. Truth is, bringing that empty reminder into the house is something I'm not quite ready to do.

I hear LaVera pulling shades, telling my guests where they could find clean towels, and that they don't need to set an alarm. She'll call them when lunch is ready. Doors close, then LaVera tromps down the stairs and I brace myself for the conversation I've been dreading.

She huffs into the kitchen carrying an armload of bedding. "You know we need to call Charlotte, right?" She plops the load onto the counter.

"I do."

"She's flown through the night, then rented a car and is frantically searching the highways and byways for you now." LaVera pulls out a chair and joins me at the table. "According to Winnie, Charlotte's worried sick."

"She thinks I'm crazy."

"If breakin' out of a nursing home doesn't prove it, I don't know what would."

"Actions have consequences." I swirl the dregs of my tea. "Time I faced up to mine. I knew this little shenanigan would give my daughter the nail she needed to seal my coffin."

"Why'd you do it then?" LaVera asks. "You were on the mend. Probably could have talked her into springing you parole-free in a few weeks."

Suddenly very weary, I closed my eyes. Lauralee's face appeared on the back of my lids.

I open my eyes and smile at LaVera. "Life is short, my friend." I take her hand and try to sound upbeat. "Go ahead and call

Charlotte." I push up from the chair.

"Where are you goin'?"

"There's something I've got to do."

Chapter 38

Too Late

Charlotte peered through the iron beams of the bridge that forded the span of the Frio. Although LaVera had assured her that Mother was fine, tired but no worse for the wear, she half-expected to see a blue Cadillac floating downstream.

But she couldn't shake the feeling that something bad was about to happen. Especially when she pulled up to the old farmhouse and Winnie's VW, Tucker's Gas & Tire tow truck, and Raymond's van were among the two sheriffs' vehicles parked alongside an old blue Cadillac.

She and Aria leapt from the car and bounded up the front porch steps. "Mother!" Charlotte screamed as she burst through the door. "Mother!"

"Charlotte?" LaVera rushed to the hall, drying her hands on a kitchen towel. "You made good time."

"Where is she?"

"Calm down." LaVera noticed Aria. "Oh, my, pretty girl. Haven't you grown?"

"LaVera, I need to see her."

"She's at the river." Winnie rushed to her. "You okay, C.?"

"No, I'm half out of my mind." Charlotte grabbed Winnie's shoulder. "Why'd you let her go to the river?"

Bo stepped in. "Miss Sara said she had something she had to do before she'd let you take her away."

Fear pounded Charlotte's chest. "Stay here, Ari."

"I'm going with you," Aria argued.

"No, you're not." She wasn't about to put her daughter in the position of seeing something that would give her nightmares for the rest of her life. "LaVera, would you mind fixing Aria something to eat?"

"Of course not, but the sheriff and his deputy are having coffee and waiting to talk to you."

"They've got to make a report and I'm trying to convince them there isn't anything to report, right?" Winnie said. "Miss Sara was out with friends. No law against that, right?"

"Thanks, Win." Charlotte dropped her keys into her purse. "Keep them busy."

"I can come with you," Bo offered.

"No." Charlotte said emphatically. "I've got to do this alone."

"Mom—" Aria said.

"LaVera, can I ask you to help me out one more time?" Charlotte pleaded.

"Come with me, sweetheart." The old woman draped a

protective arm around Aria's shoulders. "There's still a couple of eggs in the fridge."

"But, Mom—"

"No." Charlotte cupped Aria's worried face in her hands. "I love you." She kissed her daughter's forehead and flew out the front door.

She raced around the house and sprinted toward the giant live oak that hung over the bluff and prayed she was not too late.

Chapter 39

Time to Fly

I'm perched on the edge of the river bluff. The toes of my grass-stained slippers hang over the crystal waters swirling thirty feet below. Our family swimming hole is so clear I can see the fossils that line the rocky river bottom. For centuries, the Frio has behaved much like Raymond Leck, following the path of least resistance and ambling along on its journey through life.

In the same way my unexpected confrontation waylaid Raymond, this lazy river struggles to break free of the barn-sized fissure beneath my bluff. The deep hole is a double-edged sword. Wonderful for strong, confident swimmers. Deadly for anyone who is not. That's how creatures from long ago became part of the fossil record. They couldn't hold on until the rains upstream infused the current with enough force to set them free.

I've been swirling in this deep eddy, going nowhere, for far too long. Time to cut bait or sink into the fossil record.

"Come on, Sara." The voice calling to me from the river sends a familiar tingle through my arthritic limbs.

I'm glad to know that I can still hear him here. "Martin?"

"Jump, Sara. I'll not let you drown. I promise."

I crouch forward, clutching my secret close to my breasts. "I'm coming."

"Mother! Stop!" Charlotte skids to a stop a few feet behind me, out of breath and from the high pitch of her voice, terrified. "Can you step away from the edge, please?"

Bracing for a lecture, I rise slowly but keep my back to my daughter and my focus on the water. "You sound tired, Charlotte Ann."

"That's what happens when a person spends the night flying across the country to track down her mother."

I turn my head and see that her clothes are wrinkled, her mascara is smeared, and her hair could use a comb. Her expression tells me emotions waver between love and compassion to anger and terror for what I've put her through. "I'm sorry I caused you worry."

"Worry? Mother, your continual refusal to take my advice could have cost not only your life, but the life of those two seniors you had in that car."

"No one was hurt."

"Ira's family is worried sick. We'll be lucky if they don't sue us."

"I came home to put an end to your worries. Once and for all."

"No, Mother. Don't." Charlotte's palms fly up in surrender. "You still have reasons to live. Aria needs you. I need you." Her head is shaking slightly as she inches closer. "I'm the one who should be apologizing. The Reserve was a bad choice. You tried to tell me what you needed, but I didn't hear you."

I clutch what I'm holding tighter to my chest. "I've been obstinate to the point of endangering not only myself but others. I've refused to accept life for what it is." The leather in my hands is old and cracked. "The bad has seemed so very bad, but when I really sift through the memories, there's also been a whole lot of good." I think about what Lauralee would say at this particular moment and find some much-needed courage. "Too many wasted days have tumbled into too many wasted years."

"Mother—"

"Let me finish." I wait until Charlotte agrees with a nod. "Anger and bitterness is not the legacy I want to leave you. For my final lesson, I want to teach you how to age well, but more importantly how to live well."

"Good." Hope flickers in Charlotte's eyes. "But remember, Mother, I'm a slow learner. It could take several years for you to pound these points through my thick skull." She inches closer, slowly extends her hand, and motions me forward. "Let's go back to the house and talk about where to start."

"We start here."

Her breath catches and the color drains from her face. "Not here, Mother."

"It must be here, Charlotte."

"Could you at least step away from the edge? I'm afraid you're going to fall like..."

Her unfinished sentence is a curtain that hangs between us, a curtain I'm determined to bring down, no matter how painful. "Your father?"

"Yes."

"Martin didn't fall, Charlotte."

"What do you mean?" Charlotte dares to inch closer, which is big since she hasn't been back to the river since we buried her father in the little family plot on the other side of this giant live oak. "Are you saying someone pushed him?"

"Not physically." I turn completely to face her, Martin's boots clutched to my chest.

Charlotte's mouth falls open as her gaze rakes over me. "Are those Daddy's Red Wings?"

"Yes."

"How did you get them? I thought the river pulled them from his feet."

"I found them before I found him." I point to the base of the live oak. "Here. Tucked beneath the broken rope that dangled from this tree." I look up. All that remains of the tire swing is a frayed rope loop around the branch that the bark has nearly grown over.

"Are you saying he took off his shoes and...jumped?"

"A year to the day after Caroline died."

"And you knew he was going to do this?"

I shake my head. "When he didn't come in for supper, I came looking for him. I found his boots and then I found him floating face down in the swimming hole. I called the sheriff and then I called you."

"Why didn't you tell me?"

"You deserved to keep your father on a pedestal. He deserved a pedestal."

"But you didn't tell me about the boots."

"You were already so eaten up with guilt over Caroline, I couldn't let you add your father's suicide to shoulders."

"I'm a big girl, Mother."

"I'm counting on it." I clutch the boots tighter. "Now that I've told you he jumped, I need to tell you one more thing."

Charlotte flinches, but from the rise of her chin, she's not backing down. "I'm tired of the secrets."

Hope tugs at the frayed corners of my heart. "Shortly after we married, your father ordered grapevine cuttings from Italy. He said he'd done his research and the hill country soil was perfect for vineyards. He was going to be the first in Texas to make fine wine. But that year, we had a late frost and the vines were too new to survive. We lost the vines and every penny we'd saved for this investment. We would have lost the ranch if Wilma Rayburn hadn't hired me to teach third grade."

Charlotte's face softens. "No wonder you can't leave this place."

I hear her heart finally softening toward me, which makes confessing what I must say all that much harder. But Charlotte deserves the truth and I must tell it while the details are still clear in my mind. "My unwillingness to let go of this ranch...killed your father."

"I don't understand, Mother."

"My desire to stay here reminded your father of his failure every single day. Martin had so wanted to prove to my father that he was going to amount to something, but when his wife had to go to work to put bread on the table, he was humiliated. Embarrassed. Somehow, your grandfather found out about our financial struggles and Martin didn't feel he could show his face in town. He became so disappointed in himself, he started to drink. A lot. So much, he couldn't look for a job let alone keep one. But in those rare moments when Martin was sober, he was a good father and the man I'd fell in love with. I wanted his big plans to sell photos to magazines or bowls and furniture crafted from downed trees to tourists to succeed. We built the barn and filled it with tools for his workshop. But none of his projects ever made a dime." I brush the image of him sitting on the porch smoking his pipe and staring at the river from my mind.

"After Caroline died and you left for college, he didn't have any reason to hide his disappointment or his demons anymore." I pull a bottle from the pocket of my robe. "I found this empty Jim Beam bottle stuck inside one of his boots." I could see her questions swirling into denial.

"You're making this up. I never saw daddy drink."

"He was drunk the day Caroline died." Releasing the secret that's been festering inside me all these years is like opening a boil. It hurts worse than sticking a knife in my heart, but I can't stop until all the pus is pushed out. "It's why he couldn't help you get the rope untangled. It's also why he couldn't forgive himself."

Charlotte's eyes are darting from her father's grave to the river as she struggles to grasp this horrific information. Her ability to bury things deep is more like me than I've realized. Her dreams. Her love for her father. Her memories of that day. If I can't help her bring them to the surface, they'll drag her down and bury her in the fossil record.

I step from the ledge and come to stand between her and the river. "Charlotte Ann." Confusion glazes her eyes. I set Martin's boots on the ground and take her by the shoulders. "Listen to me, Charlotte Ann. You have always been stronger than your sister."

Charlotte shakes her head, mulling what I've said. "No."

"Yes." I say. "The stronger student and the stronger swimmer." I grip her a little tighter and continue. "Caroline gave up that day. You never did. You never will. It's why you've stayed married to that no-good son-of-a-gun. It's why you call to check on *me* every Monday morning. It's why I know your daughter is going to be okay. You'll never give up on Aria." I swallow. "We're peas from the same pod. Your father gave up on us a long time before the day he let your sister drown. And though I've let our anger push us apart, I've never given up on us being family and I never will."

"Oh, Momma." Charlotte's eyes fill with tears. "I was so afraid you were going to leave me, too."

Suddenly, out of nowhere, there she is. My Charlotte Ann. The little girl I used to hold in my arms, the one who never had a moment of colic or kept me awake at night worrying about what she was doing with a boy in the backseat of a car. The daughter who used to beg me to play the piano or traipse along the riverbed in search of fossils. The eager student I taught to tie her shoe, to count to one hundred, and how to read before she started school. The teenager who dreamed of teaching other children to love music. The girl who used to throw her arms around my neck and tell me she would never leave home.

I've been waiting twenty-four years for her to return and now, here she is. Maybe she's been here all along. It was me who disappeared below the murky waters of grief.

Something powerful, a love I thought long dead, awakens. It pushes me toward the surface. My head bursts through the watery memories. I gasp for air, and suck in my first deep breath in years.

The relief is sweet and clear as the river that cuts through my land.

"I'll have to leave you one day, my love." I say, staring deep into her eyes. "But not just yet." My heart feels too big for my chest. "I came here to toss these boots as far as I can throw them. I'm going to free us both. Once and for all."

"I'm so sorry, Momma. For everything." Charlotte's phone rings. She glances but doesn't answer. "It's Ari."

"Charlotte Ann." My fingers dig into her shoulder. I don't want her to miss a word of what I must say…should have said years ago. "What happened to your sister was not your fault. It's just the painful way life went…for all of us." I inhale the clean tang of river air. "But, it *is* my fault if I continue to let the pain come between us. I'm the one who is sorry."

I'd hoped for reluctant forgiveness, but when my daughter falls into my arms and we wrap each other tight, I know it is love, with no strings attached, that binds us.

We stand there, in the dappled sunlight of the live oak, holding on to the only other living soul in the world who understands what the other has lost. Our tears flow hard and fast as the river in spring. Birds flit in the branches overhead. I hear the laughter of two sisters as their sweet father pushes an old tire swing and I smile.

I don't know how long Charlotte and I remain entwined. I want to hold my baby forever, except my legs are about to give out.

"I'm ready to make it up to you," I whisper in her ear.

She pushes away slightly, her face confused. "What do you mean, Momma?"

"I got lost tonight, Charlotte Ann."

"I know."

"It was only by the grace of God and the kindness of a stranger that I made it back to Fossil Ridge. I need help...your help. I don't want you to continue having to choose between me or your family or your job. I'm ready to come to Washington."

"Mom!" Aria's voice cuts through the sounds of our blubbering, water splashing over rocks, and birds calling. "Mom!" she rushes our huddle, cell phone in her hand and screaming, "Geez, Mom, you scared me to death. Why didn't you answer your phone? I thought Nana was dead or something."

Charlotte and I laugh, a true hearty, free laugh.

"Not yet, kiddo." I can't contain my joy at Charlotte's willingness to bring her daughter and open my arms wide. "What a wonderful surprise!"

"Nana!" Aria throws herself at me and I hang on to the years I let slip past.

"Nana's going to be around us and us around her for a long time," Charlotte adds. "What would you say to us moving to Fossil Ridge?"

My mouth falls open. "What? But Charlotte, I—"

Aria pulls free of my hug and turns her unbelieving eyes on her mother. "Live with Nana?"

"Yes," Charlotte says.

"Dad too?"

Charlotte's face sobers. "No, Ari."

My granddaughter looks so much like a young Charlotte as she mulls over what her mother is saying. "Can we change my last name to Slocum?"

"No," Charlotte says. "No more secrets, from each other, or the world."

"Do I still have to write that paper for the principal?"

"Yes." Charlotte smiles. "But I'll mail it with my check."

Aria's face brightens. "Can we get a horse?"

"Maybe," Charlotte says.

"Absolutely," I say at the same time.

"We'll see," Charlotte reclaims her maternal authority, but not the sharp edge she's worn for years. She opens her arms. "Come here, you two."

Our joint hug pulls my beautiful granddaughter between me and Charlotte like ham in a generational sandwich. I soak in the scent of my girls and the touch of their arms around my shoulders.

Like Lauralee said, life is a series of short stories. I may not be able to choose the moment of my end, but I can choose how my story ends...with my sins and secrets forgiven, my sense of humor restored, and my family healed. In the end, I want to teach my greatest lesson of all...how to die well. Until then, I intend to give to the people I love until I have nothing left to give.

I'm lost in the glory of this group hug, until Aria's squirming indicates she can't breathe.

Charlotte and I ease up and Aria wiggles free.

Aria looks at us like this newfound togetherness means I'm not the only one who's lost her mind. I start to clarify, to say that I have the market cornered on dementia, but then she grins and says, "Nana, did you really bust out of an old folk's home and steal a car?"

"Technically, your grandmother borrowed a car," Charlotte explains.

"But the State police were looking for her, right?" Aria's face is Charlotte's at thirteen. Naïve. Smart. Full of life. "So, technically, Nana's been in trouble with the law."

"Technically," Charlotte concedes.

"So, technically, Mom, you can't say a thing about my criminal record now that Nana has one."

From the smirk on Charlotte's face, she's tossing this teachable moment squarely into my lap. "I'll let you handle this one, Momma."

A bigger love swells inside me, pushing aside the last of my horrible fears of aging. To my surprise, there's suddenly all of this room for what could possibly be. What my final years might look like if I could have Charlotte and Aria around.

Close.

Family taking care of family.

I take a deep breath and put a firm hand on Ari's shoulder. "I can see I've got a few holes to plug in your education, young lady."

TO MY READERS:

Thanks so much for joining Sara and Charlotte on the first leg of their life journey. I hope you laughed and cried as they struggled to find each other again.

Remember **reviews** help an author so much. When readers take the time to leave an honest review, it causes the digital book fairies to give this book the love and attention it needs to be discovered by others. Please share your love of this story and **leave a review** on the retailer site where you purchased your copy. Thanks.

Did you know I have another book in this series?

FINALLY FREE lets you come along when Charlotte and Aria move back to the Fossil Ridge Ranch to care for Sara. While the idea is good in theory, in practice merging the lives of these three strong-willed women will take a whole lot of unconditional love and a lot of laughter as Sara slips further into dementia.

Sign up for my newsletter so you won't miss a single new release in this series or any of my other works. PLUS, you'll receive a bonus gift from my Mt. Hope Southern Adventures series: www.lynnegentry.com

In the meantime, here's a sneak peek at the next book:

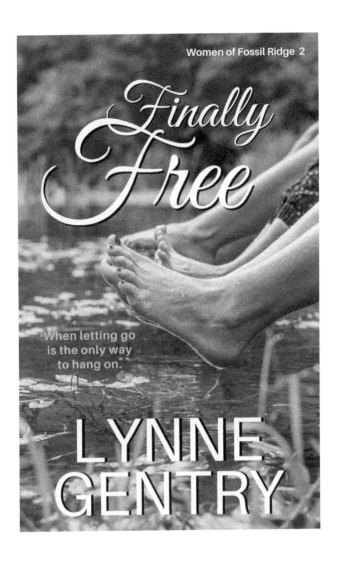

FINALLY FREE EXCERPT

CHARLOTTE COMES HOME

"Family is not always flesh and blood, Charlotte Ann." My mother clutches the porch railing and glares at the senior citizen van lumbering up the lane. "Ira and Teeny belong here...on the Fossil Ridge...with us."

I cast a weary glance at the small U-Haul trailer still hitched to my rental car. Maybe it was a mistake to press a pillow to the face of my dying marriage, pull my daughter away from her friends, and flush my financial stability down the toilet to move home. I wish doing the right thing didn't give me such heartburn. Like it or not, Momma's recent accident and subsequent escape from an assisted living facility proves she can no longer fare for herself. There is no one else to assume her full-time care. I'm it.

This is not the first time I've completely remodeled my life to do right by my mother, to somehow make it up to her for failing to save my sister. My old college roommate and long-time friend Winnie— at least I think we're still friends—says I'm a glutton for punishment. She also says there's really not a sacrifice big enough to make up for not drowning that day.

Winnie's opinions aside, I moved home for three reasons. One, my daughter deserves a shot at a normal family, if the Slocum women can ever be *that* again. And two...

"Charlotte Ann, I want them to stay," Momma repeats.

I can't allow Momma to pile a couple of extra geriatrics on my plate. The added weight would bury the needs of my thirteen-year-old. I'm not shortchanging Aria again. Navigating my mother's descent into dependence and my daughter's ascent toward independence will take everything I've got. I have to draw the line at taking on senile strangers.

And two, I tell myself as I mentally review my list, taking care of my aging mother is the right thing to do.

"Momma," my exhausted sigh pushes out the reprimand I've been holding back for two days. "We've talked about this...several times." Guilt immediately swamps me. Condescension is exactly the opposite of what my mother needs. "The director at The Reserve agreed to let Teeny and Ira *visit* here for a few days, but they can't stay."

"I haven't forgotten what it takes to run a household, Charlotte." Momma shakes her pointer finger at me like the wooden ruler she once used to control her students. "I'm simply asking you to look beyond how this affects you and help my friends."

I'm pleased that my mother is finally asking for my help, but the implication that I've *never* done anything for her before nicks my resolve to do the right thing. "Momma, do you realize that I left a very lucrative career on Capitol Hill, pulled my thirteen-year-old away from her school and friends, and drove a U-Haul half-way across the country so that *you* wouldn't have to spend your last days away from your ranch?"

"My friends shouldn't be punished. I'm the one who planned the entire prison break. I won't let you send them back."

Momma's determined expression reminds me of the disapproval she expressed on my wedding day. "Marrying James McCandless is a mistake," she'd said right before she reluctantly dropped the veil over my face in the stuffy little nursery of the Addisonville First Baptist Church and marched out.

It's been nearly fifteen years since I walked myself down the aisle. Less than a year after the exotic honeymoon my mother-in-law paid for, I caught James and a beautiful woman model in X-rated affection. Momma was right. James McCandless was a mistake. One of many. Making up for my mistakes is the *third* reason I've circled back to this ranch.

I turn and gently clasp my mother's shoulders. "Momma, we got lucky this time. Teeny doesn't have any family left to press charges against you, and Ira's threatened to disinherit his kids if they even think about taking legal action."

"Geez, Mom." Aria sits wedged between Ira and Teeny on the porch swing. "They're sitting right here." She strokes the Siamese cat curled in her arms. "Nana's friends are old, not deaf." Her hostile stare pushes me deeper into what's fast becoming a very lonely corner.

No matter what I do, it's not going to be right for someone. I'm destined to be the bad guy. "Everyone needs to understand the seriousness of this situation." I'm the only one who blinks. "Leaving your assisted living center...in the middle of the night...in a stolen car was...a dangerous thing to do. You're all very fortunate that you eventually found your way here and that no one was hurt." There I go with the reprimands again and, as usual they fall harder on everyone than I intended.

Ira pulls his little lap dogs close to his chest. "How can anyone claim that I stole my own car?"

"When my mother drove your Cadillac off the premises, it was considered stolen," I explain...again.

"Sara only drove because I can't see good no more," Ira points to his thick glasses. "Heck, I gave her the keys and got in...of my own free will."

"And that's the only reason Momma's not in jail." Bless Ira's bald head, the fact that he no longer has a driver's license is obviously a sore spot so I try a different angle. "Ira, your children let you keep your car at The Reserve only—"

"To keep me busy." Ira sets his dogs at his feet then drags a palm over his shiny head. "Tinkering on an old car ain't the same as nurturing the land or watching things grow." His rheumy gaze lights on my mother. "Helping this fine woman fix a few things around here these last few days has been more fun than polishing my whole fleet of antique cars."

"Fun." Teeny's voice is rusty from lack of use. According to Momma, this Yankee wearing a huge pink hairbow on the side of her snowy-white head has become a chatterbox since Momma planted her in Hill Country soil.

"Mom," Aria deposits her cat into Teeny's arms and leaps from the swing. "Nana's right, why can't you pull one of your fancy, lawyer tricks? Become their legal guardian or something?"

My jaws clench at how quickly Aria's loyalty has landed squarely with my mother. Shoring up either relationship is going to be harder than I thought. "How do you know about legal guardianship?"

Aria holds up her phone. "I Googled it."

"Have you Googled how Texas frowns on lawyers practicing law who are not licensed in their fair state?"

"I did." She swipes her screen. "Here's the short version: Until you pass the Texas bar exam, you can get another lawyer to vouch for you." Aria dramatically waves her musically-gifted fingers in the direction of Momma's fellow escapees. "You've got to do something to make money. While you're getting your Texas license, Ira can pay you to live here and to represent him. Right, Ira?"

"I can," he says.

"Ari, let me worry about our finances, okay?"

My daughter's eyes blaze with the same stubborn streak I've seen in the mirror. "If *these* people are part of Nana's family, doesn't that make them part of *our* family?"

"We'll visit Nana's *friends* often." I land hard on the differentiation.

Aria jams her hands on her hips. "How often?"

"As often as we can, okay?"

"More than we used to visit Nana?"

The Reserve's shiny-white-people-mover comes to a stop in front of the porch, but four sets of pleading eyes stay glued on me, waiting for my answer. "I don't know, Ari. There's no set plan. We're going to have to make this up as we go along."

"Teeny and Ira won't be any trouble." Aria's tears are a tow truck wench on my heart. "Nana and I will do everything. You won't even know they're here."

This child has always had a special attachment to her Nana, but her willingness to hatch a secret plan with her grandmother proves that it's grown even stronger in just the few days that we've been here. No question about it, Aria has always brought out the best in my mother—the softer side—the side that I remember but haven't felt or experienced since my older sister Caroline died.

I want my daughter to know *that* woman...the one I lost.

But until this very moment, I hadn't considered the emotional blow my mother's inevitable passing will have on my daughter. I was eighteen when I lost my sister. I know the damage of tragic loss at a young age. Allowing Aria to attach herself to my mother's elderly friends sets my little girl up for two extra heartaches.

The driver pokes his head from the van. "Morning. This the Slocum residence?"

"It is," I turn, smile, and chirp like we're all so excited to see him that we've baked a cake. "I'm Charlotte McCandless."

He steps from the folding door dressed in blue scrubs. "I'm the nurse sent to pick up two wayward Reserve residents."

I don't know why, but the term *wayward* doesn't set well with me. "You'll be transporting Ira Conner and Teeny McElroy. They're lovely people."

"Are they packed and ready?" he asks like that's all he cares about.

"Yes," I say.

"No, they're not." Aria snaps, then rapidly corrects herself after I shoot her a confused scowl. "Ready to go, I mean."

The driver's conflicted gaze jumps between me and my daughter. "Why don't I get my clipboard...give everyone a minute to say their goodbyes?"

"That would be great," I smile despite the visual daggers being plunged into my back.

His gaze slides toward my mother. "I have a few papers for you to sign, Mrs. Slocum."

Momma crosses her arms and presses her lips into a thin, defiant line.

"She's not signing anything!" Aria shouts.

"Ari!" While the nurse slips back inside the van, I take my daughter aside. "Listen to me." I assume the exact same parental clasp of the shoulders I'd just taken with my mother. "There's twenty minutes of dusty road between the Fossil Ridge Ranch and the nearest milk and bread. What do you think would happen if Ira or Teeny needed emergency medical care?"

Aria rolls her eyes at me as if I'd left all of my brain cells in DC. "We'd do the same thing for them we'd do for Nana. We'd call an ambulance."

"Help could take too long to get here."

"If it's so dangerous, why are we letting Nana live out here?"

"It's her home." I shake off Aria's belligerent glare. "Honey, Ira and Teeny deserve to be in a home where qualified professionals can look after them and get to them immediately."

Momma steps between me and Aria. "Then you might as well send me back, too."

From the corner of my eye, I see the well-built nurse making his way up the sidewalk. Provoking my mother in front of a muscled, medical professional probably isn't the wisest choice, but for Aria's sake I can't let Momma's ridiculous demand go unchallenged.

"What do you mean send *you* back?" At the strain in my voice, the nurse stops in his tracks. I don't care if this stranger thinks I'm the one who needs a seat on the senile bus, this has to be said. And I'm going to keep saying it until my mother finally hears me, no matter how long I've put off changing from daughter to caretaker. "We're trying to be a family here. Not a retirement village. I can't raise my daughter, take care of you, and babysit two failing geriatrics."

Momma sets her shoulders. Her don't-mess-with-me stare pins me to a porch pillar. "I used to manage twenty-five third graders with varying family lives, IQs, and behavioral issues. And I did it all by myself. I'm more than capable of taking care of two wonderful friends." My mother marches over to the swing and plops down between Ira and Teeny. "Friends are the family you choose, Charlotte Ann." She hooks one arm around Teeny and the other around Ira. "We're a package deal. Take us or leave us."

"Don't tempt me, Momma."

AUTHOR'S NOTE

Thank you for taking this journey to Fossil Ridge with me. While this story is completely fiction, you may be wondering why I chose to tackle the subject of caring for elderly parents.

Twelve years ago, my mother was diagnosed with an aggressive form of breast cancer. She was a brilliant woman who'd spent the majority of her career in the legal field as a very sought-after court reporter. But as her disease progressed, her physical and mental health slowly declined. The woman I knew, the one who could add columns of numbers in her head and spell medical terms longer than her arm, slowly lost the ability to balance her checkbook or manage her meds. It soon became evident that us kids would have to step in and help Dad manage her care. Unlike a lot of caregivers, I was fortunate. I have two sisters and a brother. All of us agreed to give one week a month to come "take care of Mom." But I lived 8 hours away. Although I had easy access to a major airport, Mom did not. If I flew, I had to rent a car and drive almost two hours. So, most of the time, I made the long drive alone. Added to the strain of doing my part for Mom, I had a husband, a drama ministry, and two teenagers at home to manage.

For two years, I juggled Mom's care and my family. It was the most wonderful thing I've ever been privileged to do. It was also stressful, exhausting, and one of the saddest times of my life.

When Mom felt good, we'd reminisce about old times, or I'd ask questions about her childhood, and I did my best to collect her knowledge of our family tree. As cancer invaded her brain, her thinking became more like that of someone with Alzheimer's. She had little notebooks everywhere with jottings that made no sense. One day she drove her motorized wheelchair to the curb, slid into her old Lincoln, left her scooter on the side of the road, and drove herself to Walmart. When she got to the store, she realized that without help, she couldn't get to the motorized cart she needed to navigate Walmart. She sat in the Walmart parking lot for thirty minutes, had a good cry, then turned around and drove home. Fortunately, her scooter was right where she left it.

To keep from crying about Mom's deterioration, I learned to laugh. Humor became my key to surviving the horrible process of watching pieces chip off of the person I'd always thought was invincible.

I learned a lot about how I wanted to die by watching Mom deal her impending death. Most importantly, I gained a deeper appreciation for each day and the importance of faith and family.

While I counted the extra time with Mom as a blessing, I hated every minute I was away from my own family. My teenage children were adjusting to a new home, new school, and trying to make new friends. The stress of carting them to all of their activities fell to my husband. Every time I missed a game or special program, I was swamped with guilt.

When I was with Mom, I felt like I was failing my kids. And when I was with my family, I worried that something about Mom's care would fall through the cracks.

While writing this story, I realized this dilemma is not unique to me. Millions of you are currently sacrificing your time, money, and efforts to care for an aging parent. My prayer is that you will find strength to manage the hard work of dividing your time. That you will experience love on the deepest level when you give to another whether they gave to you or not. That by your loving actions you will teach your children what it means to love, even when it's hard. That you'll find something to laugh about every day. And that, in the end, you'll forgive yourself for feeling like you failed everyone who had you sandwiched between two impossible choices.

Author Bio

Lynne Gentry is an actor/director turned fiction author who loves using her crazy imagination to entertain audiences with her books. Her varied works range from the highly-praised time travel series

(Carthage Chronicles) to a laugh-out-loud romantic comedy series (Mt. Hope Southern Adventures). She recently released a co-written romantic medical thriller (Ghost Heart) with author friend Lisa Harris. RT Reviews calls Lynne Gentry a Top Pick author and one to watch. Readers say her writing is extraordinary and her stories exceptional. When Lynne is not creating enchanting new worlds, she's laughing with her family or working with her medical therapy dog.

Find out more about Lynne at www.lynnegentry.com.

BOOK CLUB DISCUSSION
QUESTIONS

We are spouses. We are parents. We are siblings. We are the adult children of aging parents. How can we possibly fill all of these roles? How can we fragment ourselves enough to give a little piece here and a little piece there? These are the questions that an ever-increasing number of people in their forties, fifties and sixties are struggling to answer.

According to the Alzheimer's Association (www.alz.org), more than 5.7 million Americans are currently living with decreased mental capacity due to dementia or Alzheimer's disease. Alzheimer's is the 6th leading cause of death in the U.S. In 2017, Alzheimer's and elderly dementia cost our nation $259 billion. By 2050, estimates put the cost at $1.1 trillion a year. Currently, approximately 15 million Americans provide unpaid care for their loved ones struggling with memory loss and reasoning capabilities. Thirty-five percent of elderly caregivers report that their own health has declined since they assumed the responsibilities of their parents. Two-thirds of caregivers are women.

1. Sara Slocum is only 72. While one in ten Americans over the age of 65 will develop memory issues before their death, Sara is still physically healthy. She treasures her independence and her ability to think. She's terrified of the possibility of losing her mind before her body gives out. If you could choose, which would you prefer to lose first: your physical health or your mental health. Why?

2. Charlotte is only 42. She's made a life for herself miles away from easy access to her aging mother. But as her mother begins to have accidents and make decisions that are completely out of character, fear that her mother's mental capacities are slipping sets in. Have you had to deal with an aging parent? What are some of the strange/funny/terrifying changes in their behavior that alerted you to the possibility that things were changing?

3. Sara's increasing inability to handle things on her ranch forces Charlotte to make the long flight home more and more frequently. These trips take Charlotte away from her job, marriage, and her 13-year-old daughter. This precarious position that Charlotte finds herself in is not unique to her. In fact, so many grown children are being forced to parents their parents while trying to parent their

own children that they've been dubbed "The Sandwich Generation." The tug-of-war between caring for her mother or tending her own life, often puts Charlotte between a rock and a hard place. As the pressure mounts, so do Charlotte's feelings of frustration. According to research, caregivers are at risk mentally and physically. Should Charlotte allow herself self-care? Why do caregivers shy away from self-care? What are some things Charlotte could have done to protect her mother, her daughter, and herself from falling apart?

4. Few families escape the damage caused by tragedies and secrets. The Slocums are an example of the power of unresolved grief. It is harder to forgive others or to forgive ourselves? Why?

5. The cost of caregiving is high. Name a few of those sacrifices caregivers often make and cite the ones that would be the most difficult for you to give up.

6. To whom do you believe the Sandwich Generation's loyalties should lie—to their parents or to their children? Is there a way to successfully balance both? If so, what are they?

7. Have you had to care for an aging parent? What was your biggest struggle? Was it the switching of roles?

Watching the slow decline of someone you always believed invincible? Or the sad reality that you no longer have the parent you once did?

ACKNOWLEDGEMENTS

Throughout my life, these three older women graciously opened their hearts and homes to me: Lib Sikes, Ruth Rushing, and Elizabeth Smith. When I was crafting Sara, she became a combination of these incredibly strong women. All of them were widowed and all of them were determined to maintain their independence for as long as possible. Elisabeth ended up having to give up her home and move to a retirement center close to her daughter. While her mind was slipping, her love of life became stronger than ever. Shortly after she settled in her little assisted living apartment, she set about to bring a breath of fresh air to the other residents. She established a writer's club and a story hour and read books to visually impaired residents. She started a campaign called: Let's Chat. Made posters. Sent out fliers. Encouraged residents to band together to make management do something to improve their living conditions. She wanted the drapes replaced. Wallpaper removed and walls painted with a rosy glow in the activity room. She wanted activities other than Bingo to stimulate her mind. She wanted movie nights, benches in the courtyard. A little garden space to get her hands dirty. I'll never forget the day I came to speak at Elizabeth's little writer's club and she introduced me to a poet Laureate and a steamy romance writer. Both were still churning out work using only old manual typewriters. I thank Lib, Ruth, and Elizabeth for showing me how to live well and, more importantly, how to die victorious.

A special thanks to Colleen Crawford and June Sikes Houston. These women were sandwiched between caring for their mothers and their children and did it so graciously. I want to thank my life group where we regularly pray for those of us currently sandwiched between family and making tough decisions for our aging parents.

I also want to thank my critique group, Kellie Coates Gilbert, and Janet Johnson for giving this story their critical eyes. As always, a special thanks to my fabulous editor Gina Calvert. Your insight blesses so many. To my family, who supported me with their love and understanding during my sandwich years. And most importantly, to God who willingly sandwiched himself between me and my tendency to become wrapped up in my own life.

EXTRA BONUS FOR MY READERS

I'd like to introduce you to my other Texas family.

Leona Harper's family lives in West Texas. Readers report laughing until they cry as they zip through this heartwarming 4-book series similar to Jan Karon's Mitford series. You can start with **WALKING SHOES** and read your way through the next three books. If you sign up for my newsletter at the end of **WALKING SHOES**, I'll gift you ACT 1 of the audio performance of this story. I spent several years performing this one-woman show. At the end of each succeeding book in the Mt. Hope series, you can collect the next audio act. Collect all three audio acts and share in the laughter with audiences around the country.

Other Books by Lynne Gentry

Walking Shoes

Shoes to Fill

Dancing Shoes

Baby Shoes

Ghost Heart

Finally Free

Here's a peek at WALKING SHOES:

Chapter One

"Living in the parsonage is not for sissies." Leona Harper's husband planted a kiss on the top of her head. "If you want to wear fancy red shoes, wear 'em, darlin'."

"Maybe I'll wait until Christmas."

"It's almost Thanksgiving. Why don't you go ahead and break them in?"

"I was fixin' to, but ..." Leona twisted her ankle in front of the mirror, imagining herself brave enough to wear trendy shoes whenever she wanted. "You don't think they might be a bit much?" She reached for the shipping box. "The bows didn't look this big on my computer screen."

"So what if they are?"

"I wouldn't dare fuel Maxine's fire."

J.D. tucked his Bible under one arm and pulled Leona to him with the other. "If Sister Maxine wants to talk, let's give her somethin' real juicy to say."

Leona loved the way this bear of a man nuzzled her neck every Sunday morning. J.D. Harper was as handsome as the day they met some thirty years ago, even with the silver streaks traipsing across his well-trained waves. Folks often guessed him a successful CEO of some major corporation rather than the pastor of a dying church in a small west Texas town.

"I can hear her now. 'Anyone who can buy new shoes doesn't need a raise.'" Leona pushed J.D. away and undid the ankle straps. "Eighteen years and we haven't even had a cost of living adjustment."

"The church provides our house."

"You know I adore living in this old parsonage, but we're not accruing a dime of equity." She buried the shoes in the box and closed the lid. "How are we ever going to be able to afford to retire?" She stashed the box next to her forgotten dreams.

"We've got equity where it counts—"

"Don't say heaven." Leona rolled her eyes at J.D.'s ability to remain slow to anger. "As long as the Board believes we're living on easy street, I don't know how we're going to make ends meet here on earth."

"The Board? Or Maxine?"

"Same thing."

"Live your life worrying about what Maxine Davis thinks, she wins." He had her, and he knew it. "Is that what you want?"

Ignoring the righteous twinkle in his eye, Leona slipped on the sensible brown flats she'd worn for the past ten years. "I hate it when you preach at me, J.D. Harper." She threaded her hand through the crook in his suit-clad arm.

"So many worries. So little time." He kissed her temple. "If it weren't for guilt trips, you wouldn't go anywhere."

"It's all we can afford." Leona scooped up the Tupperware caddie that contained her famous chicken pot pie. What good did it do to long for exotic cruises or expensive adventures? She'd given up those dreams, along with her dreams of writing, long ago. But she'd never give up on wanting her whole family together, even for just a couple of days. "Let's get the Storys and go."

Sitting on the living room couch were the blue-haired twins and founding members of Mt. Hope Community Church. They waited where they waited every Sunday morning. Today, instead of their regular offering of canned pickles, they each had a large relish tray on their lap.

"Etta May. Nola Gay. I'm fixin' to preach the Word. You girls got your amens ready?" J.D. offered Nola Gay his arm.

Nola Gay blushed, "Reverend Harper, you're such a tease."

"It's my turn to hold his arm, Sister," Etta May complained.

"Lucky for you lovely ladies, I've got two arms."

Arm-in-arm J.D. and his fan club crossed the church parking lot, trailed by the lowly pastor's wife.

J.D. opened the door to the fellowship hall. The familiar aroma of coffee and green bean casseroles assaulted Leona's nose. If only she had a nickel for every meal she'd eaten in this dingy room, maybe they could pay all their bills, save a little for retirement, and even afford the mini vacation J.D. had reluctantly agreed to take when the kids came home for Thanksgiving.

"Y'all need help with those trays?" Leona asked Nola Gay.

"We may be slow, but we can still handle a few pickles," Nola Gay assured her.

"Holler if y'all need me." Leona headed for the kitchen, weaving through the scattered tables. Crock-Pots brimming with roast and carrots or pinto beans and ham lined the counter.

While J.D. checked the overloaded power strip, Leona deposited her contribution for the monthly potluck scheduled to follow the morning service. She glanced at the dessert table. Maxine's coconut cake was not in its usual place. "I'm going to my seat."

"You can't avoid her forever," J.D. whispered.

It wasn't that she was afraid of the sour elder's wife; she just hadn't figured out the best way to address Maxine's latest attack on J.D.'s attempt to make the worship service a little bit more relevant, something that would help an outsider feel welcome.

Truth be known, Maxine and Howard didn't want outsiders to get comfortable on the pews of Mt. Hope Community Church. Especially anyone they considered to be "the less fortunate." With the addition of the highway bypass, the community had experienced an influx of vagrants. Most of them needed help. Howard and Maxine preferred these interlopers to just keep walking.

Why God had seen fit to park a generous man like J.D. Harper at a church where the chairman of the elder board's wife loved only two things—having the last word and adding to her list of complaints against the Harpers—was first in a list of pressing questions Leona intended to ask when she did get to heaven.

"I don't want to start a fight before church," Leona said. "It would ruin my worship and I'll be hanged if I'll let her take that too."

"That's my girl." J.D.'s eyes lighted on something behind her. "Better put your game face on, Maxine's fixin' to test your resolve."

Leona turned to see Maxine prancing through the door with her coconut cake seated on a throne of beautiful cut glass and her heavy purse dangling from the crook of her arm.

"Morning, Leona!" Maxine crowed.

Leona plastered on a smile and maneuvered through the chairs. "Can I give you a hand?"

"I don't think so." Maxine pulled her cake out of reach. "Unlike that Pyrex stuff you bring your little casserole in, this is an extremely expensive piece of antique glass. This pedestal has been in our family for years."

Leona knew all about the Davis glass. Every Christmas, Leona had to practically beg Maxine to let the hospitality committee use the crystal punchbowl the Davis family had donated to the church on the condition the church insure it. The job of washing the slippery thing was one Leona tried to avoid.

Leona nipped the reply coiling on her tongue and offered her best platitude, "Your cake and platter are as beautiful as ever. Oh, I forgot I promised the Storys I'd give them a hand." She smiled and quickly moved on to help the twins fussing over how many dill or sweet pickles they should put on their trays.

Leona regretted that from behind her retreat could leave the impression of her tail securely tucked between her legs. She waited until Maxine exited the fellowship hall before she headed to the sanctuary and her regular front row pew.

J.D. slid in just as Wilma Wilkerson blasted out the first note on the organ. He winked at her and began to sing.

Still stinging from her failure at repairing her relationship with

Maxine, Leona inched along the wooden pew that vibrated from the force of her husband's resonant bass. Clutching the worn hymnal, she filled her lungs to capacity, tightened her diaphragm, and joined him in praise. Music always carried her past any earthly troubles.

Behind the large oak pulpit, song leader, Parker Kemp brought the organist and sparse crowd to a synchronized close. Blue from holding on to the last note, Leona glanced across the sanctuary aisle. Maxine Davis eyed her back with her nose wrinkled in disapproval. Leona quickly diverted her gaze.

"And the church said?" Parker flipped to his next selection.

"Amen," the Storys chimed in unison.

"Before the sermon, we'll be singing all five verses of page 156. Please stand, if it's convenient."

Solid oak pews groaned as the congregation lumbered to their feet.

Parker gave a quick nod to the organist, readying his hand for the beat. His expression morphed into that dazzling smile sure to land him the perfect wife someday.

Leona loved the Sundays this radiant young fellow led. Unlike the steady diet of first-and-third-versers, the county extension agent sang every word of every verse. Hymns that once plodded the narrow aisles danced before the Lord under Parker's direction. His ability to stir in a little spirit always gave Leona the distinct feeling rain had fallen upon her parched lawn, offering a smidgen of hope that if this congregation had a shot at resurrection, maybe she did too.

Naturally, Maxine claimed allowing such unrestrained expressions of joy during the song service might lead to who-knows-what in the sanctuary. It had cost J.D. popularity points with the elder board, but in the end none of them had been willing to remove Parker's name from the volunteer rotation. Thank God.

The congregation fidgeted as Wilma Wilkerson attempted to prod some heft into the organ's double row of yellowed keys and squeaky pedals.

Leona used the extra time to beseech the Lord on Parker's behalf. She'd always hoped their daughter Maddie would one day consider Parker more than an irritation, but Maddie was insisting on going another direction.

Perhaps the recent arrival of Bette Bob's adorable niece was God's plan for Parker. Unlike J.D., who never did anything without praying it through for weeks, she was flexible. To prove it, she made a quick promise to the Lord that she'd do her best to connect Parker and Bette Bob's niece at today's potluck.

J.D. reached for Leona's hand and gave it a squeeze, same as he did every Sunday before he took the pulpit. Some pastors prayed.

Most checked their fly. Mt. Hope's preacher always held his wife's hand during the song preceding his sermon.

Relishing her role as coworker in the Kingdom, Leona wiggled closer, her upper thigh pressed tight against her husband's. Nestled securely against J.D.'s charcoal pinstripes, Leona could hear the throaty warble of the Story sisters parked three pews back.

The blue-haired-saint sandwich had a crush on her husband, but to begrudge these seniors a little window shopping bordered on heresy.

The old girls had suffered a series of setbacks the last few months, burying several of their shriveled ranks. What would it hurt if staring at her handsome husband gave them a reason to get out of bed on Sunday mornings? Besides, Widow's Row vacancies were increasing at an alarming rate, and replacing these committed congregants seemed unlikely, given the current trend of their small town's decline.

J.D.'s familiar grip throttled Leona's errant thoughts.

She patted his hand. Her husband felt unusually clammy this chilly fall morning. Was this a new development, or something she'd missed earlier because she'd been in such a twit?

J.D. had been dragging lately. She'd just written off his exhaustion as the discouragement that hounded a man with the weight of a dying congregation on his shoulders.

What if something else was wrong? What if the elders had voted to let them go and J.D. hadn't told her? She felt her keen senses kick into overdrive. Out of the corner of her eye, she checked his coloring.

"Are you okay, J.D.?" Leona whispered.

He kept his eyes on Parker, but Leona knew he wasn't just waiting for his cue to take the stage. He slipped his arm around her trim waist, drawing her close. He whispered, "Who by worrying can add a single hour to her life?" His breath warmed the top of her color-treated head. A tingle raced through her body.

J.D. had promised her he'd take off for the entire week of Thanksgiving. He needed a break and they both needed the time to reconnect their family.

Both kids had finally agreed to come home from their universities. Leona wanted to believe David's and Maddie's hearts were softening, but she knew they'd only consented to a family gathering because it was their father's fiftieth birthday. For him, they would do anything. For her? Well, that was a prayer the Lord had yet to answer.

The song ended, but the glow lighting Parker's dark eyes did not. "You may be seated." He gathered his list and songbook and left the podium.

J.D. ascended the stage steps as if taking some faith mountain.

He removed the sermon notes tucked inside a leather-bound Bible and surveyed the crowd's upturned faces.

Leona recognized the tallying look in her husband's eyes. He would know the dismal attendance count before Deacon Tucker posted the numbers on the wooden board in the back of the sanctuary.

J.D. unbuttoned his coat, ran his hand down his tie. "Mornin', y'all." He greeted his congregation of eighteen years with the same determined expression he had his first Sunday in this pulpit. Filleting the worn pages of his Bible with a satin ribbon, he opened to the day's chosen text.

The rustle of people settling into their favorite pews rippled across the sanctuary.

The Smoots' tiny addition fussed in the back row. Newborn cries were rare here. Leona was grateful the Smoots had decided to stay in Mt. Hope. Other than Parker, most of the young people, including her own children, left after high school and never came back.

The sound of children was something Leona missed. She'd loved the days of diapers, sleepless nights, and planting kisses on the exquisite soft spot right below tiny earlobes.

If only dispensing love could remain that simple and teething remain a mother's biggest worry.

Leona offered a quick prayer for the fertile mother of four. Maybe the Lord would spare that young woman the mistakes of her pastor's wife.

Leona reined in her wandering focus and aimed it on the man standing before the congregation. No matter what became of her relationship with her children, she could always take comfort in the fact that at least she had J.D.

Uneasiness suddenly intruded upon her admiration. Something wasn't right. A shimmering halo circled her husband's head. Surely the unnerving effect was the result of the flickering fluorescent stage lighting. J.D. would surely lampoon her overactive imagination, but Leona couldn't resist scanning the platform.

Four dusty ficus trees and two tall-backed elders' chairs were right where Noah left them when he exited the ark.

Leona smoothed the Peter Pan collar tightening around her neck. Her hand froze at her throat, her breath trapped below her panicked grasp.

Glistening beads of sweat dripped from J.D.'s brow. He removed a monogrammed handkerchief from his pocket and mopped his notes. With a labored swipe, he dried his forehead and returned the soaked linen to his breast pocket. As he clasped the lip of the pulpit, his knuckles whitened.

Leona stood, ready to call out no matter how inappropriate, but her husband's warning gaze urged her to stay put.

J.D. cleared his throat. "There was one who was willing to die—" the pastor paused—"that you might live." A pleased smile lit his face. He placed a hand over his heart and dropped.

Get your copy of **WALKING SHOES** now and start off on another small-town adventure.

CPSIA information can be obtained
at www.ICGtesting.com
Printed in the USA
BVHW031323060421
604334BV00010B/91